W9-BNQ-941

Butternut Summer

Center Point
Large Print

Also by Mary McNear and available from
Center Point Large Print:

Up at Butternut Lake

**This Large Print Book carries the
Seal of Approval of N.A.V.H.**

Butternut Summer

Mary McNear

CENTER POINT LARGE PRINT
THORNDIKE, MAINE

This Center Point Large Print edition
is published in the year 2015 by arrangement with
William Morrow, an imprint of HarperCollins Publishers.

This book is a work of fiction. The characters, incidents,
and dialogue are drawn from the author's imagination and
are not to be construed as real. Any resemblance to actual
events or persons, living or dead, is entirely coincidental.

The text of this Large Print edition is unabridged.
In other aspects, this book may vary
from the original edition.
Printed in the United States of America
on permanent paper.
Set in 16-point Times New Roman type.

ISBN: 978-1-62899-543-5

Library of Congress Cataloging-in-Publication Data

McNear, Mary.
   Butternut summer / Mary McNear. — Center Point Large Print edition.
   pages cm
   Summary: "Daisy is back in Butternut Creek for the summer helping her
mother run her coffee shop and preparing for her final year of college. A
chance encounter with Will, the bad boy from high school, and the return
of her absentee father will cause mother and daughter to come to terms
with the desires of their hearts"—Provided by publisher.
   ISBN 978-1-62899-543-5 (library binding : alk. paper)
   1. Mothers and daughters—Fiction. 2. Large type books. I. Title.
   PS3613.C585945B88 2015
   813'.54—dc23

                                                      2015003688

For David

Butternut Summer

Chapter 1

When Daisy Keegan heard the high-pitched squealing sound coming from the engine of her mother's pickup truck that morning, she did what her mother had taught her to do in situations like this: she turned up the radio. There. Problem solved. If she couldn't hear the noise, the engine wasn't making it. It was that simple.

Except that it wasn't. Because damned if the noise didn't get louder. She turned the radio up all the way, but she could still hear it. "This is not happening," Daisy muttered. Not today. She glanced at the dashboard clock. She had exactly thirty minutes to get home, unload the truck (it was full of the restaurant supplies she'd bought that morning at the wholesale warehouse in Ely), and change into something halfway presentable to wear to lunch with her parents.

Lunch with her parents, she thought, working hard to ignore the engine noise that was getting harder to ignore. What a strange concept; not for everyone, of course, but for her anyway. The fact was, to the best of Daisy's knowledge, she'd never once, in her twenty-one years of life, had lunch with both her parents at the same time. And maybe, her subconscious told her now, there was a perfectly good reason for that.

But an alarming new development interrupted her thoughts. The truck was losing power. Fast. She pumped the accelerator, but nothing happened. She checked the rearview mirror. It was blessedly empty. There wasn't a lot of traffic on the county road she'd taken as a shortcut back from Ely. Still, she couldn't stay on it—not if the truck was about to stall out.

Think, Daisy. Think. There was a service station about a mile from here, right outside the town of Winton. With a little luck—and God knows she deserved a *little* luck—she could coax the truck all the way there. Then, maybe, with a little *more* luck, she could persuade someone to repair the engine while she waited, or, if there wasn't time to repair it, rig something up that would last long enough to get her home. She probably wouldn't have enough time then to unload the truck, or change her clothes, but she might have enough time to pull into a parking space on Main Street, dash into Pearl's café, slide into a seat at the lunch table with her parents, smile sweetly, and say something like, "You know, we really should do this more often."

No, she wouldn't say that, she decided, turning off the county road onto a local street and passing a WINTON, UNINCORPORATED sign. Sarcasm wasn't her style. Instead, she'd say something like, "We should have done this sooner." Or "I know we've never done this before, but maybe now we can do it more often. Start a new tradition . . ."

Daisy was still rehearsing possible conversational openings when she pulled into the service station. The truck was practically crawling by now, and the engine's squeal was so loud that a guy came out of the office to investigate. Daisy turned down the radio and rolled down the window, wincing at the blast of hot air that immediately overtook the truck's admittedly feeble air-conditioning system.

"That doesn't sound good," he said with a friendly smile, coming over to the driver's-side window. He was young and blond, and he was wearing a baseball cap.

"It's not good," Daisy agreed. "I'm losing power, too. Do you think you could take a look at it?" *Please, please say yes.*

"No," he said. "I'm not a mechanic." Then he added, "But Will is," pointing with his chin in the direction of the service bay. "Are you in a hurry?"

Daisy nodded her head emphatically. "A *huge* hurry."

"Well, let's go then," he said with another smile, motioning her out of the truck. "Leave it running. I'll take it from here. You can wait in the office, if you want. Out of the heat."

"Thanks," Daisy said gratefully, opening the door and sliding out.

"Daisy, right?" he asked, taking her place in the truck.

"Right," Daisy said, realizing that he looked vaguely familiar, but unsure of why. "High school," he said, answering her unasked question as he pulled the door closed behind him. "I was a couple of years ahead of you."

"Oh, right," Daisy said, placing him now, but still mentally searching for his name.

"Jason," he said, "Jason Weber." He smiled again, then drove the truck, which was still squealing, into the service bay.

Jason, she thought, walking across a pavement so blisteringly hot she could feel it through the soles of her rubber sneakers. That's right; she did remember him. Daisy's hometown of Butternut, Minnesota, five miles from here, was too small to have a high school of its own, so instead it merged with four other towns in the area, Winton being one of them. She tried to picture what Jason had been like in high school, but she could only conjure up the faintest image of him. Their social lives hadn't overlapped. Then again, between maintaining a perfect grade point average and playing varsity volleyball, Daisy hadn't had much of a social life anyway.

She tugged now at the glass door to the office and entered its air-conditioned coolness. Then she sat down on a metal folding chair, crossed her legs, and tried to simulate calmness. She quickly gave up, though, and started pacing up and down the small room instead, stopping only when a calendar hanging on the wall caught her attention. It was a calendar for an engine parts company, but the blond, bikini-clad model on display for the month of June didn't look like someone who knew the difference between an alternator and a carburetor. Daisy leaned closer, frowning at the photograph, and wondering if the model's glistening body owed its bronze color to a spray tan or to a good, old-fashioned, carcinogenic suntan. The former, she decided, thinking of her own almost preternaturally pale skin. It wasn't humanly possible to get that tan naturally. And, judging from the photo, her tan wasn't the only thing that model hadn't come by naturally. *Honestly,* Daisy thought, leaning closer, *this calendar would be more appropriate hanging in a plastic surgeon's waiting room than in a service station office.* But her disapproval was mixed with curiosity, and she was flipping the calendar to July when Jason came back into the office.

"Oh, hi," she said, dropping the page on the calendar and taking a little jump back. Jason, though, didn't seem to notice what she'd been doing.

"Jeez, do you think it could get any hotter?" he asked, yanking the door closed behind him. "And it's only the beginning of June."

"It's hot all right," Daisy agreed.

"So Will's looking at your engine," Jason said, crossing the room and sitting on the edge of a gunmetal gray desk piled high with papers.

"Did he say how long it would take to fix it?"

He shook his head. "No. But he'll know as soon as he figures out what's wrong with it."

"But it could be really quick, right?" she asked, glancing at her watch and fighting down a new wave of panic. She had fifteen minutes to get to her lunch.

"Could be quick," Jason said. "It depends on what the problem is. And whether it needs a new part, and whether or not we have the part in stock."

"Could I . . . could I go see for myself?"

"Sure," he said, shrugging. "Will won't mind. Do you remember Will Hughes? He went to high school with us."

She thought for a moment. "Not really," she said. "But his name sounds familiar." She was leaving the office when Jason asked, "Hey, your mom owns that coffee shop in Butternut, doesn't she? Pearl's?"

Daisy turned back and nodded, her politeness overriding her impatience. "That's right."

"Best blueberry pancakes I've ever had," Jason said, a little wistfully.

"I know. It's famous for them," Daisy said. *And it's where I should be right now, staking out a table in the middle of the lunch rush.*

She gave Jason a quick smile and walked out of the office and into the blinding sunlight. Then she skirted around the station to the service bay and ducked inside, blinking as her eyes adjusted to its relative dimness. It was surprisingly cool in there, and it smelled pleasantly of motor oil and rubber and damp concrete.

When her eyes had had a moment to adjust, she saw a young man—Will, presumably—standing in front of her truck. He had the hood up and was poking around in the engine with some kind of wrench.

"Will?" she said, coming closer.

He glanced up and nodded, and Daisy felt a little jolt of recognition. As it turned out, she *did* remember Will. Almost better than she liked to admit. In high school, he'd been what Daisy and her friends had thought of as a bad boy. (Not that a boy had had to be very bad to get that designation from them. From their perspective on the student council, anyone who cut the occasional class or got the occasional detention qualified as bad.) Still, in her innocence, Daisy had found Will just different enough, just *dangerous* enough, to be appealing—from a safe distance, anyway. And, looking at him now, she saw an image of him as he'd been then, sitting in the bleachers at the athletic field with his friends, smoking cigarettes.

"Hey," she said, feeling suddenly shy. "Jason

told me it'd be okay if I came back here."

Will looked over at her again. If he recognized her, it didn't register in his expression. Daisy came a little closer. He looked different, she thought. His dark hair had been on the longer side in high school, long enough to brush against his neck, but now it was cut short, very short, and its shortness called attention to his wide, gold-brown eyes. She watched while he wiped his sun-tanned forehead with the back of his suntanned wrist.

"Do you know what's wrong with the engine yet?" she asked, coming to a stop. She was careful to leave a few feet of space between them.

"As a matter of fact, I do," he said, reaching for a greasy rag to wipe his hands on. He wasn't wearing one of those coveralls that mechanics usually wore. Instead, he had on a T-shirt and a pair of blue jeans, and as he reached to put the rag down, the movement stretched the fabric of his T-shirt against the outline of his shoulders. They were nice shoulders, Daisy thought. She shook her head, trying to dislodge the thought; she needed to stay focused.

"Your fan belt's broken," Will said. "It needs to be replaced."

"Can you do it now?"

"Uh-huh."

"How long will it take?"

"Five or ten minutes."

"That long?" Daisy asked, panic-stricken.

"That's pretty fast," he said, pulling on a pair of gloves. "In my world, anyway."

Daisy looked at her watch. There was no way she was going to get there on time now, which left her with only one option: cancel the lunch. She walked a short distance away from Will and the truck, slid her cell phone out of her pocket, and turned it on. Nothing happened. She tried again. Still nothing. She stared at it in disbelief. Was it possible she'd forgotten to charge the battery? Yes, it was entirely possible, especially given the way this day was already going. In a wave of uncharacteristic fury, she slammed the phone down, loudly, on a nearby worktable. Will stopped what he was doing to her engine and looked over at her.

"The battery's dead," she mumbled, gesturing to her phone on the table.

"That's probably not going to help it, though," he said, mildly, and Daisy felt her face flush hotly. She was behaving badly, and she knew it.

She walked back over to Will, feeling contrite. "I know that's not going to help it."

"Jason'll let you use the phone in the office," he said, not looking up from the engine.

She considered the offer, then decided against it. Her father's cell-phone number, which she didn't yet know by heart, was trapped inside her cell-phone's directory. That left calling her mother. And if Daisy did that, what exactly would she say to her? Her mother didn't even know yet that Daisy had planned this lunch. And now, Daisy didn't know if she was brave enough to tell her.

She sighed and shook her head. "No, that's okay. I don't need to use the phone in the office. And thank you for replacing the fan belt. I'm sure you're doing it as fast as you can." Coming closer to him, she added, "It's just . . . it's just I'm running late for this lunch. It's very important that I be there on time."

"Yeah?" Will said, looking over at her again. "What is it, some kind of high-powered, corporate lunch?" he asked, and his eyes, amused and skeptical, traveled from her faded, Minnesota Twins T-shirt, to her cut-off blue jean shorts, to her slightly battered Converse sneakers, one of which happened to be untied.

"No, nothing like that," Daisy said, her cheeks flushing again. "But it's still important. It's sort of a . . . a family reunion." *Is that what it is?* she wondered, anxiously. And then, for reasons she didn't entirely understand, she decided to tell Will more about it, even though his attention had shifted back to the truck's engine.

"I mean, it's not exactly a family *reunion,*" she qualified, brushing a strand of strawberry-blond hair off her face, "It's more of a *homecoming,* I guess. For my dad, anyway."

He glanced at her, quickly, just long enough to let her know he was listening to what she was saying.

"My dad left my mom and me eighteen years ago," she continued. "And then, a year ago, he got in touch with me again. He came down to Minneapolis—I go to the university there—and we had coffee. I hadn't seen him since I was three, but when I met him again, I liked him. He seemed like a nice guy. He *is* a nice guy, actually."

Will looked at her. She had his full attention now. "A nice guy who left?" he asked. "And didn't come back?" Now he wasn't amused and skeptical, he was just skeptical.

"Yeah, I know," Daisy said. "And believe me, I had trouble with that. I really did. I was *so* angry at him at first." She shook her head at the memory of their first meeting. "In some ways, I'm *still* angry at him. But you know what? I was curious about him too. I mean, who wouldn't be, right?"

But Will only shrugged, as if to say, *I wouldn't be*. He didn't say that, though. He went back to work on her engine instead.

"Anyway," Daisy continued, "I got to know him over the last year, and I realized he's changed—for the better. He's not the same man now he was when he left. And when he told me he was moving back here, back to Butternut, I suggested that the three of us, my mom and my dad and me, have lunch together today. The thing

19

is, though, my mom doesn't know about it yet. I mean, she knows she's meeting me for lunch. But she doesn't know he's going to be there." Slightly breathless, she finished, "Which is why it's so important I be there on time." She glanced at her watch again. Ten minutes to go.

"So let me get this straight," Will said, looking back at her. "You've seen your dad since he left. But your mom hasn't?"

Daisy shook her head.

"And she hasn't talked to him since he left, either?"

She shook her head again.

"And she doesn't know she's going to be having lunch with him today?"

"No," Daisy said. "It's going to be a surprise."

"A surprise, or an ambush?" Will clarified.

"An *ambush?*" Daisy repeated, frowning. She didn't like the sound of that word. "Why do you say that?"

He hesitated. "Well, I'm just guessing here. But from what you've said, it sounds like your mom probably wouldn't have agreed to this lunch if she'd known your dad was going to be there."

"That's probably true," Daisy said. *Probably* true? *Definitely* true.

"But you still think it's a good idea?"

"Well . . ." Daisy started. But then she stopped. She stopped because she hadn't thought to ask herself that question yet. Well, no, that wasn't true. She had *thought* to ask herself that question, but then she hadn't let herself answer it. And she hadn't let herself because she'd already known the answer: the lunch wasn't a good idea. It was probably, in fact, a very bad idea.

"Hey," Will said. And when she looked over at him, his gold-brown eyes were resting on her. "Don't worry about it. It'll be all right."

"You think so?"

"Sure. I mean, it's not going to be like one of those daytime talk shows where family members have to be held apart by security guards, is it? Your parents aren't violent people, are they?"

"Violent?" Daisy repeated. "No, not as far as I know." Her father didn't seem violent to her, and of all the charges her mother had leveled against him over the years, his being violent had never been one of them. She'd never known her mother to be violent either. But then again, the woman had her limits, and now Daisy wondered if this lunch might actually push her beyond them. "I don't think they'll have to be held apart," she murmured, more to herself than to Will.

"That's good," Will said. "And do you know what else is good?"

"What?"

"I'm almost done with your truck."

"Really?" she said, feeling a rush of gratitude. He nodded.

"You know, I remember you from high school,"

21

she said suddenly, edging closer. Because there was something about this place—the coolness, the dimness, the quietness—that made her feel almost brave. "You used to sit with your friends on the bleachers at the football field and smoke cigarettes."

"Yeah, that was me then."

"Is that you now?" she asked.

"Uh, no," he said, not looking up. "I haven't been back to the bleachers since I graduated. And I quit smoking a few years ago."

"Why'd you quit?" she asked, unabashedly curious.

"Smoking's an expensive habit," he said, with a shrug. "Working here," he added, looking around, "I can't afford it."

"Well, that's good," Daisy said. "I mean, good that you gave it up," she added, quickly. "Not good that you couldn't afford to keep doing it." She blushed then, afraid that she'd offended him. But he didn't look offended. In fact, she thought she saw one corner of his mouth lift in amusement.

She watched him work for a little while longer, strangely comfortable with the silence between them. She noticed a smudge of grease on his neck, and she thought, idly, about reaching over and trying to wipe it away with her fingertips. But she came to her senses almost immediately, wondering why she would even consider doing something like that. It was the heat, she decided, and she took a little cautionary step away from him.

"I remember you, too," he said, glancing over at her. "You were a cheerleader, weren't you?"

"A cheerleader? No," Daisy said, faintly appalled. "I was on the volleyball team." *I was the captain,* she wanted to say, but didn't.

He shrugged. "Well, same thing, right?"

"Wrong," Daisy said, crossing her arms across her chest. "Very different thing."

"Huh," he said, stopping his work long enough to pull his gloves off. And Daisy saw then that his eyes were amused again. Amused enough to make her think he knew damn well that being a cheerleader and a volleyball player was not the same thing. Amused enough to make her think he was teasing her, and, what was more, that he was enjoying teasing her.

"That's it," he said, stepping back and slamming the engine's hood. "Normally, I'd take it for a test drive, but you probably don't want to stick around for that."

"You're right, I don't," Daisy said. "But thank you."

"Anytime," he said, with a smile. His smiles, she saw, were harder to come by than his coworker Jason's were. But they were worth waiting for. *Nice eyes, nice smile, nice shoulders,* she thought, taking a mental inventory of Will.

But when she realized that he was looking at her, quizzically, she blushed. He was probably wondering why she was standing there, staring at him, when she was supposed to be in such a hurry, when she *was* in such a hurry.

"Well, I'd better get going," she said, backing away from him.

He nodded. "You can pay Jason in the office. I'll pull your truck out. And, uh, good luck with the lunch."

"Thanks," she said, turning to go. But as she walked out of the service bay she looked at her watch. The lunch was starting right now. She felt her earlier panic ebb away, only to be replaced, almost immediately, by an ominous foreboding. Because they were going to have to have this lunch without her.

Jack Keegan sat in his pickup truck, which he'd parked on Butternut's Main Street across the street from Pearl's, and considered the possibility that he was crazy. And not just sort of crazy, either, but completely and totally crazy—insane asylum, straitjacket, padded-cell crazy. How else to explain his actions today? He was back in a town he'd sworn he would never return to. He was following the advice of a daughter who, until a year ago, had been a stranger to him. And he was waiting to have lunch with an ex-wife who, he was pretty sure, still hated his guts.

24

But it got worse. Much worse. Because Jack, who'd given up gambling two years ago, was taking the biggest gamble of his life. He'd decided to move back here, into a cabin an old friend of his—an old drinking buddy of his, really—had left Jack in his will. Jack had quit his job at an oil refinery in South Dakota, given up his apartment, sold all his furniture, and given away anything he couldn't fit in the back of his pickup truck. And then he'd gotten into that pickup truck and driven five hundred twenty-five miles to this lunch date.

But there was no turning back now, he reminded himself, running his fingers through his hair. Besides, there was no life for him to turn back to anyway. So depending on what happened next, he'd either risked it all for everything. Or nothing.

And that was assuming, of course, that this lunch actually took place. He and Daisy had agreed to meet at twelve thirty in front of Pearl's, and it was already twelve thirty-five. Under ordinary circumstances, five minutes barely qualified as late. But these weren't ordinary circumstances. Besides, Daisy had suggested this lunch a month ago, when they'd last met in person, then e-mailed him a reminder last week, and then confirmed by cell phone last night. Now for her to be late? Or to not show up at all? It didn't make sense. What was more, it seemed completely out of character for her.

Here, though, he had an uncomfortable thought: What if he didn't know Daisy well enough to know whether this was out of character for her or not? Maybe being late, or not showing up at all, was *in* character for her. As soon as he had that thought, though, he rejected it. Because whatever else could be said about Jack Keegan—and a lot of things *had* been said about him over the years—he was a good judge of character. He'd never have won so many poker games if he hadn't been. And he knew, when it came to Daisy, that she was as good as her word. As good as gold, really; if she said she would be here, she would be here. That was all there was to it.

He reached for his cell phone on the seat beside him and punched in her number again. But it went straight to voice mail. He didn't leave a message, since he'd already left one when he'd parked here an hour ago. He pressed end on his cell phone and tossed it back onto the seat. Then he blew out a breath, ran his fingers through his hair again, and tried to think about something, anything, really, other than this lunch.

So, instead, he thought about Butternut, Minnesota, population 1,200. He'd hated this town when he'd left it, hated everything about it: its hypocrisy; its small-mindedness; its gossipy mean-spiritedness. It hadn't helped, of course, that so much of that gossip had been about him. Still, when he'd seen Butternut receding in his rearview mirror that morning eighteen years ago, he'd felt a grim satisfaction. *There. Take that, stupid little town. I'll be damned if I'll live here anymore, and damned if I'll ever come back again either.*

But the joke was on him, apparently. Because judging from Main Street's tidy storefronts and well-swept sidewalks, Butternut had done just fine without him. Better than fine. *So much for the supposed disintegration of small-town life in America,* Jack thought, looking up and down the block at businesses and shops with cheerful striped awnings on them and brightly painted wooden benches sitting in front of them. And there were old-fashioned streetlights, too, every half block, with big baskets of flowers hanging from them. *Very pretty,* Jack thought. *Very Butternut.*

But unlike some towns in summer communities, which seemed to be staged simply for the benefit of tourists, Butternut had more to offer than fudge shops and ice cream parlors. It still had Johnson's Hardware, for instance, which had been owned by the same family for over a hundred years. And there was Butternut Drugs, where generations of teenage girls had spent countless hours poring over lipsticks and glossy magazines. And there, too, was the Butternut Variety Store, whose original five-and-ten-cent sign had been amended to also include "$1 and up."

There were some changes, of course. Even Butternut, whose northern Minnesota location was several hours by car from the nearest city, couldn't escape change forever. Where a ladies' dress shop had once been, there was now a place called the Pine Cone Gallery, a chic-looking little shop that wouldn't have been out of place in the Twin Cities.

For the most part, though, the businesses on Main Street had stayed the same. And none of those businesses, Jack knew, was more important to the social fabric of Butternut than Pearl's. He studied it now from across the street, marveling that from the outside, anyway, it looked exactly the same: same red-and-white-striped awning snapping in the breeze, same hand-lettered BEST PIE IN TOWN sign hanging in the window, same little bells jingling on the door as customers came in and out. He couldn't really see inside; the glare from the afternoon sun was too bright on the windows. But he didn't need to see inside to know what the rest of it looked like. He already knew, by heart, every scuff on the linoleum floor and every scratch on the Formica countertop. Not that Pearl's wasn't well-maintained; it was. His ex-wife, Caroline, was a stickler for that kind of thing. The whole place, he knew, was scrubbed and buffed and polished to within an inch of its life. Still, it would be showing its age a little, showing it in a

28

way that only added to its charm and its warmth.

He closed his eyes now and imagined himself walking through the front door at Pearl's, past the red leather booths that lined the front window, past the smaller tables for parties of two and four in the middle of the restaurant, and up to the counter, with its row of chrome swivel stools that children loved to spin on. And there, at the counter, he imagined Caroline, a smile on her face, a pot of coffee in her hand, saying "Hello there. What can I get for you?"

But that smile wasn't for him, he realized. It was for another customer. And so were the friendly words. Because when she saw him, she'd be shocked. Shocked and angry. And instead of saying "What can I get for you?", it was more likely she'd say something like, "What the hell are you doing here?"

No, not hell, he decided. She wouldn't say *hell;* she wasn't a big one for swearing. She'd say something *like* hell, something that let him know, in no uncertain terms, that his being here was not a good thing and that she wanted him to leave. The sooner the better. He felt a trickle of perspiration start to work its way down from his temple to his jaw. Just thinking about seeing her was making him, quite literally, sweat.

He reached over now and turned the air-conditioning up and pulled the visor down against the noonday sun. But it didn't help. He

29

glanced at his watch again. Daisy was now ten minutes late.

He swallowed, hard. His throat was parched, his mouth as dry as sandpaper. He reached for the water bottle in the drink holder and saw that it was empty. Not that it really mattered. It wasn't water he wanted, anyway. He wanted a drink, a real drink, a neat tumbler of single-malt whiskey. It swirled around the glass in his mind's eye, its amber color the loveliest thing he had ever seen. No, not the *loveliest,* he corrected himself. Because the loveliest thing he'd ever seen was in Pearl's, right now. She was the reason he was here, sweating in the arctic chill of his air-conditioned truck. He'd give Daisy five more minutes, he decided. Then, with or without her, he was going in.

At the exact moment Jack Keegan made that resolution, Caroline Keegan was sitting in her cramped office behind the coffee shop, staring at a monthly bank statement on the desk in front of her. She'd already reviewed it carefully, committed it to memory even. But she kept staring at it, hoping the numbers would somehow magically rearrange themselves. They didn't. She sighed, stretched, and bent to examine it again. Nope. Still the same. She'd have to make that appointment, after all. The one with the bank, the one she'd been absolutely dreading having to make.

But before she could do that, her cell phone rang. She glanced down at the display. It was Buster, her boyfriend of three years. She hesitated, then let the call go to voice mail, then felt guilty about letting it go to voice mail. Of course, Buster never minded when she didn't take his calls, though sometimes, honestly, she wished he *did* mind. Just a little. But that wasn't fair, she told herself. He didn't mind because he knew she'd call him back when she found the time. And she would. It was just that, lately, it seemed to be getting harder for her to find the time. Well, she'd think about that later, she decided, scrolling through her cell-phone's contacts for the bank's number. But she was interrupted again, this time by a light tap on the door.

"Do you have a minute?" Frankie, who was the cook at Pearl's, asked as he opened the door just wide enough to poke his head in.

"Yes, of course," she said, though she suppressed a little flicker of irritation as she said it. She wasn't irritated at Frankie—the man was a saint—but at the constant interruptions that every workday brought with it. Normally, she didn't mind those interruptions; she even welcomed them. They were what kept her from getting bored. Not today, though. Today she needed to do something about the problem staring up at her from her desktop.

Still, she smiled at Frankie as she simultaneously motioned him into the office and locked the bank statement back in her top desk drawer.

"What can I do for you, Frankie?" she asked, as he lumbered in, immediately filling the entire space with his massive bulk.

"Um, well, it's not for me. It's for the customers. They're complaining—whining, really—that it's too hot in Pearl's," he said, in a tone that suggested they were being unreasonable. Frankie was so loyal to Caroline, and to Pearl's, that he took even the most minor customer complaint personally. "*I* don't think it's that bad, though," he added. "I mean, we're having a heat wave; what do they expect?"

"They expect to eat their breakfasts in an air-conditioned coffee shop," Caroline said, automatically.

"It *is* air-conditioned," Frankie objected. "The system's just a little old."

"Frankie, that system is more than just a little old. It's ancient. It needs to be replaced. You and I both know that. Now our customers know it, too."

Frankie sighed, an enormous sigh, and shoved his gigantic hands into his apron pockets. "Well, what do you want me to tell them?"

"Who's complaining?" she asked.

"Mr. and Mrs. Sylvester, and Cliff Donahue."

She frowned. They were all good customers.

"Just . . . just comp their lunches and turn up the fans," she said. "And ask Jessica to put extra ice in all the water glasses."

He nodded and turned to leave.

"And Frankie? I'll ask Bill Schelinger to take another look at the air-conditioning. Maybe there's something he can do with it, at least until I can . . ." Her voice trailed off. She had no idea if, or when, she'd be able to afford a new system, not when Bill Schelinger had already told her it would cost over ten thousand dollars.

"Hey, don't worry about it," Frankie said, flashing her one of his rare smiles. "It'll all work out. You'll see."

"Thanks, Frankie," she said, gratefully. And then, with a little frown, "Is Daisy back yet?"

"Not yet."

"Well, she's late then," she said, her eyes traveling to the clock on her desk. "Which is strange, because believe it or not, she wants me to have lunch with her here today. A sit-down lunch. She made me put it in my date book and everything."

"That's nice," Frankie said. And it *was* nice, Caroline thought, but it was also a little odd. Of course, she and Daisy had lunch at Pearl's every day in the summertime, but they usually just grabbed it whenever they could. They rarely had either the free time, or the free table, to have it together. Maybe, Caroline thought now, Daisy

33

was trying to make some time for them together in an otherwise hectic summer. And she couldn't argue with that, could she? Since Daisy had started college, their time together had felt all too brief to Caroline.

"Well, I'll be getting back to work," Frankie said, and then he was gone. And Caroline was left to chew distractedly on her lower lip and add the faulty air-conditioning to her list of worries. But she was interrupted again, almost immediately, by another knock on the door.

"Come in," she called out, her impatience flaring at this latest interruption.

The door opened, tentatively, and Jessica, her waitress, leaned in.

"Caroline?"

"Yes, Jessica?" Caroline said, steeling herself for this exchange. Jessica was Daisy's best friend, and although the friendship between the two of them had long been a mystery to Caroline—Daisy, the perennial honor student, on the one hand, and Jessica, the hopeless scatterbrain on the other—she tried to be respectful of it. She'd hired Jessica six weeks ago, after she'd failed out of cosmetology school, as a favor to Daisy. But Caroline had regretted it ever since. Of course everyone had a learning curve when they started waitressing. But Jessica's was all curve and no learning.

"Um, there's a problem with a customer,"

Jessica said hesitantly, her brown eyes wide in her heart-shaped face.

"Yes?" Caroline said, impatiently. Every minute Jessica spent standing here was a minute she wasn't waiting on tables.

"Well, it's kind of awkward, but . . ." She shrugged her shoulders helplessly and fidgeted with her apron strings.

"Jessica," Caroline said, closing her eyes and willing herself not to lose her temper, "please tell me this isn't about one of your ex-boyfriends eating here again. Because I've told you before you're going to have to wait on them the same way you'd wait on any other customer." And she sighed wearily, because the way Jessica waited on any other customer was with a fairly consistent level of incompetence.

"Oh no, it's not one of *my* exes," Jessica said now, tucking one of her unruly brown curls behind an ear. "It's . . . it's actually one of *your* exes. I mean, not *one* of them," she qualified, shifting her weight nervously from one foot to the other. "Just your ex. Your *ex*-husband, I mean. He's sitting at one of the tables. And he says he wants to see you."

"My ex-husband? Here?" Caroline said, her mind a perfect blank.

Jessica nodded emphatically. "Uh-huh." But Caroline only stared at her, and Jessica, feeling some explanation was in order, went on. "See, what happened was, I went to take this customer's order. And I said the patty melt was on special, and he said 'no, thank you,' he didn't want the patty melt, he wanted to see you. And I said you were in your office, and I wasn't supposed to disturb you there unless it was absolutely necessary. And I said it had already been absolutely necessary three times this morning, and I was hoping it wouldn't be again, because the last time I interrupted you, you seemed a little irritated. So I told him if I bothered you again, I might get fired, and I really need this job. And he said—"

"Jessica, stop," Caroline said. Her brain was finally starting to work again. And her brain told her that Jack Keegan could not be here. "Just back up, honey. Where, in all of this, did this man say he was my ex-husband?"

"I was getting to that."

"Well, get to it faster."

"He said he didn't want to get me in trouble, but I'd still need to tell you that Jack Keegan, your ex-husband and Daisy's father, was here. And that he wanted to see you."

Jack? Here? After all this time? It took a lot to shock Caroline. But this did it. This completely, and totally, shocked her.

"What do you want me to tell him?" Jessica asked now. "Because I'll tell him anything you want me to, Caroline. Even if it's not true. I mean,

36

I try not to tell lies, I really do. Especially big lies. But small lies are different; sometimes you can't help telling them. Well, you can help telling them but—"

"Jessica, please. Just . . . just stop talking. Just for a minute," Caroline said, needing it to be quiet in the office. Needing to think—and think quickly.

"No," she said, after a moment of silence.

"No, what?"

"No, I won't see him, Jessica," she said, knowing that it was the only possible answer to his request to see her. "Tell Jack—Mr. Keegan—that he has no business turning up here, without warning, in the middle of the workday. And, furthermore, that I can't imagine why he's here, or what he could possibly want."

"I, I don't know if I can remember all that," Jessica said worriedly. "I mean, not exactly the way you said it. Should I write it down?"

"No," Caroline snapped. "Just tell him I can't, *I won't,* see him."

"Okay," Jessica said, scurrying out of the office and closing the door behind her.

But it seemed to Caroline that not sixty seconds later she was back, knocking on the door again.

"Yes, Jessica?"

Jessica opened the door, slightly breathless. "Caroline, I told him what you said, and he said to tell you he's not leaving until after you see him. He said he'll sit at that table all afternoon if necessary."

"He actually said that?" Caroline asked, her face flushing with anger.

Jessica nodded anxiously. "Do you want me to have Frankie ask him to leave?" This was generally how they dealt with the rare unwanted customer at Pearl's. Frankie asked them to leave. He never had to do more than ask them either. Having people listen to you was one of the perks of being six feet six inches tall and weighing three hundred pounds.

"No, don't tell Frankie," Caroline said. "It's tempting. But Jack is just brave enough—or stupid enough, I should say—to take Frankie on. And I don't want there to be a scene. I'll ask him to leave myself."

So she was going to see him again, she thought, after eighteen years. And then something occurred to her, something that made the corners of her mouth twitch up in a smile. She'd often wondered, since he'd left, if the passage of time would be kind to Jack's looks, and she'd decided that it probably wouldn't be. After all, all those years of hard living would take their toll on anyone, even someone as good-looking as Jack. She pictured him now with a receding hairline, a spreading waistline, and a jowly neck.

"How does he look?" she asked Jessica suddenly. "Does he, you know, look bad?"

"Bad how?" Jessica frowned.

"Bad like . . . well, like old and kind of broken down. You know, bloated. Puffy. The way a man looks when a lifetime of bad habits finally catches up with him."

Jessica looked perplexed for a moment, but then she shook her head. "I don't know what he looked like before. But he looks good now. I mean, *really* good. When I first walked over to his table—before I knew he was Daisy's father, because now, of course, it feels a little strange to think this—but when I first walked over there, I thought, 'This guy's not from around here. If he were, I'd remember him.' We don't have that many—"

"Okay, that's enough, Jessica," Caroline said with a flash of annoyance. "You can get back to work now. I'll handle Mr. Keegan."

Jessica nodded and started to leave, but Caroline called her back. "Where's he sitting, hon?"

Jessica considered. "At table five, I think. Or maybe it's table seven. I get them mixed up. It's the one—"

"Never mind," Caroline said distractedly. "I'll find him." Jessica nodded and closed the door behind her. And Caroline stood up from her chair and then immediately sat back down again. She wasn't just angry, she realized; she was nervous, too. Which was ridiculous, really. *She* had nothing to be nervous about. *He* was the one who should be nervous. He was the interloper here, not her. And not Daisy. *Daisy!* In all the tumult following Jessica's news, she'd completely forgotten about Daisy.

Thank God she was late, she thought, glancing at her watch. Thank God she hadn't seen her father. Hadn't seen her father *yet,* she corrected herself. And just like that, her nervousness was gone, replaced by a pure, blind fury. She practically catapulted herself out of her chair, flinging the office door open and running down the narrow hallway to the coffee shop's back door. It was one thing for Jack to spring himself on her, she thought, her mind racing as fast as her body; it was another thing for him to spring himself on their daughter. After all, Daisy had long since accepted the fact that her father was a father in name only. The last thing she needed now was for him to reappear, opening up old wounds and bringing back old memories.

Caroline opened the back door to Pearl's and came out from behind the counter, her eyes scanning the room. There he was, at table five. *Table five, Jessica,* she thought, gritting her teeth and heading straight for him. He didn't look up. Instead, he leaned back comfortably in his chair, glancing casually at the menu, acting as if his being here were the most natural thing in the world, as if the only thing on his mind was

40

whether to order the BLT or the turkey club.

When Caroline reached him, she stopped abruptly, and, resting her hands on the tabletop, she leaned across it toward him.

"Jack," she said, not bothering to lower her voice. "What the *hell* are you doing here?"

He looked surprised, shocked even, but only for a second. After that, he recovered his equilibrium, his infuriating equilibrium. "Caroline," he said, putting down his menu, "I don't remember you ever swearing before."

"Well, I don't remember ever having as good a reason to swear before, Jack," she said, leaning a fraction of an inch closer to him. "But we don't have time to discuss that now. You need to leave before Daisy gets back. And I *mean* it," she added. "She's not going to see you here today. Today or any day. Is that clear?"

"Caroline, calm down," he said. But she saw a worried expression flit briefly over his face.

"I will *not* calm down," she said, bringing her fist down on the table hard enough to make the ice jump in Jack's glass of water, hard enough to make the customers at the table next to theirs stop their forks in midair and turn to stare. But Caroline, usually the consummate professional, didn't care if she was making a scene.

"Caroline, it's all right," Jack said, his tone placating. "I've already seen Daisy. Not today.

But recently. And she knows I'm here now. She's supposed to be here now, too."

"What?" was all Caroline could say.

"Look," he said, almost gently. "Sit down, okay? Just for a minute. And I'll explain it all to you. Or I'll try to, anyway."

Caroline, moving mechanically, pulled out the chair across from him and sat down on it. Not because she thought sitting down at the same table with him was a good idea. She didn't. But because she couldn't think of anything else to do right at this moment. She was, quite simply, in shock.

"Miss, excuse me," she heard Jack say, at the periphery of her consciousness. "Can you bring Ms. Keegan a glass of ice water?" A moment later, Jessica was back with the water and, looming up behind her, was Frankie.

"Is there a problem here?" Frankie asked, towering over their table. Caroline took a sip of the water and watched while Frankie gave Jack the once-over. She'd seen Frankie do this to men before, with predictable results. But Jack, she saw, more than held his own, returning Frankie's stare with a cool, levelheaded one of his own. Jack, she knew, was an excellent poker player. Whatever else you could say about the man, he knew how to bluff.

"There's no problem," Jack said. "I'm just meeting my ex-wife for lunch."

Frankie's face registered surprise, something it

rarely did. "Is he . . . is he who he says he is?" he asked, looking at Caroline.

She nodded dumbly.

"Do you, uh, do you want him to stay?" Frankie asked.

She hesitated, then nodded again.

"Well, okay," Frankie said uncertainly. "But let me know if you change your mind," he added. He glowered at Jack again and left the table. Caroline, meanwhile, sipped her water and felt her shock beginning to recede. That was when she looked over at Jack and saw him—*really* saw him—for the first time that day.

There was no receding hairline, she noted with regret, and no expanding waistline, either. No bloating or puffiness. Jack Keegan was still very much the man she'd remembered him to be. He still had more than his share of tousled brown hair, for instance, none of which looked like it would be going anywhere anytime soon. And his dark blue eyes were brighter and clearer than they had any right to be, too, especially when you considered how little the man slept, and how much time he spent in dark, smoky rooms. Add to those his healthy suntan and lean athletic build, and he was a disappointment to her all around. But she consoled herself with the thought that, unlike Jessica, she knew enough about Jack Keegan to take some of the shine off all that handsomeness.

He looked at her now, looking at him, and shrugged apologetically. "Maybe this was a mistake," he said. "I don't know. But I think Daisy thought—no, I *know* she thought—it was the only way for the three of us to be together. I mean, let's face it, if you'd known I was coming, you would have headed for the hills."

"You're damn right I would have," Caroline said, without hesitation.

Jack's mouth lifted at one corner. "Another swear word, Caroline. That's two more than I ever heard from you the entire time we were married."

Caroline ignored that remark. She could feel herself slowly returning to her senses. As angry as she was at him for coming here, there were still things she needed to know from him. "Jack," she said now, knowing Daisy could be there at any moment, "when did Daisy get in touch with you?"

But he shook his head. "Daisy didn't get in touch with me, Caroline. I got in touch with her."

"Really?" Her eyes widened with surprise, then narrowed with suspicion. "Why, Jack?"

"Why? She's my daughter, Caroline. Do I need to have a reason for wanting to see her again?"

"You do when you've waited almost two decades to do it," she said.

He shrugged. "I disagree. After all, there's no statute of limitations on being a parent."

"Maybe not. But don't you think it's a little late for you to start playing that role?"

He lifted his shoulders in another shrug. "I think it's up to Daisy to decide whether or not it's too late."

She sighed, exasperated. They were talking in circles. She wanted—*needed*—more information from him.

"How did you get in touch with her, Jack?" she asked, her jaw tightening.

"I Googled her," he said, a little sheepishly. "Her name was mentioned in her student newspaper. The intramural volleyball team she played on won a league championship. I figured if she was going to the University of Minnesota, she was probably living in Minneapolis. So I looked up her phone number there and asked her if she wanted to meet me for coffee."

"How long ago was this?"

"A year ago."

"And that was the last time you saw her?"

He shook his head. "No. I've seen her every month since then. The last time, just a few weeks ago."

"What?" she said, trying to take it all in. And then she shook her head. "I don't believe it, Jack. I just don't believe it."

"Why not?"

"Because the Daisy I know would never keep something like that from me. Not for a whole

45

year. Especially since we've never kept secrets from each other before." But even as she said that, she realized it wasn't true. She was keeping a secret from Daisy right now, a secret that she'd just locked in the desk drawer in her office. Who was to say Daisy wasn't keeping a few secrets of her own, she mused, especially after being away at college for three years.

She watched now as Jack took a drink of his water. He looked uncomfortable, something she'd rarely seen him look in the past, and it pleased her. A little.

"I don't think Daisy meant to keep a secret from you," he said carefully. "I think she was afraid that if you knew she was seeing me, you'd be upset."

"That's ridiculous," Caroline said stubbornly. "Daisy's a grown-up. She's free to see whomever she pleases. She doesn't need my approval."

"Maybe not. But she'd *like* your approval. And she wasn't going to get it this time, was she?"

No, Caroline almost said, because it was the truth. But she opted for silence instead.

"Anyway, we're here now," Jack said lightly. "All that's missing is our daughter, who's running a little late. But when she gets here, Caroline, I think we should both make an effort to be civil, don't you?"

At that, she shot Jack an irritated look. Since when had he played the role of the adult in their relationship? But still, he had a point. "Okay, fine," she said. "I can do that. Be civil, I mean. It's just one lunch. And you probably need to be getting back to . . . where is it? Elk Point, South Dakota? That's a long drive, isn't it?"

"Actually, I'm not going back there," he said, watching her a little warily. "I'm staying here, Caroline. In Butternut. Wayland left me his cabin when he died a few years back. I'm going to be living in it and fixing it up, at least for the foreseeable future." With a hint of a smile, he added, "They're going to have to change that sign, from Butternut, population 1,200, to Butternut, population 1,201."

Caroline stared at him, rendered speechless for the third time that day, and it was at that moment that Daisy appeared, apologetic, embarrassed, and breathless, her strawberry-blond hair disheveled, her shoelace untied on one Converse sneaker.

"I'm so sorry," she said, sliding into a third chair at the table. "The truck broke down, Mom. It was the fan belt. I got it replaced. But my cell-phone battery was dead and . . ." But she stopped, then, and looked, slowly, from Caroline to Jack and back to Caroline again. "So what did I miss?" she asked, in a way that suggested she didn't really want to know.

Chapter 2

"Don't you have anything better to do than watch me work?" Will asked Jason, looking up from the alternator he was repairing.

"Not really," Jason said, lounging against a nearby car.

It was three o'clock in the afternoon, and, as usual, Will was working and Jason was . . . well, *not* working. This was because Jason's personal philosophy was never to do more at the garage than was absolutely necessary. And, so far, his philosophy was working for him. But only because his father owned the garage.

"So Daisy Keegan, huh?" Jason said, apropos of nothing. "Do you remember her, Will?"

"I remember her," Will said, noncommittally, not looking up.

"What do you remember about her?"

"Not much," Will said, hoping that would end the conversation. But Jason persisted.

"She was some kind of athlete, wasn't she? She played some sport."

"Varsity volleyball," Will said, without thinking. "She was good, too. Her sophomore year, they went all the way to quarterfinals." He stopped. He'd said too much.

"I thought you said you didn't remember that much about her," Jason said, suddenly alert. "And since when did you follow girls' volleyball in high school?"

"I didn't *follow* it," Will said, carefully. "I just went to a few home games our senior year. You know, I didn't want to go back to my house, so it was either watch one of those games or go to the library."

"Yeah, well, I don't blame you for not wanting to go back to your house," Jason said. "I mean, not if your dad was actually *in* your house."

Will chuckled, but he didn't say anything. This was the best part of knowing someone your whole life. You could joke about things that were hard to joke about—like Will's father.

A pickup truck pulled up outside, and Jason pushed himself lazily off the car he was leaning on and went to investigate. And Will, relieved the conversation was over, tried to focus on the alternator. Concentration wasn't generally a problem for him. He liked working on engines, and he was good at it. It was usually just varied enough, or just challenging enough, to keep him interested. But this afternoon he was off his game. And he knew why; it was seeing her again, seeing Daisy.

He hadn't exactly been honest with Jason when he'd told him he didn't remember that much about her. But he had been honest with him when he'd told him why he'd watched her volleyball games. Or why he'd watched the *first* one, anyway. Because that first game, he'd just kind of stumbled onto.

It was a gray day in early October, and Will, who had just slept through another detention, was leaving his schoolbooks in his locker. (He tried, whenever possible, not to take these books home, since studying occupied an even lower priority in his life than attending classes.) Usually, at the end of the day, he enjoyed this little ritual at his locker. Dump books in, slam door shut, spin combination lock—and get the hell out of there.

On that day, though, even the sound of metal colliding with metal as he banged the locker door shut didn't give him any real pleasure. Mainly, this was because he had nowhere to go. Jason, whose house he practically lived at, was on a father-son hunting trip, and going back to his own house this early in the day wasn't even an option. The library was out too, as he'd already read the entire supply of automotive magazines for that month and had pretty much consumed all the aviation magazines as well. Besides, the librarian, a dried-out prune of a woman, was always nagging him, saying things like, "If you're so curious about the way things work, why don't you try going to your physics class sometimes?"

But as he was hesitating at his locker that afternoon, he heard a burst of cheering from the gymnasium next door, and he decided on a whim to investigate its source. When he pushed open the gym's swinging door and saw it was a girls' varsity volleyball game, he almost went right back out again. All school sports were lame, as far as Will was concerned. But volleyball, he thought, was especially lame. Still, something made him stay. Maybe it was the thought, again, of going home. Or maybe it was just that on this gloomy October day, the gym, which was bright and warm and noisy, seemed strangely cheerful to him.

In any case, he climbed up to the top of the bleachers, sat down, slumped against the back wall, and waited for boredom to set in. It never did. For one thing, the game was much better than he'd expected it to be—fast paced and suspenseful—and not at all like the clumsy coed volleyball he and his classmates were periodically forced to play in PE. Even more important, though, it was a *girls'* volleyball game, and if there was one thing that interested Will besides cars, it was girls. And this team had some exceptional girls on it.

There was Jenny Holmes, for instance, a junior whose blond-haired, blue-eyed beauty and year-round tan made her look more like a Southern California surfer girl than a midwestern volleyball player. And there was Hazel Bell, too, a pretty, dark-haired senior who was that rarest of high school combinations: an athlete *and* a bad girl. Because while Hazel could hit a mean spike shot, she could also drink a pint of Jack Daniel's straight from the bottle. She had a very nice body, too, a body that Will was already intimately familiar with, given that drinking was only one of Hazel's two favorite activities.

As he was watching Jenny and Hazel, though, he noticed another player, number 17. He liked watching her, too, he decided. He liked the way she moved, with the easy grace of a natural athlete. He liked the way her strawberry-blond ponytail bounced up and down whenever she made a play. He liked the way her creamy white skin seemed to almost glow under the gym's fluorescent lights. And he liked the way her body seemed to be both hard and athletic, and soft and feminine, at the same time. He liked, in fact, everything about number 17, whose name, he learned, was Daisy. Soon, he stopped watching Jenny and Hazel and all the other players and watched only her, which wasn't a bad strategy. Even as a sophomore, she was already the best player on the team. Except that, after a while, he watched her even when she wasn't playing. Even on those rare occasions when she sat on the bench.

Will went to Daisy's next game. And most of her home games after that. He never told any of his friends where he was going, and, once there, he was always careful to blend in with the crowd and leave as soon as the game was over. But he was there, week after week, game after game, and, as he sat there, watching Daisy play, he became aware of a feeling that was sometimes right below the surface of his consciousness, and, at other times, right on the surface of it. The feeling, he decided, was lust, pure and simple, and it was made all the more acute by the knowledge that where Daisy Keegan was concerned, it would most likely never be satisfied.

It wasn't because Will had any trouble with girls. He didn't. Even then, they came as easily to him as the engines Jason's father was already letting him tinker with at his garage. But a girl like Daisy? She wasn't just in a different league than Will. She was in a different *world*.

It was a world at their high school that Will knew almost nothing about, the world of students who studied, played team sports, and participated in extracurricular activities. They didn't just *have* to be there, like Will; they actually seemed to *want* to be there, which for him was a complete mystery. Will hated high school. Hated the boredom, the routine, the sameness of it all. Hated being herded from one class to another, hated being constantly told what to do, hated all the stupid rules—the stupid rules he broke whenever he got the chance to break them. The only relief for him came in automotive class and on the weekends, when he and his friends would convince someone's older brother to buy them beer, and then they'd drive to the Butternut Town Beach where they'd build a bonfire and have a party.

Daisy never came to those parties. She never came to *any* parties, as far as Will could tell. He never saw her outside of school. And when he saw her inside of school, she was either playing volleyball or engaged in some similarly wholesome activity. She was studying in the library between classes, a tiny frown of concentration on her pretty forehead. Or selling tickets to a school dance. Or volunteering at a bake sale—croissants only—to raise money for the French club.

He wanted to see more of her—he really did —but since he wasn't about to join the French club, and Daisy, apparently, wasn't about to get detention, he figured their paths would never cross. And, except for those volleyball games, they never did.

Then volleyball season ended, and Will thought about Daisy less. When he graduated that spring and started working full-time at the garage, he thought about her even less. Until today. Today, when she walked into the service bay, and walked back into his life, bringing with her all the memories of those autumn afternoons five years ago.

And here was the amazing thing. *It was still there*. That irresistible pull he'd felt toward her then. Only this time it was stronger, because now she was real. He thought now about the way she'd been that morning. Flustered, impatient, funny, though the funny part, of course, was largely unintentional. Still, she'd been adorable in an innocent, tomboyish way, and as sexy as hell . . .

"Damn, Will, what do I have to do to get your attention?"

Will jumped a little. Jason was standing right next to him.

"What?" Will asked, a little embarrassed. He'd been completely lost in thought.

"I said, 'Can you service Mrs. Elliot's Camry tomorrow?'"

"Yeah, okay," Will said, going back to work.

But Jason didn't move. "You're thinking about that girl, aren't you? Daisy?"

"No, I'm not," Will said, irritated that Jason, for the first time in his life, was being perceptive.

"Yes, you are," Jason said, grinning. "Too bad you're not going to see her again anytime soon. Because if you're as good a mechanic as you say you are, that fan belt could hold out for a *long* time."

"Oh, I'll see her again," Will said nonchalantly. "She'll be back. If not today, then tomorrow."

Jason raised an amused eyebrow. "You're pretty sure of yourself, aren't you?"

Will shrugged.

"What, you think she's not going to be able to resist those big brown eyes of yours?"

"No, I think she's going to want her cell phone back," Will said, gesturing at the shiny silver rectangular object Daisy had left lying on a nearby worktable, right next to a pile of greasy rags.

When Jack drove out to the lake that afternoon, he missed the turnoff to Wayland's cabin. But about fifty yards down the road from it, he was struck by a sudden sense of familiarity, and he braked, threw the truck in reverse, and backed up to an overgrown dirt track that looked as if nature was trying, hard, to reclaim it. It was Wayland's driveway, though, he decided, squinting down it. He'd driven down it a hundred times before. He turned into it and started to drive down it again now, but he stopped when he saw a mailbox, smashed in on one side and lying on the ground. Were kids still doing that? he wondered, getting out of the truck. Still leaning out of the windows of speeding cars and knocking over mailboxes with baseball bats? He'd done this himself before, during a rural adolescence spent on the edge of juvenile delinquency.

Still, he thought, grabbing the mailbox, it seemed wrong to have done it to Wayland, especially when you considered all the bad luck he'd run into at the end of his life. Jack stood the mailbox up and tried to plant the post back into the ground. But when he let go of it, it tipped right over. The whole thing was rotted right through. He picked it up and tossed it into the woods. He wasn't expecting a lot of mail here this summer, anyway.

He got back in his truck then and kept driving, but he had to stop again almost immediately to clear a fallen tree branch blocking his way. The driveway, it turned out, was littered with branches that needed to be moved, and by the time Jack had reached the final bend in it, his T-shirt was yoked with sweat, and his arms were covered with scratches. Still, he didn't mind. He wasn't afraid of physical work; there was something familiar about it, reassuring even. What wasn't reassuring was his first sight of the cabin.

"Oh hell," he muttered, as it came into view. He braked and slid out of his truck without bothering to turn off the engine or close the driver's-side door. He started to walk up to the cabin, then stopped, not wanting to go any closer. He rubbed the sweat out of his eyes, hoping it would improve the view. It didn't. The cabin looked . . . the cabin looked like a teardown. He blew out a long breath. He was good with his hands; he knew how to fix things and build things. There were a lot of things, in fact, he knew how to do. But he wasn't sure if salvaging this cabin was one of them.

He squared his shoulders, though, and walked up to the cabin's front porch, or what was left of its front porch, which, admittedly, wasn't much. Most of it had simply fallen away. But someone had built a set of makeshift cinder-block steps that led up to the front door, and Jack climbed them now, craning his neck to look into one of the windows that flanked the door. But he couldn't see anything through it. It was cracked and streaked with dirt. He tried the front door; it was locked. He frowned. There'd never been any mention of a key. Then again, details had never been Wayland's strong suit.

As it turned out, though, Jack didn't need a key. One good shove with his shoulder and the door gave way. He started to go inside, then stopped. The airless cabin felt like a blast furnace in this heat. He opened the front door wider and forced himself to go inside, opening windows as he went. Several of them were stuck, but a couple of them opened, and so did the back door, which faced out onto the remains of a small deck. *There,* he thought, *maybe that'll get a cross breeze going.*

He stood then, for a moment, in the open back door, looking down toward the lake, which was only partially obscured by tall grasses and overgrown weeds. Here, at least, was one view that couldn't be spoiled: Butternut Lake, the crown jewel of Butternut, Minnesota, twelve miles long and, in some places, one hundred and twenty feet deep. It was one of the clearest, cleanest lakes in Minnesota, and it was ringed with tall pines, magnificent maples, and oaks and birches. Today, Jack thought, it was at its best, smooth and sparkling in the afternoon sunlight, and so blue it almost hurt his eyes to look at it.

It was still early in the season, and only one motorboat puttered lazily over the water on the far side of the bay. As Jack watched it, the heaviness and the stillness of the day weighing down on him, he got that feeling he sometimes got in the summer—that time itself was slowing down and that it might, eventually, stop altogether.

It reminded him of an afternoon, more than twenty years ago, when he'd gotten that same feeling. Wayland, who'd worked with him at the mill in town, had invited him to come out here. It had been a day like today, though not so hot, maybe, but still, drowsy and heavy and slow. And he and Wayland had sat out on this deck, which was new then and still smelled like freshly cut pine, and they'd talked and talked, and drank and drank, though maybe, in retrospect, there'd been a little less talking, and a little more drinking.

But Jack remembered now that he'd left the engine running in his pickup, and he went back outside to turn it off. When he came into the cabin again, he forced himself to go through it, slowly and methodically this time. He flicked the light switches on and off. Nothing. He turned on the water in the kitchen tap. There was silence, then an ominous gurgling sound, and finally, the faucet spit out something that looked like coffee. He waited until it ran clear, or as close to clear as it was going to get, and then he stuck his head under it, looking for some relief from the heat. But the tepid water didn't give him much. He turned off the tap, looked around for something to dry his face with, and settled for his T-shirt.

He finished inspecting the kitchen. There was a refrigerator and a stove, both disconnected, both covered with an ancient layer of grime. And that was about it. That and some old pots and pans, and some chipped crockery in the cupboards, and a box of macaroni on a dusty shelf in the pantry. Jack turned and left the little kitchen before he got too discouraged, but the living room wasn't much better. It held a couch with the stuffing poking through, a scuffed coffee table, and a lamp whose shade had an ominous burn mark on it. The corners of the room were full of dust bunnies and festooned with spider's webs as intricate as May Day streamers.

Jack remembered now there were also two bedrooms, and he went to find them. The smaller one was empty, except for an old box spring, but the larger one was the only room in the cabin that looked as if someone had put any care or thought into it. It had a bed with a patchwork quilt spread neatly over it, a doily-covered bedside table, and a rocking chair in one corner. There was a little framed needlepoint hanging on the wall, too. "God Bless this House," it said. *Strange,* Jack thought. Wayland hadn't seemed like the religious type to him, and there certainly wasn't much to bless about this house, but still, you never knew about people. They could surprise you.

He left that bedroom, and, after poking his head into a small but apparently serviceable bathroom, he made his way back to the living room. He had some idea about bringing the rest of the gear in from his truck now, but he didn't. Instead, he went and lay down on the lumpy couch and stared up at the ceiling. Noticing a chink of blue sky between one of the rafters, Jack sighed. He'd actually brought some camping gear with him —a sleeping bag and a few lanterns. But now he was wishing he'd thought to bring a tent, too. It would have offered better protection from the elements than this cabin. Oh, well. What difference did it make, really. He closed his eyes. He hadn't come back for this godforsaken place, anyway. He'd come back for Caroline . . .

Caroline. He'd told himself he was prepared to see her again today. But he'd been wrong. He hadn't been prepared at all. Because the moment he'd seen her, all his preparations had gone straight out the window. Maybe it was because she'd been so angry, much angrier than he'd expected her to be. Had he ever seen her that angry before? he wondered. But then he realized he had, a couple of times, when they were still married, and he'd stayed out all night drinking, playing poker, and . . . but he pushed the thought of the other women out of his mind. He would concentrate on the present, not the past. He wouldn't think about the past any more than was absolutely necessary. He couldn't; it was too dangerous for him.

So instead he pictured Caroline as she'd been today, angry, yes, but beautiful, too, beautiful in a wholly unexpected way. And he almost winced, remembering that, as a young man, he'd believed that as a woman aged she got less attractive, as if she were a carton of milk with an expiration date stamped on her. How wrong he'd been, how stupid. Not to mention shallow. Because in the years since he'd last seen her, Caroline hadn't gotten *less* attractive, she'd gotten *more* attractive. There had been some changes, of course. There were some tiny lines now around her eyes and mouth that hadn't been there before. But they didn't make her any less desirable. And the other changes, the changes that were harder to put his finger on, made her more desirable. Her face, for instance, seemed just slightly softer and fuller now than it had been before. And her strawberry-blond hair, her gift to their daughter, Daisy, was just a shade darker, her blue eyes just a shade brighter. He wasn't sure what it was, exactly, but whatever it was about her that had changed, she was lovelier now than she'd ever been before. And it was killing him.

He thought about getting up now, and starting his life here, such as it was—bringing his gear in from the truck, making a run to the grocery store, maybe even stopping in at the hardware store to get some of the stuff he was going to need to get started on this place. But he didn't move. Didn't open his eyes, either. Instead, Jack was paralyzed by a new fear. He'd been afraid to see Caroline again, but he hadn't been afraid of failing, not in the long run. Now he wasn't so sure. It was possible he'd underestimated the depth of her dislike—no, *her hatred*—for him. And the way he and Daisy had set it all up might not have been the best idea they'd ever had.

Poor Daisy. She must be getting an earful from her mom now. He'd make a point, the next time he spoke to Caroline—and there *would* be a next time—to shoulder more of the blame. To shoulder *all* of the blame, if he possibly could. Because the last thing he wanted was to somehow interfere in Daisy and Caroline's relationship. He knew they were close. They'd had to be; for all those years, they were the only family either of them had had.

He felt a familiar stab of guilt now, so sharp this time it made him open his eyes and sit up on the couch. He blinked and looked around the room, as if seeing it for the first time. *God, this place is hopeless,* he thought. And he'd been a fool to think it might be otherwise. But then something else occurred to him. Because if the cabin wasn't the way he remembered it being twenty years ago—what with all the basic amenities, like a roof that would keep out the rain—it also didn't have any of the fringe benefits that it had had back then. Like a refrigerator full of ice cold beer waiting to be emptied out. And that, Jack Keegan knew, was a very good thing.

"Daisy, what were you thinking?" Caroline asked that night, back at their apartment above the coffee shop. She was in crisis mode now, doing what she always did when she was in crisis mode: sitting at the kitchen table and drinking black coffee.

"I *wasn't* thinking," Daisy admitted. "I'm sorry. In retrospect, it was a bad idea."

"In retrospect?"

"Okay, it was *always* a bad idea. But, Mom? Tell me the truth. If I'd told you he was coming, would you have agreed to see him?"

Caroline closed her eyes and exhaled slowly. "No," she said.

"I didn't think so."

She opened her eyes again and looked at Daisy. Daisy, who suddenly seemed so young, so anxious, and so . . . *so hopeful*. And Caroline relented—but only a little. Because while she knew her daughter's intentions, however misguided they might seem, had been good, she was also hurt that Daisy had kept a secret like this from her, and kept it from her for so long. Still, feeling disappointed with Daisy was such an unfamiliar feeling to her that she tried to brush it away.

"Look, I'm not angry," she said. "Or at least I'm trying very hard not to be. But, Daisy, there's a whole history between your father and me that you can't possibly understand. And I have to believe that if you did understand that history, you would know that it could never be erased over a single lunch."

"Mom, I know that. I do, really. And I don't want you to erase it. I just want you to . . . to give him a chance, I guess," she said, with a little shrug.

"A chance to what?" Caroline asked, immediately tensing.

"A chance to prove to you he's different. I mean, different from how he was when you were married to him."

Caroline frowned. There was something about Daisy's choice of words that bothered her. And she was suddenly reminded of a movie that Daisy had loved as a child, a movie she'd watched over and over and over again. In it, twin daughters had schemed, successfully, to get their long divorced parents back together again. God, how Caroline had hated that movie, and its easy, fairy-tale ending.

"Daisy, your father and I have lived apart for eighteen years," she said, carefully. "We've been divorced for more than sixteen of those years. And we got divorced because we were completely, and totally, incompatible." *Well, that and your father was a serial adulterer.*

"So," she went on, "even if I didn't already have someone else in my life whom I care about—and I care about Buster very much—there would be no possibility of your father and me getting back together again. None whatsoever. And I know your father feels the same way. You understand that, don't you?"

"Of course," Daisy said, flushing with either embarrassment or disappointment, Caroline wasn't sure which.

"Because I've heard of the children of divorced parents fantasizing about their parents getting back together again," Caroline continued pointedly. "And you need to know, that is not going to happen here."

"Mom, please, I'm twenty-one. I'm old enough to know the difference between a Disney movie and real life," Daisy objected. But her cheeks were still pink.

"Good," Caroline said, only slightly mollified. "Now, if you want to continue the . . . the friendship you and your father have begun, then obviously, that's different. I can't tell you what to do with your own life." *Although God knows, in this case, I'd like to.* "But I can warn you, Daisy, that your father is not reliable. Or trustworthy." Here Caroline flashed on a memory of Jack coming home at six o'clock in the morning. Still slightly drunk, still reeking of perfume—some *other* woman's perfume. "When it comes to your father," she added, "you should proceed with caution."

"I will," Daisy said. But then her chin jutted out stubbornly, and she said, "But I'll remember what you taught me, Mom. That everyone deserves a second chance."

Well, not everyone, Caroline thought, but didn't say.

Daisy, sensing her skepticism, persisted. "I mean, you thought Frankie deserved a second chance. And Frankie's an ex-con."

"Frankie was a very special case," Caroline said.

"Mom, he *killed* a man."

"Yes, he did," Caroline said, calmly. "But you know as well as I do, Daisy, that there were extenuating circumstances." Extenuating circumstances that Frankie had only recently told her about. "Frankie did what he did in self-defense. He was trying to protect his sister from an abusive husband, and that husband, it turned out, had a knife. Even so, Frankie paid the price for his actions. He did his time. And there's nothing now he wouldn't do for you, or for me, or for Pearl's, for that matter."

Daisy nodded. "You're right, Mom. When it comes to second chances, Frankie *is* a special case. But, Mom, people change."

Caroline sighed. Daisy was just young enough, and just naive enough, to actually believe this. And now she worried that all the time Daisy had spent in libraries over the last several years had taught her a lot about academic subjects, but not a lot about the real world. Because in Caroline's experience, most people didn't change; most people stayed the same. And, as she poured herself another cup of coffee, she remembered an old adage about this.

"Daisy, do you know what my grandmother Pearl used to say?"

"What?"

"She used to say 'a leopard never changes its spots.' "

Daisy rolled her eyes. "Mom, this is the same woman who made her husband drink cream every day because she thought it was good for his heart."

"Well, yes. She did do that," Caroline admitted. "But she had a point about those spots."

"Maybe for some people that's true," Daisy allowed. "But Dad's changed, Mom. I know he has."

"Dad?" Caroline echoed. The surprises just kept coming today.

"Yes, Dad," Daisy said, a little defensively. "Because that's what he is, Mom. My dad."

"Well, *biologically,* yes," Caroline started to say, but something about the set of Daisy's chin made her stop. Instead, she sipped her coffee.

"I didn't call him that right away," Daisy said, after a moment of silence. "I didn't call him *anything* right away. But that felt strange. So after I'd seen him a few times, I started calling him Jack. And that felt wrong, too. Then, one day, this spring, I just . . . I just called him Dad." She blushed again but added stubbornly, "And despite what you say, Mom, he *has* changed."

"Okay, then," Caroline said, changing tack. "How has he changed?"

"He just has," Daisy said evasively. "I'll let him tell you how."

"But that's where you're wrong, Daisy," Caroline said. "Your father's not going to tell me how he's changed. He's not going to tell me *anything*. Because I'm not going to ask him anything. I'm not interested in him, or his life, anymore, except as it pertains to you."

Daisy started to say something, then stopped. She knew Caroline well enough to know that they'd reached a stalemate on this topic. "If it's okay with you, Mom," she said, after a moment, "I think I'll go to bed early."

"Of course it's okay."

"And you and I . . . *we're* okay?" Daisy asked.

"We will be. Just . . . just give me a few days. And, Daisy . . . no more surprises, all right? Not for a little while, anyway."

"You have my word on that," Daisy promised, reaching for Caroline's hand on the tabletop and giving it a quick squeeze. They stood up then, Caroline to take her coffee cup to the sink, and Daisy to leave the kitchen. But in the doorway, Daisy stopped and turned back.

"Mom, you know the mechanic who repaired your truck today?" she said, coming over to Caroline. "I went to high school with him."

"Really?" Caroline said distractedly, washing out her coffee cup. She was thinking about Jack again.

"Uh-huh. His name is Will. Will Hughes. We weren't friends back then. I think he used to . . . you know, get into trouble a lot."

"Well, no wonder you weren't friends," Caroline said. "That doesn't sound like someone you'd have had anything in common with."

"No, but . . ." Daisy lingered there for a moment, then shrugged and said, "Well, I'll see you in the morning."

"All right, honey," Caroline said, putting her coffee cup in the dish rack. She was relieved when Daisy went into her bedroom and closed the door. God knows, Caroline adored her, but right now, she needed to be alone. She needed to think. And although she generally did her best thinking at the kitchen table, the bathtub, she decided, was a close runner-up. So she went to her room, undressed, and put on her bathrobe. Then she went into the bathroom and ran lukewarm water into the tub, pouring a generous stream of jasmine bath oil under the faucet. Soon, its soothing fragrance filled the room, and Caroline felt some of the tension ebb out of her body.

She turned the faucet off and started to slip out of her bathrobe, but she stopped and turned instead to look at herself in the mirror above the sink. Caroline wasn't a vain woman, not by any stretch. And, as a general rule, she spent very little time staring into mirrors. But tonight, she studied herself in the mirror carefully, critically, trying objectively to see who it was Jack had seen when she'd first sat down across the table from him that afternoon.

Still no gray in her red-blond hair, she thought with satisfaction, ruffling it with her fingers, though that would probably change soon. And her eyes, she decided, leaning closer, her eyes were still her best feature, still a vivid blue. But her skin, unfortunately, was beginning to show her age. It was still creamy white—she'd always been careful to avoid sitting in the sun—but there were a few wrinkles, she thought, with a frown that only deepened those wrinkles. Well, there was nothing she could do about those.

She turned her head slightly to the side now, and, lifting her chin a fraction of an inch, studied her profile. Was the skin there, under her chin, softening just a little? she wondered. Getting just a little less firm? Would she look like her grandma Pearl one day? Grandma Pearl's droopy under-the-chin skin had always reminded Caroline of a turkey's wattle.

She sighed and let her eyes travel down, to her neck, to her collarbone, and then to her breasts, partially obscured by the pink fabric of her bath-robe. And she was tempted, for a moment, to slide her bathrobe down, over her shoulders, and continue her inspection. But she wasn't brave enough to do it. She was still, after all, Pearl's granddaughter, and Grandma Pearl would never have approved of anyone—let alone a middle-aged woman—examining herself naked in the mirror. Still, Caroline thought her body had held up pretty well over the years. Not that she believed in exercise. She didn't; she hated it with a passion. And she'd be damned if she'd get on a treadmill when she already walked at least five miles a day between tables in her coffee shop. But she hadn't gained any weight, as far as she could tell. There was no scale in the apartment, but there was an ancient pair of ripped blue jeans in her closet that were too comfortable to give away, and they still fit her. So that was some-thing, wasn't it?

But then she came to her senses. "Oh, for God's sake, Caroline, stop being such an idiot," she mumbled, turning away from the mirror and dropping her bathrobe on the floor. *You look exactly like what you are, which is a forty-two-year-old woman.* A forty-two-year-old woman who doesn't get facials, or Botox, or . . . or whatever other treatments women used today to turn back the clock, or at least slow it down a little. And that was fine, she thought, stepping into the bathtub, and easing herself down into it. She was perfectly attractive as she was, perfectly attractive to the only man who mattered to her, and that was Buster.

Buster! She sat bolt upright in the bathtub. She'd forgotten to call him back. She looked at her watch; it was too late now. Buster belonged to the "early to bed early to rise" school of thought. It had been something of a sticking point, in fact, in the early days of their relationship, though she'd learned to appreciate the fact that if she didn't have any late nights with Buster, she also didn't have any bleary eyes at Pearl's the next morning. In any case, she decided, lying back down in the bathtub, she'd call him in the morning and bring him up to speed on everything that had happened today. He'd be as surprised as she'd been to discover her ex-husband was back in town. Buster had never met Jack before, of course. He'd only moved up here three years ago, when he'd retired from the military and bought a cabin on Butternut Lake. But he'd heard about Jack from her, heard about him and disapproved of him heartily. But then Buster and Jack were as different as two men could be. Buster would never do anything impulsively, never shirk a responsibility, never count on his looks, or his charm, to get the job done when hard work and discipline would do it just as well.

Still, she thought, easing down a little more into the water, she couldn't pretend Jack wasn't living here now. Butternut was too small for that. And even living out at Wayland's cabin, Jack would be making frequent trips into town. He wouldn't have any choice, if that cabin was as run-down as Caroline remembered it being. Besides, Jack had never been one for seclusion, or quiet reflection—not when there was a bar, or a poker game, within driving distance.

She'd get his cell-phone number from Daisy, she decided, and call him tomorrow. Then they could meet and establish some ground rules. Chances were Jack wouldn't stay long in Butternut anyway. He wasn't much on follow-through, wasn't much on what he'd once told Caroline was the "boring part" of life, the day-to-day in and out that most people not blessed with Jack's good looks had no choice but to be part of—paying bills, running errands, just generally taking care of business. Of course, Jack's business, when Caroline had last known him, had been having a good time. And, as she recalled, he'd been very good at that, though he'd been less good at picking up the pieces that having a good time left behind.

She sat back up and took a sea sponge off the bathtub ledge. She squirted some bath gel onto it and started to wash away the faint scent of bacon grease that always clung to her skin by the end of every workday. And, as she was rinsing herself off, the first real breeze of the day rippled the bathroom window curtain. It felt delightful on her bare skin, and it led her to hope that tomorrow, at least, might be cooler. Then maybe, just maybe, the air-conditioning wouldn't have to work so hard, and it would hang on a little bit longer, until . . . until what? Until she found the money to replace it under her pillow? Or until a customer left her a gargantuan tip, tucked beneath his or her water glass? She sighed. She'd better make that appointment with John Quarterman, the bank's executive vice president, tomorrow, she reminded herself. With all the craziness today, she'd never gotten around to it.

But she pushed the thought of that future meeting out of her mind and lay back down in the bathtub, letting the now cool water lap over her. She'd think about something else, she decided. She'd think about . . . Daisy. But thinking about Daisy, which usually brought her so much pleasure, brought something else with it tonight. She was still hurt that Daisy hadn't told her about Jack coming back into her life, and she was surprised, too, that Daisy didn't seem to share any of her resentment toward him. Then again, she reasoned, if Daisy didn't resent Jack, it was probably because Caroline hadn't *wanted* her to resent him. She'd always been careful, in the years since he'd left, to shield Daisy from any of the bitterness she'd felt toward him. She hadn't done this because she'd thought Jack would ever come back. She hadn't. No, she'd done it because she hadn't wanted to sour Daisy on the institution of marriage. Because despite her own experience with it, and her own reluctance to try it again, Caroline still believed in it, and she hoped Daisy would believe in it too, someday.

Now, though, she wondered if she should have been more honest with Daisy. And not just honest with her about the years before Jack left, but honest with her about the years after Jack left, too. Honest about the loneliness she'd felt then, a loneliness so overwhelming that there were times she was afraid it would simply swallow her whole. Honest about the exhaustion she'd felt; raising a child and running a business by herself, she'd sometimes been so tired that she'd literally fallen asleep on her feet. And maybe she should have been honest about the constant anxiety over providing for their little family, especially when the check that Jack sent every month never seemed to stretch far enough.

But no, she decided, she'd been right not to tell Daisy how difficult those years had been for her. Besides, Daisy wasn't a fool. She knew how hard Caroline had worked. She'd told Caroline, many times, how much she'd appreciated it, too. If she wanted to get to know her father now, well, that was her decision. And if he hurt Daisy, as he probably would, well, then Caroline would just have to strangle him herself. That was all there was to be done about it.

Another breeze blew now, stirring the window curtains again, and feeling, on her skin, like the gentlest caress of summer. *Summer,* she mused. She'd been looking forward to it all year, since last summer, actually. It was always a hectic time at Pearl's—the summer tourism season saw to that—but it was also an uncomplicated time, too. Sure, she worried about whether the "Butternut Burger" special would last through the lunch hour, but beyond that, her biggest worry was how soon she and Daisy could close up Pearl's and head out to Butternut Lake for a late-afternoon swim. Now, suddenly, everything seemed uncertain, unstable—as if the ground had shifted, ever so slightly, beneath her feet. And between the looming deadline with the bank, her ex-husband's return to town, and her daughter's relationship with that ex-husband, Caroline realized that, for the first time in years, she had no idea what to expect of the summer ahead of her.

She exhaled, closed her eyes, and sank a few more inches into the water. And, as she did so, an image of Jack came, unbidden, into her mind. It was an image of him smiling, smiling *that* smile. She hadn't seen that smile today. He'd been too nervous to smile that smile. But the truth was, when Jack smiled, *really* smiled at you, he had a great smile. It was a slow smile, a smile that seemed to say that he had all the time in the world. And you, the woman he was smiling at? You were the only other person in that world with him. She had loved that smile once, and she wondered, now, if he still had it . . .

Caroline sat up abruptly and yanked the plug out of the bathtub. What was she doing, thinking about Jack that way? If she started daydreaming about him again, the way she had when she'd first met him, she'd know it was time to go straight to a mental health professional. Because only a crazy person could go through what she'd gone through with Jack Keegan and still feel any attraction to him at all.

"Jason, seriously, are you going to take the shot or not?" Will asked. They were playing pool at the Moccasin Bar that night, and Jason had already lined up his shot three times.

Jason sighed with mock exasperation and straightened up. "Will, you broke my concentration. Now I'm just going to have to start all over again."

"Yeah, well, they're not going to let us have this table all night," Will pointed out, taking a swig from his beer bottle. "And I do mean *all* night, the way you're playing."

"Patience, Will, patience," Jason said, setting up the shot again, this time even more carefully than before. Will groaned, but only on principle. He didn't really care how long this game stretched out for, not when playing pool at his favorite bar with his best friend seemed as good a way to spend the night as any other.

"Three ball in the side pocket," Jason said, finally taking the shot. As Will watched the balls scatter, he felt a tap on his shoulder. Although he knew who it was without turning around, he turned around. "Hi, Christy," he said, and he saw, immediately, that there was something in his expression, or in his tone of voice, that she didn't like.

"You don't seem that happy to see me," she observed, her pink lip-glossed lips forming a pout. Oddly enough, Christy's pout was one of the things that had initially attracted him to her. But tonight, for some reason, he found it mildly irritating.

"No, it's not that," Will said. "It's just, I'm in

the middle of a game." He looked over at Jason, who was setting up another shot. He was used to these interruptions from Christy.

"Are you mad at me?" Christy asked. Her pout had gotten poutier.

"I'm not mad at you."

"Are you sure? Because I know it's been a while. But, Will, I can't help that."

"I know you can't help that."

"Good," she said, and after a quick look around to see if anyone was watching them, she reached out and gave his T-shirt a tug. "So let's go," she said. "Now." He saw then, objectively, how pretty she looked, with her wide blue eyes and her long, shiny blond hair. Saw it, but for some reason, tonight, he didn't feel it.

"I'm going to finish this game," he said, shifting his pool cue to his other hand.

A frown creased Christy's smooth, suntanned forehead.

"Look, it's not a big deal," he said.

"This is the first time we've been able to see each other in what, two weeks, and it's 'not a big deal'?"

Will closed his eyes, just for a second, bracing himself for what was next. Christy, he knew, did not take rejection well, since, like most exceptionally attractive people, she'd had very little experience with it. And, in fact, when Will opened his eyes, he saw there was a little muscle working in Christy's tightly clenched jaw.

"Okay, Will, I'll tell you what I'm going to do," she said. "I'm going to go sit at the bar and order a drink and drink it while you finish your game. Not because I understand why you need to finish it but because I've missed you, and I don't know when I'll be able to see you again after tonight. So when you and Jason are done, come and get me and we'll leave. All right?"

"No," Will said. He didn't know who that single word surprised more, him or Christy.

"No what?" she asked, her blue eyes, with their heavily mascaraed lashes, opening wide.

"No, I'm not leaving here with you tonight."

"Why not?"

"You don't need to know why not, Christy," he said, trying to keep a lid on his exasperation. "I'm a free agent. I'm not your husband; you already have one of those, remember?"

She flinched, visibly. They both knew Will had never said anything like that to her before. But then again, they both knew Will had never not wanted to go home with her before either. He watched, uncomfortably, as the expression on her face turned from shock to hurt to anger.

"That wasn't very nice, Will," she snapped, and then she walked away.

"What was that about?" Jason asked, mystified, when Will rejoined him at the pool table.

"Nothing," Will mumbled, setting up to take his shot.

"That didn't look like nothing," Jason observed. "But I have to say, Will, she looks hot when she's angry. Then again," he added, drinking his beer, "she looks hot when she's not angry too."

Will set up his shot and took it. It was a lousy shot.

"Hey, Will, if you want to take off with her, that's fine," Jason said, watching as the pool balls scattered ineffectually. "I'll find someone else to play with."

"No, I don't want to go. But you know what? I don't really want to play pool, either. Let's get another round at the bar."

They both sat down at the bar and ordered a beer, and Will drank his moodily as he thought back to the night he'd met Christy. He and Jason were at a different bar, a dive bar called the Mosquito Inn, where they went sometimes just for the hell of it. Christy was there too, with a friend, and the two of them had sat down at the bar with Will and Jason. Will had seen her wedding ring right away, and he'd been on his guard. He didn't have many rules in his life, but not getting involved with married women was one of them.

Still, it had seemed to him, at first, that if getting involved was the farthest thing from his mind, it was the farthest thing from Christy's mind too. She wasn't flirtatious—except, maybe, for that adorable pout—she was just unhappy. Very, very unhappy. She'd gotten married too young, she told Will, to a man who didn't really love her. Mac, her husband, was a salesman who traveled a lot on business, and she was lonely when he was away, but she was even lonelier when he was home. Most of the time, he just ignored her. When he wasn't ignoring her, he was being mean to her. She started her story sitting at the bar with Will and finished it sitting in his pickup truck in the bar's parking lot. By then, she was crying, and even with mascara-blackened tears running down her cheeks, she'd still looked ridiculously beautiful. He'd comforted her, as best he could, getting cocktail napkins from the bar for her to dry her tears with, holding her, stroking her back. But when none of these worked, he'd taken her home to her lonely house and made her feel less lonely—all night long. And leaving her house the next morning, Will hadn't felt especially guilty about it either. He figured if her husband was as big a jerk as she said he was, he probably didn't deserve her fidelity, anyway . . . That had been a year ago.

Since then Christy had seemed happier. She rarely mentioned Mac anymore, though that was partly because Will, who tried not to think about him, didn't want to talk about him either. He'd never met him before, and, except for the pictures of him at Christy's house, he wouldn't have recognized him if he had. But sometimes, Will felt bad for the guy. And that wasn't the only problem with their arrangement. Because between the coded messages Christy insisted they use when they texted each other, and the sneaking around, and the lying, he was starting to feel like Mac wasn't the one who was the jerk here. He was.

He had a bitter taste in his mouth now, and he took a slug of his beer, hoping to wash it away, but it stayed there, and thinking about the first night he'd met Christy wasn't helping. He was wondering if she'd ever been as unhappy as she'd said she was, wondering, too, if Mac had ever treated her as badly as she'd said he had. And, most of all, he was wondering why this was the first time he'd bothered to ask himself either of these questions.

"Christy's still here," Jason said now, breaking into his thoughts.

"Yeah?" Will said.

"Uh-huh. And I don't think she's ready to give up on you yet," Jason observed, looking down the bar.

Will followed his eyes and saw Christy talking to two men sitting at the other end of the bar. She was pointedly ignoring Will and Jason, but she was lavishing attention on her two new friends, tossing her long blond hair, and laughing exaggeratedly at whatever they were saying. Will looked away, but Jason was fascinated by her performance.

"She keeps looking over here, Will. I think she's trying to make you jealous."

"It's not working," Will mumbled into his beer.

"Okay, she just walked away from those two guys. One of them, by the way, looks like he's about to cry in his beer. I think he thought he was gonna get lucky. Let's see, what's she doing now. She's walkin' over to the jukebox, she's puttin' some quarters in—"

"Hey, Jason," Will broke in. "I don't need the play by play."

Jason shrugged and was silent for a few minutes, but then Will heard him whistle softly under his breath. "Will, you have got to see this," he said.

Will glanced over to where the jukebox was and saw that Christy was dancing, suggestively, by herself. Even Will couldn't quite bring himself to look away, which meant he was in good company, since by now the whole rest of the bar was staring at her too.

She was dressed tonight in a tiny, vintage rock concert tee, denim cutoffs that were so short the linings of the pockets peeked out from beneath their fashionably ragged hems, and high-heeled wedge sandals that made her long suntanned legs look even longer. Her arms were above her head, her head was thrown back, and her eyes were closed, as she swayed and swiveled to an '80s rock anthem that everyone in the bar knew by heart.

"Will, seriously, *just go with her already,*" Jason said. "I can't take much more of this."

"Yeah, well, you're pathetic," Will said, making a point of staring into his beer.

"I'm not pathetic," Jason said, unperturbed. "It's just . . . her legs, Will. What's up with them? Seriously. How does she get them so shiny?"

Baby oil, Will almost said. This was true. He knew for a fact that Christy rubbed it into her legs to make them softer and smoother because he'd seen her do it on more than one occasion. But he didn't tell Jason this; he'd never hear the end of it if he did.

"You know what?" he said suddenly, taking out his wallet and throwing some money on the bar. "Let's go."

"Go?" Jason objected. "The show's just getting started."

"Well, it's over for us," Will said, sliding off his bar stool.

"Will, I haven't even finished my beer yet."

"We'll stop and buy a six-pack," Will said. "Then we'll go back to the garage and play some darts, and I'll try really hard not to beat you."

"Okay," Jason said reluctantly, taking a final swig of his beer and giving Christy one last look. "But you're paying for the beer."

An hour later they were back at the garage. They'd finished their dart game, and they were sitting outside in a couple of beat-up old lawn chairs, drinking beer.

"I thought you said you were going to let me beat you at darts," Jason said, a little sulkily.

"Did I say that?"

"Yep," Jason said, reaching into the cooler between them and grabbing another can of beer. "You said that, Will." But Will could see he'd already forgotten about it. This was why he could spend as much time with the guy as he did; Jason was the most easygoing person Will had ever met.

Jason started to open his can of beer, then changed his mind and held it up against his forehead instead. Even now, with a decent breeze finally blowing, it was still at least ninety degrees outside.

"By the way, you were right about that girl," Jason said, taking the beer can away from his face and popping it open.

"Which girl?"

"That girl from today. Daisy. She called right before closing to see if her cell phone was here. I said it was, so she's going to pick it up tomorrow."

"Why are you just telling me this now?" Will asked, annoyed.

"I don't know. Is it that important?"

"Maybe."

"Why?"

"I might ask her out when she comes back," Will said casually, swatting at a mosquito.

Jason stared at him, then shook his head. "I don't think that's a good idea."

"Why not?"

Jason leaned back in his chair. "Well, for one thing, Christy won't like it."

"Christy doesn't have a say in the matter."

"Okaaay," Jason said slowly. "Well, then, there's your MO, Will. It's not going to work with a girl like that."

"My MO," Will said, amused. "What's my MO?"

"Well, let's see," Jason drawled. "It's been a while. But before Christy, you'd pick up a girl in your truck, drive her out to the lake, and split a six-pack of beer with her while you watched the sun set. Then you'd climb into the back seat for the evening's entertainment."

Will smiled. "Sounds good to me."

"Well, it wouldn't sound good to Daisy."

"How do you know that?"

"Because I just know." Jason shrugged. "You can just tell from looking at her. It's going to take a lot more than a few beers to get her into the back of your truck—if she'd *ever* even go back there, which I seriously doubt she would."

"Okay, so I'd have to work a little harder with someone like her," Will allowed.

"A *little* harder? Try *a lot* harder, Will. There are

still some girls like that, you know. Girls where, if you want to get anywhere with them, you have to date them. Do you even know how to do that, Will? Do you know how to take a girl out, and, you know, do stuff with her? Like, show her stuff? And buy her stuff?"

"It can't be that difficult," Will said, amused by Jason's description of dating. It wasn't something either one of them knew a lot about, seeing as how they'd both worked so hard to avoid doing it.

"Besides," Will added, finishing his beer, "I think you're wrong about Daisy. I think she's the kind of girl who could appreciate life's simple pleasures."

Jason laughed. "Is that what you're calling it now? 'A simple pleasure'? I don't know, Will. Maybe she'd appreciate it, but you'd have to wait for her to. And I don't think you'd be willing to wait that long."

"Maybe," Will said, distractedly. But he wasn't really listening. He was thinking about Daisy brushing a strand of strawberry-blond hair off her cheek today. It was such a small thing to do, an ordinary thing, an uninteresting thing, really, on the face of it. So why couldn't he stop thinking about it now?

Chapter 3

When Daisy walked into the office at the garage the next afternoon, Jason was leaning back in a swivel chair, his feet up on the desk, reading a video-gaming magazine.

"Oh, hi," he said, when he saw her. He took his feet off the desk. "You're here for your cell phone."

She nodded and waited for him to reach into one of the desk drawers and pull it out. But instead he pointed in the direction of the service bay. "It's right where you left it yesterday."

"Oh," she said, hesitating.

"Will can get it for you," he said with a smile, and then he went back to reading his magazine.

"Thanks," Daisy said, feeling a combination of relief and nervousness as she left the office. Relief because she'd been worried she wouldn't see Will today; nervousness because, at the same time, she'd been worried she *would*. When she came around the corner of the service bay a moment later, she expected to find him working on a car, but instead he was rummaging around in a cooler filled with ice.

"Hey," he said, straightening up when he saw her.

"Hi," she said, hanging back. It had only been twenty-four hours since she'd last seen him, but already he looked different. He looked *better*. He wiped his hands, wet from the cooler, on his blue jeans.

"I came to get my cell phone," she said, wishing there was a more interesting way of saying that.

"Right over there," he said, pointing to the worktable where she'd slammed it down when she'd realized the battery was dead.

Daisy went over and picked it up.

"The battery's probably still dead," Will said, his eyes playful, and Daisy blushed at the mention of her near temper tantrum.

"Well, thanks," she said, backing away.

"Anytime," he said, rummaging in the cooler again. She started to leave, then stopped and turned around. She didn't want to go, but she didn't have an excuse to stay, either. He looked at her for a moment, standing there, then smiled.

"Do you want something to drink?" he asked.

"Okay," she said, edging closer.

"What do you want?" he asked. "Water? Soda?"

"Um, do you have Diet Coke?"

"Nothing diet. But regular Coke."

"That's fine," she said, coming closer.

He reached into the cooler again and brought up two cans of Coke. He handed one to her, and she opened it immediately and took a sip. It was so sweet, she almost winced. But it was also cold and fizzy, and it felt good going down her suddenly dry throat.

Will opened his can and took a long drink, then asked, "How did it go yesterday?"

"With my parents?"

He nodded.

"It didn't actually go that well," she admitted. "You were right, by the way. My mom did feel ambushed."

"But no one needed to pull them apart, did they?" he asked, his gold-brown eyes never leaving her face.

"No," she said, sipping the sweet drink and wondering if it was possible for her parents to be any further apart than they already were.

"They're actually going to meet again today," she said. "Without me there. This way, I guess, my mom can say exactly what she wants to say to my dad."

"Maybe that's good," Will said. "You know, to clear the air."

"Maybe."

"Jason told me your mom owns that coffee shop in Butternut," he said. "Pearl's, right?"

She nodded.

"I went there a few times in high school. But I don't think my friends and I were very good customers. One of them, I remember, knew how to do this thing where you left the tip—some change—under an upside-down glass of water."

"You're not the first high school students to do that."

"No? Well, we probably weren't very original. Do you work there?" he asked. "When you're home in the summer?"

"Uh-huh."

"Do you like working there?"

"It's . . . it's okay," she said. "I mean, I grew up there, so I don't really think about it. I just do it, I guess. My mom says I could waitress in my sleep, and she's probably right."

After a pause, Daisy asked, "What about you, do you like working here?" That curiosity she'd felt about him yesterday surfaced again, only now that curiosity was mixed up with another feeling too, a feeling she didn't want to examine too closely.

"I like it," he said, with a shrug. "I just wish it was a real business."

"A real business?" she echoed. "You mean, it's not a real business?"

He shook his head.

"So, it's like . . . it's like *a front?*" she asked, lowering her voice and coming closer.

"A what?" he said.

"A front. You know, for money laundering?"

He looked at her quizzically, and for a moment she was afraid he was going to be angry, or offended. But then he laughed. "No, it's not a front. What I meant was, Jason's dad, who owns it, doesn't take it that seriously. He doesn't need to. He's made some money on other investments, and this place is more of a sideline for him. You know, it gives Jason something to do, something other than sitting on the couch all day playing video games."

"Well, you seem pretty busy here," she said, glancing around.

He shrugged. "I could be a lot busier. But without some real investment in equipment, and some more training for me, we can't compete with the dealerships in Ely, or with the big automotive chains, either."

"So why don't you go someplace else?" Daisy asked, then regretted asking it. It was a pretty personal question to ask someone she barely knew. But again, he didn't seem offended.

"I don't know," he said. "I guess I feel like I kind of owe it to Jason, and his family. I basically grew up over at their house. Plus, Jason's dad taught me almost everything I know about engines. And the pay here might not be great, but it has some fringe benefits. Like free rent," he added, pointing behind them.

"You live here?" Daisy asked, surprised.

"Yeah. There's a little apartment back there. It's not much to look at. But it has the basics, a refrigerator, a microwave . . ." He shrugged again.

So it's like a dorm room, Daisy almost said. But she didn't, because when you thought about it, it wasn't anything like a dorm room.

"There's another upside to working here, too," Will said now, finishing his soda and tossing the can into a nearby bin. "Come here. I'll show you." Daisy followed him over to the other side of the garage. She knew very little about cars, but she knew that the one Will stopped next to was a vintage model. It was a bright, cherry red, and its lines were sleek and graceful.

"This is a 1960 Chevy Impala," he said, running his hand along one of its fenders. "Not bad, huh?"

"It's beautiful," she said honestly.

"It is, isn't it?" he said. "It's Mr. Phipps's. You probably know him. He owns the lumber mill in Butternut."

"Two eggs, over easy, sausage, sour dough toast," she murmured, without thinking.

"What?"

She blushed. "That's Mr. Phipps's breakfast order."

"Oh, right," Will said, chuckling. "Is that how you see the world, Daisy? In breakfast orders?"

"Sometimes," she admitted. "In the summertime, anyway. When I go back to college, in September, I try to forget how people like their eggs."

Then she added, "But it turns out I don't know everything about Mr. Phipps. I didn't know he drove this car."

"Oh, he doesn't drive it. Not that often, anyway. He collects cars like this—classic cars. He has something like twelve of them now, twelve and counting."

"And you work on them for him?"

He nodded. "After he buys them, I help him restore them. I mean, it pays. But mostly, it's just fun. You know, scrounging around for parts; it's kind of like a scavenger hunt. And then, when I get the parts, working on the engine is totally different from working on a new car engine. Here, I'll show you," he said, going around to the hood of the Chevy, lifting it up and propping it open. Daisy came over and stood beside him. "I mean, look at this," he said. Daisy looked at it politely. It looked like an engine.

But Will was captivated by it. "In cars today," he said, turning to Daisy, "a lot of engine diagnostics are done by computer. But with a car like this, built fifty years ago, it's just you and the car. And you really have to listen to its engine. You know, pay attention to it. Because if you do, it'll talk to you." As soon as he said that, though, he averted his eyes back to the car's engine and started tinkering with it, as if he were embarrassed, as if he thought he'd said too much.

Daisy didn't say anything. Instead, she looked at the place on his neck where she'd seen the smudge of grease yesterday. It was gone now, washed away. But she still longed to touch the

96

skin there, to run a finger over its smooth, suntanned warmth. That urge—the strength of that urge, really—surprised her, and she looked away from that place on Will's neck and back at the Chevy Impala.

"So engines talk to you?" she asked.

He shrugged and fiddled with something in it.

"Because I'm pretty sure an engine has never talked to me before. Not even to say hello."

He glanced back at her and smiled an almost smile. "You don't know anything about cars?"

"Wasn't that obvious yesterday?"

He shrugged. "Well, you don't need to know what I know. But you'd be surprised how easy it is to learn some basic automotive maintenance."

"I would be surprised," she said.

The corner of his mouth quirked up in another almost smile. "Do you know how to change your oil?" he asked.

She shook her head.

"Do you know how to *check* your oil?"

Again, she shook her head. "No. Joey Riggs does that for us at the gas station in Butternut."

"Okay. But what if Joey Riggs can't do it for you one day?"

"Then . . . then we'll get someone else to do it?" she offered.

He raised his eyebrows, more amused than exasperated. "Look, let me at least show you how to check your oil," he said. "That way, even if you can't change it yourself, you'll still know when someone else needs to change it. The dipstick in your truck is in a slightly different location than it is here"—he gestured at the Chevy's engine—"but if you can find it here, you'll be able to find it there, too." He took a pair of gloves off a nearby worktable, saying as he handed them to her, "Why don't you put these on."

She put her can of Coke and her cell phone down on the same worktable and slid on the gloves. They were too big on her, but the leather felt cool against her skin. As Will showed her where the dipstick was, she thought about the fact that he'd worn these gloves, perhaps recently, and that their soft leather had touched his skin, too, and she felt what she knew was an adolescent thrill.

He talked her through checking the oil and watched while she pulled the dipstick out, wiped it clean, stuck it back in the engine, and read the meter on the end of it. He explained then how much oil to add, and how to tell when the oil needed to be changed. It seemed silly to her that she hadn't already known how to do something so simple, but when Will was done, he seemed satisfied.

"See," he said, pulling the gloves off her hands in a strangely intimate gesture. "You already know more about engines than you did five minutes ago."

Daisy smiled at him, and he smiled back at her, a real smile this time, before he turned serious. And for a split second, Daisy had a crazy feeling that he was going to lean down and kiss her. But instead, he asked her, "Would you like to go out with me sometime, Daisy?"

"Yes," she breathed, and then she blushed furiously, wishing she'd taken a moment to at least pretend to consider the offer.

But Will only smiled again. "Good," he said. "When are you free?"

Tonight, she wanted to say. But she caught herself. "How about Saturday?" she said.

"Saturday's good. Where should I pick you up?"

"Around the corner from Pearl's. On Glover Street. There's a separate entrance for our apartment. Just ring the buzzer," she said, her face warm under his steady gaze.

"Okay," he said. "How's seven o'clock?"

"Seven's fine," she said, realizing that her voice had sunk almost to a whisper. She got that feeling again that she'd gotten yesterday, that the two of them were alone in their own private world.

"Well, I better be getting back," she said, after a long moment. She tried to speak louder this time, and her voice sounded almost normal.

"I'll see you Saturday," he said.

She started to go, but she hadn't gotten very far when Will called out to her. "Daisy?"

"Yes?" she said, turning around.

"You forgot your phone."

Driving back to Butternut in her mom's pickup, Daisy replayed their conversation in her mind. *Funny,* she thought, directing the air-conditioning vent to blow on her still warm face, summer, to her, had always felt as predictable as Mr. Phipps's breakfast order. But she was getting the feeling that this summer was going to be more interesting—*a lot* more interesting.

"Caroline, are you sure you don't want me to stay for this?" Buster asked, leaning on the counter at Pearl's.

"Yes, Buster, I'm sure." She was unscrewing the lids on all the salt and pepper shakers and lining them up on the countertop to refill. Whenever Caroline was nervous—and she was very nervous right now—she liked to keep her hands busy with some task or other.

"Well, I don't like it," Buster said, shaking his head.

"I know you don't like it," Caroline said, pausing in her work and studying him. He was fifty-eight now, his thick salt-and-pepper hair cut in a longer version of a crew cut, his blue eyes crinkling appealingly in his pleasantly weather-beaten face. He'd retired from being an army transport pilot three years ago, but Buster still projected an air of calm, unflappable confidence, that sense that no matter what happened, he'd be prepared for it. He'd know exactly what to do.

Except, possibly, today; today he looked a little bit at a loss, as if he was waiting for orders that hadn't come yet. He'd been that way, she imagined, since she'd called him and told him that her ex-husband was back in town. Caroline paused now, and, putting down the carton of salt she was holding, she put her hand on his arm, which was resting on the counter. It was a nice arm, she thought, patting it. An arm that, like everything else about Buster, was reassuringly solid.

But as much as she appreciated Buster being here now, in all his solidity, she hadn't counted on him staying so long. She glanced at the clock on the wall behind the counter and saw it was 3:25. Jack would arrive in five minutes. She'd already flipped the Open sign on the door to Closed, already banished Daisy, just back from picking up her cell phone, to the apartment upstairs, and already begged Frankie to leave work a half hour early, something he rarely, if ever, did. But she hadn't counted on Buster still being here.

"Sweetheart," she said, gently, "look, I can't just pretend Jack isn't here now. I mean, I can, but it'd be awkward, sharing this town with him, without actually acknowledging his presence in it. And another thing, I don't think this situation is good for Daisy."

"What's wrong with Daisy?" Buster frowned. He was very fond of Daisy, even though he hadn't spent a lot of time with her. By the time he'd met Caroline, Daisy had already left for college.

"Nothing's *wrong* with Daisy," Caroline said, carefully, though she was remembering Daisy's stubborn defense of Jack last night, and her hopefulness, however naive, that Caroline would see how much he'd changed for herself. "Daisy's fine," she said. "I just think if Jack and I can reach some kind of understanding, it would be better for her." Squeezing his arm, she added, "And better for us, too, Buster. Because if Jack's going to stay here, even for a little while, we all have to find a way to peacefully coexist together."

Buster nodded. "Look, Caroline, I know you're doing the right thing. You always do the right thing. It's just . . ." His voice trailed off.

"Just what?" Caroline prompted.

"It's just that I'm jealous, I guess," he said, a little sheepishly.

"Buster," Caroline said, with a rush of affection. "You have nothing to be jealous about. You know that."

"I do know that," he said. "But I remember what you told me about him—how charming he is; how persuasive he can be; how he swept you off your feet and made you do all these crazy things."

"You mean, like ever going out on a date with

him in the first place?" Caroline asked wryly.

Buster nodded.

"Well, that *was* crazy. No doubt about it. But that was over twenty years ago. I like to think I've grown up *a little* since then. And as for Jack, well, that's not what Jack wants either. I don't know why he's back here, but it's not because of me. Trust me. He was as unhappy in that marriage as I was. And Buster? Even in the very unlikely event that he did want us to get back together again? Well, I have you now." She leaned over and kissed him on the lips. He was surprised. When she was at Pearl's, Caroline was usually all business. But today, she thought, taking her time with the kiss, she needed to make a point.

She pulled away. "Better?" she teased.

"Much," he said, smiling.

"Good. Now, you should get going. I happen to know you're due at the driving range soon," she reminded him. After dating Buster for three years, Caroline knew his schedule like the back of her hand. On Tuesday afternoons, weather permitting, Buster went to the driving range outside of town and hit exactly one hundred golf balls. After thirty years in the military, the man thrived on routine.

"Okay, I'll go," he said, a little reluctantly, sliding off his stool. "But I still don't like it." And then he was gone, and Caroline was left alone with her anxiety. She thought, fleetingly, about checking her appearance in the mirror in her office, then dismissed the thought. *This is not a date,* she reminded herself. *This is a . . .* But as she was mulling over *what,* exactly, it was, she heard the tinkle of little bells, and Jack Keegan walked through the door.

"Hello, Caroline," he said, smiling a little uncertainly. And Caroline was surprised to see that he was as nervous as she was. She didn't remember Jack ever being nervous before, even when he *should* have been nervous. Like the time she'd brought him home to meet her disapproving parents, or the time, after their marriage, he'd tried to explain to her how meeting a friend for a beer had somehow turned into a three-day game of poker.

"Hello, Jack," she said coolly, screwing the lid back on a now full saltshaker. But then she remembered her promise to herself to be civil to him, to be, if not friendly, then at least polite. Because she was afraid if she let her anger seep out, even a little, she'd end up drowning in it.

"Would you like something to drink, Jack?" she asked him now. "An iced tea? A lemonade?"

"Actually, if you've still got some, I'd love a cup of coffee," he said, coming up to the counter and standing, disconcertingly, where Buster had stood only moments before.

"Coffee is the only thing we never run out of here," Caroline said, reaching behind her for a clean cup. "Why don't you choose a table and I'll join you in a minute," she added.

He nodded and went to sit down at a table while Caroline poured him a cup of coffee, adding plenty of half-and-half, and poured herself a glass of iced tea with a lemon wedge. Then she carried them over to the table, set them down, and sat down across from him.

"Thanks," he said with a smile. Not the slow smile she'd thought about in the bathtub last night, but a quick, easy smile that touched his blue eyes and reminded her again of what a good-looking man he still was. *Damn him,* she thought with annoyance, sipping her iced tea. She watched while he took a sip of his coffee, then said, with surprise, "You remember how I like it."

"I remember how *everyone* likes it, Jack," she said, staring back at him impassively. "It's my business to remember."

"Of course it is," he agreed, unfazed. "And if there's one thing you know how to do, Caroline, it's run a business."

She thought of her most recent bank statement, which would seem to dispute this assertion, but to Jack she said simply, "Let's skip the compliments, all right? I didn't ask you to come here so that we could exchange pleasantries, Jack."

"No?" he asked innocently. *Too innocently.*

"No," she repeated, crossing her arms over her chest. "So let's cut to the chase, all right?"

"All right," he said, leaning back in his chair, his dark blue eyes resting on her.

"What are you doing here, Jack? In Butternut?"

"I told you. I'm living here."

"At Wayland's old cabin?"

"That's right."

"And you say Wayland left it to you?"

Jack nodded.

But she was skeptical. "I didn't know you and Wayland had stayed in touch, Jack. I mean, when was the last time you even saw him?"

A shadow crossed his face. "I went to visit him in the hospital in Duluth when he . . . when he was sick. Really sick, toward the end."

Caroline nodded somberly. "He had cancer, didn't he?"

"Liver cancer," Jack said. "Terminal cancer's never good, obviously," he said, quietly. "But this . . . this seemed especially bad, somehow."

Caroline sighed. Poor Wayland. He'd been a sweet, though ineffectual man. And unlike Jack . . . well, unlike Jack, all the good times had finally caught up with him.

"Anyway," Jack said. "Wayland didn't say anything about a will when I visited him in the hospital. Honestly, I would have been surprised to know he even *had* a will. But then, about a year ago, I got a call from his lawyer. I didn't know he had one of those, either. Anyway, it wasn't until this summer that I was able to move back up here and, you know, actually live in it."

"You can't be serious, Jack."

"About what?"

"About living in that . . . *place,*" she said, because *cabin* suddenly seemed to be too kind a word. "I mean, is it even habitable?"

"Depends on your definition of the word. But it's *going* to be, by the time I get through with it. I've never done anything quite like this before, but I figure, what the hell. I know my way around a tool belt."

"A *tool belt,* Jack? I think a *bulldozer* might be more apt, don't you?"

There was that little shoulder lift again. If he was intimidated by what lay ahead, he wasn't saying so.

"Okay, so you're going to fix up that cabin. But with what money, Jack? And what are you going to live on while you do it?"

"I've saved some money over the past couple of years, working at the refinery."

She'd taken a sip of her iced tea, and now she practically choked on it. "Oh please, Jack," she said, trying not to laugh. "You've never saved a penny in your life." *Not if you could sink it into a card game instead.*

But Jack didn't argue the point. He only lifted his shoulders a little, as if to say, *We'll see.*

"All right then," she said challengingly, "what

do you do when you're done with the cabin? Sell it to some unlucky soul?"

"Or I stay," Jack said casually. "Put down roots in this fine community."

"This fine community that you've always *hated*, Jack," Caroline pointed out. "Or have you forgotten?"

But he sidestepped the question and said, with his infuriating nonchalance, "Towns change, Caroline. So do people."

"Trust me, Jack, this town hasn't changed."

"Then maybe I have," he said, his dark blue eyes suddenly serious.

"That's what your daughter thinks," Caroline said. "But I know better. And, Jack, I give you two weeks here; a month, tops."

"We'll see," he said, sipping his coffee again. "But in the meantime, I'm looking forward to spending the summer here."

"And seeing my daughter?" Caroline asked.

Jack hesitated. "Yes, Caroline. And seeing *our* daughter."

Caroline flinched. *Our daughter*. That sounded strange. That sounded . . . *wrong*. It had been years since Caroline had thought of Daisy as anything other than *her* daughter. She squeezed her lemon wedge, angrily, into her glass of tea and tried to organize her thoughts. Because what she was going to say next was the real reason she'd asked him to come here today—and the real reason, too, she hadn't been able to sleep last night. So she chose her words carefully now, or as carefully as she could when you considered how furious she was.

"Look, Jack, I don't know why, after all this time, you've resurfaced in Daisy's life. And I don't know why she has developed such a touching faith in you either. But I don't share that faith, Jack. I know how this is going to end. And it's going to end badly."

"You can't know how this is going to end, Caroline. None of us knows that." And there was that shadow, again, crossing so quickly over his face she wondered if it had been there at all.

"Look," she said, changing tack. "I can't tell you what to do, Jack; I never could. Just don't . . . don't hurt her, okay?"

He nodded slowly, his blue eyes serious. "I have no intention of hurting her, Caroline; at least not any more than I already have. And don't think I don't know how much I've already hurt her," he added. "I'm not an idiot, Caroline. And even if I were one, Daisy spelled it out for me the first time I saw her again."

"She did?" Caroline asked, surprised. Since she'd found out about these meetings, Daisy had volunteered very little information about them, and Caroline hadn't wanted to pry. But the truth was, she was curious, damned curious.

Jack nodded. "She was so angry that morning I

109

met her for coffee," he said, "in this little dive coffeehouse near the university, that it put the fear of God in me. She told me she hadn't known until the last minute whether she'd come and meet me or not. She said that I was a sorry excuse for a father, and that if I thought I could just walk back into her life again after all these years, I was dead wrong. She told me, too, that the two of you had done just fine without me the whole time she was growing up, and if you hadn't needed me then, there was no reason you needed me now." With an admiring smile, he added, "There was more, but that was the gist of it."

"Daisy said all that?" Caroline asked, wonderingly. She'd never even guessed at the depth of Daisy's anger toward Jack. But, then again, she hadn't wanted Daisy to guess at the anger *she* felt toward him either.

"She said all that and more," Jack said. "Much more. That was when I realized how articulate she was. It didn't surprise me, later, when she told me she'd been on the debate team in high school."

"What did you do, Jack, while she was saying all this to you?" Caroline asked, genuinely curious.

He shrugged. "I sat there and listened to her. What else could I do? Every word she said was true. I couldn't argue with her, so I just tried to take it like a man."

Caroline squeezed her already pulverized lemon wedge into her iced tea again and tried to imagine Jack sitting there and taking it. But she couldn't. The Jack she remembered had hated being on the receiving end of a lecture. He'd hated it so much that as soon as he'd felt one coming on, he was out the door.

"Anyway," he continued, "things got better between us, eventually. The third or fourth time I met her, we had an actual conversation. It was good, Caroline—really good—just talking to her. She was less angry, and I was less nervous. But I was still awed by her."

"Awed?"

He nodded. "Awed by the person she'd become. And humbled, too, by the knowledge that I couldn't take any credit for her becoming that person."

Caroline felt confused. Because the Jack she'd known had had many qualities, some of them even good qualities, but humility? Humility had never been one of them.

"But you know what, Caroline?" he continued now. "*I* might not be able to take credit for the person Daisy has become, but you can. And you should. Because you've raised one hell of a daughter."

"I . . . need to get a refill on my tea," she said abruptly, feeling disconcerted by the direction the conversation had taken. And by seeing a side of

Jack that felt wholly unfamiliar to her. She stood up. "Would you, would you like more coffee?" she asked.

"No, thank you," he said, chuckling. "And you still can't take a compliment, can you, Caroline?"

But she ignored that question, took her glass to the counter, refilled it, and brought it back to the table. The forty-five seconds it took her to do this was crucial, because it allowed her to collect herself, refocus herself.

"Okay, let's assume, for the time being anyway, that you're going to stay in Butternut, Jack," she said. "If that's the case, then we need to establish some ground rules."

"Ground rules, huh?" he repeated, a smile playing around his lips. He was back, the old Jack. "That sounds serious, Caroline."

"It *is* serious. Because long after you've decided your little experiment here has failed, *I'll* still have to live here and work here. So I'd appreciate if you'd take this seriously, Jack."

"All right," he said, "I will, Caroline. In fact, just tell me what the rules are, and I'll follow them."

"Well, for one, I don't want you coming in here anymore," she said, gesturing around the coffee shop. "If you need to speak to me again— although I don't think that will be necessary— you can call me here and we can meet. Privately. I'm not giving this town any more opportunities to gossip about us, and that's exactly what they'll do if you start coming in here."

"And where am I supposed to get my morning coffee?"

"Anywhere but here," she said, without missing a beat.

He hesitated. "All right, fine. If it makes you uncomfortable, I won't come in here anymore. Unless you invite me in, of course."

"I won't invite you in," she said crisply. "Which brings me to the second ground rule, Jack." She looked down now, away from his dark blue eyes, which she found distracting, and focused instead on the small triangle of bare, suntanned chest visible above the top unbuttoned button of his blue work shirt. But that was distracting, too. So she looked down at her own iced tea, stirring it vigorously with the straw. "I'm seeing someone now, Jack," she said. "I have been for the last couple of years."

"I know."

"You do?" she asked, looking up with surprise.

He nodded. "His name is Buster, right? Buster Caine. He's retired. Ex-military."

She frowned. "How do you know all that?"

"Daisy told me."

"Daisy discussed my personal life with you?" she said, feeling another rare flash of anger at her daughter.

Jack saw that anger, and his face fell. "No,

Caroline. She didn't. It wasn't like that. That's all she told me. And the only reason she told me that was because I asked, asked if you were seeing anyone, I mean."

"Well, I still don't like it," Caroline said, wondering, with irritation, why Jack was probing into her love life.

"Okay. Don't like it. But blame me. Not Daisy."

She stirred her tea again, but didn't say what she was thinking, which was that as far as she was concerned, there was plenty of blame to go around for both of them. When she started talking again, she could hear the irritation in her own voice. "Well, whatever Daisy told you, Jack, Buster and I have been dating for a couple of years now and—"

"Is it serious?" he interrupted her.

She looked at him sharply, surprised by the question. "That, Jack, is none of your business. But even if it were, I don't think you'd understand my relationship with Buster."

"Why not?"

"Because it's an adult relationship, Jack, a mature relationship based on mutual respect for each other. I don't think Buster and I have ever even had a minor disagreement, let alone a real argument." Here she flashed on an image of her shouting at Jack after one of his late nights out, so angry at him she could have throttled him. "Anyway, Buster and I have settled into a routine—again, something you wouldn't know anything about. We see each other every Wednesday and Saturday night. It's something—"

She stopped then, because she'd seen the corner of Jack's mouth twitch up in an involuntary smile.

"What is it, Jack? What's so funny about two grown-ups dating each other?"

"Nothing," he said, but there was that twitch again. "It's just . . . don't you ever see each other any other day of the week. On a Tuesday maybe? Or a Thursday?"

She glared at him, not least of all because Buster's way of scheduling their relationship had always been a sticking point with her. But she was damned if she'd let her ex-husband see that. "Look, like I said, Jack. I don't expect you to understand this. We're getting off track, anyway. We're supposed to be discussing ground rules, remember?"

"Okay," he said, holding up his hands in mock surrender. "So what's the ground rule about you and Buster?"

"It's . . . it's not a *rule,* exactly. It's just that I want you to be respectful of him. Respectful of *us*. It's a little awkward for him, having you back in town. I think he might feel . . ." She struggled here. She didn't want to give Buster's feelings credence by repeating them to Jack, but then again, they *were* his feelings, however misplaced they might be. "I think he might feel

115

threatened by your being here," she said. "I told him that was ridiculous," she added quickly. "That we don't have feelings for each other anymore. But still, he's worried, I think." She waited for Jack to say something, something about how crazy it was for Buster to worry that they still had feelings for each other. But when he didn't say anything, she glanced up at him.

He was looking at her, thoughtfully, almost gently, it seemed. "Tell Buster that I'll be respectful of him, and of his relationship with you," he said quietly.

"I will," she said, feeling disoriented again, this time by Jack's sudden seriousness. "I'll tell him that."

"Good," he said. "Now you probably want me to get going."

"That . . . that would be nice," she said. "I've got some things I need to do around here."

"Okay," he said, reaching for his empty coffee cup.

"Just leave that, Jack," she said distractedly.

"All right," he said, pushing his chair back. "But thank you. It was the best cup of coffee I've had in a long time." Then he smiled at her. He smiled that smile, that slow, I-have-all-the-time-in-the-world-for-you smile she remembered so well. Only this time, she wasn't having it.

"Don't smile that smile at me, Jack," she snapped.

"What smile?"

"And don't pretend you don't know what I'm talking about either," she said, her eyes narrowing. "I'm not some girl you just met in a bar," she added. "I know you, Jack; I know you better than you know yourself."

He looked at her for a long time, an unreadable expression on his face. "I hope that's not true anymore, Caroline," he said finally, and he got up and walked out the door.

She sat there then, thinking about what he'd said. She didn't understand it; she didn't understand *him*. And she didn't understand herself right now either, because seeing Jack again had dredged up so many old feelings for her. Most of them were easily identifiable—anger, disbelief, exasperation—but some of them . . . some of them were harder to classify.

Why had he come back? she wondered, using her straw to play with the ice cubes in her glass. Why had he *really* come back? And why now? After all this time? "What are you up to, Jack?" she murmured to herself, clinking the ice cubes together. "What in the hell are you up to?"

Chapter 4

When Will picked Daisy up for their date that Saturday night, he felt a twinge of guilt.

"You look really nice," he said, glancing sideways at her as he drove down Butternut's Main Street. *You look too nice to just be going to the town beach,* he added to himself.

"Thank you," she said, and she smiled shyly and looked out the passenger-side window of his pickup.

"What do you think about driving out to the beach to watch the sunset?" he asked, stealing another look at her. She was wearing a sundress, and her reddish-gold hair was smooth and shiny. As she turned to face him now, it brushed against her bare, creamy shoulders in an especially distracting way.

"I think watching the sunset sounds nice," she said, smiling again.

He felt another twinge of guilt. "You don't mind that we're just going to the beach?"

"Why would I mind?"

"I mean, you wouldn't rather be going out for dinner?" he asked, thinking about what Jason had said about dating a girl like Daisy.

"Oh, God no," she said. "The last place I want

to go at the end of the day is to another restaurant."

"I bet," Will said, and he made a mental note to tell Jason he'd been wrong about Daisy. She was going to be a cheap date after all. No, not a *cheap* date, he amended. *Cheap* wasn't a word he'd associate with her; she was going to be an *inexpensive* date.

They drove in silence the rest of the way out to the lake. When they turned into the parking lot at the Butternut town beach, Daisy drew in a breath. "It's beautiful," she said, of the sunset over the lake, which was a swirl of pinks, oranges, and reds. *Inexpensive* and *easy to please,* Will thought, sliding into a parking space that faced the water and cutting the engine.

"I come here, sometimes, in the late afternoon for a swim," Daisy said now. "But it's so different at this time of day, isn't it? Without all the cranky toddlers? And the Popsicle wrappers?" And Will laughed, because he knew exactly what she meant. By day, the beach belonged, for the most part, to families with children, and to their damp beach towels, and soggy swim diapers, their peanut butter and jelly sandwich crusts, and lopsided sandcastles, and their inflatable rafts that refused to stay inflated. Even now, hours after the last stragglers had left, there were still signs of their presence: garbage cans overflowing with picnic remnants, a set of sand toys forgotten by the water's edge.

But as night fell, the beach took on a different quality. It seemed less domesticated somehow— wilder, and more mysterious. A soft wind blew off the lake, carrying with it the clean, tangy smell of deep, green water; the great northern pines that fringed the beach seemed to sway, almost imperceptibly, in that wind, their branches an inky black against the pale pink sky. From across the bay, a loon's call echoed mournfully, and a little eerily, over the water.

"Are we going to get out?" Daisy asked now, a little shyly.

"Sure, if you want to," he said, even though getting out of the truck hadn't actually occurred to him.

"That'd be nice," Daisy said. "Do you have anything to sit on?"

"Yeah, I've got a blanket," he said. "Let's go." They got out of the truck, and he reached into the back seat for the blanket and a cooler. Then Daisy slipped off her sandals and, carrying them in one hand, walked with Will across the now cool sand.

"How's this?" he asked, stopping about ten yards from the lake's edge.

"It's fine," Daisy said. Will put the cooler down, and Daisy helped him spread the blanket out on the sand. Then she sat down on it, and he sat down beside her, careful to leave a little space between them.

"Do you want a beer?" Will asked, sliding

the cooler open and reaching into its icy depths.

"No, thank you," she said.

"Oh," he said, surprised. "Do you not like beer? Because if you don't, I could get something else. A bottle of wine, maybe."

"That's okay," she said, watching him twist the lid off his beer bottle. "I don't really drink alcohol."

"Not at all?"

"Not really. Is that a problem?"

"A problem? No, of course not." It wasn't a *problem*. It was just that the second part of the night, the part spent in the back seat of the truck, was more or less dependent on the first part of the night. And the first part of the night involved the two of them drinking enough beer to sufficiently overcome whatever inhibitions they might otherwise have toward each other.

"Why don't you drink alcohol?" he asked.

She lifted her pale shoulders in a shrug. "I don't like the way drinking makes me feel."

"How does it make you feel?"

"Well, my experience with it is pretty limited. But my freshman year, I went to a party and they were serving these little drinks, and they were so sweet, you could barely tell they had alcohol in them . . ." Her voice trailed off.

"But they did have alcohol in them."

She nodded ruefully. "Anyway, I somehow ended up drinking too many of them. And I didn't like that feeling . . . that feeling of being out of control, I guess."

"No?" Will said, putting his beer down. "Because some people get to like that feeling."

"Well, I don't think I'll ever be one of them," she said with a frown, her blue eyes narrowing almost imperceptibly. And then Will frowned too, because it occurred to him that the second part of the night might not actually happen. *Score one for Jason,* he thought, taking another sip of his beer.

"How's your dad doing?" he asked, feeling like a change of subject was in order.

"He's doing okay. Better than my mom's doing, anyway. She's furious."

"At you or at him?"

"At both of us," Daisy said with a little sigh.

"But you're not mad at him, are you?" Will asked, suddenly interested.

She looked at him, in surprise, and then thought about it. "No, I'm not mad at him," she said. "Not really. Not anymore. I was, at first, when he got in touch with me again. But that was a year ago. We've talked a lot since then, about why he did what he did. And while I haven't *completely* forgiven him—I don't know if you can ever do that, really—I think maybe I understand him, and maybe even . . . admire him a little. Especially for coming back here."

"Why would you admire him for that?"

"Why? Well, because leaving is easy, Will. But coming back? Coming back is hard."

Will thought about that while he took another drink of his beer and watched the sun hang just above the horizon on the opposite shore of the lake. He'd never thought about leaving here before. It wasn't because he wanted to stay, necessarily, but because he didn't give the future a lot of thought, the future or the past. It seemed better—safer—to stay in the present. Repairing engines. Shooting pool. Coming to the beach . . .

"What about your parents, Will?" Daisy asked.

He tensed. Why was she asking him about his parents? But then he realized it was for the simple reason that he'd asked her about *her* parents. "Umm, my mom's not around," he said, vaguely. "And my dad's around somewhere. But we're not . . . we're not in touch with each other."

"Your mom's 'not around'? What does that mean?"

He shrugged. "It means she left. Like your dad. Only I was a little younger than you were, I think. Two, two and a half years old. Young enough to not remember her being there."

"Did she stay in touch?"

He shook his head. "Nope. I have no idea where she is. Or what she's doing."

Daisy looked appalled.

"What?" he said, a little defensively. "Your dad left, too."

"I know. But still. I mean, maybe it's not fair to hold mothers and fathers to a different standard. But a mother leaving a young child? That seems worse, somehow, than a father leaving one."

"Maybe," Will said. "But maybe it was better that she left when she did, before I could remember her. You can't miss someone you don't remember." But the part about not remembering his mother wasn't entirely true. He *did* remember her—or at least he thought he did. He remembered sitting on the steps of the little house he'd grown up in, with someone, a woman, sitting beside him. She was singing to him softly, a song he couldn't remember the words to now, and she was resting a hand protectively on his back. And that was it—that was the only image of her he could summon up. And the worst part was, he wasn't even positive if it was her, his mother. But he had a feeling that it was.

"So your dad raised you?" Daisy asked, interrupting his thoughts.

"If you could call it that," Will said warily. "But I don't think he was reading any child development books or anything."

"Well, you seemed to have turned out all right," she said gently.

He shrugged. "Maybe. But no thanks to him."

"Why, Will, what's he like?"

He hesitated. He wasn't used to answering personal questions about himself. But Daisy seemed so genuinely interested that he decided to try.

"Well, let's see. He lives off by himself, in the woods, and since I've moved away from home, he has almost no contact with anyone."

"What does he do all day?"

"He hates the government, basically. That's his chief occupation. The rest of the time, he's waiting for some kind of global catastrophe to happen. You know, something he'll be prepared for but the rest of us won't know anything about until it's too late."

"Is he a survivalist?" Daisy asked.

"I, I don't know what you'd call him, exactly," he said. Then he chuckled. "Why, what do you know about survivalists, Daisy?"

"Nothing personally. But I saw a program about them on the Discovery Channel. It was interesting."

Something occurred to him then, and it made him laugh.

"What?" Daisy asked.

"Nothing. It's just that first you thought the garage I work at was laundering money, and now you wonder if my father is a survivalist."

"And?"

"And the truth about both of them is a lot less interesting than either of those things. Are you in the habit, Daisy, of finding the world more interesting than it actually is?"

"But the world *is* interesting, Will," she said seriously. "Don't you think so?"

"I think *you're* interesting," he said. And, all at once, he realized he was exhausted. Talking, it turned out, took a lot of energy, and he and Daisy had just talked more in one evening than he and Christy had probably talked in the last six months.

So instead, he anchored his beer bottle in the sand beside him and did something he'd wanted to do since he'd first seen her again at the garage four days ago. He kissed her. He leaned over, put a hand on her shoulder, and kissed her on the lips. She was surprised, for a moment, but then he felt her lips relax beneath his, and she kissed him back. Her lips were so soft, he marveled, and, in that moment, he forgot to go slowly, as he'd planned, and he pushed his tongue into her mouth instead. And when it touched her tongue, he felt her whole body stiffen, just for a second, as if he'd given her a tiny electric shock. But again, she relaxed, and he pushed his tongue farther into her mouth.

And her mouth tasted so good, too. So sweet. He thought of all the things girls' mouths had tasted like over the years. Beer. Wine. Lip gloss. Chewing gum. But Daisy's mouth didn't taste like any of those things. It just tasted delicious.

He slid his arm around her shoulders, and, without breaking the kiss, he pulled her against him. He kissed her more deeply, then, and, feeling the silkiness of her shoulder under his hand, and the rise and fall of her chest against his, he stroked her tongue with his tongue. He couldn't go slowly, he realized. Pulling her more tightly against him, Will took her tongue, greedily, into his mouth and sucked on it a little. He heard Daisy make a little noise in the back of her throat then, and at first he thought it might be a sign of protest. But then he realized it was a sign of excitement, of arousal.

"Daisy," he said, pulling away and breathing hard. "Let's go back to the truck, okay?"

"The truck?" she said. She was breathing faster, too, and she had a slightly dazed expression on her face.

He nodded. "We'll have more privacy there."

He saw her hesitate, so he kissed her again for good measure. "What do you say?" he asked, taking his mouth off hers and nuzzling her neck with his lips.

"I say yes," she said, a little shakily.

Daisy helped Will shake the sand out of the blanket and let him lead her by the hand back to the pickup truck. Her heart was pounding, and her breathing was shallow. She knew she should be asking herself why they were going back to Will's truck when they'd come here to watch the sunset. But what she was really asking herself was, *What the hell kind of a kiss was that?* She'd been kissed many times before, of course, but never like that. Never with that kind of intensity. That kind of . . . *of skill,* she realized. That was the only word for it, really. What else would you call it when someone kissed you exactly the way you wanted to be kissed, without your even knowing you wanted to be kissed that way?

They got to the truck, and, instead of opening the front passenger door for her, Will opened the back door. She hesitated for a moment. Why were they getting into the back? And then she realized, with an inward groan at her own stupidity, that they were getting into the back so they could lie down. So they could follow that kiss to its natural conclusion. And a kiss like that only had one natural conclusion.

She hovered there, just for a second, but long enough for Will to look at her questioningly, and then she thought, *What the hell,* and climbed into the back seat. Will followed her, closing the door behind him and putting the blanket on the seat beside him.

"Did I tell you how pretty you look tonight," he asked now, his eyes moving over her. She shook her head wordlessly and concentrated on breathing normally. Hyperventilating, she decided, was not an option.

"Well, you look pretty—*really* pretty. I like that you're not tan, that you're so pale. It's . . . it's different."

She swallowed. "I don't really have a choice. I don't get tan. I just burn."

He nodded, as if he was thinking about that. Then, slowly, with careful deliberation, he took the blanket from the seat beside him, unfolded it, and spread it out on the back seat.

"Come here," he said, reaching out his hand for her.

She gave him her hand again, and he pulled her, gently, toward him, and then he lay down and eased her onto the blanket beside him. He looked good too, Daisy thought, his suntanned skin contrasting with her own pale skin, his brown eyes mixed with gold. And he smelled wonderful too, she decided, inhaling him. Clean and masculine, like soap and like something else . . . like summer.

"Look up there," he said, pointing to the sunroof above them. Daisy looked up at the square of dusky, violet sky visible through it.

"I put that in myself," he said of the sunroof. "For nights like tonight. So I could lie back here and look up at the stars. In another hour, we'll be able to see them." He turned on his side then, so that he was facing her, and Daisy turned to him, too. Only a few inches separated their bodies now.

"Do you know a lot about the stars?" she asked, and immediately regretted the question. It sounded completely inane.

But Will only smiled and leaned closer to her. "No, Daisy," he murmured. "I don't know anything about them." And he kissed her again.

This kiss was different from the kiss on the beach, though. Where that kiss had been deep and urgent, this kiss was slow and almost leisurely. She felt her body begin to relax, felt her guard slip down a few notches. Will felt it too, because he circled an arm around her waist, and, resting his hand on the small of her back, he drew her, almost imperceptibly, against him, so that the softness of her breasts was barely touching the hardness of his chest. His other hand reached around to her shoulder, bare except for the thin strap of her sundress, and started caressing it with an almost feather-light touch.

When Daisy felt his hand there, she sucked in a surprised little breath, right through their kiss. But he didn't take his hand away, didn't stop stroking her shoulder, and, gradually, she gave herself over to this new sensation too. *No wonder he's such a good mechanic,* she thought, as he slipped down one and then the other strap on her sundress, so that her shoulders were completely bare. *He never makes a wrong move with his hands.* Then again, she thought, the same could be said of his mouth.

He pulled his mouth away from her mouth then, and, before Daisy could even register her disappointment, he started kissing her shoulder instead, gently, unhurriedly. The sensation of his lips, and his tongue, on her skin was exquisite, and Daisy almost squirmed with anticipation in his arms. But Will took his time, kissing first one shoulder, and then, using his lips to follow the line of her collarbone, settling into the hollow at the base of her neck. He stopped there for a long moment, letting his tongue play over this indentation, and soon it was all Daisy could do not to let out a little moan of pleasure.

How had he even learned to do this? she wondered. *Practice,* her subconscious answered. *Lots and lots and lots of practice.* But she didn't want to think about that right now; she didn't want to think about anything right now. She wanted to concentrate on the way his lips and his hands felt on her—especially since they were both in constant, gentle motion.

She felt one of his hands now, for instance, move to the neckline of her dress, feeling for a button. But there were no buttons, and no zipper, either, Daisy realized. And, after a moment, Will realized it, too. The only way this sundress was going to come off was up over her head. For a moment, in the hesitation of his fingers, she felt Will wondering if this were an option. But she knew he'd decided against it when he started running his hand over the top of her sundress, feeling her breasts right through the thin fabric of her dress. Daisy stopped breathing, just for a second. But if her lungs weren't being responsive, the rest of her body seemed not to have this problem. She felt her nipples, for instance, hardening under his touch, and she knew he could feel them, too, right through her bra and her sundress. She was embarrassed by their pebbly hardness, but if they embarrassed her, they seemed to please him, because his fingers lingered on them, caressing them so lightly, but so insistently, that pretty soon she forgot to be embarrassed, and just went with the feeling.

He stopped kissing and touching her then, but only long enough to sit up, pull his T-shirt off, and drop it onto the floor of the truck. Then he lay back down beside her and pulled her back into his arms, his mouth closing over hers again, his bare skin touching her bare shoulders and arms. And his skin was so warm, she thought, wriggling against it. It was as if he'd been in the sun all day and now, at sunset, he still held the warmth of it within him and was releasing it, slowly, against her. She moved her hands up tentatively and laid them both, palms down, on his bare chest.

She felt the beating of his heart and the rise and fall of his chest quicken beneath them. He liked her touching him, she thought, pleased by the realization, and she started to move her hands now, over his skin, over his hard but smooth shoulders and chest and back. She didn't have his confidence, she knew, or his sureness. But what she lacked in experience, she more than made up for in curiosity.

"Oh, Daisy, that feels good," Will said, taking his mouth away from hers and kissing her neck. "Your hands are so soft."

Daisy kept touching him then and imagined what it would feel like if there was nothing between them, if her sundress magically disappeared, and there was only his bare skin against her bare skin. Will apparently had the same thought, because now his hands started moving again, only this time, they didn't move up, they moved down, down to the hem of her sundress and the bare legs underneath it. Daisy tensed up again, but not for long. His hands on her legs, and then her thighs, as he edged up her sundress, were so patient, so gentle, so insistent, but really, *so right,* that she relaxed again into him, into his bare chest and into his lips, which were still doing such interesting things to her neck.

But then something occurred to her, something that intruded, almost rudely, on this little, private world they'd created in the almost cavelike back seat of his truck.

"Will, what if somebody comes," she said, against his ear.

"Nobody will," he said, taking his lips only far enough away from her neck to form the words. "Nobody comes here at night anymore. Not since the Forest Service banned campfires here."

"But if somebody does come?" she persisted, her hands stopping their movement and resting on his chest.

"If someone comes, we'll stop," he said, lavishing more attention on her neck, and then he moved his lips lower, until they were dangerously close to the neckline of her sundress.

We'll stop, Daisy repeated to herself as Will ran his tongue along that neckline. Then, leaving one hand under her dress, where it was stroking the inside of her thighs with deliberate slowness, and maddening gentleness, he brought the other hand back to one of her breasts, cupped it through the dress, and, finding the nipple, took it between his fingers and caressed it again. If you could call it a caress, which she wasn't sure you could. There was a lot more hunger in his touch now, and a lot less gentleness, too, but the friction between his fingers and her nipple was delicious, and when he increased it, fractionally, she arched her back and moaned softly.

If someone comes we'll stop, she reminded herself again, her hands running over his back. But stopping was easier said than done, wasn't it? Because how would she stop at this point? *Why* would she stop? Why would anyone stop doing anything that felt this good? And if what they were doing *now* felt this good, what would what they did later feel like?

As if in answer to this question, Will moved the hand that had been on one of her thighs up to her navel, up to the elastic waistband of her panties, and started skimming softly over the skin there.

Daisy felt herself tense again, just for a second, but it was enough, enough to kick-start that part of her brain that had been turned off for most of the night. *Are you really going to do this? Right here? Right now? In the back seat of a pickup truck? At a public beach?*

Maybe, her body answered, as the hand that had been on her breast left and came up under her sundress. *Maybe I will,* she thought, as both hands started to ease her panties down, gently. Slowly. Maybe she would just let this happen. And why not? She could do a lot worse than Will Hughes. For one thing, he obviously knew what he was doing. There wouldn't be any fumbling around, any wrestling with stuck zippers, or accidentally poking her in the eye with his elbow. No, he would make love to her properly, definitively. And afterward, there'd be no doubt in her mind, or her body, for that matter, that she'd been made love to.

On the practical side, too, he was a good choice. Because a guy like him would have protection. A guy like him, in fact, wouldn't even

135

get out of bed in the morning without a condom tucked into his blue jean pocket. And afterward? Afterward, she'd never have to see him again, if she didn't want to. Though, she didn't know, honestly, if that was the case. She thought, in fact, that maybe she *did* want to see him again—very badly.

Maybe that was why, as his hands eased her panties off, she finally felt a belated little wave of panic.

"Will?" she said, pulling away from him a little. "Will, I don't know . . ."

"Don't know what?" he answered into her neck, kissing it again.

"Don't know if I want my first time, *our* first time"—she caught herself—"to be in the backseat of your pickup truck."

Will kept kissing her neck for a moment longer, then stopped, and lay very still beside her. "What did you say?" he asked, and he took his hands, very slowly, out from under her dress.

"I said . . ." She stopped. She was suddenly almost painfully embarrassed. He was looking into her eyes now, their bodies still touching, his chest rising and falling rapidly against her own. It occurred to her, then, in that moment, that before she'd interrupted them, he'd been as aroused as she had been. "I said," she started again, barely above a whisper, "that I don't want our first time to be in the back seat of your pickup truck."

But he gave his head a tiny shake. "No. Before that. What did you say before that?"

Her heart sank. So he'd heard her. "I didn't say anything," she lied. Already she missed what they'd been doing only moments before, missed the feel of his body against hers, missed the touch of his hands on her skin. She wondered if she could coax him back into a kiss now, but decided she couldn't. His expression, and his body, were alert, tense. Sex, it seemed, was suddenly the farthest thing from his mind.

"You said something else, Daisy. You said something about 'my first time.' "

She blushed and looked away.

"Daisy, did you mean that?"

She lifted her shoulders noncommittally. But she didn't look back at him.

"You've never done this before?" he pressed. "With anyone? You're a . . ." He stopped. He couldn't even bring himself to say the word, she realized, with dismay.

"A virgin," she supplied, trying to keep the dismay out of her own voice. Because right now, she couldn't believe it, either.

"Jesus, Daisy," he said, sitting up and looking down at her, suddenly wary. He looked at her as if she were a danger to him, a poisonous snake that could strike at any moment.

"Will, it's okay. It's not contagious," she said, sitting up. "I said I was a virgin. Not a leper."

He ignored her remark. Instead he continued to watch her, running his fingers through hair that was too short to run his fingers through and looking for all the world like a man trying to solve an unsolvable problem—in this case, her virginity.

"Daisy," he said finally, giving up on the problem, "why don't you get in the front seat. I'll take you home."

"Now?"

He nodded, reached for his T-shirt, and pulled it back on.

"So that's it. Our date is over?"

"Yes, it's over."

She felt dismay giving way to anger. "Why, Will? Because I've never had sex with anyone? Or because I won't have it with you?"

"Neither," he said, shaking his head.

"Then why?" she asked, and she was horrified to feel tears burning in her eyes. *Don't cry,* she pleaded with herself.

"Because Jason was right about you."

"Jason from the garage? What did he say about me?"

"He said you were different. He said you didn't just, you know . . . sleep around."

"And that's a bad thing?"

"No, it's not. It's just . . . it's just that we want different things, I guess."

"Will, you barely know me. How could you possibly know what I want?"

"I *don't* know what you want, Daisy," he said quietly. "But I'm willing to guess it's more than *this*." He made a gesture with his hand that included the two of them and the back seat of the truck. Then he reached over and, very carefully, without touching her skin, tugged first one strap up on her sundress, and then the other. When they were both back in place, he said quietly, but firmly, "Come on. Let's go."

Daisy knew it was useless to argue. So she slid out of the back seat, awkwardly pulling up her panties as she did so, got into the front seat, and fastened her seat belt. She was careful not to look at Will, careful to look out the window as he started up the truck and headed back to town. The tears that had threatened to come had arrived now, running silently down her cheeks, and she was convinced that if he saw them, it would put the final seal on her humiliation. She could almost hear him telling Jason. *First, I found out she was a virgin. Then she cried the whole way home. It was a nightmare.*

By the time Will turned his truck onto Main Street, though, her tears had stopped and her embarrassment had turned to anger.

"You can let me out here," she said stiffly when they were a block from her building. "I'll walk the rest of the way."

139

He slowed down but didn't stop. "Can I take you to your front door?"

"No, Will, you can't," she snapped. "And don't worry about being rude, okay? Because you couldn't set that bar any lower than you already have tonight."

He stopped the truck, and she got out and slammed the door behind her. She knew he was waiting there, though, in the idling pickup, while she walked up the block and let herself into the building's side door. But if that was his last-ditch effort to be polite, she thought, starting up the stairs to the apartment, it was too little, too late. Hopefully, after tonight, she'd never have to see him again.

But she did have to see her mother again. She was on the phone in the kitchen when Daisy let herself into the apartment, but she poked her head out as Daisy walked by; instantly, Caroline's face registered her concern.

"Allie, hold on a second," Caroline said, putting the phone aside. "Daisy, what's wrong. What happened on your date?"

"Nothing happened," Daisy said, knowing that her red eyes and blotchy skin had given her away. "It's just that, Will and I . . ." She shrugged. "We just didn't have that much in common. But that's *not* why I'm crying, Mom. I'm tired and, and it's been a crazy week."

"It *has* been a crazy week," her mother agreed.

"Do you want to talk about it? I can call Allie back."

"No, thanks," Daisy said, already heading into her bedroom. "I'll see you in the morning, okay?"

She closed the door behind her, crossed to her bed, and swiped impatiently at the textbooks scattered across it. They were for a senior seminar she'd be taking in the fall, and she'd meant to get started on them early, but now she pushed them off the bed, listening with satisfaction as they thudded onto the floor.

Then she lay down on the bed and buried her face in its pillows. She considered crying again, but she didn't. The situation was just too ludicrous, even to her. So instead, she pictured the expression of almost abject horror on Will's face when he'd found out she was a virgin, and she almost, *almost* laughed. But she couldn't do that, either. She was too hurt, too disappointed.

She'd thought when she and Will talked at the garage and then again at the beach that there'd been something between them. An attraction, yes, but something else, too. *A connection,* she decided, though she knew that word belonged to the province of cheesy reality dating shows. Still, she'd felt it. And she'd thought he'd felt it, too. And now? Now she knew it hadn't been there. Or, if it had been, it had been completely one-sided, on *her* side.

Will hadn't taken her out to the beach because

he wanted to talk to her or get to know her better. No, he'd taken her there for one reason and one reason only. And was that *so* surprising? Like most people their age, he lived in a world of casual hookups, and sexting, and friends with benefits. It was *Daisy* who was the anomaly, Daisy who was the throwback to another time. Because, like it or not, she was still burdened with the almost arcane idea that *sex should mean something, be the product of something.* Maybe not the product of true passion—because she'd always suspected this was an overrated commodity, anyway—but the product of something deeper, and more meaningful than two people killing a couple of hours together on a Saturday night.

But her mind had caught on that word, and it went back to it now. Passion. She'd never felt anything close to it before, had she? No, she hadn't. Except for . . . well, except for tonight, she realized with surprise. Tonight, in the back seat of Will's pickup, she'd gotten a little preview of what it might be like. The way he'd kissed her and touched her had made her feel like . . . like she was standing on the edge of something, something incredibly pleasurable but also, at the same time, incredibly scary.

She thought about that for a while, picking at a loose thread on one of her pillowcases. Was it fear, she wondered, that had held her back, fear that had kept her clinging stubbornly to her virginity?

She remembered what Will had said tonight about how people could learn to like the feeling of being out of control. Maybe she was afraid of that feeling, afraid of letting go, afraid of sliding, sweetly but dangerously, off the edge of everything she knew and understood.

But she pushed that thought away. It was dumb. Her biggest fear in life wasn't losing control; it was getting into a good graduate program in psychology after she finished college. Besides, what was wrong with a little self-control, anyway? She would never have gotten as far as she'd gotten if she hadn't exercised self-control. The academic awards, the volleyball championships, the scholarship—those had all required self-discipline. And she was going to need a lot more of it to get her through these next few years. She'd be the first person in her family to graduate from college, the first person, too, to go on and earn an advanced degree.

She stopped picking at the thread now and pressed her too-warm cheek against the cool cotton of the pillowcase. Her virginity wasn't her problem, she decided; her naïveté was. No more trips out to the beach with guys like Will, she vowed, unless, of course, she wanted a casual hookup, too. And no more thinking that the way Will had kissed her tonight—however amazing it might have been—was any different from the way he'd already kissed a hundred girls before her.

Chapter 5

Almost three weeks after Caroline's meeting with Jack at Pearl's, she brought a lunch order over to a customer. It wasn't just any customer, though. It was quite possibly the most important customer she would ever have—and certainly the most important customer Pearl's would ever have.

"Here you go," she said, sliding the order on the table. "One freshly squeezed orange juice, and one tall stack of blueberry pancakes with a side of extra-crispy bacon. Did I get that right?"

"Have you ever gotten it wrong?" John Quarterman asked, with amusement.

"Probably not," she said. "But then again, it is what you order for lunch every time you come in here. More coffee?"

"No, thanks. Not yet," he said. He'd already taken his suit jacket off and draped it over the back of his chair, and now, as he loosened his tie, he stared longingly at the pancakes.

This order of them was especially good, too, Caroline thought with satisfaction. They were fluffy, and golden brown, and studded all the way through with perfectly ripe local blueberries. Caroline had made these pancakes herself. Not that Frankie wasn't a wonder at the grill. He was.

But she wasn't leaving anything to chance today.

"All right then," she said, resisting the urge to get the coffeepot and pour a few more inches of coffee into his cup. She'd brewed the coffee herself, too, in a small batch, just for him. "I'll leave you to it, and, when you're done, I'll come back and we can talk for a minute, all right?"

"All right," John agreed cheerfully as he drenched his pancakes in maple syrup.

Caroline left him and went back behind the counter. Frankie, who was at the grill flipping a perfectly browned grilled cheese sandwich, looked up.

"Everything okay?"

"Everything's fine," she said distractedly, watching John and trying to gauge what kind of a mood he was in.

"Frankie," she asked. "How does Mr. Quarterman look?"

"How does he look?" Frankie repeated, glancing over at him. He shrugged. "He looks . . . he looks like a man eating pancakes. Why? How's he supposed to look?"

"Like a satisfied customer," Caroline murmured.

"Isn't that the only kind we have?" Frankie said, sliding the grilled cheese sandwich onto a plate.

Fifteen minutes, and one coffee refill later, Caroline was back at John's table. "Are you ready to talk?" she asked.

"Sure," John said, indicating the chair across from him. Caroline pulled it out and sat down. She was glad she'd told Daisy she could go back up to the apartment after the lunch rush, and glad, too, that at two o'clock on a weekday afternoon, the tables closest to her and John's table were empty. This way, she figured, they'd have a modicum of privacy. Privacy was important because it had occurred to her that she wasn't beyond shedding a few well-placed tears if she thought they might help her cause.

"I know why you wanted to meet here, Caroline, instead of at the bank," John said now, forgoing the small talk.

"Well, I figured you had to have lunch."

"And you figured if I had it here, before our meeting, it would be harder for me to say no to a reset on your loan?"

"Something like that," Caroline admitted, slightly taken aback. She'd been expecting a little small talk first. But she could be direct, too. "I wanted to remind you that you were raised on those pancakes, John," she said now. Her remark wasn't even an exaggeration; his father, John Sr., had brought him here for breakfast every morning when he was a child.

"I *was* raised on them, Caroline," John agreed. "Which is why every single bite of them tastes like childhood to me." And Caroline, who was only ten years older than John, nonetheless flashed on an image of him as a little boy, spinning wildly on one of the swivel stools at the counter, his mop of blond hair flying around his head like an unruly halo.

"But, Caroline," he said, brushing that same blond hair, now slightly thinning, off his forehead, "I'm not going to reset your loan. I'm sorry; I can't. My family doesn't own the bank anymore. I'm an employee there, like everyone else."

"But you're the executive vice president," she objected, in a voice that was louder than she intended.

"It's a title, Caroline; it doesn't mean anything. Besides, I did what I could. I made my recommendation to the loan committee, and they overruled me. That's it. It's out of my hands."

"But . . ." Caroline shook her head, feeling helpless. She'd thought he'd at least give her time to make her case. She hadn't expected him to preempt her like this.

"I'm sorry," he said, again. "I can give you the reason why we're refusing to reset your loan in bank jargon, if you'd like me to. But I think you'd prefer that I give it to you straight, Caroline. And the bottom line is this: you're not a good risk. Even if it were my decision to make, which it's not, I'd be reluctant to reset the loan."

"So . . ." Caroline stopped, at a loss for words. She'd rehearsed this conversation many different times in her mind, but it had never ended this way before. She'd always been able to make the case for Pearl's, make it elegantly, persuasively, and, ultimately, successfully. Failing this quickly, and this completely, had never even entered her mind.

"Look, Caroline," John said, rubbing his temples. "I know this is hard for you to hear. It's hard for me to say. But you're not without options."

"Options?"

"Well, yes," he said, and for the first time in this conversation, he looked uncomfortable. "You could borrow the money to pay us back. Borrow it privately, I mean—from a friend."

Caroline shook her head. "My friends don't have that kind of money."

He shifted in his seat. "Then you could sell the building. And Pearl's, of course. That should cover the loan."

"And then what?" she asked, shaking her head in disbelief.

"And then . . . well, obviously, that would be up to you. But I'm not worried about you, Caroline."

"Why's that, John?" she asked, not bothering to keep the sarcasm out of her voice.

He drained the last of his coffee, then leaned back in his chair. "I'm not worried because I remember what my father used to say about you, Caroline. He said you were, bar none, the smartest person in this town."

"Well, a lot of good it's done me, if I can't even keep a business afloat."

"That wasn't you, Caroline. That was the recession."

She sighed. Because what difference did it make, really, at the end of the day, if the outcome was the same? Still, she didn't feel angry or upset right now. Just . . . just numb, she decided.

"Can I get you another cup of coffee, John?" she asked, suddenly wanting their meeting to be over.

"That'd be great," he said, with an attempt at a smile. "And, Caroline?" he added, as he pulled on his suit jacket. "I wish I could have done more. I really do."

"I know," Caroline nodded, standing up. "Let me get you that coffee."

"Are you all right?" Frankie asked when she came to get the coffeepot. "You look a little pale."

"No, I'm fine." She knew he didn't believe her. "Frankie," she said, "I'm going to pour John another cup of coffee, and then I'm going to head upstairs. I'll send Daisy down, though, to take care of the rest of the lunchtime stragglers."

"Sure," he said, and the worried expression on his face told her that no matter how hard she tried to keep this all from him, he'd still figured most of it out for himself anyway.

As Will was entering Pearl's, another man was leaving it. Will stepped back to let him pass.

149

"Excuse me," he said, and Will nodded, taking note of the man's suit. You didn't see too many of those around here, especially in this hot weather. He walked into the coffee shop and looked around. He'd tried to time his arrival for after the lunch rush, but there were still several customers sitting at the counter and at tables scattered around the room. He glanced at his watch. Two thirty. And these people hadn't eaten lunch yet? Then again, he thought, he hadn't eaten lunch yet either.

He walked over to one of the red leather booths in the front window and slid into it. There was no sign of Daisy, he saw, as he scanned the room. The only person behind the counter right now was a gargantuan man working the grill. Will had seen him before, he realized, playing pool at the Mosquito Inn. He was rumored to have killed a man once, with his bare hands, and looking at him now, it wasn't that hard to believe.

The cook saw Will looking at him and nodded at him, almost imperceptibly. It wasn't a friendly nod, though. It was more of a warning nod. A "you better not be giving us any trouble" nod. Will nodded back and looked away. The food must be good here, he decided, if people were willing to stare that man down for the privilege of eating some eggs.

Will took a menu out of the menu holder on the table and tried to read it, but he couldn't concentrate. It hadn't occurred to him that Daisy might not be here, and now that she wasn't, he had no backup plan. But when he glanced toward the counter again, a few minutes later, he saw her coming into the coffee shop through a back door, and, as she did, her eyes met his across the room. She looked first surprised, and then flustered, but she didn't look angry, so Will relaxed a little. She wavered there for a moment, unsure of what to do, and then she turned and said something to the cook. He turned around and looked at Will again, and Will felt himself tense involuntarily. Had she told the guy to throw him out? he wondered. But the cook made no move toward him. Instead, he turned back to Daisy, nodded, and put something on the grill. Will exhaled slowly. He wasn't a coward, not when it came to a fight, but he wasn't stupid, either.

After Daisy spoke to the cook, though, she ignored Will, and he watched as she went back to work, refilling customers' water glasses, taking a party of four their check, and clearing away plates from an empty booth in the back. He sighed, fiddling with the menu. Here was another contingency he hadn't planned for. It had occurred to him that Daisy might still be angry at him, but it hadn't occurred to him that she wouldn't even speak to him. He'd thought if he came here as a paying customer, the least she would do was take his order. But he couldn't force her to wait on him. If she was enjoying his banishment to this booth, there was nothing to stop her from leaving him there until closing time.

Just when Will had decided this was her game plan, Daisy poured a soda from the soda dispenser, picked up an order from the grill, and headed directly for him.

"Hi," she said, with a neutral smile, setting a Coke and a sandwich with fries down on the table in front of him.

"Hi," he said. "I didn't order anything yet."

"I know," she said. "I brought you the hamburger club. It's on special today. If you can wait while I do a few more things, I can come back and talk for a minute."

"All right," he said, and she walked away. *God, she was even prettier than he'd remembered her being*, even in a big white apron that covered her slender frame, and even with her hair pulled back in a rather severe ponytail. He flashed, for an instant, on an image of her bare white shoulders and bare white thighs. But he shook his head impatiently, putting the image out of his mind, and reached instead for the hamburger club. It was good, really good. And he must have been hungrier than he realized, because by the time Daisy came back five minutes later, it was gone, and so were half of the french fries. Eating here, he decided, was definitely worth facing down the potentially homicidal cook.

"Hi," she said again, a little uncertainly, as she slid in across from him.

"Hi." He smiled. "The special's great, by the way," he said, indicating his almost empty plate.

"I'll tell Frankie you said so."

"Frankie? Is that his name?"

She nodded.

"Is it true . . ." Will leaned in closer. "Is it true he killed a man once?"

"Oh, that again," Daisy said, rolling her eyes. "Don't believe everything you hear, Will. But you didn't come here to talk about Frankie, did you?"

"No," he said, shifting in the booth, and wishing he was better with words. "I came here to . . ."

"To apologize?" Daisy suggested, raising her eyebrows.

"That's part of the reason I came."

"Well, I'll save you the trouble," Daisy said, leaning forward, elbows on the table. "You don't owe me an apology."

"I think I do," Will disagreed. "I'm not . . . um, proud of the way I acted the other night. You didn't do anything wrong, Daisy. There's nothing wrong, either, with your being a, you know . . ."

"A virgin?" Daisy supplied, her mouth lifting at the corners.

"Yeah, okay," Will said, glancing around to make sure that no one had heard her. But Daisy, he saw, was amused. "Anyway," he continued, "what I meant to say is, it's nothing to be ashamed of. If I made you feel that way, I'm sorry." He stopped, disoriented. Were they really sitting here, in public, in broad daylight, discussing her virginity? He got a feeling then that he'd stepped off the edge of something, and that there was nothing underneath his feet.

"Will, look, it's okay. I'm not angry anymore," Daisy was saying, when his brain caught up with conversation again. "I was on the drive back, but after I got home, I calmed down. I was even able to see a little humor in the situation," she said, emphasizing the words *a little*. "I know that my, um, *situation* is a little unusual. I mean, how many twenty-one-year-old virgins have you met before me?"

Not many, Will thought. *Maybe not any.* But to Daisy he said, "I don't know."

She took a french fry off his plate and nibbled on it. "Well, I'll tell you something, Will. We're a very select group of people, sort of like a club that no one wants to be a member of. Sometimes, even *I* don't know if I want to be a member of it anymore."

He frowned. "But, I mean, I thought the whole point was that people like you were proud of what you were doing. Don't you take some kind of vow? And wear some kind of ring? A promise ring?" He looked reflexively at her hands. He didn't know what a promise ring looked like, but she wasn't wearing any rings.

"Is that what you think, Will?" Daisy asked, surprised. "That I'm saving myself for marriage?"

He nodded. Since she'd told him she was a virgin, it had never occurred to him that there might be any other reason for it.

But she shook her head. "There's no promise ring. I didn't plan it this way, Will. It just sort of happened."

"But how?" he asked, and then, added, quickly, "I mean, you've had boyfriends before, obviously."

"I've had boyfriends," she agreed. "One or two of them were even serious. Or *could* have been serious. But I have this annoying habit of overthinking my life, to the point where it's hard to be spontaneous and hard to do something that feels big, or important, without worrying that I'll regret it later. Do you know what I mean?"

"About overthinking things?"

She nodded.

"Not really," he admitted. "I'm more of an underthinker myself."

"Well, maybe that's better sometimes," she said musingly. "Overthinking definitely has its drawbacks. But that's probably not the only reason I'm . . ."

"A virgin?" Will said, getting the hang of it. "Why, what's the other reason?"

She smiled, then paused. "Well, what it comes

down to, I guess, is expectations. Because either mine are too high, or most men's are too low."

"What do you mean?"

"Well, take our date, for instance," she said, picking up another one of his french fries and taking a bite of it. "I mean, was that the whole plan, Will? The beer, the back seat, the . . ."

He sighed inwardly, but he decided to go with honesty. It was the simplest, if not always the best, policy. "Yeah, that was more or less the plan."

"And you thought that was enough for a first date?"

I've never had any complaints before, Will almost said. But he caught himself. His plan was not to antagonize her; his plan, in fact, was to do the opposite. So he raised his shoulders, noncommittally, in an answer that was no answer at all.

Again, Daisy saw through it. "Huh," she said thoughtfully. "I mean, no offense, Will. It just seems that today, in the twenty-first century, you might offer a woman a little more than that."

"Well, don't knock it till you've tried it," Will said, without thinking, and he was instantly annoyed with himself. He watched warily as the surprise registered on her face, and he waited for that surprise to turn into annoyance. Or anger. But after a moment, she laughed. "You may have a point there, Will," she said. Then she glanced over at Frankie, still standing at the grill, and some wordless communication passed between them.

"Look, I've got to get back to work," she said. "But, Will? Thank you for stopping by. And, um, apology accepted." She smiled then, a smile that was so pretty and unaffected that it immediately reminded him of the other reason he'd come here.

"Yeah, about that," he said, quickly, as she started to slide out of the booth. "There was something else, too."

She hesitated.

He took a swig of his Coke, plagued by an unfamiliar feeling—nervousness. "I wanted to know, Daisy, if you'd like to go out with me again."

She raised her eyebrows. "On another date?" she asked skeptically.

"Yeah, but not like the first one. We could go out for dinner or—"

But she interrupted him. "Will, don't. Really. It's not necessary. You apologized. You don't need to take me on some pity date now."

"Pity date?" he repeated. "I don't know what that is."

"You know, a second date to make up for the lousy first date. So when you never see me again after the second date, you can have a clear conscience."

He shook his head. "No, I don't mean a pity date. That's not what I had in mind. I wanted to take you out again on a real date."

"Why?" she asked.

"Why?" he said, caught off guard by her again. She was such an odd combination of shyness and directness. "Well, because . . ." But he struggled a little here, unsure of how to put this. She was waiting, though, so he said, "I want to take you out again because I like you, Daisy. And because I've been thinking about you. I've been thinking about you *a lot*." *To the exclusion, it turned out, of almost everything else in his life.*

He watched now while she blushed, her cheeks a lovely mingling of creamy white and soft pink. "Well, I've been trying *not* to think about you," she said softly. "But I've been doing it anyway."

"Good," he said, and he wanted to lean over and kiss her, right here and right now, but he sensed the cook was still watching him. "So what do you say? Could we try that again?"

She studied him thoughtfully. "We could, but . . . I'm not going back to the beach with you, Will."

He smiled at her double meaning. "No, we won't go back to the beach," he said. "In fact, let's take that whole subject off the table. But I have to warn you, though. What you said about dating, and about our expectations being different? Part of it, Daisy, is that I don't *have* any expectations. I've never really dated anybody before."

"No?" she said, surprised. But then something occurred to her. "So this is one area where I have more experience than you?" she asked, a smile playing around her lips.

"Definitely."

"All right, then. Yes, I'll go out with you again, Will—on one condition."

He raised his eyebrows.

"You let me plan what we do on our date."

He thought about that. "Yeah, okay," he said. Why not? It wasn't like he had anything in mind anyway, other than just being with her.

"Good." She smiled. "When should we go out?"

"Tomorrow," he said, without hesitation.

"Okay," she said, and she seemed suddenly shy again. "Do you want to come here around eight o'clock?"

He nodded.

"I'll see you then," she said, starting to slide out of the booth again.

"Oh, wait," he said, reaching for his wallet. "Let me give you some money for my lunch."

"No, that's okay. It's on the house."

He shook his head and took some bills out. But when he put them on the table, Daisy pushed them back. "Will," she said, "I wish I could say that giving away the occasional free meal was *one* of the perks of working here, but the truth is, it's the *only* perk of working here." She smiled again, and then she was gone. And Will was left there, eating a cold french fry and thinking about the fact that, for the first time in a long time, he had no idea what he was doing.

Chapter 6

"Storm's coming," Jason said, later that afternoon, leaning against a car in the service bay.

Oh, a storm is definitely coming, Will thought, looking up from the engine he was working on. It had been hot and overcast all day. But since he'd gotten back from Pearl's a few hours ago, it had gotten even hotter and the sky had gotten even darker. And now the air was so heavy and still, so full of the hum and taste of electricity, it had you almost praying that the rain would start and break the tension. Will put his wrench down, pulled off his gloves, and, sliding his cell phone out of his back pocket, checked the latest text from Christy. *I'll be there in five minutes.* He sighed. It was going to be one hell of a storm.

"Jason," he said, wishing now more than ever that Jason actually worked during his workday. "Isn't there something you could be doing in the office?"

"Probably," Jason said, "but you're better company than the radio in there."

"Yeah, that's great," Will said, coming over to him. "But Christy's going to be here soon, and we'll need some privacy. To talk," he added pointedly.

"Oh, right. Because you two spend so much time talking," Jason said with a smirk.

"Out," Will said, exasperated, pointing in the direction of the service bay door.

"All right, all right," Jason said, holding his hands up in surrender. "As it turns out, I do have some work to do. I need to read some new video-game reviews."

"Knock yourself out," Will said, searching for a bottled water in the cooler and wishing Jason would leave.

But when he left, Will wished he would come back, if only to take his mind off the conversation he was about to have with Christy. He was nervous again, for the second time that day, and nervousness was an unfamiliar feeling for Will, who rarely left his comfort zone.

He walked over to the door to the service bay now and looked out at the ominous sky. In the distance, he saw a first flash of lightning, followed several seconds later by a low rumble of thunder. And, as if on cue, Christy's silver Mustang sped into view and turned, a little too fast, into the service station driveway. It was a beautiful car, Will thought, watching her park, but judging from the faint rattle he heard coming from the engine, there was a loose heat shield in the exhaust system. He wondered if he should offer to tighten it up for her while they talked, but he decided against it. Given that he'd never worked on her car before, now was probably not the time to start.

"Hi, Will," Christy said, opening her car door. She unfolded her long, baby-oil-soft legs and followed them out of the car.

"Hi, Christy," Will said, and if his voice sounded a little strange to him, it was probably because he was surprised by her appearance. She was wearing a short, tight dress that barely skimmed the top of her thighs and high-heeled sandals. Her blond hair was piled up on her head, and in place of the pink lip gloss she usually wore was bright red lipstick. She looked . . . she looked like a woman with one thing on her mind, and one thing only. And for once, it wasn't the same thing that Will had on his mind.

"Is anyone else around here?" Christy asked, glancing over her shoulder as she came into the service bay.

"Just Jason," Will said with a shrug.

"Good," Christy said. "I told Mac I had to run some errands." She smiled mischievously.

In that dress? Will thought.

"You know, Will," she said, turning to face him once they were inside, "it would have been easier if you could have waited for Mac to leave on Wednesday."

"Yeah, I know. But it couldn't wait that long."

"That's what I thought," she said, looking pleased, and Will realized he needed to choose his words more carefully.

"Well, I'm glad you couldn't wait to see me this time," she said. "Because the last time you saw me, you got mad at me for interrupting a game of pool."

"I wasn't mad at you for that—"

"I know, Will," she said, stepping closer. Close enough so that he could smell her sweet, fruity perfume. "But you were mad. And you know what?"

He shook his head.

"I don't blame you. I know it's been hard for you—all of this. Especially the part about not being able to see each other whenever we want to. It's been hard for me too." She pouted, then reached out and put one perfectly manicured hand on his arm.

He looked down at her hand, feeling a strange sense of detachment and wondering if this conversation could be going any worse than it already was. Or if he could have expressed himself any more inadequately than he already had. How was it, exactly, that he'd planned to tell her what he needed to tell her? He couldn't remember now, but he needed to say something else—fast.

"Christy, I'm seeing someone."

She blinked.

"What?"

He said it again.

She took her hand off his arm. Her pout

straightened itself out into a thin line, a thin red lipsticked line.

"How long?" she asked, quietly.

"Not long. Not long at all," he said, which, God knows, was the truth.

"So it's not serious, then?" she asked.

He hesitated. "No. It's not." So why did he feel, in some strange way, that he was being disloyal to Daisy by discussing it with Christy?

"Who is she?" Christy asked now, and the thin red line that was her mouth got thinner.

"That's not important."

"It is to me."

"Well, that's too bad," he said, feeling the first spark of irritation. "Because I don't owe you that information."

A flush spread across her face then, over-laying her too-tan cheeks. "Oh, right, Will. You just spend the night with me, what, like a hundred times? And now you don't owe me any-thing?"

"I didn't say I didn't owe you *anything,* Christy. I just said I didn't owe you *that.*"

"What *do* you owe me, Will?"

"Well, I think I owe it to you to be honest with you," he said, although as he said this, it occurred to Will that it was a little late for that in a relationship that had been built on dishonesty.

She thought about this for a long time, and he saw a muscle working in her jaw, like she was concentrating. Hard. He heard another rumble of thunder, closer this time.

Then Christy did the strangest thing. She put her hand back on his arm and gave him a light, caressing touch. "Okay, that's fair," she said, brightening a little. "I get it. I do. I mean, obviously, there are certain . . . limitations built into our seeing each other. And I don't blame you for feeling frustrated with them, and for wanting, sometimes, to see someone openly. But, Will, I don't understand why we can't keep seeing each other, even if you do have a girlfriend now. I mean, I won't tell if you won't tell." She gave him a little smile and leaned closer to him.

"What? No," Will said, shaking his head.

"Why not?" she said, her fingers running suggestively up his arm. "That way, we'd both have a secret."

"Christy, no," he said. "That wouldn't . . . that wouldn't be fair to her."

"Fair to her," she repeated softly, like she was testing out the words. Christy took her hand off Will's arm. She was angry now, very angry, as angry as he'd expected her to be. And for some reason, it came as a relief to him.

"And what about Mac, Will? Was it fair to him all those times we were together without him knowing it?"

"No, Christy. It wasn't."

He saw her whole body tense with anger, and,

for a second, he thought she was going to haul off and hit him. But she didn't. Instead, she leaned closer, so close that she was almost touching him, and she said, very quietly, "Go to hell, Will." And then she turned on her high heels and walked rapidly out of the garage.

Will didn't go back to work after she'd driven away. He didn't do anything except listen to the sounds of the approaching storm. It was getting closer now, bringing with it gusts of wind that shook the trees out front and smelled like cool, damp earth. It was raining somewhere, not far away, and soon it would be raining here, too.

"Jesus, Will, she looked pissed," Jason said, coming into the service bay and shaking Will out of his torpor. "I think she peeled out of here going sixty. What'd you say to her?"

"Not now, Jason," Will said warningly, pulling on his work gloves.

"Hey, I was just trying—"

"Well, don't," Will snapped. "I mean it. Get out of here; go pretend to work somewhere else, all right?"

"All right," Jason said, backing away. He was surprised, but so was Will. He and Jason never fought, and they only rarely departed from the easy banter they'd spent years perfecting.

Jason left, and Will tried to work, but he couldn't. He wandered over to the service bay door to watch the first big raindrops splash

166

down onto the parched concrete. The wind blew, stronger this time, blowing rain onto him. But he didn't move. He was thinking about what he'd said to Christy, and to Jason. He felt like a jerk, on both counts, but he felt like a jerk on his count, too. Because he realized now that for a long time, he'd been drifting, drifting in a relationship that wasn't really a relationship, and drifting in a job that wasn't really a job.

Jack was on the roof of the cabin when he saw the storm approaching from across the lake. He'd known it was coming. He'd heard the faraway thunder, annoying but persistent, like a mosquito buzzing in his ear, and he'd seen the distant lightning, benign and random, like a child flicking the lights on and off. But he'd told himself he still had plenty of time to patch the hole in the roof. He'd already pulled up the old shingles, now all he needed to do was put down the piece of wood he'd cut that morning and nail the new shingles over it.

But as he looked out over the bay, to where the gray line of the rain was beginning to move over the grayer line of the water, he decided he only had five minutes left to do it in. No, three, he amended, as a lightning bolt traced a jagged line down to the opposite shore. He'd have to finish it later. He grabbed the plastic tarp from behind him, opened it up, and shook it out, trying to spread it back over the hole. But the wind was picking up now, and it kept catching the corners of the tarp and yanking them up again. Finally, though, he managed to wrestle it down, and anchor its four corners with cinder blocks. That would hold, for now, he thought, if the wind didn't blow too hard, and the rain didn't last too long.

Trying not to let his nerves get to him, Jack carefully worked his way down the steep slope of the roof. He wasn't afraid of heights, but he'd fallen off a roof once when he was about eleven or twelve, and the memory had stayed with him. He'd been helping his uncle, who, along with his aunt, had raised him, and he'd lost his footing and slipped right off the edge of their farmhouse roof. He'd been lucky, he supposed; he'd only broken an arm and a couple of ribs, but what he remembered about that day now was sitting in the back seat of his uncle's pickup on the way to the hospital, trying hard not to cry, and even harder not to throw up, and having his uncle turn to him and say, "You just cost me a whole morning's worth of work."

Jack reached the ladder, climbed down it, and ducked under the roof's overhang about ten seconds before a deafening crack of lightning split a nearby tree. That was followed, almost immediately, by a boom of thunder and a whoosh of rain as the sky above the cabin opened up. He knew he should go inside and see whether or not the roof was leaking, but he stayed where he was, leaning against the side of the cabin and watching the storm. He loved storms—he always had—especially their fury and unpredictability. And besides, on a day like today, a good thunderstorm was likely to be the only entertainment he was going to get.

Not that he minded; he didn't. His life had taken on an almost monastic quality since he'd moved out here, and he found that it suited him—sleep and work, work and sleep. The sleep part, of course, wasn't going that well; more often than not, he was awake at night. But the work part had paid off. He'd already built a completely new front porch, rebuilt the back deck, and replaced the rotted-out planks on Wayland's old dock.

He'd done all this by starting early in the morning, before it got too hot, and continuing well into the evening, when it got too dark to see and the mosquitoes were threatening to eat him alive. He was exhausted by then. But he liked the tiredness, even if it didn't let him sleep. He liked the new calluses on his hands, too, and the new ache in his shoulders, and the new sunburn on his neck. It felt right somehow, all of it. It felt like penance. And Jack knew he had plenty to atone for.

It wasn't all work, of course. He went into town, too, to the hardware store, or the lumber mill, or the grocery store, and, two or three nights a week, to the Redeemer Lutheran Church, or more specifically, to the basement of the Redeemer Lutheran Church. And there was the time he spent with Daisy. Jack had let her call the shots; he didn't want her to feel like she had to see him. But she usually drove out a couple of times a week, in the late afternoon, and they'd sit on the front porch, on the smooth, new, yellow pine steps, and talk. Yesterday, she'd had the day off from work, and she'd brought over an impromptu picnic lunch. Jack had felt a little guilty, knowing that the iced tea and the ham sandwiches they were eating were too good to have come from anywhere but Pearl's; he hoped Daisy hadn't had to sneak them out of there like some kind of contraband. But mostly, he'd just been happy to be with her.

But Daisy wasn't the problem right now, he thought, almost oblivious to the storm raging all around him. The problem was Caroline. They'd had no contact at all since that morning at Pearl's, and to be this close to her—his cabin was less than ten miles from Butternut—without ever actually seeing her was harder than he'd have thought possible. But he'd been true to his word. He hadn't gone into Pearl's, and he hadn't tried either to frequent the places he thought she might go in Butternut. If he came back into her life, he knew it would have to be on her terms. In the meantime, he channeled all his energy into the cabin, savored every second he spent with his daughter, and prayed—yes, prayed—for some realignment of the universe to bring him and Caroline back together again. Because when he was honest with himself, which he hoped was most of the time, he knew that a realignment of the universe was about what it was going to take for the two of them to have a future with each other.

The storm was moving on, he realized then. The intervals between lightning and thunder were lengthening, and the drumming of the rain on the eaves above him was slowing. Soon it would be over, and the air would be sweet with the smell of pine needles, and the evening breeze would be cooler and fresher than it had been all of this hot, muggy week. And Jack? Well, he couldn't go back up on the roof; it would be too slippery now. He thought, instead, that he might spend the rest of the day ripping up the cabin's floors. It would be hard, knuckle-scraping, back-breaking work. And he couldn't wait to get started on it.

Chapter 7

"Lemonade?" Caroline's friend Allie asked, holding out a tray with three tall glasses on it.

"Thank you," Caroline said, reaching up and taking one. "I can't tell you how nice it is to have someone wait on *me* for a change." She leaned back on her deck chair and took a sip.

Caroline was sitting with her two best friends, Allie and Jax, on the deck of Allie's cabin, overlooking Butternut Lake. It was a lovely, twilit evening. Yesterday's storm had left the pale, lavender sky so crystalline and the air so sweet that it was as if it had washed away all the hazy humidity of the last week. And Caroline, rearranging herself on her deck chair for the umpteenth time, was trying to relax and enjoy the lovely evening. Trying, and failing. It was a shame, really, when you considered how much she looked forward to these girls' nights out, or, in their case, girls' nights *in*.

They had started three years ago, when Allie and her son, Wyatt, had moved to Butternut, and they'd continued ever since, always with the same simple set of rules: the three of them met once a month, alternating houses; there were no men or children allowed; dinner was low maintenance, usually takeout. And the nights went as late as they needed to go, which, by their standards anyway, were usually pretty late.

But on this particular night, Caroline couldn't relax. She couldn't ignore the nagging sensation that all was not right in her little world, which, of course, it wasn't. And it wouldn't be right, either, not until she could figure out how to repay the bank loan, and not until Jack Keegan gave up whatever game he was playing and left Butternut for good.

She sighed now, sipped her lemonade, and tried to think about something else, something besides Pearl's, and something besides Jack. So she thought instead about her friend Allie, who had put down the empty tray and was lowering herself onto a deck chair beside Caroline. There was something about the way she did this—some almost imperceptible carefulness to her movements—that made Caroline wonder if she would have guessed Allie was pregnant even if she hadn't already known she was. Yes, she decided, she would have known. If not because of the way she was moving, then because of the way she looked. Allie had already been lovely, with her honey brown hair cascading down her shoulders, and her golden complexion bringing out the green in her hazel eyes, but lately, she seemed to have been infused with a special light. Maybe the whole pregnancy glow thing wasn't just a cliché after all, Caroline thought.

"How many weeks are you now?" she asked Allie.

"Almost twelve," Allie said, lounging back against the deck chair's yellow-and-white-striped cushion. "We're almost ready to tell people outside of our immediate family." Caroline flushed with pleasure to think that Allie considered her and Jax immediate family.

"How are you for maternity clothes?" Jax asked from her deck chair, her blue eyes serious in her pert, freckled face. Jax, who had four children, was something of an expert on maternity wear.

"Funny you should ask that," Allie said, tucking a strand of honey-colored hair behind her ear. "Because this morning, for the first time, I couldn't button my favorite pair of blue jeans. I told Walker I've reached the point of no return," she mused. "And that it'd be pretty grim from here on out."

"Don't say that," Jax protested. "I bet you looked beautiful when you were pregnant with Wyatt. And I love the dress you're wearing now. Did you save that from last time?"

"This?" Allie said, gesturing at her slightly blousy cotton sundress. "No, this isn't maternity; it's just very forgiving. I didn't save any maternity clothes from my pregnancy with Wyatt. I mean, I did, initially, but later, I gave them away."

A silence fell over the three of them. By "later" Allie meant when her first husband, Gregg, had died in Afghanistan. That had been five years earlier, when Wyatt was three. She'd thought at the time she would never marry again, let alone have children again. That was before she'd moved to Butternut and met Walker Ford, her current husband, and now, Wyatt's adoptive father.

"I'm sorry," Jax murmured. "Of course you didn't save them."

"Jax, I hope you know by now you don't need to apologize," Allie chided her gently.

"I know, but still," Jax said softly. Then, brightening, she said, "Allie, why don't you come raid my closet? I have enough maternity clothes to take you through three pregnancies."

"Jax, please tell me you haven't saved all those clothes," Allie said, her eyes widening.

"Why not?"

"Because it means you're at least entertaining the possibility of having a fifth child."

"Well, it's not in the works," Jax said, with a mischievous smile. "But, you know, 'never say never.' "

"Oh, honestly, Jax," Allie said, her affection mingling with exasperation.

"No, seriously," Jax said, "I wouldn't dream of having another baby until I finish my degree." Two years earlier, Jax, who had never been to college, had started making the twice weekly drive to the University Extension in Ely, where she was working toward a degree in accounting.

"How are your classes going?" Caroline asked, finally jumping into the conversation.

"They're going really well," she said, drawing her knees up to her chin and wrapping her arms around them. "But I feel so old sometimes. In one class, Cost Accounting, there's no one else over the age of twenty in the room, never mind thirty."

"Oh, please, Jax," Allie said, rolling her eyes.

"You still look barely old enough to drive." It was true. Even at thirty-three, Jax could still have passed for a teenager. Partly, it was her size; she was barely five feet tall, and even after four pregnancies, she was still only approaching the one-hundred-pound mark. But partly, too, it was her sense of fun and liveliness. Even with all her responsibilities—her daughters, the hardware store she ran with her husband, Jeremy, and now, her college classes—Jax never took herself, or her life, too seriously.

"Okay, maybe I look *a little* younger than I actually am," she admitted. "Because the other day, a guy in one of my classes asked me out."

"Didn't he see your wedding ring?" Allie asked.

Jax shook her head, and her jet-black ponytail swung back and forth. "I wasn't wearing it. I forgot it and left it on the sink when I was washing the dishes that morning."

"So what did you say?" Allie teased.

"I said no, of course," Jax said, shooting her an amused look. "I told him I was married. That, actually, didn't seem to discourage him. But when I told him how many children I had, that did the trick. He looked positively ill."

Allie laughed, but then noticed that Caroline wasn't laughing. "Hey, are you okay?" she asked gently. "You haven't been saying much tonight. And you look a little . . . a little tense."

"Oh, no. I'm fine," Caroline said, too quickly,

too blithely. Both her friends stared back at her, unimpressed. She sighed.

"Is it hard having Jack living here again?" Allie asked.

"Hard?" Caroline echoed. "I don't know about *hard*. But it's unsettling, knowing I could just bump into him at any time."

"I bumped into him yesterday, at the hardware store," Jax volunteered. "Jeremy says he's in there almost every day. Buying tools, ordering supplies, asking about home repairs. I think he's serious, Caroline, about fixing that place up."

"We'll see," Caroline said skeptically. "I mean, he probably likes the novelty of it, for now, but once that wears off . . ." She shrugged. *He'll be out of here.* Jack had never been one to stick around for long, not after the fun ended, anyway.

"But he's kept his word, right? About not coming into Pearl's?" Allie asked.

"He's kept his word. So there's that—but still, knowing he's there . . . it's making me a little crazy," she admitted.

"What about Buster?" Jax asked. "Is it making him a little crazy, too?"

Caroline shook her head. "No, Buster's been great, as usual." That didn't explain why she kept forgetting to return his phone calls. Or why, the last time she'd had dinner with him, she'd been unable to concentrate long enough to have an actual conversation with him. This hadn't irritated Buster, but it had irritated Caroline to no end. She hated feeling this preoccupied, this unsettled. But she knew that when Jack had come back, it had been, for her, like opening an old box she thought she had stored away a long time ago. And now, now that she'd popped the lid off the box, she found that she didn't particularly want to examine its contents.

"What about Daisy?" Jax pressed. "How's she doing with the whole situation?"

"Daisy, believe it or not, seems happy to have him here. She's forgiven him apparently, which is more than I can do."

"You don't think you could ever forgive him?" Jax asked.

"Forgive him?" Caroline said, surprised, and a little hurt that Jax could even suggest this. Jax had only been a teenager when Jack had left, but she'd been close to Caroline's family and old enough to know how hard that time had been for Caroline. "Jax, the man left me alone to raise a child and run a business. I mean, forgiveness is all well and good in theory. But in practice? Some things can't be forgiven."

Jax looked penitent. "I'm sorry. You're right, of course. It's just . . . it's just I've been in Jack's position before. I've been the person who needed to be forgiven."

"Oh, sweetie," Caroline said gently, reaching over and patting Jax's small hand. Because now they were all remembering a time a few years earlier when Jax and her husband, Jeremy, had separated briefly after the birth of their fourth child. Caroline had intervened then and had pleaded with Jeremy to forgive Jax, not so much for a lie Jax had told him, as for the truth she'd withheld from him.

"Jax," she said now, "you deserved to be forgiven. And if your roles had been reversed, if there was something you needed to forgive Jeremy for, you would have done it too. It's in your nature to be forgiving. You're like Daisy that way. Even as we speak, in fact, Daisy is forgiving some boy who took her out on a lousy date a couple of weeks ago. She's having him over to our apartment tonight."

"Who is he?" Allie asked.

"His name is Will. Will Hughes," Caroline said. "He went to high school with Daisy. He graduated a few years ahead of her."

"Well, you don't look too thrilled about her seeing him," Allie observed with her usual perceptiveness.

"I'm not," Caroline said bluntly. "Daisy came home from their first date in tears. She said he hadn't done anything wrong. She said she was just tired. But still . . ."

"You don't believe her?" Allie frowned, knowing, as Caroline did, that if she didn't believe Daisy, it would be a first.

"It's not that I don't believe her," Caroline hedged. "I just don't like him." Then she amended quickly, "I mean, I don't like what I've *heard* about him. I've never actually met him. But I . . . I did a little checking up on him."

"How?" Jax asked.

Caroline took a sip of her lemonade, partly to kill time; she wasn't particularly proud of what she was about to tell them. "I asked Jay Niles about him when he came into Pearl's the other day. He's the counselor at the high school," she added, turning to Allie. "He's been there forever. Anyway, I asked him about Will and he told me—"

"Wait, he discussed a former student with you?" Allie interrupted.

Caroline nodded, a little sheepishly.

"But isn't that protected by some kind of confidentiality?"

"Oh, please." Jax snorted. "There's no confidentiality in Butternut. You should know that by now, Allie."

"Look, I know it was wrong of me to ask," Caroline said quickly. "And, just for the record, I've never done anything like that before. You know I trust Daisy implicitly. But she said something about him being a troublemaker in high school, and then there was that first date, and, I don't know, I've been feeling so protective of her lately. What with Jack back in her life and all." Jack, who was sure to disappoint Daisy in the end.

"All right, so what did Jay say Will was like in high school?" Jax asked.

"He said he had a bad attitude."

"Oh, well. High school. Who didn't have a bad attitude?"

"Daisy didn't," Caroline said.

"Well, Daisy's perfect," Jax said, without a trace of sarcasm. "But not everybody else is."

"That wasn't all he said, though. He said Will got suspended several times. He said once he almost got expelled. And he said"—this had bothered Caroline the most—"that 'he was one of those kids who was going nowhere fast.' I mean, what would Daisy even see in someone like that? She's the exact opposite of that."

"Oh, I don't know," Allie mused. "Bad boys can be very exciting."

"It's true," Jax agreed. "And then there's this little thing that can happen between two people. It's called chemistry, Caroline."

Caroline nodded distractedly. She knew all about chemistry, because she and Jack had had it in spades. In the beginning, they couldn't even be in the same room together without practically combusting. But it hadn't been enough. If it had been, he never would have left her, three years later, high and dry.

"Or maybe it's not just chemistry," Allie offered.

"Maybe he's different than he was in high school. People change, you know."

Ugh, Caroline thought. There was that word again. *Change.* She was actually starting to hate it.

"What's he doing now?" Jax asked.

"Um, he's a mechanic over at a garage in Winton," Caroline said.

"Is he any good? Jeremy and I can always use a good mechanic."

"I don't know," Caroline said honestly. "But he can't be making much money. Daisy tells me he lives right there, in a little apartment, behind the garage."

Neither Jax nor Allie had anything to say about this, and it was only later that it occurred to Caroline that both of them were either too tactful, or too polite, to point out that Will wasn't the only person they knew of who lived at their place of work. Caroline did, too.

"Caroline, seriously," Allie said, after a little while. "Don't worry about it. If they really have nothing in common, this thing will probably just burn itself out over the summer."

"Probably," Caroline agreed. But the truth was, she didn't feel sure of anything anymore. Since this summer had begun her whole world had begun to feel as if it was tilting, steeply, on its axis. And she felt a longing again for past summers, simpler summers, summers when an evening like this, spent with friends lounging on deck chairs in a soft, purple twilight, would have been an end in itself, and not a fleeting distraction. She didn't know how to articulate this, though, to Allie and Jax, and it didn't matter anyway, because at that particular moment the conversation was interrupted by Walker and Wyatt coming up the steps from the lake.

"Hey," Walker said, as the two of them hurried across the deck to the cabin's sliding glass door. "I'm sorry. I know we're not supposed to be here. We took the new boat out for a test drive, and we got a little carried away. We're going out for pizza right now. And we'll stay out for as long as you need us to. Right, Wyatt?"

"Right," Wyatt said, grinning a hello at Caroline. She'd become close to him the summer he and Allie had moved to Butternut. The timing had been perfect, actually, with Caroline missing Daisy, who'd just left for college, and Wyatt missing his friends from back home in Eden Prairie.

"Hey, it's okay, you two," Allie said. "I'm sure Caroline and Jax are willing to tolerate your presence for a few minutes."

"Absolutely," Caroline agreed, and when Wyatt came over to her, she gave him a hug and a kiss, though she was careful to not rumple his curly brown hair the way she had when he was five. Wyatt said hello to Jax, too, and Walker asked Allie solicitously if there was anything he could do for her before they left.

Allie smiled and shook her head. "I have everything I need," she said, tipping her face up to him. And as he bent down to kiss her, brushing her honey-colored hair off her suntanned face, Caroline felt a little stab of jealousy. Jealousy because the kiss Walker gave Allie was so much more than a polite, husbandly kiss. It was gentle, yes, but it was sensual, too. Sensual in a way that made Caroline think that the six months Allie had told her it had taken her and Walker to conceive their child had not exactly been a hardship for either one of them.

Caroline looked away, ashamed of herself for feeling envious of Allie. Allie, who'd had so much sadness in her life, deserved all the happiness she'd found now. Besides, who was she to be feeling sorry for herself when it came to love and lovemaking? She had Buster, didn't she? And he wasn't just kind, and loyal; he was the tenderest, and most considerate, of lovers. Still, she thought, as she sipped her lemonade, there was Buster's tendency to regiment everything in his life, including the time he spent with her. And she heard Jack, maddening, infuriating Jack, teasing her about her and Buster's dating schedule: *Don't you two ever see each other on a Tuesday or a Thursday?*

After Walker and Wyatt left, Allie and Jax and Caroline started talking again, though it was mainly Allie and Jax who talked and Caroline who listened, or sort of listened, as she lapsed in and out of attention. They were talking about Allie buying the Pine Cone Gallery, where she'd worked for the past three years, from the woman who owned it. The sale would be complete this summer, and Allie was excited about the changes she wanted to make and the new artists whose work she wanted to show.

"Should we have dinner?" Allie asked after a little while, when the dusky sky had gotten a shade darker and the first pinpricks of stars had become visible.

"Not quite yet," Jax said. "It's so pretty out here right now. Did you know there's supposed to be a meteor shower tonight? The best time to see it, apparently, is going to be around two thirty A.M."

"Really? Well, there's no way I can stay up that late," Allie said. "Nine o'clock feels like a stretch to me now."

"I might be up then," Jax said, repositioning herself on her deck chair. "If my back keeps me awake."

"Your back? What's wrong with your back?" Allie asked.

"Nothing," Jax said, a little guiltily. "It just hurts like hell."

"Jax," Allie said sternly, "are you still carrying Jenna around everywhere you go? Because you know you can't do that anymore. She's three now, and she's getting heavy."

185

"Oh, no. That's not the problem," Jax said. "It's not Jenna. It's Jeremy."

"You haven't been carrying him around too, have you?"

"No," Jax replied, laughing. And then she glanced over her shoulder, and into the cabin, to make sure Walker and Wyatt were truly gone. "It's just . . . Jeremy and I had sex on the kitchen floor last night. And I think I might have bruised something or pulled something."

"Is this something you do often, Jax?" Caroline asked, feeling a little envious.

"No," Jax said. "Definitely not, not with four inquisitive girls in the house. But the three oldest were sleeping over at friends' houses last night, and Jenna was asleep upstairs, and Jeremy was drying the dinner dishes for me and . . . well, one thing led to another."

"And you two couldn't even wait long enough to get to a bed?" Caroline asked.

"Well, we *could* have waited long enough, I guess. But we didn't want to."

And now Caroline was more than a little envious. Because she could remember that feeling. That feeling of not being able to wait even one-tenth of one second longer to be with someone. But she hadn't had that feeling with Buster, she realized, her disloyalty making her face feel suddenly hot—she'd had it with Jack.

"I think I'm going to need another lemonade," she said, standing up abruptly.

"Kitchen counter," Allie said.

When she got back with her lemonade a minute later, still feeling warm, and strange, Allie was saying, "We've done that before, the whole sex-on-the-kitchen-floor thing. Not recently, though. And I'm guessing not for another six months, at least."

"Caroline, what's wrong?" Jax asked, studying her. "And don't say 'you're fine.' Because we don't believe you."

"But I *am* fine," Caroline insisted, sitting back down on her deck chair. "It's just . . . it's just that it's not like that for Buster and me. The 'not being able to wait' part." Then she added quickly, loyally, "I mean, it's nice, and it's pleasant. It's even a little exciting, sometimes. But mostly"— Caroline finished a little forlornly—"our being together, it's just . . . *comfortable,* I guess you'd say."

"Nothing wrong with that," Allie said gently. "You two care about each other, Caroline. That's what counts."

"I know," Caroline said. "But you and Walker, and Jax and Jeremy, you have *both*. You care about each other, *and* you have sex on the kitchen floor."

"*And* I have a back that's killing me," Jax reminded her, smiling.

"Maybe." Caroline sighed. "But you can always take some Advil for that, can't you?"

Will, who'd never been early for anything in his life before, was five minutes early for his date with Daisy that night. He parked his pickup on Main Street outside of Pearl's, then he walked around the corner to the side entrance to the building and rang the doorbell. A moment later, she was there, opening the door for him, slightly breathless, and prettier somehow than he'd remembered her being. He always felt that way when he saw her again. When it came to Daisy, he decided, his imagination failed him every time.

"Hi, come on up," she said, smiling, and as they went up the stairs he stole a sideways look at her. There was no sundress tonight, the way there had been at the beach, only a cotton blouse with little blue flowers on it (flowers that matched the color of her eyes) and a pair of slightly faded blue jeans. Her hair, which had been straight and shiny on that last date, was loose and tousled on her shoulders now. He liked it that way, he decided, a little messy. It made him want to make it messier.

But when they got to the door to the apartment, which Daisy had left open, he had another, less pleasant thought. What if Daisy's mom was home tonight? Will's avoidance of commitment in general, and of dating in particular, meant that he'd never had to meet a girl's parents before. And now that he might have to, he wasn't exactly thrilled by the prospect.

Daisy noticed him glancing around the apartment. "My mom's not here," she said, amused. "She's at a girls' night out. So you're off the hook, for now."

"I guess so," he said, relieved.

"Would you like something to drink?" she asked.

"Sure. What are you having?"

"Diet Coke. But we have regular, too."

"I'll have one of those." He followed Daisy into a bright kitchen with lemon yellow walls and black-and-white-checked flooring. She took a Coke and a Diet Coke out of the refrigerator, handed him his can, and popped hers open. She started to say something then, but her cell phone, which was sitting on the kitchen counter, rang, and Daisy picked it up and frowned at the display.

"I need to take this," she said apologetically.

"That's fine," he said.

She answered it. "Hi, Jessica," she said. She listened for a long time, with what Will could see was forced patience. "Jessica, hold on one second." Daisy put the phone down and said to Will softly, "I'm sorry. I have to talk to my friend." She added, with an apologetic little shrug, "Boyfriend trouble."

"Sure," Will said, backing out of the kitchen. "I'll wait out there."

189

Out there was back in the front hall. He stood there for a few minutes, then looked down a short hallway, where one of the doors was cracked open. He knew, intuitively, that it was the door to Daisy's room, and he walked hesitantly over to it and pushed it gently open. It was a nice room, he saw, looking inside, a pretty room, a girl's room. The furniture was all white wood, and there were pale pink walls, a fluffy pink rug on the floor, and pink curtains hanging in the windows. He edged into the room, thinking about how different this apartment was from the house he'd grown up in. There hadn't been a single feminine touch in that house, he realized, though whether that was because his mother hadn't stayed long enough to leave any or because his father had purged the house of them after she'd left, he didn't know.

He walked farther into the room, drawn to a bookshelf whose top two shelves were almost collapsing under the weight of the trophies they held. He studied them now. Most of them were for volleyball, including two from Daisy's junior and senior years for most valuable player.

On a lower shelf was a collection of Daisy's high school yearbooks, and Will pulled out the one from her senior year. He opened it and flipped through it, looking for pictures of Daisy. They were everywhere. There she was with the Honor Society, the Student Council, the Debate Team, and the French Club. He shook his head. That part of high school was a complete mystery to him. He flipped through some more pages: spirit rallies; homecoming; senior prom. He wondered now, for the first time, if he'd missed anything when he'd boycotted all those things in high school. At the time, he'd never even given it a second thought. He and his friends had just done it on principle, though what principle that was, exactly, he didn't quite know anymore.

He kept turning the pages until he came to one of Daisy with the volleyball team. There she was, in the front row, her hair pulled back in a ponytail, her uniform showing her pale, supple arms and legs to what Will thought was their best advantage. As he was looking at the photo, he noticed Daisy's bed out of the corner of his eye and turned to stare at it. It was a double bed, and its pink, ruffled coverlet was piled high with puffy pink pillows. He wondered, idly, what the chances were of him ever spending the night with her on that bed. *Nonexistent,* he told himself, and he pushed the thought out of his mind. He turned back to the yearbook and had just found a candid photo of Daisy at a charity car wash when he sensed, rather than saw, her standing in the doorway.

"Oh, hi," he said, simultaneously turning around and closing the yearbook. He put it back in its place on the shelf. "I hope it's okay that I came in here."

"It's okay," she said, coming over to him. "I just wish my room wasn't so embarrassing."

"Why? It's nice. It's very . . ." He looked around. "Very pink."

She laughed. "I know. My mother and I decorated it when I was in the third grade. Now she won't let me change anything. She won't even let me put those trophies away. It's as if, ever since I went to college, she's turned it into a shrine to me or something."

"I like the trophies," he said. "But where are the ones from college?"

"Oh, I'm not on the team there."

"Why not?"

"I didn't make it."

But you were so good— he started to say, and then, remembering she didn't know about his watching her games, he amended it to, "But you won all those trophies."

She shrugged. "It's really competitive at the college level. They recruit players from all over the country. But it worked out all right. I still play, but now I play in a universitywide coed league. It's less competitive, but it's more fun, too."

"A coed league?" He pictured Daisy playing on a team with other students, *male* students. It bothered him.

"Coed," she repeated. "That means both sexes."

"Yeah, I know what coed means," he said, giving her a quick smile and glancing around the room again. Something hanging on one of the walls, a framed, typed letter, caught his attention and he sidled over to it. But before he could take a closer look at it, Daisy angled herself between him and the letter and blocked his view.

"Please don't read that," she said, blushing.

"Now I'm really curious," he said, straining to see it.

She sighed and moved away. "My mom again," she mumbled. "I asked her not to hang that in here, not to hang it *anywhere,* but . . ." Her voice trailed off.

Will read the letter. It was dated three years ago that spring, and it was from the University of Minnesota, offering Daisy a full academic scholarship.

"You're really smart," he said, turning to her.

But she shook her head. "No. I get good grades."

"Isn't that the same thing?"

"Not really. Getting good grades is about ten percent intelligence, and ninety percent hard work."

"That doesn't sound right," Will objected.

"No, it's true. I mean, there are those people— those very *few* people—who are naturally brilliant. But I'm not one of them. And neither are most of the other people I know who're good students. We just study harder than everyone else."

"But why?" Will asked, genuinely curious. "Why do you study so hard?"

Daisy frowned, as if she'd never asked herself that question before. "I don't know," she admitted. "I guess in the beginning, in grade school, I studied because my mom and I had a deal. If I was studying, I didn't have to help out with any of the work at Pearl's. So I studied—I thought it was better than wiping down counters or refilling ketchup bottles. Then, later, when I was in high school, I had to help her anyway, but by then, studying had become a habit. Besides, I liked what I was learning. I understood it. As opposed to everything else in my life."

And Will nodded. Because he understood; he'd felt the same way when Jason's dad had shown him how to take apart, and then put back together, a car engine. Nothing else at that time had made sense to him. But that engine had.

Still, it was hard to believe that Daisy's home life had been quite as . . . *complicated* as his had been during high school. "What was it that you didn't understand about your life?" he asked.

"Why my dad left," she said, simply.

"You missed him," Will said. It was a statement, not a question.

"I did miss him," she said. "I was only three when he left, so I didn't have a lot of memories of him, but the ones I did have were so . . . *so good*. Which is kind of strange, when you think about it, because my mom said my dad was almost never around then, and that when he was around, all they did was fight. But I didn't remember any of that. What I remembered was being with my dad and, you know, feeling safe with him. And feeling like, well, feeling like he loved me. I think that's why I felt so confused when he left. And I know that's why I wanted to study psychology in college. I wanted to know more about why people do the things they do."

She blushed then, and Will could tell she was suddenly self-conscious about telling him so much. "Sorry about taking that phone call before," she said, changing the subject.

"How's your friend doing?" Will asked, taking a step closer to her. He was so close to her now he could smell her shampoo.

"She's okay."

"So she's not heartbroken?" he asked, reaching out and taking a strand of her hair between two of his fingers. It was so soft. He gave it a little tug and let go. He saw her swallow slowly.

"No, she *is* heartbroken," she said. "But she's always heartbroken. It's a habit with her. But it's also kind of her own fault. She has bad taste in men."

"That's too bad," he said, bending down and kissing her, very softly, on the lips.

"It *is* too bad," Daisy breathed, as soon as he took his lips off her lips.

"So are you going to tell me what we're doing on this date?" Will asked.

Daisy smiled. "Yes, I am. Because tonight, Will, it's dating 101 for you."

"Dating 101, huh? Is there going to be a test at the end of the night?"

"No test, Will. Just a classic, all-American date."

"And what might that be?" he asked, wanting to kiss her again.

"Pizza and a movie."

"Are we going out?"

"No, we're staying here. I ordered the pizza, and I rented the movie."

"What's the movie?" he asked, sliding his arms around her waist. He didn't just want to touch her; he *needed* to touch her.

"That one about zombies," she said, putting her hands on his shoulders and looking up at him shyly. "It just came out on DVD."

"Oh, yeah. I want to see that. But I didn't have you pegged for a zombie kind of girl, Daisy."

"No? I like horror movies."

"But are they intellectual enough for you?" he teased.

"Oh, I think I can slum it for one night," she said, smiling.

"All right, but next time we'll choose a movie for you. Something for someone in your IQ range. A documentary," he said, kissing her lightly on the lips again. "With subtitles."

She laughed, right as the doorbell rang. "That's the pizza," she said, and this time she kissed *him* on the lips.

"Let me pay," Will said, sliding his wallet out of his pocket.

"Next time," she said, and she went to answer the door. *So there would be a next time,* he thought, with a half smile. And he was careful not to look at her bed again as he left the room.

The rest of the night was easy, and fun, even if it all felt a little unfamiliar to Will. They sat on the couch in the living room, ate pizza, and watched the movie. Will was on his best behavior. He put his arm around Daisy, which he thought was acceptable, under the circumstances, and he kissed her, twice, on the lips. When the credits started rolling and it was time for him to go, Daisy walked him downstairs. Standing there in the little vestibule was the only time that night he let himself do what he'd wanted to do since he'd gotten there. He backed her up against the wall, tilted her chin up to him, and kissed her, deeply, tasting the sweetness of her mouth. He stopped when he found himself thinking, again, about the pink bed upstairs.

"I want to see you again," he said, brushing his lips against her ear.

"I want to see you again too," she said, and he could actually feel her heart beating through the thin cotton of her blouse.

"Good. Are you free tomorrow night?"

She nodded, and he stroked her cheek, and then he left quickly before he started kissing her again. When it came to Daisy, he decided, as he drove back to the garage, he'd draw a line for himself. And as long as he didn't cross it, he figured they'd be fine. But the problem with that line, as he soon discovered, was that it was a *very* fine line, and it kept moving around. So that soon, all it took was a single word or a single look from Daisy, and he'd completely forget where the damned thing was.

Long after midnight, Jack lay on the dock he'd recently rebuilt and looked up at the sky. He'd heard on the radio today there was going to be a meteor shower tonight, but that wasn't why he'd come down here. He'd had the dream again. He'd been having it almost every night lately, and after he woke up from it, he could never go back to sleep again. So he'd started coming down here. He figured if he was going to be an insomniac, this was a pretty good place to be one, surrounded by sky and trees and water. Besides, if he spent too much time in the hovel he called a cabin, he got claustrophobic.

He squinted at the sky now, looking for signs of meteors, but he couldn't find any. Sometime after he'd gone to sleep, the wind had picked up, and it was blowing wispy white clouds across the dark sky, obscuring most of the stars. Jack didn't mind, though. The wind felt good on his skin, and it was keeping the mosquitoes away, too. What he minded was the dream. Not the dream itself, but the fact that it was just a dream, the fact that it wasn't real.

In the dream, it was nighttime, and Jack was back at the apartment above Pearl's, walking down the hallway to Caroline's bedroom and then opening the door to it. And she was there, waiting for him, in her bed, in *their* bed. Sometimes in the dream, she was wearing one of the nightgowns she'd worn when they were married, a simple, sleeveless, white cotton nightgown that barely hinted at the lovely nakedness it concealed. And sometimes in the dream, she'd already taken the nightgown off, and her bare skin was emitting a faint, almost otherworldly glow. But in both versions of the dream, she smiled at him, and peeled back the covers, and welcomed him into the bed beside her. And then, just as he took her into his arms, just as he crushed her sweet-smelling softness against him, just as he felt the warmth of her skin against his skin, he woke up abruptly and looked around. And he was stunned, and bereft, to discover himself, once again, alone in his cabin.

Jack missed Caroline so acutely then that he experienced it almost as a physical pain. He'd had a way to treat that pain once, to numb it almost beyond recognition, but now he had no choice but to feel it, to feel it filling up his chest, settling in his rib cage, gnawing at his stomach. When he first started having the dream, he'd lain there with the pain for a while, letting himself feel it, and then he'd tried to go back to sleep. But now he knew better; he didn't try anymore. He came down to the dock and waited there for the pain to lessen or, if not to lessen, then at least to change. Because usually, right around the time the sky started to lighten in the east, he'd feel a tiny flicker of hope.

That's when he'd tell himself, it'll work out, one way or another. They'd be together again. He couldn't turn the clock back, he knew that now. He wouldn't even try to. He would just love her, love her the way she deserved to be loved. He'd love her the way he would have loved her the first time if only he'd known how, if only he'd been a real man, and not some sorry excuse for one.

Now, right above him, the gauzy layer of cloud cover lifted just long enough for him to see a smattering of stars, and then, a moment later, a falling star, streaking across that same patch of sky. He decided to take it as a good omen.

Chapter 8

On a muggy evening in early July, a week after the girls' night out at Allie's cabin, Caroline found herself standing at her apartment's living room window, staring down at the street below. It wasn't that there was anything to see down there —there wasn't—but she was completely at a loss as to what to do with herself tonight. This was surprising, really, when she considered that she'd spent a whole lifetime staying busy.

Tonight, though, she'd exhausted all her options. Thanks to Frankie, who'd insisted on staying late again today, there was nothing to do downstairs at Pearl's. The tables had been wiped down, the chairs stacked neatly on top of them, and the floors mopped to within an inch of their lives. The napkin dispensers had been refilled, so had the salt and pepper shakers and the ketchup and mustard bottles. The industrial coffee machines, the heartbeat of Pearl's, had had their filters changed and freshly ground coffee shoveled into them. They'd been programmed, too, to start brewing at exactly six A.M. the next morning.

And upstairs? Well, there was nothing that needed doing up here, either. Caroline found herself wishing, for once, that she and Daisy weren't both such naturally neat people, and that there was some big cleanup job just waiting for her to roll up her sleeves and get started on it. But there wasn't; the dish rack was empty, the laundry was folded, and the living room rug was vacuumed. She thought, for a second, about cleaning out the lint screen in the dryer, but then realized she'd already done that tonight—twice.

She sighed, still watching the street below. It was quiet in the apartment, but even quieter, it seemed, on Glover Street. Where was everybody? Well, Daisy was on a date, for the third time that week, with Will. Buster was home, at his cabin, watching a baseball game. Allie and Jax were home with their families, and, if her conversation with the two of them last week was any indication, they were probably waiting for their children to go to sleep so they could be alone with their husbands. And Jack? What was Jack doing? She had no idea. She wondered, idly, if he was lonely living out at Wayland's cabin, then quickly dismissed the thought. Jack, lonely? Not likely— the man had never been lonely in his life, as far as she could tell. She pictured him now, sitting on a bar stool somewhere, talking to a pretty girl, smiling that slow smile of his at her . . . But then she stopped herself. She couldn't take that image of him any further.

Caroline felt a heaviness settle over her then, a slowness, a sleepiness almost. It was as if she suddenly had more than her fair share of gravity binding her to the earth. She recognized this feeling. She knew it very well, in fact, even though she'd only felt it a few times in her life. It was the feeling she got when she had to do something she really didn't want to do. Something that would be hard, and messy, and painful. She'd felt it when she'd had to tell her parents, who couldn't stand Jack, that she was marrying him. She'd felt it when she'd had to say good-bye to her father, a few years after that, on his deathbed. She'd felt it when she'd had to fire a longtime employee, who she knew was going through a hard time, when she'd caught him stealing money from her. And she felt it now.

She sighed again and left the living room, picking up her handbag from the hall table on her way out of the apartment. As she walked around the corner to where her pickup was parked, she felt that same resistance settling on her limbs again, as though she was walking under water. And when she got into her pickup, pulled out of her parking space, and drove out of town, she imagined that her pickup felt slow, too, and sluggish in its handling. She gave it a little gas, though, and after what felt like an eternity, she was turning onto gentle, meandering South Butternut Lake Drive, then onto a private dirt road, and, finally, into Buster's long gravel driveway.

She wondered briefly if he would mind her

surprising him like this, since, as a general rule, he didn't like surprises. But when she pulled up in front of his cabin and he came out on the front porch, he didn't look irritated. He looked worried.

"Everything all right, Caroline?" he asked, coming down the steps to meet her.

"Everything's fine," she said, giving him a kiss on the cheek. But it wasn't, of course. And Buster knew it wasn't.

"Why don't you come inside, Caroline, and I'll pour you something to drink," he said. And the way he said it told her that now they were both dreading the conversation they were about to have.

"Okay. Thank you, Buster. I'd love a glass of water," she said.

The two of them went into the cabin together, and Buster went into the kitchen, leaving Caroline alone in the living room. She sat down on the couch and looked around her. This living room should have been utterly familiar to her after three years of dating Buster, but tonight, for some reason, she felt as if she was seeing it for the first time. It was neat and orderly, with not a thing out of place, not a speck of dust anywhere. She didn't mind that, of course. But she minded *something*. Her eyes traveled over to the card table, where Buster played gin rummy with friends one night a week, then over to a dining table that Buster had commandeered for one of the jigsaw puzzles he loved to do, and finally over to the bookshelf where Buster kept his prized collection of military history books. And she suddenly realized what it was about the room that she minded: it never changed. Not really, not in any meaningful way.

It was like their relationship, she suddenly understood. Their relationship was comfortable too, and pleasant, and predictable. But it never changed, and it was never going to.

Her eyes settled on Buster's armchair then. There, on its arm, was today's paper, neatly creased and waiting for Buster to return to it. And on the small table beside the armchair was a single glass of scotch, waiting for Buster to drink it. He always had exactly one glass of scotch, never more. Not like Jack, she thought; his philosophy had always been if one was good, then more was better. He'd been that way about their lovemaking, too, she remembered, and then, realizing she was sitting in Buster's living room, and thinking about being in bed with Jack, she had the decency to blush.

But Buster was back then, carrying a glass of ice water, and as Caroline took it from him, she smiled. Or she tried to, anyway. Buster sat down on the couch and smiled back at her gently, a little sadly. And Caroline understood that when he'd gone to the kitchen, he hadn't just poured her a glass of ice water, he'd accepted, in some fundamental way, what was going to happen next.

"Buster," she said softly.

"Yes, Caroline," he said with the same gentleness.

"I . . ." she stopped.

"I know," he said quietly. "I know why you're here. It's been coming for a while now, hasn't it?"

She nodded, feeling miserable.

"I'm sorry, Caroline."

"*You're* sorry?"

He nodded.

"Buster, this is *not* your fault."

"Yes, it is, Caroline," he said, his blue eyes pained. "I couldn't give you what you needed."

But Caroline shook her head. "No, Buster, *I* couldn't give you what you needed," she said, her eyes glazing over with tears. And it was true, she thought. Because what Buster needed was so simple: affection, companionship, respect, and yes, predictability and routine. And what was wrong with that? Nothing, she told herself. There was nothing wrong with that. It had been enough for her until . . . until when? When had it stopped being enough?

"Look, Caroline, I appreciate that," Buster said now, his face pained. "But I think we both know I'm just an old bachelor, too set in my ways for my own good. I wish I'd met you when I was younger. But I was married to the army for so long"—he gave a little shrug—"it's hard to shake."

She blinked, and a tear rolled down her cheek. "You loved the army, Buster," she said softly.

"And I love you," he said quietly. "But that doesn't change anything, does it?"

She shook her head, slowly, knowing he was right.

"Now, if you don't mind, I'll walk you out to your truck," he said, his expression stoic.

"Of course," Caroline said, wiping a tear off her face with the back of her hand. She saw she'd been wrong about one thing. Breaking up with Buster may have been hard and painful, but it hadn't been messy. He was too dignified for that. Whatever grieving he would do, he would do privately.

Caroline let Buster walk her out to her pickup, but when he opened the door for her, she turned to him. "Buster," she said, a little sob escaping her. "Just for the record? It's been a good three years."

"It's been a great three years," he corrected her, reaching over and hugging her gently. She was so tempted then to tell him she'd made a mistake, that she'd changed her mind, that she wanted to stay with him here, tonight, at his cabin. But she knew in her heart that it wouldn't work. She knew that she needed something different, something more, than Buster could give her.

So she climbed into her pickup, and Buster closed the door for her. But he left his hand on the door frame for a moment.

"Caroline, promise me something?" he said.

"Of course."

"Promise me you won't let him hurt you again?"
She stared at him. "You mean . . . Jack?"
He nodded.

"What? Buster, no," she said, shaking her head.
"Is that what you think? That I did this because
I'm going to get involved with him again?
Because I'm not. I haven't even seen him since
he came to Pearl's that day."

But Buster looked unconvinced. "Drive safely,"
he said, taking his hand off the door frame and
stepping back.

And she started to say that he was wrong about
Jack, and that none of this had anything to do
with him, but then she stopped herself. If Buster
was going to believe that, there was nothing she
could do to persuade him otherwise.

She pulled her seat belt on and turned the key
in the ignition, and, as she turned her truck
around, Buster went back up onto the front porch.
She saw him there, in her rearview mirror, until
she went around the bend in his driveway. How
like him, she thought, to be concerned about her
when she was the one who had broken things off.

"Oh Buster," she said, fighting back tears. And
as soon as she turned out of his driveway, she
pulled over to the side of the road and let herself
cry, really cry. Most of those tears, of course,
were for Buster, and for what they had had

together, but a few of those tears were for herself. Because ever since the day when Jack had
walked into Pearl's, nothing, *nothing* had gone as
planned. Sometimes she felt as if she was letting
go of everything that was safe and familiar to her,
and sometimes she felt as if it was being taken
away from her.

The next day, after closing time at Pearl's, it was
Jessica who was crying.

"Daisy, what are you doing?" she asked, sniffing
loudly as she wiped her tearstained face with a
napkin.

"I'm making you a root beer float," Daisy
said, standing behind the counter and scooping
vanilla ice cream into a tall glass of root beer.
"Remember how much you used to love these
when we were kids?"

"I remember," Jessica said, and another sob
escaped her.

Daisy brought the glass, a spoon, and a straw
over to Jessica and set it down in front of her on
the counter. "Here, drink this. Or eat it or
whatever. I promise it'll make you feel better."

"You think so?" Jessica said doubtfully. "You
think it can cure a broken heart?"

"Why not?" she said, thinking that the only
upside to Jessica's heart being broken so often
was that it had learned to repair itself so quickly.
Daisy poured herself a Diet Coke from the soda

dispenser, came around from behind the counter, and slid onto the stool next to Jessica's.

"Come on, Jessica," she coaxed when her friend only stared at her root beer float. "Just try it."

Jessica sighed, but she picked up her spoon and dipped it tentatively into her glass. "I thought it would last this time, Daisy," she said, lifting a spoonful of ice cream to her mouth. "I really did. I thought this was it; I thought we'd be together forever."

But you always think that, about everyone you date, Daisy wanted to say. Instead, she reminded herself that her role as Jessica's friend was to support her, not to judge her.

So she patted her on the back and listened patiently while Jessica recounted, again, her brief, tumultuous relationship with Steve Owen, which had ended the same night that Will had come over to Daisy's for their first date.

"God, I really know how to pick them," Jessica said, depositing another spoonful of ice cream into her mouth. "But he seemed like such a nice guy."

No, he seemed like a jerk, Daisy thought, but she nodded sympathetically.

"Daisy, seriously, why can't I meet a *real* nice guy?" Jessica asked, using her spoon to fish around in the root beer float for some more ice cream. "Just one?"

Because you have lousy taste in men, Daisy

said to herself, but to Jessica she said, "I don't know why you haven't met one yet, Jessica. But you will. Just . . . just be selective, okay? Try . . . try not to jump into things too quickly." Even as she said it, Daisy knew this advice was lost on Jessica. She was a true romantic, falling in love as often as she did her nails.

"But it's not only that," Jessica said, putting a straw into the root beer float where the melted ice cream was puddling on top and taking a long pull on it. "Nothing else is going well for me this summer. I mean, I'm not getting the hang of this whole waitressing thing, for one. Your mom was so mad at me this morning, Daisy, I thought she was going to fire me on the spot."

"Yeah, about that, Jessica," Daisy said worriedly. "You're going to have to be on your toes for the next couple of days. No more mistakes, all right? Or at least as few of them as possible. Because my mom's mood this morning might be the new norm around here for a while."

"You think so, Daisy? Because your mom's bad moods usually blow over pretty quickly."

"Well, not this one." Daisy sighed. "My mom and Buster broke up last night."

Jessica's mouth dropped open. "They did?"

Daisy nodded.

Jessica thought about that, and then asked, "Who broke up with who?"

"My mom, I think, broke up with Buster."

211

"Why?"

"I don't know," Daisy said. Actually, she had a theory about it, but she wasn't about to share it with anyone else. "I came home last night," she said to Jessica, "and there was my mom, sitting at the kitchen table, drinking coffee, in full crisis mode. She didn't want to talk about it, though. And this morning, well, you saw her this morning."

"I saw her," Jessica said with a shudder. "But still, poor Buster."

Daisy nodded, a little sadly. She'd always liked Buster, partly because he was a nice guy, and partly because, for a long time, he'd seemed to make her mother happy.

"Do you think he'll still come in here?" Jessica asked.

"I don't know," Daisy said. "Probably not right away." Which meant that now there'd be two men in Butternut who wouldn't be coming into Pearl's.

"He was such a good tipper, too," Jessica lamented. "I mean, he even left *me* good tips." She finished her root beer float with a majestic slurp, and she seemed to feel better, too, because when she pushed her glass away and turned to face Daisy, her big brown eyes were free of tears and they only looked a little bit swollen.

"All right, change of subject," Jessica said. "What about you, Daisy? How's your love life?"

212

"Mine?" Daisy asked, feeling suddenly self-conscious.

Jessica nodded. "You never told me how your date with Will went last week."

"It was . . . it was good," Daisy said, evasively.

"So what did you two do? On your first date, I mean?"

Daisy shrugged. "Not much. He came over, and we had pizza and watched a movie."

"And . . ." Jessica prompted.

"And that was it," Daisy said. *Well, that and he kissed me. Five times. Not that she'd counted. And not that she'd replayed every single one of those kisses over and over in her mind, because obviously, she hadn't.*

"Well, have you seen him since then?" Jessica asked.

"Uh-huh," Daisy said. "A couple of times."

"So what did you do?"

"Oh, we just went out," she said vaguely. After Will had come over to watch the movie, he'd taken her the next night out to dinner at a nice restaurant in a nearby town. It had felt a little like an apology to Daisy, almost as if Will was saying, *This is the date I should have taken you on that first night.* But the best part of the night wasn't the dinner; it was after the dinner, and after Will had driven her home and walked her to her front door. Because that's when he'd brushed a strand of hair off her cheek, leaned down, and given her a long, lingering kiss that seemed to hold the promise of the whole summer in it.

The next time they'd gone out, a few nights later, Will had had to work late and by the time he'd picked Daisy up, she'd already had dinner. So he'd taken her for a drive on South Butternut Lake Drive, which followed the curving shoreline of the lake. And Daisy had been perfectly happy, alternately watching Will drive—he was an amazing driver, the kind who drives with the same naturalness most people breathe with—and looking out the window at the soft, twilit night. Will had the radio tuned to a classic rock station, and the windows opened to the sweet, piney air, and just when Daisy had thought things couldn't get any better, he'd smiled at her and reached over and taken her hand. He'd held it there, too, resting on the seat between them, until he'd driven, one-handed, all the way back into town again. But after he'd parked on Main Street, he'd made no move to walk her to her door. Instead, he'd pulled her into his arms and kissed her, gently at first, and then harder, pouring so much desire, finally, into that kiss that it had left Daisy half wishing he'd take her out to the beach again. But he'd stopped kissing her as suddenly as he'd started, and when he'd kissed her again, at her front door, it had been a chaste, almost polite kiss.

"Honestly, Daisy," Jessica was saying now, a

little impatiently. "I don't know why you're being so secretive. You've always told me everything before."

"I know; you're right. I'm sorry, Jessica," Daisy said, feeling guilty. She didn't want to hurt her friend's feelings, but she also wanted to be alone with her own feelings for Will a little bit longer.

But Jessica didn't look hurt now. She looked bemused. "You really like him, don't you, Daisy?" she asked.

And Daisy sighed, because she really did.

Jessica studied her, frowning slightly. "But what do you like about him, Daisy?"

"What do I like about him?" Daisy repeated, a little stymied.

"Yeah. Like with Steve, for instance, I liked his abs. That's basically why I was going out with him."

"Oh," Daisy said, a little taken aback.

"In retrospect," Jessica said seriously, "it might not have been enough to base a relationship on."

"No, maybe not," Daisy said. But the memory of Steve's abs seemed to have sent Jessica into another funk, because she got up to make herself another root beer float, leaving Daisy to ask herself the same question Jessica had just asked her: What *did* she like about Will? Well, *everything,* she admitted, even his abs, though her exposure to them had been limited to that first night at the beach. Still, she'd be lying if she said she didn't like the way he looked. She did. She liked all the things she'd noticed about him that day he'd repaired the pickup: his gold-brown eyes, his athletic shoulders, his worth-waiting-for smile.

But there were other things she liked about him, too, things that were harder to quantify. She liked his quietness, for instance. It wasn't the quietness of someone who had nothing to say. It was the quietness of someone who didn't feel the need to fill every silence with empty conversation, especially since the silences, with him, never felt strained or uncomfortable. They felt right, somehow. And he was a good listener, too. He really paid attention to what Daisy said, and when he commented on it, or responded to it, he didn't say a lot, but he always said something that was insightful, or perceptive, or funny.

"Daisy, honestly, you're acting like me," Jessica said, coming back with her new root beer float. "I'm the one who falls in love after three dates. Not you."

"Oh, I wouldn't say I was *in love,*" she said, thinking that, crazily enough, she might be. "But I think when I told you not to jump into things too quickly, I was being a little hypocritical."

"Daisy," Jessica said, her brown eyes widening. "Did you two, are you . . . ?"

"Oh, no," Daisy said, shaking her head emphatically. "Not even close." Since the night at the beach, they'd only kissed, and Daisy understood that that was all they would do, too, unless she told him or, more likely, showed him that she wanted to do more. And she *did* want to do more. But she was afraid of the more; well, not the more itself, but the feelings that came with it. Because even Will's kisses left her feeling like she was being pulled into something, like the time she'd gone swimming in Lake Superior as a kid and she'd felt as if the lake's current was pulling her in. It had been scary and exciting, all at the same time. Will's kisses made her feel exactly the same way.

"Daisy, are you all right?" Jessica asked, clearly worried. "You have the strangest expression on your face right now."

"What? No, I'm fine," Daisy said, trying to keep the memory of those kisses at bay, at least temporarily.

"This really is different, though, isn't it? This thing with Will."

"It is," she said, and something about the expression on Jessica's face made her add, "Why, is there something wrong with that?"

"No, it's just . . . ." She shrugged. "I mean, I don't know Will that well, obviously, but you two seem so different. And I . . . I don't want you to get hurt."

"Why would I get hurt?"

"You wouldn't, necessarily. But I . . . I heard something about Will recently. You know, gossip.

About someone he was . . . not *dating,* exactly. But, you know, more like *seeing.*"

"You mean, seeing right now?"

"I don't know," Jessica admitted. "But it wasn't that long ago that I heard about it."

Now it was Daisy's turn to be worried, because the thought of Will with another girl left a sudden, hollowed-out feeling in her stomach. But then she remembered something. "Will's not seeing anyone but me, Jessica," she said calmly.

"How do you know that?"

"Because I asked him, the night we went out to dinner. I said 'are you seeing anyone else right now?' and he said 'no, I'm not.' "

"And you believe him?"

"Well, he hasn't given me any reason not to." *Yet.*

"So you don't want to know what I heard?"

"No, I don't want to know," Daisy said, unconsciously squaring her shoulders. "It's probably just a rumor, anyway."

"You're right," Jessica said, visibly relieved. "Besides, if you don't have trust in a relationship, what do you have?" Saying this seemed to remind Jessica of her own recently ended relationship with Steve, and Daisy, watching her, realized her tear glands were warming up again.

Fortunately, Frankie chose that moment to interrupt them, coming through the back door of the coffee shop and wiping his hands on a rag.

"Hey," he said to both of them. Then to Daisy, "Tell your mom I got the air-conditioning working again. For now, anyway."

"Thank you, Frankie, I'll tell her," Daisy said, wondering, for the one-millionth time, what her mother would do without him.

"Hey, Jessica, what's wrong?" Frankie asked, coming over to them.

"I'm fine," Jessica said. But even with the remnants of her second root beer float in front of her, she dabbed her eyes with a napkin.

"Well, I hope you're not upset about the mix-up here this morning," Frankie said. He was referring to Jessica's confusing so many orders that the grill had come to a standstill while Daisy and Frankie had tried to help her sort them out. Caroline, barely hiding her fury, had given all the customers free coffee. "Because that kind of thing could happen to anyone," he continued. "I make mistakes like that all the time."

No, you don't, Daisy thought. *You almost never make a mistake.* But when she saw Jessica's face brighten, she was grateful to Frankie for saying it anyway, and when he turned to wash up at the sink, Daisy leaned over and gave Jessica a hug and whispered in her ear, "You'll be okay, Jessica. You just need to find a guy who's as nice as Frankie."

Chapter 9

Caroline yanked open the door to the commercial freezer and stared glumly at the economy-sized tubs of ice cream on the top shelf. It had been a busy day today at Pearl's, and there were only two flavors left now, vanilla and butter brickle. She preferred vanilla, but they might need it all tomorrow, when apple pie à la mode was on special, so butter brickle it was. She reached up and slid the tub off the shelf, then lugged it upstairs to her apartment, feeling slightly ridiculous as she did so.

If eating ice cream was going to become a nightly ritual, she decided, hefting the container onto the kitchen counter, then she was going to have to start buying quarts of ice cream at the grocery store, like a normal person. Then again, since ending things with Buster ten days ago, she'd felt like anything *but* a normal person.

The days, at least, were busy. She didn't have a lot of time to think about anything other than work. But the nights? The nights were interminable; the nights were when she missed Buster. Because while she knew she'd made the right decision, it didn't stop her from missing him, missing him enough to have almost called him and told him how much she missed him. But she hadn't done it. It wouldn't have accomplished anything, and it would have been unfair to Buster. After all, the impasse they'd reached would still be there. He still couldn't give her what she needed, and she still couldn't give him what he needed. And whatever comfort they might find now in each other's words, or even in each other's presence, they'd only be postponing the inevitable. From now on, they'd have to live their lives without each other. Maybe one day they could be friends again, but that day hadn't come yet.

Still, as she peeled the lid off the tub of ice cream, a part of her wished she hadn't forced the point with Buster. What had been wrong with what they'd had? *Nothing,* she thought bitterly, swiping a spoon out of a kitchen drawer, nothing at all. Everything had been fine, or, if not fine, then *fine enough.* Until she'd somehow gotten it into her head that she needed more. More passion, more spontaneity, more . . . *more love,* she realized with surprise.

Caroline tested the ice cream with a spoon, but it was still too hard to eat, so she put the spoon down on the counter and stood there, waiting for the butter brickle to soften. And, as she waited, she felt an ache of loneliness so deep that she wished, for a moment, that she'd taken Daisy up on her offer to stay home with her again tonight. But she hadn't; she'd figured there was no point in both of them having a bad time. Even so, Daisy had been conflicted, and when Jessica had invited her over to her house to spend the night, Caroline had had to practically push her out the door.

She sighed, poked at the ice cream with the spoon, and wondered if Buster felt as lonely as she did. She thought not; Buster was good at being alone, good at not being lonely. And there'd been times in her life when she'd been good at those, too, though being alone and being lonely could be two very different things. You could be surrounded by people, and still be lonely, or be completely alone, and still feel perfectly content. But tonight, tonight she felt both alone and lonely.

There were only two other times in her life she'd felt this way. One of them was when Daisy had left for college, and the other was when Jack had left for good. Of those two, though, Jack's leaving had been the worse. She'd felt so lonely then that she'd thought her loneliness would swallow her whole. And it might have, too, if she hadn't had a three-year-old daughter to raise and a business to run. Even so, though, it was years before she learned to keep the loneliness at bay, years, too, before she stopped missing Jack with an intensity that was like a physical hunger. Because for all the craziness in their marriage— all Jack's craziness, really—all the drinking and the lying and the cheating—she'd loved him.

Loved him and the way he'd made her feel. Because when things were good, when they were happy, which, admittedly, was less and less often as the marriage progressed, she'd felt so . . . *so full*. So full of life, and so full of love. And that had been the opposite, she understood now, of being lonely.

Caroline suddenly felt a flash of exasperation with herself. *Stop doing this. Stop dredging up all these old feelings. And for God's sake, stop thinking about Jack.* She'd already spent enough time thinking about him since he'd come back this summer, and it hadn't done her a bit of good. That story was over now; it had been over for a long time. And the only part of it she needed to remember was this: he'd left her, *left them*. And he was the same man now that he'd been then, the same man who had left them. Daisy could give him the benefit of the doubt—Caroline wasn't going to.

She tried, again, to dip the spoon into the ice cream but discovered its surface was still virtually impenetrable. *My God, it's like Arctic permafrost,* she thought, chipping away at it in vain. She considered putting it in the microwave. But no, the tub was too big to fit in there. She'd just have to wait some more, even if waiting wasn't part of her plan. Her plan, such as it was, was to eat as much ice cream as was humanly possible while watching the worst television program she could find. (She'd narrowed it down to two possibilities: one about toddlers in beauty pageants, and the other about mob wives in New Jersey.) Then, when her brain and whatever was left of the ice cream had both sufficiently melted, she would get into bed and slide, gently, into a sugar-induced coma.

She tested the ice cream, again, with her spoon. It was still frozen solid. *Oh, for heaven's sake, I can't wait all night to eat this,* she thought, especially when she wasn't even really looking forward to it. What flavor, exactly, was butter brickle anyway? She got the butter part, but the brickle? She made a mental note not to order it from their supplier anymore, then dumped the tub of ice cream, unceremoniously, into the sink and tossed the spoon in after it.

She walked out of the kitchen then and, grabbing her handbag from the hall table, hurried out of the apartment. She went down the stairs, out the door, and turned right onto Main Street. Then she walked up the quiet block, seeing, without really seeing, its businesses and shops, shuttered for the night. She knew this town so well she could have navigated it with her eyes closed, and sometimes, like tonight, she all but did. This familiarity with the town, Caroline knew, could make her feel by turns both comforted and claustrophobic. But tonight she felt comforted by it. There'd been enough unpredictability in her life this summer to make her crave the predictable.

Two blocks up Main Street, Caroline stopped at the Corner Bar, its neon sign blinking on and off in the dusky evening light, and, before she could change her mind, she pushed open the front door and walked inside. She was immediately enveloped by a dim, air-conditioned coolness, and by the soft clink of glasses and the quiet murmur of conversation. Jack had liked this bar, she remembered, hesitating in the doorway. She wondered if he might be here tonight, but a quick look around told her he wasn't. She felt a twinge of disappointment then, which she could only attribute to temporary insanity.

She closed the door behind her and walked over to the bar, then leaned on it, a little self-consciously, while she waited for Marty, the Corner Bar's longtime bartender, to finish serving another customer and look over in her direction.

"Caroline?" he said when he did.

"I'd like a drink, Marty," she said, since this was the new plan, the plan to replace the recently thwarted eating ice cream/watching television plan. She was going to have a drink. She was going to have several of them, actually.

Marty frowned. "You want a drink?" he repeated, coming over to her.

"Yes, Marty," she said, annoyed by the defensiveness she heard in her voice. "You do sell alcoholic beverages here, don't you?"

"I do," he said slowly, picking up a glass and polishing it with a cloth. "I've just never sold one to you before."

"Well, I've been known to have the occasional drink," she said. *Very occasional,* she added, silently. Once or twice a year, she'd have a beer at a picnic, or a glass of eggnog at a holiday party. But that didn't mean she couldn't drink alone on a weeknight if she felt like it, did it? Besides, it wasn't like she was going to get drunk, drunk as in fall-down, pass-out, sleep-with-your-shoes-on drunk. No, she was going to get pleasantly, woozily, just-drunk-enough-to-forget-all-your-problems drunk.

"So what'll it be, Caroline," Marty asked now, looking at her speculatively. "We have a nice chardonnay you might like. I just opened a bottle of it."

"No, I don't think so," she said, because chardonnay sounded too polite. She'd go for the hard stuff, she decided. But here her knowledge of liquor failed her. She glanced up at the bottles neatly lining the back of the bar behind Marty.

"I'll have a vodka," she said, her eyes resting on one of the bottles.

"A vodka and what?"

"Just a vodka."

"A vodka straight up?" Marty frowned.

"Straight up," Caroline said. She liked the

way that sounded. It sounded like a serious drink.

Marty didn't make any move to pour her one, though. "How about a screwdriver?" he suggested, after a moment. "That's vodka and orange juice."

"I know what a screwdriver is, Marty," Caroline said, resisting the urge to roll her eyes. "And I don't want one." The orange juice, she figured, would take up too much space in the glass, and it would take her that much longer to feel the vodka's effects.

"All right, well, then, how about a vodka tonic?" Marty suggested. "That at least should taste better to you than just plain vodka."

"Marty, do I tell you what to order when you come into Pearl's?" Caroline asked, a little frostily.

He shook his head.

"I didn't think so. Now, I'd like a glass of vodka. *Please.*"

He sighed and reached for a glass under the bar and a bottle behind him. Then he scooped some ice into the glass. "Vodka on the rocks," he announced resignedly as he poured the vodka over it. He set the glass down on the bar in front of her.

"How much will that be?" she asked a little contritely, hoping now she hadn't been rude to Marty.

"For you, it's on the house," he said.

"That's not necessary." Taking a ten-dollar bill

out of her wallet, Caroline left it on the bar. She had no idea, actually, what a drink cost, but she figured that ought to cover it, with a generous tip thrown in on top. Because if there was one thing Caroline couldn't stand, it was a bad tipper.

Now she took her vodka and a cocktail napkin over to a shadowy table in the corner and sat down, relieved to be away from Marty's censorious gaze. Jeez, the man was a bartender. Who knew she'd have to practically wrestle him to the ground to get a drink? She looked around, noting with satisfaction that she didn't recognize any of the other patrons sitting at the small tables scattered about the room. Summer people, she decided. They came in June, moving into the rental cabins, crowding the aisles in the grocery store, and taking over the town beach. And then, in August, they departed as suddenly as they'd arrived, leaving an odd, empty feeling to settle over the town and the lake, while all the locals adjusted to life without them for another nine months. But Caroline never complained about the summer people; they were her bread and butter. Or, more accurately, she and Pearl's were *their* bread and butter.

Caroline turned her attention back to her drink, raising the glass to her lips and taking a tentative sip. *Ugh,* she thought, as it burned first her throat, and then her stomach. She thought about asking Marty for a glass of wine instead, but when she glanced over at him, she was irritated to see he was watching her uneasily. So she took another sip, a bigger sip, for good measure, and forced herself to smile at Marty afterward. *See Marty, I'm fine,* she wanted to say. But he looked away then and went back to polishing glasses.

So Caroline sat there and drank her vodka one reluctant sip at a time, and she wondered why it wasn't making her feel better yet. The problem, she decided, was that the vodka wasn't turning off her brain; she was still thinking. And worse, she was still feeling. Feeling lonely, yes, but feeling sad, too. Because so far the theme of this summer seemed to be one of loss. She'd lost Buster, obviously, or, more accurately, the two of them had lost each other. But she felt, in a way, as if she'd lost Daisy, too, at least temporarily. Because ever since Daisy had started dating Will Hughes, Caroline had felt as if she wasn't really there anymore. Either she was with him, or thinking about being with him, and they both added up to the same thing. *It's like she's a million miles away,* Frankie had observed the other day, watching Daisy bus an empty table with a dreamy, faraway expression on her face. And Caroline had nodded somberly. Because that million miles, it turned out, was much farther away than the two hundred fifty miles that separated Caroline from Daisy when Daisy went back to college every fall.

And then there was Pearl's, the one constant in her life, threatening to close. If she couldn't make the balloon payment on her loan come September, and there was no reason to think she could, that would be gone, too. The thought of it was enough to make her finish her first vodka and order a second.

But halfway through the second, she realized she was still disappointed by the result. The vodka blurred the edges of her sadness, and made her worry feel a little further away, but the sweet release she was waiting for never came. Besides, it was making her mind wander dangerously, and when she found herself thinking about Jack's long, slow smile, she decided it was probably time to stop drinking. She was about to leave, in fact, when the actual Jack Keegan walked up to her table, pulled out a chair, and sat down across from her.

"Jack? What are you doing here?"

"What am I doing here? I was going to ask you the same question," he said, with the same disapproving expression that Marty had had when he'd poured her drink.

"I'm having a drink, Jack," she said. "Would you like to join me? Oh, that's right, you already have." She was trying for sarcasm, but she didn't quite succeed. Maybe because her tongue, which felt clumsy and heavy in her mouth, was having trouble enunciating the words she'd said.

"No, thank you," he said. "I'm not drinking, Caroline. And, frankly, you shouldn't be either."

"Why shouldn't I have a drink if I want one?" she said indignantly. *And who the hell are you to tell me not to drink?*

But Jack only shook his head and said patiently and a little wearily, "You shouldn't have a drink because you're not a drinker, Caroline."

"Says who?" she shot back, but the effect was undercut, again, by the fact that her voice sounded thick and slurry.

"Says me, Caroline." Jack sighed. "Trust me. I know something about this. The world is divided into two kinds of people. Drinkers and nondrinkers. And you, Caroline, are a nondrinker. Don't question your destiny, all right?" he added, with a bleak smile.

She thought about what he'd just said, but it seemed unnecessarily complicated to her, and when she couldn't quite untangle it, she dismissed it. Then something else occurred to her.

"How did you know I was here, Jack?"

"Marty called me," he said.

"Marty?" She frowned. "Why would he do that?"

"Because he's an old friend of mine. I ran into him the other day at the gas station, and I gave him my cell-phone number. So when you came in here, hell-bent on getting drunk, he called me and asked me to come over here. He was worried about you, obviously, and now so am I."

"Humph," she said, irritated by Marty's and Jack's meddling. "He shouldn't have called you, Jack. But you know, it's funny, I thought I might see you here tonight. I remembered how much time you used to spend in bars like this one."

"I haven't been to a bar in two years, Caroline," he said, running his fingers through his hair.

"Why not, Jack?"

"Because I'm an alcoholic, Caroline. A recovering alcoholic. And bars are generally acknowledged as bad places for us to be."

Alcoholic. That word, somehow, cut through the fog in Caroline's brain. She tried to focus now on what he'd said. Tried to, but couldn't. But it didn't matter anyway, she decided, because she didn't believe him.

"You're not an alcoholic, Jack."

"No, Caroline? You lived with me for almost five years. You never noticed how much I drank?"

"Oh, you *loved* to drink, Jack. No doubt about it."

"I did love to drink, Caroline. But more important, I *needed* to drink."

"Needed to drink?" she repeated. "I don't know about that, Jack." She tried to think clearly. "I mean, you drank all right. Don't get me wrong. But it just sort of went with the territory, didn't it?" Shaking her head at the memory, she went on, "You know, the drinking, the fighting, the women—they were all just part of the Jack Keegan package."

He started to interrupt her, but she ignored him. She was just getting started.

"My God, you were trouble," she added, almost to herself. "The first time my mother met you, Jack, she said, 'That boy is trouble . . .'" Caroline's mind seemed to slide away from her then, away from Jack and away from the bar, and back to the memory of bringing Jack home to meet her parents. It had not gone well, as she recalled. She hadn't cared, though; she was crazy in love with him by then. So crazy, in fact, that— but Jack broke into her thoughts.

"Caroline, you're dead wrong about me. I wasn't just some rabble-rouser, if that's what you're thinking. Some guy who liked to stir up trouble. I was a drunk. And everything else I did," he said, waving his hand, "that was all a part of it, too. The collateral damage, I guess you could say, of my alcoholism."

Caroline frowned, trying to accept this. But she shook her head. "No, Jack. You weren't an alcoholic. You never drank during the day, and you always had a job."

"Oh, for Christ's sake, Caroline," he said, exasperated. "Haven't you ever heard of a *functional* alcoholic?"

She looked at him blankly. She'd heard of that, but it didn't seem to fit Jack either.

He sighed impatiently. "How can you know so little about this, Caroline?"

She shrugged, a little helplessly.

"I mean, haven't you ever seen one of those shows on cable about addiction and recovery?"

"I, I don't think so . . ." she mumbled.

"Not even when you were changing the channels?"

"Oh, I guess I saw them," she said, a little befuddled. "But I didn't watch them. They always seemed so . . . *depressing*."

He sighed. "Well, mostly, they *are* depressing. But sometimes, if you stick around until the end, they can be uplifting, too."

"Is that what your life is like now, Jack? Uplifting?" Caroline asked, as she tried to bring him into focus. But he still looked a little blurry, as if his edges had been ever so slightly smudged.

"No," he said, closing his eyes for a second. "No, my life isn't uplifting, Caroline. I haven't gotten there yet. Now, if you don't mind, I'm going to get rid of this." He gestured to her half-drunk glass of vodka on the table.

"I don't mind," Caroline said softly, and when he whisked the glass away to the bar, she was left to try to make sense of what he had said. Jack, an alcoholic? Was that true? And if it *wasn't* true, why would he lie about it? Still, it didn't jibe with what she knew about alcoholism. Or at least with what she *thought* she knew about alcoholism. Granted, that wasn't a lot. But still, Butternut, like any small town, had had its share of drunks, and living here all her life, she'd known them all: the sloppy drunks, the loud drunks, the sad drunks, the secret drunks (or at least the ones who thought their drinking was a secret), the dangerous drunks, the belligerent and angry drunks.

The trouble was, Jack didn't remind her of any of those drunks. Back when they were married, when they were both in their early twenties, she'd thought of Jack as a man who liked to drink, liked to drink *a lot*. But then, so had most of the men in their social circle. And Caroline had assumed at the time that it came with the territory. After all, they were all young. And they had all worked hard, by day, at the mill in Butternut or at the snowmobile factory in Ely farther north. It had seemed like their due, somehow, to go out to a bar at night and blow off some steam. Eventually, of course, it was assumed that they would settle down into marriage, and children, and the routines of family life.

Jack, though, never settled down. He seemed, in fact, to do the opposite. He didn't go out to bars less often; he went out to them *more* often. And he didn't come home from them earlier; he came home from them *later*. Eventually, of course, he stopped coming home from them at all, even after they'd closed. At first, this had led to frantic phone calls on Caroline's part. But gradually, as the extent of Jack's womanizing became clear, she'd stopped trying to track him down all the time, and instead, she'd waited at home with their young daughter, a silent fury building steadily inside her.

She looked back at him now, standing at the bar. He was talking to Marty as Marty filled two glasses with a clear, carbonated liquid. Was Jack an alcoholic then, she wondered, when they'd still been married? But again, she resisted the idea. He just wasn't like the other alcoholics she'd known. His personality, for instance, didn't change when he drank. He was almost always easygoing and fun loving, rarely dark or bitter. That was what had drawn Caroline to him in the first place. Unlike her friend Jax's father, an alcoholic who'd been famous for his explosive temper, Jack had never gotten angry when he drank. He'd never gotten angry when he *didn't* drink either. Even when Caroline had tried to start an argument with him, as she often did toward the end of their marriage, he wouldn't take the bait. More often than not, in fact, he'd just leave, something that had always driven Caroline crazy.

She looked back at him now, a little blearily, as he left some money on the bar, and she tried to see some sign of what he'd been through, or of what he'd had to overcome, but she couldn't see it. All she could see was Jack. And Jack looked . . .

well, Jack looked like himself, like his old self—
not like someone who was struggling with inner
demons, not like a dark or troubled soul. Unless,
unless . . .

Caroline sat very still now, trying to force
herself to think clearly. There was one thing about
Jack back then that she'd found worrying,
disturbing even. After they'd started dating, she'd
discovered that he'd never wanted to take his
shirt off, even when they were at the beach. She'd
thought that was strange, since there was nothing
wrong with Jack's body that she could see. It
appeared, in fact, to be pretty amazing. But when
she'd finally coaxed him out of his shirt once,
when they were alone, he'd asked her not to
touch his back. Only later had he let his guard
down far enough to let her see, and feel, the red,
puckered scars that ran in parallel lines across it.
Caroline had been shocked by them. But Jack
wouldn't talk to her about how he'd gotten them,
not then, not ever.

The only insight she'd ever had into the situation had come when she and Jack were making
the guest list for their wedding, and Caroline
had chided Jack for not wanting to invite his
aunt and uncle. She'd never met them before, but
she knew that after Jack's parents had died in a
car accident when he was very young, they'd
raised him on their farm a couple hours south of
Butternut. Jack, though, had been adamant about

not inviting them to their wedding, and when she'd pressed him on it, he'd lost his temper. She still remembered it vividly, because it was one of the few times she'd ever seen Jack angry. *Caroline, just drop it, okay? I said no. They're not coming to our wedding.*

"Here you go," he said now, setting a glass down in front of her and forcing her back to the present. "It's club soda. Drink it."

Caroline sipped it obediently, and she had to admit, it tasted good—clear and cold and fizzy— but even so, her head was starting to spin a little. And her stomach, which was churning uncomfortably, didn't feel like it was doing much better than her head.

"What's wrong?" Jack asked, watching her from across the table.

"I don't feel that well," she admitted.

"No? When did you last eat?"

She thought about it, and she honestly couldn't remember. It wasn't like her to skip meals, but Pearl's had been especially hectic today.

"What time did you have dinner?" Jack prompted.

"I didn't," Caroline confessed.

His jaw tightened. "Lunch?"

She shook her head.

"Caroline," he said with a groan. "Come on. That's the first rule of drinking. Never drink on an empty stomach."

"Too late for that." She sighed.

He studied her speculatively for a moment. "Let's go," he said suddenly. "I'm taking you home, and I'm not leaving until you've got something solid in your stomach."

Caroline wavered, not sure whether Jack coming home with her was a good idea or not. But he overruled her misgivings.

"We're leaving," he said, standing up. *"Now."*

"Oh, all right," she grumbled, and she followed him out of the bar.

Chapter 10

"Here you go," Jack said, setting a cup of coffee and a grilled cheese sandwich down on the table in front of her. "I told you I still knew my way around this place."

Caroline, sitting in one of the red leather booths at Pearl's, looked down at her plate and frowned. "Jack, that is, bar none, the ugliest grilled cheese sandwich I have ever seen."

Jack chuckled and slid into the booth across from her. He had to admit, this slightly scorched grilled cheese sandwich would never be served at Pearl's. But he figured it would do the trick. "Just eat it," he said. "And drink your coffee, too. Drink it black."

"Will that sober me up?" she asked, taking a sip of the coffee and wrinkling her nose at its harshness.

"No, not really. That's a myth, by the way, that drinking black coffee can counter the effects of alcohol. It can't. Neither can taking a cold shower. But sometimes, what we think something can do is more important than what it actually can do. So drink your coffee, and eat your ugly sandwich."

Caroline sighed resignedly, but bit into her slightly burned sandwich anyway. "It's pretty good, actually," she said, taking another bite. "Where'd you learn to cook, Jack?"

"Um, I don't know if you'd call that cooking. But living alone for eighteen years, you learn how to make a few things."

She paused and looked at him thoughtfully. "Did you though, Jack? Live alone, I mean."

"Most of the time," he said evasively. Because of course there had been women, over the years, who'd come to spend a night and ended up staying longer; some of them, much longer. He didn't want to talk about that now, though, so instead he asked a question of his own. "So why, exactly, were you trying to get drunk tonight, Caroline?"

"I wasn't trying to get drunk," she said, eating her sandwich and not looking at him.

"You're a lousy liar, Caroline."

She glared at him, but then relented. "Oh, all right." She put her sandwich down. "I *was* trying. I just didn't know it would be so hard."

He smiled. "Oh, I'd say you did all right for yourself. You were slurring your words pretty well by the time I got there. You sound better now, though. You look better, too."

"My head still feels funny," she admitted a little sheepishly. "Like it's buzzing or something."

"That'll go away," he said. "But I want to know what sent you running for a vodka bottle tonight."

She studied him for a long moment, and he knew she was trying to decide whether or not to tell him the truth. Then she shrugged, a tiny shrug. "For the record, Jack, it's none of your business. But . . . Buster and I ended our relationship."

He looked at her sharply. He hadn't seen that coming, not so soon. But he'd be lying if he'd said he hadn't wanted it to come.

"Oh, don't look so pleased with yourself," she said. "It had nothing to do with you, Jack, if that's what you're thinking."

"No?" he challenged.

"No. It had to do with Buster and me. We decided we'd reached some kind of . . . natural break point, I guess, and that it was time for us to move on. That's all. We're both mature adults, Jack, and we made the decision together."

She looked down at her plate. The woman

241

couldn't lie to save her life, he thought. So it hadn't been a mutual decision; she'd ended it, obviously. And thinking about that, Jack felt a tiny, welcoming flicker of hope.

"And now I have a question for you, Jack." Caroline looked him directly in the eyes and seemed, for the first time that night, to be completely sober. "Why'd you come back here? Why'd you *really* come back here? And don't say you came back here because Wayland left you his cabin, because you've already tried that one out on me."

Jack leaned back against the booth, watching her and weighing his options. He hadn't meant to tell her this yet, so soon after moving back here. But he wondered if now wasn't as good a time to tell her as any; after all, timing was everything. But perfect timing? That was rare.

"I came back here," he said, finally, "because I wanted to be with you. I've always wanted to be with you. I just . . . I just lost sight of it for a while."

Her eyes widened with surprise. "Jack," she said softly, questioningly. But after a moment she recovered herself, and her wonder was replaced with cynicism. "Lost sight of it for eighteen years," she said. "I don't think so."

He shifted again and thought about how to respond to her skepticism, her justifiable skepticism. He decided to just go for broke and tell her everything. It seemed simpler, somehow, than serving the truth up to her one spoonful at a time.

"Okay, I didn't lose sight of wanting to be with you," he said. "Not exactly. I just didn't think there was anything I could do about wanting to be with you, not while I was still drinking. So I just, I just put that hope away, I guess. Or I tried to. But it was always there, Caroline. Every single second of every single hour of every single day. And then, a couple of years ago, I got a phone call from Wayland. We'd lost touch, by then, but he was sick, really sick, and when he asked me to come visit him in the hospital, what could I say?"

He rubbed his eyes now, trying to erase the memory of how Wayland had looked in that hospital bed. "Anyway, I drove out to see him. He'd told me on the phone he wanted to reminisce about old times, but by the time I got there, he was too weak to talk. So I . . . I just sat there and held his hand, until . . ." He shook his head. "It was a hell of a way to die. Nobody there but me, and I hadn't even known he was sick until a few days before."

"I'm sorry it had to be that way for him," Caroline said quietly. "But he'd burned a lot of bridges by then."

Jack nodded. If there was one thing drunks did well, it was burn bridges.

"But, Jack, I still don't see what this has to do with us," Caroline said.

"I know. I'm getting to that." He sighed and rubbed his eyes again. "I stayed with Wayland until he died, and then I drove straight to Elk Point, straight to my first AA meeting. And that was it. I haven't had a drink since."

"So you were afraid if you didn't stop drinking, you might die that way too? With only an old drinking buddy to hold your hand? Or worse, maybe all alone, with nobody to hold your hand?" And her skepticism, he saw, was back.

"No, Caroline. I wasn't afraid I'd die alone; I was afraid I'd die without trying to get you back—you and Daisy. So I dragged myself to an AA meeting every night, and I sat in some musty church basement, wanting a drink so badly that I could only measure my sobriety in minutes, and I told myself that if I could stay sober for a year, I could get back in touch with Daisy. And if I could stay sober for two years, I could come back here, to Butternut, and be with you. Or *try* to be with you, I should say. Because I knew, even then, it wasn't going to be easy. And you, Caroline, have not disappointed me." He smiled at her, a little nervously, not knowing how she'd react.

For a moment, she didn't react to it at all. Then Caroline pushed her plate with the half-eaten sandwich on it abruptly away from her and said angrily, "I don't believe you, Jack. I believe you, I guess, about the getting sober. But I don't believe you when you say you spent eighteen years pining away for me and Daisy. Do you remember how you left here, Jack? Do you?"

He nodded, ashamed at the memory.

"You woke up one morning," Caroline said, her face flushed with anger, "and you threw your clothes in a suitcase, and you were gone. Just like that." She snapped her fingers for emphasis. "And you never said good-bye. Not to me, not to Daisy. You called us from the road, Jack, from some gas station. You said you needed a 'break,' and except for our divorce, and your child support checks, I didn't hear from you again until this summer. So either you're a liar, for saying you cared so much, or you're a complete idiot, for caring so much and waiting almost two decades to do anything about it."

"The second one," Jack said quietly.

But Caroline only shook her head in exasperation.

"Look, I remember the morning I left, Caroline," he said, resting his elbows on the table and leaning forward. "But I remember it a little differently than you do. I'd been up for most of the night before, drinking and playing poker with friends, and I'd just crawled into bed when the alarm went off. I could barely open my eyes; I mean, I felt like I'd been hit by a Mack truck. I know you've never had a hangover before

245

Caroline—though that may change now—but, trust me, some of them are their own special form of torture. Anyway, I dragged myself out of bed and stumbled into the kitchen. You were there, already showered and dressed and headed downstairs, but you asked me to look in on Daisy.

"So I go into her room, and she's climbing out of that new toddler bed you'd just bought her, and I pick her up. I can tell right away she's sick. She has a fever, and her nose is running, and she's miserable, poor kid. So I try to comfort her, and the next thing I know you come back upstairs and say the dishwasher's broken, and it's going to be a busy day, and we're going to have to hand wash all the dishes. So I ask you to take Daisy for a second, because she's really fussing by now, and I go into the bathroom to splash some cold water on my face, and, as I'm doing that, I look at myself in the mirror above the sink. It isn't pretty. I look like hell. And I feel like hell. And I know I'm useless to you two—worse than useless, really. Because I'm holding you back; you'd both be better off without me."

"Oh, I see, so you were actually doing us *a favor* by leaving, Jack?" she said bitterly. "You were actually being selfless. How convenient for you to remember it that way for all these years."

"No." He sighed. "No, I wasn't being selfless. I know that now. I was being a bastard, and a cowardly one, to boot. If I'd been a better man, I would never have left. Or, if I had, I would have come right back."

"And now, Jack?" she asked, her pretty mouth hardening. "Are you a better man now?"

"I sure as hell am trying to be," he said honestly. "But as to whether I am or not, you'll have to be the judge of that."

Caroline looked at him, long and speculatively, and Jack could feel the coffee and the grilled cheese doing their work. She was sobering up, a little.

"I don't know Jack," she said finally. "I just don't know. I can't get past the fact that you never came back before now. Not once. In all those years."

"Actually, I did come back once," he said quietly. "I just didn't tell you I'd come back."

"What do you mean, 'you didn't tell me'?"

"I mean, I saw you and Daisy, but you didn't see me," he said reluctantly. He'd never talked about this—ever. Not even in his AA meetings.

"Are you saying . . . are you saying you spied on us?" Caroline asked, her blue eyes narrowing.

"I guess you could say that," Jack said, studying the pattern on the Formica tabletop. "But I didn't mean to spy on you. It just sort of happened that way." He looked up at her and kept going before he lost his nerve. "It was about six months after I'd left. God, I missed you two. I missed you two like crazy. And I had this idea that maybe you missed me, too. Maybe you even *needed* me, crazy as that seemed. So I drove back here. It was the Fourth of July weekend. I was going to go to the fairgrounds for the fireworks and try to find both of you there. But I got to Butternut before all the festivities started, and I didn't know what to do. I didn't want to just show up at your front door, but I couldn't wait to see you either, you or Daisy. So I parked on Main Street, across the street from Pearl's. And I just sat there, sweating bullets. I was so goddamned nervous. I was alone, and I wasn't drinking. And I prided myself on not drinking alone. You know, it's one of the lies I told myself then. 'I can't have a problem with alcohol if I never drink alone.' But I remember thinking, as I sat there all afternoon, well, maybe I could have just one beer by myself.

"Finally, I saw you two. You came out of the building and turned down Main Street and walked right by my truck. By some miracle, you never saw me, even though you were close enough for me to reach out and touch you."

"Why didn't you, Jack?" Caroline asked suddenly. "Not reach out and touch us, I mean. Why didn't you do something, or say something, if you'd missed us so much?"

He smiled, a little sadly. "Because you weren't alone, Caroline. You had another man with you."

"Another man?" she murmured softly, and he watched her face as she searched for and then retrieved a memory.

"Oh," she breathed, understanding. "Todd? Todd Macomber?"

"Was that his name? Who was he?" he asked, still desperately curious, even after all these years.

Caroline sighed, a little sadly, he thought. "He was new in town. He was a shop teacher at the high school. Still is, actually. I'd met him when he came into Pearl's. I wasn't ready to date then, I really wasn't. It was so soon after . . . But he was a nice enough guy. And Daisy liked him, I remember. She liked him a lot. So I thought, why not? You were never coming back. As far as I knew," she added, with a little shake of her head.

"Well, I watched the three of you walk down the street together," Jack said, when he realized Caroline was done talking. "I didn't know anything about this guy, obviously. I didn't recognize him. But he looked nice enough, as far as I could tell; you know, clean cut, neatly dressed, that kind of thing. And the three of you, you looked, you looked . . . *so normal* together, so happy. Daisy was between you two, and she was holding both of your hands, and you were both swinging her into the air. And she was laughing . . ." His voice trailed off, as he lost himself in the memory. But Caroline, he could see, was waiting for more, so he kept going.

"I can't quite explain what it was like, seeing the three of you together. It was strange. I mean, on the one hand, it hurt like hell; it was like someone twisting a knife in my gut. Seeing you with someone who could replace me, who maybe already *had* replaced me. But on the other hand, I felt glad, in a way. I thought 'Good for you, Caroline. Good for both of you. Because you both deserve someone better than me.'

"After that, I drove home. Straight through the night and into the next day. I was trying to be happy for you, Caroline. I really was. But all I could think about, for some reason, was the little dress Daisy had been wearing. It was a sundress, white with little red cherries on it. I don't know why, but thinking about that dress just about killed me."

"I remember that dress," Caroline said suddenly. "She loved that dress. She wore it that whole summer. I was lucky if I could get it off her long enough to put it in the washing machine once in a while." She smiled now, at the memory of that dress. But then something else occurred to her.

"Jack," she said. "What you saw that day, parked in your car, it was a date. And not a very good one either, as I recall. Not that Todd wasn't a nice guy. He was; *is,* I mean. He still comes in here sometimes. But it was too soon for me. I ended it a few weeks after that, I think."

"That's not what I thought, Caroline. I thought, when I got served with those divorce papers six months later, that it was because you wanted to marry him."

"Marry him?" she said, with surprise. "Why would you think that?"

"Because never, in a million years, did it occur to me that you wouldn't get remarried. That you two wouldn't finally have the husband, and the father, you deserved. I was counting on it when I left. It was the only thing, really, that made me think I'd done the right thing by leaving."

Caroline had been tentatively sipping her cup of what by now must have been cold coffee, but when Jack said this, she slammed the cup down on the table, hard enough to make him jump back a little bit in the booth.

"Stop it, Jack," she said, her face flushing. "Stop doing that thing again. Stop pretending to be so noble. First you say you left because you thought we'd be better off without you. Now you say you didn't come back because you thought we'd be better off with someone besides you. I'm sorry, but it's too easy. And it lets you off the hook completely. Your leaving was selfish—and a lot of other things, too. None of them good."

"I agree," he said, simply. "Because over the last couple of years, I've learned a lot about the lies we tell ourselves, the lies that get us through the night when nothing else can. Not even eighty-proof bourbon." He was quiet for a moment, knowing what he needed to do and gathering his courage to do it.

"Caroline," he said finally. "I've said a lot of

251

things to you tonight, but I haven't said the most important thing yet, which is that I'm sorry. I'm sorry for all the things I ever did to hurt you and Daisy."

"That's it? You're sorry? And I'm supposed to forgive you?"

"Again, Caroline, that's up to you."

She said nothing for a long moment, but then her face softened a little, and some of the anger, he saw, ebbed out of her. It gave him the courage to ask her a question he'd wanted to ask her since he'd come back to town. "Caroline, why didn't you get remarried?" he asked. "If not to that guy, then to someone else?"

"You think eligible bachelors grow on trees in Butternut, Jack?" she said, with a hint of amusement.

"No. But I don't think the guy I saw you with that day was the only person who pursued you either."

She considered that, then shrugged. "No. He wasn't. There were one or two others over the years, but by then Daisy and I were getting the hang of it. Being on our own, I mean. It turns out, we were a good team; we *are* a good team. And when it came to the men . . ." She stopped.

"Yes?" he persisted.

"I wasn't in love with any of them," she said. "Not really. Not enough to rearrange my whole life for them."

"What about Buster?" he said, knowing he was pressing his luck.

"Buster?"

"Were you in love with him?"

"Buster was . . . different," she said thoughtfully. "I don't know about love. But there was respect there. Tremendous respect on both sides, understanding, too. When I met him, I was old enough to know that what you feel for someone when you're younger—that attraction, or infatuation, or whatever you call it—isn't always as important as just liking someone, being comfortable with someone. I actually think I might have married Buster, if he'd wanted to get married." She fiddled with her coffee cup.

"Buster didn't . . . didn't want to get married?" he asked, surprised.

"No," she said, looking at him, her blue eyes still soft. "He didn't. I understood, though. He's widowed. His wife died many, many years ago, when their daughters were still young. His daughters are grown up now, of course, and have families of their own, families that Buster absolutely adores. But I think, like me, he got used to not being married. He liked his independence. The same way I liked mine," she added, quickly. Jack nodded and said a silent thank you to Buster Caine for valuing his independence so much.

"All right, Jack, now I have a question,"

Caroline said. "You agree your leaving was cowardly. But after you left, why didn't you call, or even visit? After that first time, I mean."

"That was another lie I told myself. That it would be easier for the two of you if our break was a clean break."

"Well, that really was a lie," Caroline said, her bitterness surfacing again. "Because you try telling a three-year-old child that the father she misses thought a clean break would be easier for her."

He closed his eyes, just for a second. This part hurt, more than the rest—the part about Daisy, Daisy in that little dress with the cherries on it, missing him.

But when he opened his eyes again, he saw that Caroline was rubbing her own pretty blue eyes.

"It's late," he said, reaching for her dishes. "And you're tired. Why don't you let me clean up?"

But she held out a hand to stop him. "No, leave those for a minute," she said. "I want to know how this works, Jack. The whole recovery thing."

"Well, basically," he said, shrugging, "I try not to drink."

"No, seriously. Do you still go to meetings?"

"Absolutely. I'll always go to them. Right now I go to a meeting here in Butternut, at the Redeemer Lutheran Church. I meet with a sponsor, too, Walt Dickerson. I think you know him."

Caroline made a face. "Of course I know him. He's so cranky, though. Whenever he comes in here, he complains about the coffee. Really, Jack, I don't see how he could be helpful to anyone, let alone a recovering alcoholic."

"Well, he's not long on charm," Jack agreed. "But he's been clean and sober for twenty-five years, so that's something."

"I suppose," she said distractedly. "But, Jack, can I . . . can I ask you something else about it? About your drinking?"

"All right."

"Does your drinking . . . does it have anything to do with the scars on your back?"

"What?" he said, totally unprepared for that question. He felt it, then, the cold, prickly sensation he felt on his scars whenever he thought about how he'd gotten them. It was as if the hair on them were standing straight up. Of course, it wasn't—hair doesn't grow on scar tissue.

"Why are you bringing this up now?" he asked.

"Because it occurred to me that if you were . . ." She struggled a little here. "If you were abused, as a child, it might have something to do with why you became an alcoholic."

"No," he said, bluntly, wanting to put this subject to rest. "No, it's not like that, Caroline. With alcoholism, you can't connect the dots from one thing to another. I mean, a lot of people who have lousy childhoods don't become alcoholics."

"So you did have a lousy childhood?" she prompted gently.

"I don't want to talk about it," he said, trying to project a calm he didn't feel. He was starting to get that clammy feeling all over his body that he got sometimes when he thought about it.

"Okay, but just tell me one thing. Did you drink to forget something, Jack? Something from your childhood?"

"I didn't drink to forget." Jack wiped his now-sweaty palms on his blue jeans. "I drank to not remember."

"Isn't that the same thing?"

"No."

"Why not?"

"Because some things . . . some things you can't forget."

Caroline was silent for a long moment. "I'm sorry, Jack," she said finally. "I'm just trying to understand this. Trying to understand *you*."

He nodded a little and felt some of the tension start to leave his body. The subject of his childhood, it seemed, was closed for now.

Something else, though, seemed to occur to Caroline. "What about Daisy?" she asked. "Does she know about your drinking, and your . . . not drinking?"

"She knows."

"You told her before you told me?"

"Yes."

"She never said anything about it," Caroline said, with surprise.

"No. She thought I should be the one to tell you."

Her shoulders sagged a little. "Daisy never used to keep secrets from me."

"It's not a secret, Caroline. And I would have told you before now, too, but the last two times I spoke to you, you didn't seem to want to listen to anything I had to say."

Her face softened again. "That's true enough. But, Jack? All the things you've told me tonight . . . what, exactly, am I supposed to do with them?" And she looked so tired when she said that—so tired in her own, lovely way, her blue eyes shadowed with faint circles, her skin softly flushed, whether from alcohol or emotion, he didn't know—that his heart went out to her.

"Do whatever you like with them, Caroline," he said gently. "The rest is up to you." What else could he say? He figured he'd argued his case. Maybe not argued it well, because, selfish bastard that he'd been, it was impossible to argue well. But he'd argued it honestly. It was out of his hands now.

She yawned then, a sweet, almost childish yawn, and Jack smiled and glanced at his watch. "It's getting late," he said. "I'll clean up down here. You should be getting to bed."

"I'll help you," Caroline said. And together

257

they cleared the dishes off the table and took them over to the sink behind the counter.

Jack checked to see that he'd turned off the grill, and then he wiped it down carefully while Caroline washed the dishes.

He heard her giggle then, and he glanced over at her.

"What is it?" he asked.

She paused in what she was doing. "I was remembering another night here, Jack. A night when we were dating, and we came back here, late, and tried to make something to eat, but we were laughing so hard, we woke up my dad. He was not pleased, as I recall," she added, with another giggle.

"I remember that night," Jack said, smiling. "We'd been to a party at Joey's cabin and . . ." His voice trailed off as he remembered the details of that night. During the party, he'd taken Caroline into one of the bedrooms and locked the door. He'd wanted to make love to her on the bed, where all the guests' winter coats were piled up, but Caroline had objected. She'd said it wasn't polite of them to lie down on the host's bed. So instead he'd taken both of their coats off the bed and spread them out on the rug, and then he'd lowered her down onto them and made love to her, right then and there. She hadn't objected to that. In fact, she'd returned his lovemaking with a fervor and an excitement that afterward had left him staring down at her in wonder.

He felt that wonder again now. But the wonder wasn't over her lovemaking; it was over the fact that her lovemaking hadn't been enough for him after they'd gotten married. Why, when he'd had her, he asked himself now, had he ever wanted, or needed, anyone else?

"You'd better be getting upstairs," he said abruptly, turning away from the grill. Because the desire he felt for her now was the same desire he'd felt for her then, only stronger, if that was even possible. He skirted around her to the back door of the coffee shop, to the door that led to the stairwell to her apartment, and started to open it for her. But all of a sudden, she was beside him, leaning back against the door, and looking at him like she . . . well, like she wanted him. He felt his throat tighten.

"I'm not tired, Jack," she said, her pretty face turned up to his. Her creamy skin was tinged with pink, and her blue eyes were shining brightly. She swayed a little toward him and smiled in a way that made him think she was still a little drunk.

"You might not be tired now. But you'll be tired in the morning," he said, taking a step back.

But she ignored him. Instead, she reached out her hand and ran her fingers along his jawline in a way that made Jack inhale sharply. "Jack, I don't know what your liver looks like," she said.

"But the rest of you, the rest of you looks *so good*. Daisy's not home. Come upstairs with me, Jack. Just for tonight."

He closed his eyes and tried to ignore the sensation of her cool fingers skating over his razor-stubbled jaw. "It's not a good idea," he said, a little hoarsely, stealing a look at her.

"Oh, come on, Jack. How many women have there been over the years? Before me, during me, after me?"

He swallowed. "A lot."

"Well, I'll just be one more then." And she reached up and kissed him on the lips.

And Jack, idiot that he was, kissed her back. Tentatively, at first, because the sensation of kissing her was so strange—so familiar, and so exotic at the same time—but then harder, pressing her up against the closed door, tilting her mouth up to his and leaning into her. As his tongue tasted and touched and explored her mouth, and her tongue, too, pushed hungrily against his, he pulled her into him and felt every inch of her firm and supple body against every inch of his aching, needing body.

"Jack, come upstairs," she murmured into their kiss. "Just for one night. I don't want to think now; I don't want to think about anything. You can help me do that, can't you?"

God yes, he thought, because that was one thing he knew he could do for her. He could make love to her in a way that would obliterate every single rational thought from her brain, and his brain, too.

"Come upstairs," she said again, pulling away from their kiss and looking up at him expectantly. Later, he was grateful that she'd ended that kiss when she had, ended it when he still had a modicum of self-control.

"Caroline, no," he said, getting a grip on himself and taking a step away from her. "You've been drinking, and I don't want what feels like a good idea tonight to feel like a mistake tomorrow. And, as it happens, I know a little something about that." *Besides,* he almost added, *I don't want a one-night stand with you. I want more. Hell, I want it all.*

She blinked, then nodded, then leaned back again against the wall. This time, though, it wasn't to invite him to kiss her; it was to support her weight. It occurred to him again how tired she was.

"Caroline, it's late. You need to get to bed."

She looked at her watch and groaned. "I have to be back down here by six A.M.," she said.

"No, you don't," Jack said, making a snap decision. "I'll spend the night. On the couch," he added, quickly. "You sleep in. I'll open tomorrow. I still remember how to do that, by the way."

"Really?" she asked, raising an eyebrow.

He nodded. "Really." And then, "When was the last time you slept late?"

261

"I can't even remember," she admitted, stifling another yawn.

"Come on, let's go," he said, moving her gently away from the door and flicking off the light switches beside it. Then he led her up the stairs to her apartment and, taking the keys from her, opened the front door. She followed him in, as compliant as a child.

"I'll just get a pillow and blanket, if you don't mind," he said, going to the closet in the hallway and helping himself to both. "Good night, Caroline." Jack left her standing in the hallway as he headed for the living room, where he sat down on the couch in the dark and tried not to think about her proximity to him. Then he remembered something and hauled himself up and returned tentatively to the hallway. Caroline wasn't there anymore. She had gone into her bedroom and closed the door. He could see the bar of light visible beneath it as he passed her room, then went into the bathroom, flicked on the light, and opened the medicine cabinet. He found the Advil, unscrewed the lid, and shook a couple tablets into his hand. Then he went down the hall to the kitchen and poured her a glass of water, stopping to look for a moment at a gelatinous mass of ice cream melting in the kitchen sink. *Strange,* he thought, before he carried the glass of water and the Advil to Caroline's bedroom and tapped lightly on the door.

"Come in," he heard her say, and he opened the door. She had changed into her nightgown already, he saw, and was sitting on the edge of her bed. It was like one of the nightgowns from his dreams, he realized, only better. Better because it was real. It was white and sleeveless, with an edging of lace around the collar. And in the soft glow from the bedside table lamp, she looked impossibly young in it, and impossibly pretty.

"Here," he said, crossing the room and handing her the glass of water and the Advil. "Take these. And drink that whole glass," he said, sternly. "Trust me, you'll thank me in the morning."

She nodded and obediently swallowed the capsules with a gulp of water. And then, surprising himself, Jack knelt down in front of her and looked directly into her bright blue eyes.

"Caroline, you were right," he said. "There were a lot of women. But there was never anyone like you." With that, he kissed her gently on the fore-head and left the room, closing the door behind him.

Chapter 11

The next thing Jack knew, his watch alarm was going off and he was jerking awake on the living room couch, feeling as if he'd been asleep for about fifteen minutes. But no, it was six A.M., and he'd promised Caroline he'd get the coffee shop ready to be open by seven. He dragged himself up, folded the blanket, and left it and the pillow neatly stacked on the couch. Then he headed down the short hallway to the front door, meaning to go straight to the coffee shop. But he stopped abruptly halfway down the hallway and turned to look at the pictures hanging on its walls. They were a virtual photographic tour of Daisy's childhood, he realized, leaning closer to study a few of them. There was Daisy, looking about four years old, wearing a pair of overalls and a straw hat and riding a pony at a county fair. There was an older Daisy, maybe six or seven, perched on a stool at Pearl's, her broad smile revealing two missing front teeth. And there was Daisy in high school, wearing a volleyball uniform, holding a trophy, and already, at fifteen or sixteen, the confident, poised young woman he knew today. And here was one of Caroline, too, posing with Daisy, last year or the year before, in front of a Christmas tree in the apartment's living room. He reached out, almost unconsciously, and touched Caroline's image with his finger. Had that kiss meant anything to her last night? he wondered. Was it any indication of her feelings for him? Or was it just the product of a drunken, impetuous moment?

He took his finger off the picture and took one final look around the wall, quickly taking in the other pictures. He was nowhere to be found here.

Nor should he be, he reminded himself, feeling that sharp, but familiar pain.

Jack went down to the coffee shop then and did all the things he knew Caroline did every morning before it opened without ever complaining about having to do any of them. He was taking the chairs off the tables when he heard the rattle of keys in the front door and turned to see Frankie, the cook, letting himself in.

"Good morning," Jack said, aiming for friendly. But Frankie didn't return his friendliness. He just stared at Jack impassively and then went about his business. The two of them avoided each other for a while, but when Frankie came around behind the counter with Jack, it was close quarters for the both of them, especially given Frankie's size, and Jack could practically feel the hostility emanating off Frankie's body.

"Look," Jack said, turning to Frankie when he felt like he couldn't take it anymore. "I know you don't like me, and that's fine. You don't have to like me. But I told Caroline I'd open for her this morning, and I'm doing it, and while I'm doing it, I'd appreciate a little civility from you."

Frankie, who was standing only an arm's length away, stopped what he was doing and fixed Jack with another stare. Jack returned the stare and tried not to think about the fact that according to Walt Dickerson, his sponsor, Frankie had already killed one man.

"I know you care about Caroline," Jack said finally, hoping to ease the tension. "But, believe it or not, so do I. And if you don't like having me around, well, that's too bad, because I'm not planning on going anywhere anytime soon."

Frankie seemed to consider this, and then he took a step closer to Jack. *God help me,* Jack thought, and he tensed his stomach muscles. He knew it was unlikely he'd survive a direct punch from this man, but he was determined to improve his odds if he could.

But Frankie didn't punch him; instead, he held out a huge hand to Jack. For a moment, Jack stared down at it, unsure of what he was supposed to do, until he realized Frankie was waiting for him to shake it. Surprised, he took hold of Frankie's gargantuan hand and shook it as best he could.

"Caroline's a big believer in second chances," Frankie said, shaking his hand back. "She gave me one when no one else would. So if she's willing to let you back into her life again, Mr. Keegan, it's not for me to say she's wrong."

"Call me Jack."

"Okay, Jack. But there is one thing I don't understand," he said, letting go of his hand.

"What is that?"

"I don't understand how you could have left those two, left Daisy and Caroline. I mean, they're both, they're both pretty special, don't you think?"

Jack sighed. "Yeah, I do think."

"Huh," Frankie said, studying Jack for a moment longer. His look this time wasn't one of hostility; it was one of pity.

"Well, good luck," Frankie said then, and he went back to work.

Yeah, good luck, Jack thought grimly. Though really it was a little late for that. And thinking about that wall full of pictures, and about what Frankie had said to him, he slipped out the front door of the coffee shop and onto the quiet street. Then he slid his cell phone out of his pocket, punched a number in, and waited.

"Walt," he said, when the caller answered. "I know it's early. I'm sorry. But I need to meet with you, as soon as possible."

It was bright, too bright, Caroline thought, squeezing her already closed eyes shut even tighter, but the yellow light continued to pound unrelentingly against her eyelids. When she finally opened one eye, just wide enough to see what the source of the light was, she saw it was the sun, streaming in through the bedroom curtains she'd forgotten to close the night before. She tried to open both eyes all the way then, but she winced from the brightness and pulled a pillow over her head instead.

From under the safety of that pillow, she tried to take stock of how she felt. Her mouth was as dry as sandpaper, her head was aching dully, and her stomach . . . her stomach felt kind of queasy. She sat bolt upright in bed, wondering if she'd have to make a run for the bathroom, but after a moment the queasiness passed and she lay back down again.

Working at Pearl's wouldn't be easy today, she realized, thinking with reluctance about the bowls of gooey oatmeal and the plates of runny fried eggs she'd have to serve customers for breakfast. Maybe she could take refuge in the office, at least during the morning rush. She pulled the pillow off her head and looked at the clock on her bedside table. She was shocked to see it was already ten thirty. Ten thirty? The morning rush had already come and gone without her. Unless it hadn't. Had Pearl's even opened this morning? she wondered. But then she remembered Jack's promise last night that he'd open for her this morning, and she relaxed a little. At least she relaxed until she remembered the rest of the night: Jack's confessions to her, both about his alcoholism and about why he'd come back to Butternut, and her own rather clumsy attempt to seduce him.

She groaned and put the pillow back over her head. What had he been thinking, telling her all those things? And what had she been thinking, inviting him up to the apartment to spend the night? She reached under the pillow to massage her faintly throbbing temples and tried to sort it all out. But she couldn't; it was too much, especially on a morning like this morning, when she felt this way. She kicked irritably at the covers and thought about getting up to get a glass of water, but even the thought of drinking water made her stomach clench uneasily. Was this how Jack had felt all those mornings when he'd still been drinking? Because if it was, she could almost muster up a little sympathy for him. *Almost.*

But if she couldn't exactly feel sympathy for him, she could at least feel something else for him, she realized—gratitude. Gratitude to him for being the adult last night, for knowing that the two of them going to bed with each other would have been a mistake. Because while Jack might say he'd changed—and maybe, when it came to the drinking, he *had* changed—he still couldn't change the past. He couldn't change what had already happened to her, and to Daisy: the hurt, the loneliness, the disappointments large and small. She'd be crazy to forget those things, and crazy to open herself up to them again. Wouldn't she?

It was worrisome, though, having his feelings for her—or what he'd said were his feelings for her—out in the open like that. Caroline was worried, too, to know that when he'd told her about those feelings, and she'd recovered from her initial surprise over them, she'd also felt something she hadn't felt in a long time, something she'd thought she'd already closed the door to. Excitement? Joy? Wonder? She wasn't exactly sure what it was. And, truth be told, she didn't really want to know.

But if the emotional side of last night was something of a mystery to her, the physical side of it was not. Her attraction to Jack, obviously, was still there, still as strong as ever. She'd hoped it had dissipated over the years, disappeared even, but it had apparently only gone into hiding, and last night she'd been perfectly willing to let a few drinks coax it out again.

Her mind wandered for a moment back to that kiss. Jack could kiss like nobody's business. When she considered how many opportunities he'd had to kiss in his lifetime, though, this was perhaps not very surprising. Still, his obvious abilities aside, it was a good thing he'd stopped her when he had. With his help, she'd dodged a bullet last night. They both had.

She sighed. She'd have to see him again, and probably sooner rather than later. Even if he didn't come into Pearl's, this town was too small for them to avoid each other forever. Maybe, when Jack had last lived here, he'd been right to hate Butternut, she thought now, and, in a sudden explosion of movement, she lifted her pillow off her face and threw it violently across the room.

Chapter 12

"So no Daisy tonight?" Jason asked, sipping his beer. It was a Friday evening in late July, and Will and Jason were sitting at the bar at their favorite dive, the Mosquito Inn, on the outskirts of Butternut. The place had a nice, broken-in feel to it, and it had the added advantage of being rough enough around the edges to keep the summer people away. The same tourists who wanted to experience the local color of crafts fairs and fish frys, it turned out, thought this place, with its burly ex-cons and bearded bikers, had a little *too much* color. But even regulars like Will and Jason would have to clear out soon, since the later they stayed at the Mosquito Inn, the more likely they were to get hit by a punch thrown in somebody else's fight.

"No. No Daisy tonight," Will said. "She's with her dad at a fish fry."

"The dad who left, like, twenty years ago?" Jason asked.

Will nodded.

"Why does she even want to see him?" Jason asked, a little disgustedly.

"It's complicated," Will said. "But basically, I think, she likes him."

"And she forgives him, for walking out on them like that? I couldn't do that. And I don't think most people could either."

"Daisy's not like most people," Will said. *She's better than most people,* he almost added, but didn't.

"Well, she can't be like most *girls,*" Jason agreed. "Because you've never been like this with a girl before."

Will didn't say anything. He didn't have to; they both knew it was true. Besides, he didn't like talking to Jason about Daisy. Partly this was because he knew Jason was a little miffed about how much time he'd been spending with her, and partly it was because he liked keeping Daisy to himself. The things he felt about her, and the way he felt them, were so new, and so unfamiliar, that he didn't want to share them with anyone yet, least of all someone like Jason, who considered any strong emotion that wasn't about sports or video games to be immediately suspect.

But Jason wasn't ready to drop the subject yet. "So how long have you two been seeing each other?" he asked.

"Uh, a little over a month now," Will said. He meant a little over a month from the night at her apartment, not a little over a month from that earlier night at the beach.

"And how's the whole 'dating thing' going?"

Jason asked, making it sound as distasteful as, say, having rabies might be.

"It's good," Will said. "But it was a little strange, at first," he admitted. And it *had* been a little strange, *more* than a little strange, really, to be with a girl without actually *being* with her. This was a first for Will. In the past, his relationships had begun, and ended, with sex. He'd never misled anyone about this, never pretended that he wanted more than he actually did. And if he'd seen anyone beyond one night, as he had with Christy, it was with the understanding that what they had together was based on one thing and one thing only: the physical pleasure they could give each other.

It wasn't that Will didn't like women; he did. And it wasn't that he saw them only as sexual objects; he didn't. It was just that having a relationship with a woman, a relationship with a capital "R," was something he'd never had any desire to do before. It felt too complicated, somehow, too serious and too weighted with expectations. And it wasn't just women he'd felt this way about either. It was everything in his life. He'd worked hard to keep things easy and unencumbered, striving hard to not care too much about or invest too much in any one thing. That's why his arrangement with Christy had worked so well for so long. They'd understood each other; they'd wanted the same thing. And they'd known where they were heading, which was nowhere in particular. But things were different with Daisy. *Everything* was different with Daisy, in ways he was only just beginning to understand.

But, as it turned out, it wasn't Daisy Jason wanted to talk about anymore. "Have you, uh, seen Christy lately?" he asked now, a little too casually.

"No," Will said, shooting Jason an irritated look. "Why?"

"No reason. But I saw her the other night and . . ."

"And?"

"Will, she was so pissed at me," Jason said, with a little shudder.

"You? Why was she pissed at you?"

"I don't know. Maybe because you weren't there for her to be pissed at?"

"Maybe," Will said. *Definitely,* he thought.

"Did you, uh, did you tell her about Daisy when you broke up with her?"

Another irritated look from Will was all the answer he needed.

"And what about Daisy?" Jason persisted. "Does she know about Christy?"

Will glanced away and took a slug of his beer.

"That's what I thought," Jason said, under his breath.

Will shot him another irritated look. "Jason, seriously, stay out of my personal life," he said.

"Okay," Jason said, holding up his hands in a conciliatory gesture. "How about a game of pool then?"

"Maybe later," Will said.

"All right. Well, I'm going to see if I can pick one up now," Jason said, grabbing his beer and heading over to the pool tables.

As soon as he was gone, Will was sorry he'd gotten mad at him. But Jason had hit a nerve. Will hadn't told Daisy about Christy, even though he knew he should, even though he knew it was stupid not to. The two of them lived in the same town, and everyone who lived in a town that size knew each other, whether they wanted to or not. Of course, he and Christy had been careful to keep their relationship hidden, but there was probably still talk about it. And the simplest, smartest thing for Will to do was to tell Daisy, now, before she heard about it from someone else, namely, Christy. But he couldn't do it; he couldn't tell her.

He couldn't because he knew Daisy saw something in him, something no one had ever seen in him before. Something he'd never even seen *in himself* before. He didn't know what it was, exactly. But it was there, in her eyes, when she looked at him, and in her voice when she talked to him, and in the expression on her face when she listened to him. And when she touched him, and kissed him, it was there, too, in her tenderness, a tenderness that might have unraveled Will completely if it hadn't also aroused him so completely.

But if he told her about Christy, then what? Then, he knew, she'd be disappointed, and already, one month into their relationship, he hated the thought of disappointing her. And that was different, too. It had never particularly mattered to him before whether he disappointed anyone or not. Maybe it was because, from his earliest memories, all the adults in his life—his father, his teachers, even his mother, he suspected—were already disappointed in him. But that disappointment, Will had quickly learned, had an upside. Because the less people expected from you, the less you had to try, and the less you had to try, the less you had to care. Soon Will had made not caring a habit in his life, a religion, really. The only exception he made was to his work at the garage. Doing his job, and doing it right, mattered to him. But not much else did—until now, until Daisy.

The problem was, Christy was from the part of his life before Daisy, the not-caring part, and he didn't know how long he could keep those parts separate from each other. So far, it hadn't been an issue, because as different as he and Daisy were in some ways, there was one way in which they were alike: they only wanted to be with each other. And the amazing thing was, they'd figured out a way to do this, a way to be alone in what felt sometimes like their own personal universe.

It had started when Daisy had suggested, a couple of weeks ago, that instead of going out for dinner they have dinner downstairs at Pearl's. There were always leftovers there, she'd pointed out, and they would go to waste if nobody ate them. So they'd had dinner down there that night and most nights after that too. Daisy kept the window blinds drawn and only turned on a few, necessary lights, so that when they had their dinner at the counter, on side-by-side stools, it was under a soft pool of yellow light in an otherwise dark room. It was like being at a private restaurant, a restaurant with no frazzled waitress waiting for them to pay their bill, and no wriggling kids at the next table staring at them when Will kissed Daisy—which he did as frequently as possible.

It was around the same time they started having dinner at Pearl's that they discovered the Black Bear. They'd gone for a drive one night, and Will had chosen a back road without really paying attention to where they were going. They rarely had a destination in mind anyway. He drove and they talked, or listened to the radio, or they were quiet, letting the sweet air blow in gently through the pickup's open windows, while the moon bathed them in its soft, dappled light.

But that night, Will slowed down when they

came to a roadhouse with an enormous carved wooden bear standing on its hind legs in front of it.

"What is this place?" Daisy asked.

"The Black Bear," Will said. "I've never been here before, but I've heard Jason's dad talk about it. He and his friends used to come here when they were our age. Do you want to check it out?"

"Sure," she said.

They parked in a parking lot that had only a few other cars in it and walked into the slightly ramshackle building. The inside consisted of one low-ceilinged room, with wood-paneled walls, a small bar, a jukebox, and a scattering of tables. But its most prominent feature was a series of taxidermied animal heads—including an enormous bear's head—bolted to one wall. It was a lot of fur, and snarling teeth, but the effect was mitigated, somewhat, by the Christmas tree lights someone had thought to string between the animals' heads and even wrap jauntily around a buck's antlers.

"We don't have to stay," Will said quietly, not wanting to offend a couple of customers who were sitting at the bar.

"No, I like it," Daisy said, amused. "It reminds me a little of a movie set."

"You mean, a horror movie set?"

"Well, yes," she admitted. "But I still like it."

"Do you want to stay for a drink?"

"Why not?" she said, and while he ordered his beer and her Diet Coke Daisy wandered over to check out the jukebox.

"Will," she said excitedly when he brought their drinks over. "Look at these songs. There isn't anything here that's later than the eighties."

Will looked at the jukebox. She was right; the songs were mainly from the '70s and the '80s. Daisy loved classic rock because her mom had raised her on it.

"Will," she said suddenly, taking their drinks out of his hands and putting them down on a nearby table. "Dance with me. Please?"

"What? No," he said automatically. And then, apologetically, "I don't dance, Daisy."

"Oh, come on," she chided him playfully. "I'll put on something slow." She fished a couple of quarters out of her pocket and dropped them into the jukebox, and then, after studying the song selection, she punched some numbers in.

"Daisy," he said, shaking his head. "I can't."

"Can't or won't?" she asked teasingly, putting her hands on his shoulders.

"Both," he said, but he put his hands tentatively on her waist as he heard the record drop in the jukebox.

"Didn't you go to any dances in high school, Will?" she asked, standing on her tiptoes and nuzzling his neck with her lips. He drew in a sharp breath.

"You know I didn't," he said, looking around the bar. But nobody was paying any attention to them.

He heard the first notes of the song and sighed. It was "Night Moves" by Bob Seeger. This, he knew, was Daisy's all-time favorite song; there was no way he was getting out of dancing with her now.

"Will," she said, her voice soft in his ear. "It's not that hard. Don't think of it as dancing, okay? Just think of it as holding me."

And he sighed, again, because if there was one thing on this earth he knew how to do now, it was how to hold Daisy. He'd spent the last couple of weeks perfecting the art of it. So he circled his arms around her waist and drew her gently against him, and she slipped her arms around his neck and rested her cheek against his shoulder.

"That's good," Daisy said, after a moment. "Now all you need to do is move. But just a little, all right?" And she showed him how to sway, almost imperceptibly, to the music.

And they danced. Or they held each other. Or they did some combination of the two. And the funny thing was, Will liked it, a lot; he liked it so much that they used up all their quarters that night. Soon, going to the Black Bear, like having dinner at Pearl's, became part of their routine. It wasn't long before they felt like regulars there.

They'd walk through the door and the bartender would smile and put Will's beer and Daisy's Diet Coke on the bar, and the other customers, mostly middle-aged regulars, would nod politely at them before going back to their conversations. Then Daisy and Will would sip their drinks and put all the quarters they'd hoarded that day onto the table. And after that they'd feed them into the jukebox and dance like they were the last two people left on the planet. And as far as they were concerned, they were.

Will wondered, sometimes, if he should have gone to the dances in high school. But he decided it wasn't dancing he loved; it was dancing with Daisy. It was the feel of her soft, pliant body against his and the smell of her clean, fragrant hair, and the smoothness of her cheeks and her neck when he touched them with his lips. When he held her like that, wanting her, but not having her, and not knowing if, or when, he would ever have her, he understood, for the first time in his life, that sometimes desire had less to do with getting what you wanted than with not getting what you wanted.

There was another part of their routine too, the part after they'd run out of quarters at the Black Bear. Will would drive Daisy back to Butternut then and park his pickup on Main Street, a block or two down from Pearl's. He did this because he thought their proximity to Daisy's apartment, and to her mother—who he knew didn't really like him—was the best insurance he had that he wouldn't cross the line he'd drawn for himself. After he'd parked, the two of them would kiss, though the word *kiss* probably didn't do justice to what it was they did to each other. Because Will would kiss not just her mouth but her neck, and the little hollow at the base of her neck, and her shoulders, and her arms, and any inch of skin he could find that wasn't covered by clothing. And as he did this he'd run his hands over her body, gently at first, caressingly, but then hungrily, almost greedily, feeling as much of her warmth and her softness as he could through her thin, summery clothes.

And Daisy would be kissing him and touching him, too, her fingers splayed open, her hands traveling up and down his back, his chest, his stomach, and sometimes settling even lower, on his lap, and stroking him there, through his blue jeans, until he thought seriously about taking those blue jeans off, and every other article of clothing both of them were wearing.

That was when Will knew it was time for them to stop, time for them to say good night. And with a degree of self-control he hadn't even known he'd had, he would untangle himself from her and watch her warily from his side of the front seat while she caught her breath, and straightened her clothes, and tried to restore some order to her hair. And then he'd walk her to her front door, kiss her one more time, and drive back to the garage and his little apartment behind it. He was almost never tired then, his blood still running so hot from Daisy's feel and touch that on more than one occasion he'd literally taken a cold shower. But finally, sometime in the early hours of the morning, he'd get into bed and lie there in the darkness, staring up at the wavering shadows of tree branches on the ceiling and wondering if it was possible for someone to actually die of sexual frustration. But, apparently, it wasn't, because the next evening, at exactly six P.M., he would get off work, get into the shower, and get over to Daisy's as fast as he could, to start the whole thing over again.

"Do you want another beer?"

"What?" Will asked, startled, looking up.

"I said, 'do you want another beer?'" the bartender asked, looking pointedly at Will's empty bottle.

"Oh, no thanks," he said, glancing around the bar. He was amazed to see that while he'd been thinking about Daisy, the place had gotten crowded—and loud.

He left some bills on the counter for a tip and went to find Jason, who was in the middle of a game of pool.

"I think I'm going to take off now," he told him.

"That's all right," Jason said, taking a shot. "You were lousy company, anyway."

Will didn't disagree. Other than working on cars, there were only two things now he was able to do: be with Daisy and think about Daisy.

"I'll see you tomorrow," he said to Jason, and he turned to leave, but Jason put a hand on his shoulder and stopped him.

"Hey, Will," he said. "I like Daisy. If she's what you want, then I'm happy for you. Really, I am."

"Thanks," Will said gratefully, before an uncom-fortable silence fell over them. This was about as serious as their conversations ever got.

"See you tomorrow," Jason said, taking his hand off his shoulder.

"Yeah, okay," Will said with a quick smile. And he couldn't know it then, as he pushed open the bar's screen door and walked out into the dusky parking lot, but he would remember every single detail of those summer nights with Daisy—Pearl's, the Black Bear, the front seat of the pickup—until the day he died. Life, it turned out, didn't get a whole lot more perfect than that.

"It's crowded tonight," Jack said, sliding down to make room for more people at their table in Butternut's American Legion hall.

"It's always crowded," Daisy remarked, looking up from her fried walleye. "But you know that, don't you? You must have come to one of these the last time you lived in Butternut."

"I don't think so," Jack said, because this fish fry was exactly the kind of thing he'd made a habit of avoiding back then. Occasionally, Caroline had twisted his arm into going to some picnic, or potluck or church social, but they'd always seemed to him to be boring, gossipy affairs, and they'd always had the added disadvantage, from his perspective, of not serving alcohol.

But this fish fry tonight didn't seem so bad. For one thing, he was here with Daisy, and in between gorging themselves on the fried walleye, the biscuits, and the coleslaw, they'd been talking. Talking about everything and nothing, about all the things they'd never talked about when Jack was away. Talking was such a simple thing, he thought. But he would never take it for granted again, at least not when it came to his daughter.

And the America Legion hall was cheerful enough too. The wood-paneled walls were lined with photographs of Butternut veterans from every war since World War I, and the rafters were hung with fluttering pennants from the baseball championships this chapter of the Legion had won. Then there were the long tables, set with red, white, and blue plastic tablecloths and bunches of freshly picked wildflowers for their centerpieces.

"Well, you must have had to work pretty hard to avoid the fish fry," Daisy said, amused. "I don't know if you noticed it then, Dad, but there's not a lot to do in Butternut on a Friday night."

"Oh, I noticed it," Jack said. But he hadn't cared the last time he'd lived here; he'd made his own fun or, more accurately, his own trouble.

"Did you hate Butternut then, Dad?" Daisy asked, her blue eyes thoughtful.

"Did I hate it?" Jack repeated, sipping his iced tea. "No, I wouldn't say I *hated* it," he said, though that was a bald-faced lie. "I'd say it was more like its charms escaped me."

"And now? Do its charms still escape you?"

"Not anymore," Jack said, with a smile. But unlike his daughter, he didn't love Butternut. Not yet. He only loved two of the people who happened to be living in it right now.

"Was it the town you didn't like back then, or the people?" Daisy asked, pausing, a forkful of coleslaw on its way to her mouth.

He shrugged. "To me, they were one and the same, though I didn't dislike *all* of it, of course. I didn't dislike you, or your mom. I think what I really didn't like was . . ." He paused here, wanting to be honest with his daughter, but still learning how to be. "I think what I, yes, hated," he started again, "was the feeling I got, every time I walked into some place—the grocery store, the hardware store, Pearl's—that everyone who was in there had just been talking about me. Partly that was my guilty conscience. But partly, I think, it was because they *had* just been talking about me." *Me, and whoever I owed money to, or whoever I'd gotten into a fight with, or whoever I was sleeping with, other than my wife, of course. . . .*

"But you don't feel that way anymore, do you?" Daisy asked, frowning.

"Not really," Jack said. And it was true. Since he'd been back, there'd been some townspeople who'd been friendly, and some, fewer, who'd been unfriendly. But for the most part, they'd simply been curious about why he'd come back, and how long he was planning on staying. The first question Jack had answered, somewhat disingenuously, by explaining that he was fixing up Wayland's cabin, and the second he'd answered by saying, honestly, that he didn't know how long he'd be staying. (He didn't add, of course, that the answer to that question was up to Caroline.)

"I'll bet there are some familiar faces here tonight," Daisy said, looking around the room.

"There are," Jack agreed, his eyes following hers. "I remember Dawn Peterson," he said, nodding in the direction of an older woman in line at the buffet table. "I take it she still owns the bait-and-tackle shop?"

"She does," Daisy said. "And that man with her is her third husband, Johnny."

Jack raised his eyebrows. "Seriously?"

Daisy nodded.

"He must be twenty years younger than she is," Jack pointed out.

"Oh, at least," Daisy agreed. "Her husbands keep getting younger. But, you know, all those worms can't sell themselves."

Jack chuckled and looked around some more. "I remember the Jalowitzes, too." He indicated a man sitting a few tables down from them. "They have a big family, don't they? What, six or seven kids?"

Daisy nodded solemnly. "They had seven. But their oldest son, Don, died in Iraq. His picture's up over there," she said, glancing at one of the walls.

"I'm sorry," Jack said.

"The entire town lined the streets the day his casket came home," Daisy said softly. "Mom closed Pearl's so we could be there, too."

Jack nodded, awed, as always, by someone who could be so brave at an age when he'd been content to just be reckless.

"Do you want some more iced tea?" he asked Daisy, noticing her cup was empty.

"No, I'm fine," she said contentedly, putting down a half-eaten biscuit. "In fact, I don't know if I can eat another bite. But, Dad, seriously, how are you really doing here?"

"I'm doing fine," he said, a little evasively. He preferred to talk about Daisy when they were together.

"You're not . . . you're not lonely, are you?" she asked.

"What? No," he said, a little too quickly, and Daisy didn't miss it. Daisy didn't miss anything, as far as he could tell.

"Honey, if you're worried about me, you're worried for nothing," Jack said now. "I'm fine. During the day, I don't have time to get lonely. I'm basically rebuilding that cabin from the inside out, and, if it doesn't kill me, it'll definitely make me stronger." He laughed, shaking his head. "And then, at night, I have my meetings. I don't always want to go to them, but once I get there, I'm usually glad I did. It's kind of like working out at the gym that way. And sometimes, after the meetings, a few of us grab a cup of coffee together at the Quick and Convenient. It's nice. We're not soul mates or anything, but it helps pass the time." It was *after* he got back to the cabin that the nights were a problem. Each night, really, was its own kind of eternity, crowded as it was by guilt, and regret, and that longing, still, to do it all again, but differently this time. He didn't tell Daisy about that part of his night though.

"And how's . . . how's everything else going?" Daisy asked; "everything else" was a euphemism for his relationship with Caroline. Because even though they'd never discussed the real reason why Jack had moved back to Butternut, Daisy

289

knew what it was. And he knew that she knew. It was strange, he thought, strange and amazing, really, that even after all those years apart, he and Daisy still shared some kind of unspoken understanding with each other.

"Everything else is going fine," he said, though he had his doubts about this, too.

"Good," she said, smiling. And seeing her smile gave Jack an idea.

"Daisy, would you mind if I asked someone to take our picture together?" he asked, sliding his cell phone out of his pocket.

"No, of course not," she said, and she grabbed Bill Phipps, the first person who walked by their table, and asked him to take their picture. He took it and then he stayed to talk to Jack about the mill, where Jack had once worked, and about Wayland's cabin, which he said he'd like to take a look at once Jack was done fixing it up.

"That came out well," Daisy said, looking at the picture on Jack's cell phone after Bill had left their table.

"It did, didn't it?" he agreed. "By the way, how's Will?" he asked when they'd settled back into their conversation.

"Will?" Daisy repeated, her cheeks coloring.

Jack nodded. "That is his name, isn't it?" he said mildly.

"Yes, it's his name. But every time I hear it, Dad, even when I'm the one saying it, I feel like

I'm hearing it for the first time. And I feel like . . . like it's the most amazing name in the whole world. Does that sound stupid?"

Jack shook his head. "No, it doesn't sound stupid."

"Juvenile, maybe?"

Jack smiled. "Well, juvenile, *maybe*. But falling in love makes juveniles of all of us."

She colored again, darker this time, and Jack wondered if he'd crossed a line. Had he said something too personal? "Let's talk about something else," he suggested, picking up his fork and turning his attention to his coleslaw.

"No, I want to talk about this," Daisy said firmly. "I want to talk about Will. And about what you said, about falling in love." She looked down at her plate. "Because I have a question for you."

"Okay," Jack said, a little uneasily. "As long as you realize I'm not exactly an expert on matters of the heart. Your mom, actually, might know more about this than I do." That was cowardly, he knew. But also true.

Daisy shook her head though. "No, I can't talk to Mom about this. She doesn't like Will."

"Did she tell you that?"

"No, but she doesn't need to," Daisy said. "I know her well enough to know."

Jack didn't dispute that.

"But, Dad, it's not fair. She doesn't even know him. How can she not like him?"

Jack shrugged. "Sometimes we see what we want to see in a person. Or what we expect to see, anyway."

Daisy nodded. "Well, then Mom sees the person Will was in high school. He used to . . . you know, just kind of hang out, cut class, get detention. Stuff like that. He was kind of a . . ."

"A punk?" Jack suggested. "That's what people used to call guys like that when I was your age." Jack knew this because he'd been considered one of them himself.

"Yeah, okay, I guess he was kind of a punk," Daisy said, with a little laugh. "But he's not like that anymore, Dad. I don't even know, honestly, if he was *ever* like that. He's . . . he's different. He's not like anyone else I've ever met before. He's really . . ."

"It's okay if you can't put it into words," Jack said. "Love does that to us, too. Now, what was the question you wanted to ask me?"

Daisy looked down at her plate again and became suddenly absorbed in breaking off a piece of her biscuit. "It's about that," she said, blushing. "About being in love. Is it possible . . . I mean considering how short a time I've known him . . . is it possible that I could already be in love with Will?" She looked up at him now, her cheeks bright pink. With a telltale complexion like that, Jack thought, she was never going to be able to play poker.

"Of course it's possible you're in love with him," he said. "Why wouldn't it be?"

"Because . . . because it's so new, so fast. How could anyone fall in love that quickly?"

"I don't know *how* they can, Daisy. But they do; they do it all the time." He thought, for a moment, about telling her a story, a story about the first time he'd laid eyes on her mother. He'd only recently moved to Butternut to work at the lumber mill, and he'd walked into Pearl's one morning in search of a decent cup of coffee. And there she was, standing beside a table, taking someone's order, her expression a mixture of boredom and politeness as she scribbled on her check pad. She'd looked up though, midorder, and her eyes had found Jack's, across the room, and she'd smiled at him. And just like that, Jack had felt it, a sensation like all the air was rushing out of his body at the same time. She'd felt it too; she could barely finish taking the order, she was so flustered. He'd thought, before then, that love at first sight was a cliché. He didn't think so after that.

"But, Dad," Daisy was saying, when his mind returned to the conversation, "I'm not like those people, people like Jessica. She falls in love all the time. She's . . . impulsive—I guess that's the kindest word for it—but I'm not. I'm the opposite of impulsive."

"So you've, um, never been in love before?"

he asked, feeling again like he was in uncharted territory.

She shook her head emphatically.

"But you must have known, Daisy, that you'd fall in love one day?"

"Well, I *hoped* I would. But I thought when I did, it would happen gradually, as I got to know someone, got to know them really well. And not over a period of weeks, like now, but over a period of months, years even."

"Years?" he echoed, trying hard not to smile.

She nodded solemnly. "Yes, years. Because I wasn't going to do things the way other people did them. I was going to take my time, go slowly, make sure whomever I fell in love with was the right person. For me, anyway. You know, someone I respected, and someone who respected me, someone whom I was compatible with. It would be someone who shared my interests and my values, someone who would make a good husband and father, a good, you know, life partner. I wasn't that concerned about the whole 'being in love' thing. I thought that was probably overrated, anyway."

"Overrated?" he repeated, and now he couldn't help it; he really was smiling. She was so young. *Had he ever, ever, been that young?* he wondered. He didn't think so. But she was looking at him now expectantly, waiting for some kind of response from him, so he said, still smiling, "Daisy, did you really think all the books and songs that have been written about love would turn out to be about something that was overrated?"

She shrugged. "I don't know. But somehow I didn't think it could be that big a deal. I mean, it's one thing to read a book about something; it's another thing to actually do it."

"So how does being in love stack up against reading about being in love?"

"Oh, Dad," Daisy said, shaking her head. "It's *so* much better," and here she blushed again, a soft pink blush that made her look especially lovely, even under the American Legion hall's harsh lighting. "But, Dad? It's so much scarier, too."

Jack nodded seriously. Because now, of course, he knew what she meant. He wished he'd known that when he was her age—how big, and serious, and scary love could be. If he had known it then, he could have saved himself a lot of time.

"It *is* scary," he said. "But try not to let it scare you. Does that make sense?"

"Actually, it does," Daisy said, smiling and putting another biscuit fragment into her mouth.

They were quiet for a few moments and then Jack said, "Oh, by the way, I saw your Facebook posting today, the one about your volleyball team's reunion. That sounds like fun."

"It *is* fun. We've done that every Labor Day weekend since we graduated."

"You were a good team, weren't you?"

"We were. I mean, not to sound conceited, but it's going to be a while before that high school has another volleyball team as good as that one."

"I wish I'd seen one of your games," Jack said, without thinking.

"Me too, Dad," Daisy said, without any bitterness, but with a disappointment that seemed, for a moment, to hang in the air between them, like a thread connecting them to each other. And Jack knew that that disappointment would never, *ever,* go away. Not completely. But here was the thing about his daughter: she never let it hang there for very long. Like now, for instance, she smiled at him and said, "Dad?"

"Yes?"

"You know that other thing we talked about?" she asked. She meant him and her mother.

He nodded.

"Don't . . . don't give up on it, all right?"

"Daisy, I wouldn't dream of it," he said.

Chapter 13

"Caroline?"

"Jack?" Caroline said with surprise, turning to see her ex-husband standing in line behind her at the Butternut IGA. She felt suddenly flustered. Maybe that was because she hadn't seen him since the night a few weeks ago when she'd tried rather clumsily to seduce him. "You're the last person I expected to see here on a Saturday night," she said.

"Why?" he said, as the line edged forward. "It's as good a time to go grocery shopping as any."

"Maybe," she murmured, starting to unload her groceries onto the checkout counter. But she was thinking that the Jack she'd been married to, the old Jack, wouldn't have been caught dead in a grocery store on a Saturday night. No, she corrected herself, he wouldn't have been caught dead in a grocery store *period*. He'd been one of the least domesticated men she'd ever known, though when she turned now and saw that the only things in his grocery basket were a couple of frozen pizzas, she wondered if that aspect of his personality had changed all that much.

"Jack, one of those pizzas isn't all you're having for dinner, is it?"

His eyes followed hers to the basket. "Um, yeah," he said, a little sheepishly. "But it's fine."

"It's not fine," she said, without thinking. "And it's not real food, either."

"Well, I could always make a grilled cheese sandwich," Jack said, his blue eyes teasing, and Caroline almost smiled, but she caught herself before she did. And she didn't know what was worse: the fact that she was worried about what

Jack was having for dinner or the fact that it had been so easy for her to almost fall back into the habit of flirting with him again.

Caroline finished unloading her groceries and maneuvered her cart down to the register. But, as luck would have it, Alice Brody was working. She'd worked at the Butternut IGA forever—or at least for as long as Caroline could remember —and she was an efficient, if vicious gossip.

"Hello, Alice," Caroline said warily, sliding her wallet out of her handbag.

Alice nodded, taking in both Caroline and Jack in one meaningful look. Caroline sighed internally. This was the problem with living in a small town—everyone knew everyone else's business. By tomorrow morning, half the town would know she'd run into Jack at the grocery store the night before. Everyone already knew, of course, that Jack was back in town; she'd spent the last several weeks deflecting questions about his return from curious customers at Pearl's.

Now Alice rang up and bagged Caroline's groceries and waited, with a smirk on her face, while Caroline paid for them.

"If you wait a minute, Caroline," Jack said, "I'll help you carry those out to your truck."

"I can manage," Caroline said breezily. But she hesitated a moment too long and ended up watching Alice ring up Jack's frozen pizzas and put them in a plastic bag.

"Jack, look, why don't you come over for dinner tonight?" she asked impulsively.

"Are you sure?" he said, hesitating.

"I'm sure," Caroline said, not at all sure. But she heard Alice snicker a little as Jack paid for his groceries, and it made up her mind for her. "I have to make dinner for myself anyway, so it won't be any extra work. Besides," she added pointedly, staring straight at Alice, "there's nothing wrong with two old friends having dinner together, is there?"

"No, there isn't," Jack said, noting her tone, and her look, with amusement. "Come on, let's go."

Half an hour later, Jack and Caroline were sitting at her kitchen table, sipping iced tea and eating chicken salad on butter lettuce and slices of freshly baked French bread.

"Thank you for taking pity on me," Jack said, buttering his bread. "It's a nice change from eating frozen pizza at the cabin. It can get . . ." He shrugged.

It can get lonely eating by yourself? Caroline said silently. Because she knew all about that now, now that she and Buster had stopped going out for dinner every Saturday night. But she didn't tell Jack that. She wanted to keep their conversation on a polite, but impersonal, footing. Otherwise, Jack might think that her inviting him over for dinner tonight meant more than it did, or at least more than she *wanted* it to mean.

"Anyway, this is nice," Jack said again, and he smiled at her—smiled *that* smile at her, that long, slow smile.

Caroline put down her fork, folded her arms across her chest, and leveled what she hoped was a cool gaze at him, a gaze she hoped said, *I'm immune to that smile, Jack. Completely and utterly immune.*

"What?" he said, looking at her warily.

"Jack, I've asked you before not to smile that smile at me."

"You have asked me that. But I have no idea what you're talking about."

"You know *exactly* what I'm talking about."

"So I can't smile at you?"

"No, you can smile at me. You just can't smile *that* smile at me, that slow smile you smile when you . . ." *When you want something. Or someone.*

"Okay, no slow smile," he said, his expression playful. Then he had the wisdom to change the subject. "By the way, where's Daisy tonight?"

Caroline rolled her eyes. "At the Black Bear. Where else?"

"She told me she went there," Jack said, bemused. "I can't believe that place is still around."

"I know. Even twenty years ago it was a throw-back. But Daisy must like it; she's there every night."

"But not . . . not drinking, right?"

"No, not drinking," Caroline said, and she saw relief in his expression. It had never occurred to her before that Jack worried about Daisy drinking. "No, Daisy doesn't drink, as far as I know," she said now. "She just goes there to hang out with that guy."

"You mean Will?"

She nodded curtly.

"You don't like him, do you?"

She hesitated a moment too long.

"What's wrong with him?" he asked.

"There's nothing's *wrong* with him," she said. "He's just not right for Daisy."

"But that's your opinion, isn't it? As opposed to, say, Daisy's?" Jack said. His blue eyes were teasing again, but also gentle.

"Yes, it's my opinion," Caroline conceded. "But I don't know if Daisy knows her own opinion right now."

"What does that mean?"

"It means she hasn't been herself this summer, Jack," she said. No, since before this summer, since Jack had come back into her life, since she'd started keeping secrets from Caroline. But she didn't say this out loud.

"How hasn't she been herself?" Jack pressed.

Caroline sipped her iced tea, a little fretfully. "I don't know, Jack. It's hard to explain. It's sort of like one of those *Invasion of the Body Snatchers* movies. Remember those? She looks like herself on the outside, but on the inside, Jack, there's nobody home. I mean, she walks around all day in a complete daze. This morning, I had to ask her the same question three times. *Three times,* Jack."

"Caroline, she's in love," he said, his blue eyes gentle again.

"Did she tell you that?" she asked, and she was suddenly jealous of Daisy and Jack's new closeness. Last week, for instance, Daisy had gone to a fish fry with him, and the two of them had ended up staying for hours.

"Not in those exact words. But she's exhibiting all the symptoms. You remember what those are, don't you?" he asked, with the hint of a smile.

Caroline flushed, and so he wouldn't notice, she got up and took the pitcher of tea out of the refrigerator. But after she'd brought it back to the table and refilled both of their glasses, she was suddenly aware of his maddening proximity to her. This kitchen, she decided, wasn't big enough for the two of them—not with Jack looking so . . . *so good.* If living in a run-down cabin and subsisting on frozen pizza was his secret, then millions of other men might want to try it, too.

He brushed his hair out of his eyes now, and Caroline was reminded of how much she'd always liked his brown hair when it had started to get a little too long, and he'd have to brush it out of his eyes. *And those eyes.* They were almost criminally blue, especially against his summertime tan. He'd gotten that working outside on the cabin, obviously, but that wasn't all he'd gotten. Because through his pale blue work shirt and darker blue jeans, she could see that his body had changed this summer too. It had gotten harder, and leaner, better defined, though if she were honest with herself, there had been nothing wrong with it when he'd walked into Pearl's at the beginning of the summer.

When Caroline realized that she'd been staring at Jack for a long time and that he was staring back at her with a quiet intensity she didn't usually associate with him, she looked away and busied herself with tearing off another piece of French bread.

"So you feel like Daisy is there, without really being there?" Jack asked when they'd been silent for a little while.

"Yes, exactly. I know you'll think this is silly, and that I'm one of those parents who can't let go or who insist on living their life through their child. But that's not it, Jack. It's just . . . I miss her. I do; I can't help it."

"Caroline, she's been away at college for three years," Jack said, surprised.

"Oh, I don't mean I miss her *that* way," she said. "I'm used to her living away from home by now, during the school year, anyway. I mean I miss being close to her, Jack. I miss the way we used to talk about everything. And now, this summer . . .

303

nothing. She comes home at night and goes straight to her room. She's so secretive, all of a sudden; it's like living with a stranger."

"A stranger you happen to know very well," Jack pointed out.

"I . . . I don't know if that's true anymore," Caroline said honestly. "The other day, our lives happened to overlap for about five minutes at the breakfast table. She was sitting where you're sitting now, eating a bowl of Raisin Bran, and I looked over at her and I thought, 'Who is this person? Really, who is she?' "

"Caroline, now you're being overly dramatic."

"Well, maybe a little." She sighed. "But you didn't know her before this, Jack. Maybe you did a little, this past year, but not like I did. And you haven't known her for as long as I have. And I'm telling you, she's changed—a lot. I mean, you and everyone else, too, seems to think it's perfectly normal that she's distracted by this boy she's dating, and maybe, for most people, it would be. But Daisy isn't most people. She's always been so focused; she was born focused. I mean, she's known since the age of six that she wanted to be a psychologist. Who does that Jack? Who knows at that age exactly what they want to do with their lives?

"But now, dating this boy? She's dated boys before, of course. But she's always had something in common with them, academics or sports. She has nothing in common with Will that I can see.

And then she starts hanging out with him every night at some dive bar, while the course books she brought home to read this summer sit on her desk unopened? I'm sorry, say what you want. But she's not the same person she was before."

"Love changes people, Caroline," Jack said simply.

"Oh, love," she said, exasperated, and she started to make a dismissive gesture with her hand, but something stopped her. She was remem-bering someone else she had known, a long time ago, and another summer, a long time ago. She was remembering herself, the summer she was Daisy's age, the summer she met Jack. She sighed and closed her eyes. What had she been like before she met Jack? A lot like Daisy, actually. Not as book smart, of course, or as driven, either. But she'd been responsible like Daisy, and, in her own way, she'd been ambitious. She'd wanted to get married, have children, buy a little house, maybe, so that she and her family didn't have to spend their whole lives living above Pearl's the way her mom and dad had. And she'd wanted to build the restaurant, too, build it into something her grandmother, who'd started it, would have been proud of.

But then she'd met Jack, and everything had changed. She'd fallen in love with him, of course, and, as she recalled, she'd been much worse than Daisy. She couldn't eat, couldn't sleep, couldn't breathe almost. And her parents? Her parents had been driven almost to distraction by it. They were so worried that she'd do something crazy, or stupid, or reckless. And, it turned out, they'd been right to be worried.

She rubbed her tired eyes and wondered if history was repeating itself. It certainly seemed as if it was. Because the boy Daisy was in love with, as far as Caroline was concerned, was exactly like Jack, a young Jack—irresponsible, and shiftless, and, if the rumor she'd heard about him was true, completely unimpressed by the institution of marriage . . .

"Hey," Jack said, leaning closer and touching her hand, which was still rubbing her eyes. She stopped rubbing them, and he came into focus. "I said love changes people, Caroline. But I don't think you need to worry about Daisy. She'll keep the best of who she is, you'll see. Just give her a little time to get used to the way she's feeling now; just . . . just be patient."

"*You're* telling *me* to be patient, Jack? You, who've never been able to wait for anything?"

"I'm waiting now," he said quietly, his blue eyes resting on her.

Her face flushed hotly, and she stood up abruptly from the table. "I'll walk you to the door, Jack," she said. "I have some, um, paperwork I need to do."

"At nine o'clock on a Saturday night?" he asked, reluctantly following her out of the kitchen.

"That's right," she said crisply, standing beside the front door. "And you've probably got to be getting back, too."

"To my cabin?" he asked, the corners of his mouth tugging upward. "I think it can manage without me for a little while longer."

He came closer then, and Caroline felt a warning spike of adrenaline. *Oh, no you don't, Jack,* she thought. *Not tonight. Not* any *night.* And she took a step back so that her back was, quite literally, against the wall.

He didn't move any closer. But he looked at her in a way that was like moving closer. He looked at her in a way that was like touching her.

"Don't, Jack," she said quietly, wishing she could put more conviction into that one word.

"Don't what?" he asked, his blue eyes dark.

"Don't do what you're about to do," she murmured, already furious at herself for giving in. With Jack, forewarned was not necessarily forearmed.

"What am I about to do, Caroline?"

Her heart knocked against her rib cage. "You're about to kiss me," she said.

"Is that what you think?" he asked, and, reaching out his hand, he clasped her chin gently and ran his thumb slowly over her lower lip. "You think I'm going to kiss you? Here?" He pressed down on her lip with his thumb.

"Aren't you?" she asked.

"As a matter of fact, I am. But I'm only going to start here. Because after that," he said, running his thumb along her lower lip again, "I'm going to kiss every single inch of you. I figure it'll take, conservatively, about ten hours. But it just so happens that ten hours is almost exactly how much time we have between now and the time Pearl's opens tomorrow morning."

At some point during this little speech, Caroline stopped breathing. But Jack didn't move. He stood perfectly still, his eyes never leaving her eyes.

Finally, she sucked in a little breath. "I thought you didn't want to spend the night with me."

"What gave you that impression?"

"The night you made me the grilled cheese sandwich . . ."

He shook his head. "I *did* want to spend the night with you that night. But you'd been drinking, Caroline, and I thought under the circumstances it would be a mistake. Tonight, though, you are stone cold sober."

Actually, Caroline thought, she was feeling a little drunk right now—drunk on iced tea, drunk on Jack.

He took a step closer to her, and she put her hands behind her back as a precautionary measure, since they suddenly wanted, so badly, to reach out and touch him. Then, in a last-ditch effort to stop what was happening, she decided to try a different tack with him. "What about Daisy, Jack? She'll be home soon."

"This early?" he asked, raising an eyebrow.

"Maybe," she breathed. *Unlikely,* she thought.

"Well, we *are* her parents, Caroline. She knows we've done this at least once before." The right corner of his mouth quirked up in another almost smile.

The man has a point, she thought. He stroked her bottom lip with his thumb again, and she felt her insides quiver.

"Oh, for God's sake, Jack," she said. "Just kiss me already."

He smiled then. He smiled *that* smile, and then he took another step closer, and, keeping his hand on her chin, he tipped her mouth up to his, and kissed her, really kissed her. When they'd kissed that night at Pearl's, she realized now, he'd held something back. Something small, but important. Well, he wasn't holding anything back now— because this kiss was classic Jack Keegan. This kiss had all the bells and whistles. *This kiss has probably undressed a hundred women,* she thought. No, more, she decided. Two hundred and fifty women, none of whom had ever seen it coming; one minute Jack Keegan was kissing them and the next minute their clothes were on the floor, and they were hoping—praying—it wouldn't end soon. And, because it was Jack, it didn't. It went on and on and on, until they thought they'd die with pleasure. Except they didn't.

Because when they woke up in the morning, there was Jack, ready to start all over again.

These thoughts should have bothered her. *Did* bother her, in fact. But they didn't bother her enough to tell him to stop.

He leaned into her now, pushing the small of her back against the wall, and his kiss deepened. Deepened so much that Caroline really did stop breathing, for a moment, trying to absorb his tongue's almost relentless assault on her mouth. Then Jack stopped kissing her, stopped long enough for her to draw in a deep breath. But when he turned his lips to her neck, when she felt his warm breath against her bare skin, she shivered violently and squirmed against him.

"Oh, Caroline," he said into the nape of her neck, and his voice sounded thick and gravelly. "Let me make love to you, please. Let me take you to your bedroom now."

"I don't know," she murmured, as he kissed her neck. He kissed it lavishly, unabashedly, in a way that made her put her fingers in his hair and drag them through it a little violently. "Did you mean it, Jack?" she said suddenly. "What you said about moving back here for me?"

"Yes, Caroline. I meant it," he rasped, pulling his lips away from her neck. "I meant every goddamned word of it. Now come to bed with me. Or I'll make love to you right here. Right now." And Caroline realized, belatedly, that one

310

of Jack's hands was sliding up the front of her blouse, and the other had reached up under her skirt and was sliding up the inside of her thigh.

His hands were a little rough, she noted, probably from all the work he'd done on the cabin. But their roughness wasn't unpleasant; it was just the opposite, actually, especially when the things his hands were doing to her felt so amazing.

"We've done it before, standing up like this. Remember?" Jack said against her ear. And Caroline remembered. *Oh, God,* she remembered. She and Jack had been newly dating then, and it seemed to her now that they'd both spent every waking minute thinking about when and where they could next make love. One afternoon, when her parents were away from Pearl's, Jack had come by and Caroline had left several tables waiting and taken Jack into the storage room. She'd locked the door and turned off the lights, and he'd backed her up against the wall, pulled her skirt up and her panties down, and made love to her right then and there, while her customers waited with varying degrees of impatience.

But that was then, she reminded herself, as Jack's hands continued to work their magic. And this was now; she was older now, and wiser. Sex was one thing, but love, commitment, responsibility . . . those were other, more important things. Was Jack ready for those things now? she wondered. She had no idea. But she wasn't ready to give him the benefit of the doubt yet. And it occurred to her now, standing there, that she might never be ready.

"Jack, you need to go," she said, her fingers still wound in his hair.

He ignored her, though, and turned his tongue's attention instead to her right ear, or more specifically, to the area below and behind her right ear. This was patently unfair. Jack knew, from experience, how sensitive this area was for her, and how kissing it this way could drive her slowly, and deliciously, crazy, as it was threatening to do now. *Right. Now.*

"Jack, please leave," she said, wriggling away from him. But as soon as his lips left her skin, she thought better of it, and, pulling him closer, she kissed him on the mouth again. God, she loved the way he tasted.

He kissed her back, but then pulled away a little. "I think you're sending me a mixed message, Caroline."

"I know I am. I'm sorry. I'll stop," she said then, putting her hands flat on his chest and trying to put a little distance between them. Jack, breathing hard, reluctantly removed one hand from inside her blouse, and the other from under her skirt.

Then he ran his fingers through his hair, hair that Caroline had already left in almost comic disarray, and looking at her through slightly hooded eyes, he said, "You sure about my leaving?"

"Positive."

He nodded, kissed her quickly on the fore-head, and left, closing the door behind him.

When she heard the door to the building close behind him, Caroline leaned back against the wall and closed her eyes, her heart still pounding. *I dodged another bullet,* she thought. She waited then for the feeling of relief to wash over her, but it never did. Instead, all she felt was a burning sensation everywhere his hands, and his lips, had touched her.

A couple of days later, Caroline was sitting in her office, her chin resting in her palm, her elbow resting on the desktop. There was a stack of paperwork in front of her, which she'd ostensibly come back here to do, but she was staring at a poster on the wall instead. The poster was of a beach in Bermuda, a pink beach, and it had been hanging there for so long she could no longer remember where it had come from or who had first tacked it up there. It had been years, in fact, since she'd even noticed it. But for some reason now, she was remembering how when Daisy was a little kid, they'd both been delighted to think there could be such a thing as a pink beach. So much so that Caroline had told her that maybe, one day, they'd go there, to that very beach, on that very island. It hadn't seemed impossible then either. Caroline had figured they were one good year, maybe two good years, away from being able to do something like that.

But now she got up, walked over to the poster, and ripped it off the wall. Then she stuffed it into the little wastebasket beside her desk and sat back down again. She reached into her top desk drawer, took out a pen, and turned her attention to her paperwork. It was impossible, though, for her to make any headway on it, and, after a few minutes, she folded her arms over it and put her head down on her arms in an admission of defeat.

No sooner had she done this, though, then she remembered something her grandma Pearl had once told her. She'd said that when Caroline was feeling discouraged, she should make a list of all the things in her life that were going right. So Caroline made a list in her head right now, or she tried to, anyway. It wasn't easy. It was much easier, she decided, finally, to make *the other* list, the list of all the things in her life that were going wrong.

Let's see . . . there was, first and foremost, the future of Pearl's, which had narrowed recently to two options: default on the loan and let the bank take it, or sell it, repay the loan, and save her credit rating, if not her dignity. Neither option appealed to her. But there it was.

Then there was Jack, second on her list of what was wrong with her life. She hadn't seen him since he'd come to dinner at her apartment, but his criminally gifted mouth, and hands, had left her replaying, at odd moments of the day and night, the, um, *kiss* he'd given her in the hallway of her apartment.

Next on the list was Daisy, Daisy who Caroline needed to talk to today about a subject matter that would make both of them uncomfortable and Daisy, quite possibly, angry. And as if that wasn't enough, there was— A light tap on the office door interrupted Caroline's list. It was just as well, too, since she was already feeling much worse now than she'd felt before. *Grandma Pearl would not have approved,* she thought, hurriedly putting the papers away. If there was one thing her grandmother had had no patience for, it was self-pity, in any and all of its forms.

"Come in," she called out, forcing some brightness into her voice.

"Mom?" Daisy said, cracking the door open. "Frankie said you wanted to see me."

"Hi, sweetheart," Caroline said, feigning casualness. "I do want to see you." She gestured for Daisy to come all the way into the office, but Daisy lingered warily in the doorway.

"Mom, you don't need an appointment to see me," she said. "You see me every day, all day long. In the coffee shop, in our apartment . . ." Her voice trailed off.

"Yes, Daisy. I'm aware of that. But there's no reason we can't see each other here, in my office, too." And when Daisy still made no move to come inside, Caroline added sternly, "You know, honey, you're not *just* my daughter. You're also my employee." Here was the real reason Caroline wanted to talk to Daisy in her office. She was hoping that if they met here, it would be possible for them to maintain at least a modicum of professionalism, a modicum of civility. Because Daisy wasn't going to like what Caroline had to say to her.

Daisy sighed now, a sigh of quiet inevitability, and, closing the office door behind her, she sat down on the folding chair facing Caroline's desk. "Okay," she said, "shoot."

"All right," Caroline said, feeling suddenly uncertain. Now that she had Daisy's attention, she didn't know how to introduce the subject of Will Hughes. So she decided to stall a little and bring up a topic that was less incendiary.

"Well, first of all, I wanted to ask you how you think Jessica is doing."

"Jessica? Um, okay, I guess," Daisy said. "Why? How do you think she's doing?"

"I think, actually, she's doing a little worse, honey, if that's even possible."

"That bad, huh?" Daisy said, her face falling a little.

"I'm afraid so. I don't know how much longer we can carry her, Daisy. After all, this is a business, not a charity."

"No, Mom. You're right," Daisy said. "And, by the way, Jessica knows she's not doing well here. She already has a contingency plan for if—or, I should say, for *when*—you fire her."

"Really?" Caroline asked, a little skeptically.

"Uh-huh. She's says she's going to go to school to become a dental hygienist."

"Oh, honey," Caroline said, shaking her head. "She'd flunk right out of that program."

"I know," Daisy agreed. "But what if . . . what if, by some miracle, she didn't? What if she actually graduated from a program like that and got a job in a dentist's office?" Daisy almost whispered this last part. And for good reason. Just the thought of Jessica wielding sharp instruments destined for people's mouths was enough to make Caroline shudder.

"No, Daisy, you're right," she said. "We can't let that happen. We can't even let that come *close* to happening. She can stay, for now, but you're going to have to help her, all right? You and Frankie."

Daisy looked relieved. "We will, Mom. We *do*. Frankie, especially, is so patient with her. He's never once gotten annoyed with her, not even when she makes his job harder."

"Well, the man's a saint, obviously."

Daisy smiled, nodding her agreement. "So we'll give Jessica another try?"

"We'll give her another try," Caroline agreed, without much enthusiasm.

"And what about me? How I'm doing?" Daisy asked.

"At Pearl's?"

Daisy nodded.

Caroline paused. As waitresses went, Daisy was good, as good as they got, really. She could turn a table over even faster than Caroline could, and that was saying a lot. But since meeting Will, everything Daisy did at Pearl's she did with a dreamy, almost languid preoccupation that set Caroline's nerves on edge. Still, she couldn't fault the quality of her work. She couldn't even remember the last time Daisy had gotten an order wrong, or broken a glass, or returned incorrect change on a bill.

"You're doing fine, Daisy," she said. "Better than fine. I never have any complaints about your work; you know that."

"Good," Daisy said, pleased. She started to stand up. "Now, if my performance review is over, I think I better be getting back out there."

"Um, not quite, honey. There is one more thing . . ."

Daisy sat back down again reluctantly. "Yes?"

"Well," Caroline said, and paused. She knew she couldn't keep stalling. Still, how best to phrase this?

Daisy saved her the trouble. "Mom, I know what you want to talk to me about. It's Will, isn't it?"

"Yes, it is," Caroline said. "But it's not about Will per se. It's more about you, Daisy. About you . . . staying focused right now. You're only a year away from graduation, and you're going to be applying to graduate schools this winter, and . . ." She paused again. This was harder than she'd thought it would be.

"And what?"

"And I wouldn't want anything to interfere with your plans," Caroline said, quickly, before she lost her nerve.

Daisy flushed, not from embarrassment, Caroline saw, but from anger. "You wouldn't want anything to interfere with my plans," she repeated slowly. "Is that a euphemism, Mom, for 'You wouldn't want me to get pregnant'?"

"No, of course not. The thought never crossed my mind," Caroline said, and now it was her turn to flush. Because the thought *had* crossed her mind, and it had terrified her. Not that she thought it was likely, given how responsible Daisy was, but still, anyone could slip up once. And sometimes once was all it took.

"Daisy, look, I don't want this to turn into an argument," Caroline said, trying to diffuse the tension she suddenly felt between them. "It isn't that I don't trust you. I do; I trust you implicitly. But you're so close now, so close to getting all the things you want—a degree, a career, a whole life that will have nothing to do with Butternut or with Pearl's. Or with . . . any of this," she said, gesturing around her office. "I mean, for you, your college diploma won't just be a slip of paper. It'll be a guarantee that you'll never have to waitress here again."

But Daisy only shrugged. "I don't mind waitressing here."

"Well, no, not for a summer, maybe. But for a lifetime? I think you'd mind it, honey," Caroline said gently.

Daisy, though, seemed suddenly impatient. "Mom, can I ask you a question?"

"Of course."

"And will you answer it honestly?"

"I'll certainly try," Caroline said, a little offended by Daisy's phrasing.

"Would we even be having this conversation if I was dating someone other than Will? Someone who didn't work at a garage? Someone who was in college, for instance, or, better yet—"

"Daisy, I'd be concerned about your future whoever you were dating," Caroline interrupted her.

"Would you, Mom?" Daisy pressed. "This concerned? I don't think so. I think this conversation *is* about Will. Will, specifically. About your not liking him. And because you don't know him, Mom, because you haven't even *tried* to get to know him, I can only think of one reason why you wouldn't like him: you're being a snob."

"A snob?" Caroline repeated, and the word stung. It stung because she knew it was true. She'd never been a snob before, as far as she knew, but she was being one now.

"Yes, Mom, a snob. Admit it. You don't think Will's good enough for me, do you?"

"I didn't say that, Daisy. I just think . . . I just think you're from two different worlds."

"Two different worlds?" Daisy asked, raising her eyebrows.

"That's right," Caroline said stubbornly. "Because it's not where you've come from, Daisy. It's where you're *going*. And you're going somewhere, honey."

"And Will's not?"

Caroline hesitated, choosing her words carefully. "I don't know. But I think . . . I think he may have already gotten where he's going."

"Mom, how could you possibly know that?" Daisy asked, looking hurt again. "And even if it were true, what's wrong with where he is now? Whatever happened to what your grandpa Ralph used to say? About an honest day's work for an honest day's pay? Because that's what Will does already, Mom. And you didn't used to think there was any shame in that."

"And I still don't," Caroline said flatly. "Especially since that's all I have to show for my life at the end of every day. But I want you to have more than that; I want you to finish your education, and I want you to be successful, really successful."

"If by successful, you mean 'rich,' Mom, it's not going to happen," Daisy said. "I hate to disappoint you, but that's not important to me. I'm going to be a psychologist, not a hedge fund manager. I'm never going to be rich."

"I don't mean *rich*," Caroline qualified. "I mean . . ." She hesitated. What *did* she mean, exactly? What was it she wanted for Daisy? Well, probably what all parents wanted for their children, she thought. She wanted Daisy's life to be better than hers, *easier* than hers. She didn't want her to have to work three hundred and sixty-two days of the year, the way Caroline had had to. She didn't want her to have to wake up at five thirty every morning. Nor did she want her to live in a home that was mortgaged to within an inch of its life, drive a truck that already had two hundred thousand miles on it, or live a life full of grinding, almost constant worry about the future. But she didn't say any of this to her, because Caroline was afraid that, like her earlier thoughts, it would smack of self-pity.

So instead she said, "I don't mean I want you to be *rich*, Daisy. I mean I want you to be *secure*, at least insofar as that's possible in today's world."

Daisy said nothing for a moment. Then she asked, "And you think Will is going to stand in the way of that?" Her face was pinker now.

If he's as much like your father as I think he is, he will, Caroline thought. But she couldn't say that to Daisy. So she searched, instead, for another, less incendiary way to say it, but then realized there wasn't one. God, she wasn't used to this, she thought, this conflict in their relationship. She had no practice at it. And she had no stomach for it either. In the past, she and Daisy had always been on the same side. They'd always been on *Daisy's* side. She sighed, ready for this conversation to be over. "Look," she said, with a conciliatory smile. "Just don't lose sight of your dream, okay?" She pretended to search for a paper on her desk then, hoping to signal that the conversation was over, but Daisy stayed where she was.

"What if Will *is* my dream?" she asked, looking at Caroline steadily.

"Then you need a better dream," Caroline said, without thinking.

"Mom," Daisy said, and now she was angry *and* hurt. She stood up to leave.

"Daisy, please, sit down," she said.

But Daisy hesitated. "Mom, I think you've already made yourself perfectly clear," she said, folding her arms across her chest.

"No, I haven't," Caroline said, making up her mind. "I wasn't going to say anything about this, but I think you need to know it, Daisy."

"Know what?" Daisy asked, still not sitting down.

"Look, you know I try not to listen to gossip. If I did, I'd never get any work done around this place. But when I heard this, I paid attention. And I think you—"

But Daisy held up her hand. "Is this about Will, Mom?"

"Yes, it is. Will and . . . and someone else."

"Well, I don't want to hear it," Daisy said, her jaw set. "Really, I'm not interested in whatever's making the rounds at Pearl's, especially since there's no way of knowing if it's true or not. Besides, Mom, I trust Will." Caroline saw that Daisy's blue eyes were glazed with tears as she added, "The way I wish you trusted me. But if you can't trust me, Mom, can you at least be happy for me? I've never felt this way about anyone before. *Ever.*" She blinked then, and a tear ran down her cheek. She wiped it away with the back of her hand.

"Daisy," Caroline said, swallowing past something hard in her throat. "I want to be happy for you—"

"But you can't be this time around, can you?" Daisy said.

"No," Caroline said softly.

"Mom, I've done everything you've ever wanted me to do," Daisy said. "And the one time—"

"Daisy," Caroline interrupted her, genuinely shocked. "That's not fair. I never pressured you to do any of the things you've done, any of the things you've accomplished. That's all come from you."

"But I knew how important it was to you, Mom, that I do all those things," Daisy said, holding back a sob. "And I'm glad I did them. But I need to lead my own life now. And if you don't like the decisions I make, well, that's too bad. Because you know what, Mom? You need to lead your own life, too." She turned around then and opened the door to the office, but on her way out, she ran into the immovable wall that was Frankie.

"Whoa, Daisy," he said, catching her. "Are you okay?"

But she disentangled herself from him and kept going.

Frankie looked after her and then looked at Caroline, who was trying, very hard, not to cry, and said, "I'll come back." He reached for the door to close it again, but Caroline stopped him.

"No, Frankie. Please, come in," Caroline said, not wanting to be alone when Daisy's words still stung the way they did.

He hesitated, then came into her office, quickly filling the whole space. He started to say something, but he stopped. Caroline sighed. There weren't going to be any easy conversations in this room today.

"Is this about this morning, Frankie? About the meeting I was having when you came in to work?" she asked.

He nodded.

"I'm sorry. I asked them to come early because I didn't want you to know about it. I was hoping they'd be gone before you got to work."

He didn't say anything.

She exhaled a big breath. "They're potential buyers, Frankie. From Ely. John Quarterman put me in touch with them. They seemed nice enough, and they know their stuff, too; they already own three successful restaurants in this area. And Frankie? Their offer's fair, especially when you consider how much work this building needs."

He nodded. "What did you tell them?"

"I told them I needed time to think about it. And I told them that my accepting the offer was contingent upon them hiring you, at twenty-five percent above your current salary, and that if they closed for renovations, they'd still have to pay you while they were closed. I think that's fair, don't you?"

He shrugged. "Do you want to sell Pearl's?"

"It's not a question of *wanting* to sell it. It's more of a question of *needing* to sell it. I'll owe the bank almost forty-five thousand dollars in September when my balloon mortgage payment is due. And I don't have it, Frankie."

"What if . . . what if someone could give you some of the money, though? Would you still need to sell it?"

"That . . . that would depend. But nobody's going to give me any money, Frankie."

"Actually, I'm going to give you some money," Frankie said.

"Frankie," Caroline said, shaking her head. "That's very sweet."

"I'm not trying to be sweet," Frankie said. "I'm trying to keep my job."

"You *will* keep your job, whatever happens. I'll make them put it in writing."

"No, I mean my job working for you. I don't want to work for anyone else. Besides, I've got over ten thousand dollars. That should tide the bank over for a while, shouldn't it?"

She shook her head; it wasn't nearly enough. But that wasn't what was bothering her right now. "Frankie, where'd you get that much money?" she asked. "And don't tell me you saved it out of your salary. Because I already know for a fact you send your sister whatever you don't need to live on yourself." Frankie had gotten back in touch with his sister a few years before, the sister whose abusive husband he'd gone to prison for killing in self-defense, and he was helping to support her now.

He shifted his considerable weight from one foot to the other foot now. "It's from playing pool, actually."

She frowned.

"It's not a big deal," Frankie said. "I mean, what's a little wagering between friends?"

"A little?"

"Okay, a lot. But I like playing pool, I'm good at it, and I knew you needed the money. Or you would need it, someday. Besides, I'm lucky. Some people who play for money have trouble getting paid when they win. I've never had that problem before," he said, a mischievous glint in his eyes.

Caroline laughed. "I don't doubt that," she said.

"Look, I'll leave you alone now. Just . . . just keep it in mind, all right?"

"I will. Thank you," she said. But she was suddenly exhausted, and when Frankie left, it was all she could do not to put her head down on the desk again.

She thought about Daisy's words about letting her lead her own life. They had cut her to the quick. Probably because she knew they were true. She'd never pressured Daisy, as she'd said, but that was only because she'd never *needed* to pressure her. And she'd never interfered in Daisy's choices either, but again, that was because she'd always *agreed* with them. They'd always struck her as good choices—until now. And now, she realized, now that she disagreed with Daisy, she couldn't stand back and let her live her own life. She didn't know how to.

But Daisy had said something else, too. She'd said Caroline needed to live her *own* life, and now, belatedly, Caroline realized the truth in that statement as well. Of course, during the years since Daisy had gone away to college, Caroline had come to pride herself on her independence. On her friendships with Allie and Jax, on her relationship with Buster. But if she were honest with herself, her life during those years had still been about the same two things it had always been about: Daisy and Pearl's. In that order. She had to go back a long way, back to before Jack had left her, for her life to have been about anything else.

As she thought about all this, she did something that surprised her. She got up and took the crumpled poster out of the wastebasket and put it on her desk, and then she tried to smooth all the wrinkles out of it. When she'd done the best she could, she hung it back on the wall, and studied it again. She still liked that pink beach in Bermuda, she decided, with a weary smile. And damn it, she still wanted to go there one day.

Chapter 14

On a sultry night in early August, Will's self-control finally faltered. He and Daisy had spent their night, as usual, at Pearl's and the Black Bear. But from the moment he'd first seen her, something had been different between them. It was as if there was an added charge in their attraction to each other, an extra current of electricity running between their bodies.

He thought maybe it had to do with what Daisy was wearing, a sleeveless blouse and form-fitting blue jeans. She wasn't in the habit of dressing seductively, and tonight was no exception, but her thin cotton blouse strained just slightly against the gentle curve of her breasts and showed off, too, an almost irresistible amount of her bare, creamy arms.

And it wasn't just Will who was feeling the attraction so intensely. Daisy was feeling it too. He'd held her a little too tightly when they'd danced, for instance, and she'd let him. And then she'd pressed herself against him in a suggestive way that she'd never done before. She'd even relaxed her "no kissing in public" rule and let him give her a couple of long, hungry kisses while they danced, swaying almost imperceptibly in the flickering lights of the Black Bear's jukebox.

By the time they'd gotten into his pickup and headed back to Butternut, Will felt as if the sexual tension was pulled so tight it was about to snap. He concentrated on the road, driving with elaborate carefulness, and Daisy, who was strangely quiet, looked out the window. But when they got to town and Will started to pull into a space on Main Street, Daisy shook her head.

"Don't park here," she said. "Park outside the rec center."

Will nodded wordlessly and drove out to the

edge of town where the rec center took up a whole block that, at this time of night, was quiet and dimly lit. He parked and cut the engine, and almost before he knew what was happening, Daisy was in his arms, kissing him, hard, her tongue greedily exploring his mouth. He kissed her back, his need for her ratcheting up with every passing second, until he thought he couldn't take it anymore. That was when he let one of his hands wander over the front of her blouse, feeling her small, perfect breasts through the thin cotton material, and then, when that wasn't enough, unbuttoning her blouse and peeling it open.

He stopped kissing her then, long enough to look down at her. "Daisy," he breathed, taking in a sheer, lacy bra, whose pale violet color contrasted strikingly with the almost ethereal whiteness of her skin.

"Do you like it?" she asked, with a sudden shyness. "I bought it last weekend at the mall in Duluth."

He swallowed. Hard. "Um, yeah. I like it, Daisy. I like it a lot."

So she'd been wearing that all night? No wonder he hadn't been able to keep his hands off her. He must have known, subconsciously, how little clothing stood between the two of them. And he found himself wondering, for one wild moment, if there was a pair of matching panties that went with this bra, and if she was wearing them right now. The thought aroused him so much that he practically groaned.

Instead, he pulled her back into his arms and kissed her, harder. Soon one of his hands moved again to her breasts, and he cupped one of them gently in his palm and ran his fingers over the barely there material of her bra, feeling the warmth of her skin, and the pebbling hardness of her nipple, through it. Her breathing quickened then, and when he dipped his fingers inside her bra, and caressed her bare nipple with his fingers, she let out a little moan that pushed him right to the edge of endurance.

Without thinking, he took his hand out of her bra and slid both of his hands down and around, into her blue jeans' back pockets. Then he cupped her bottom, her delicious bottom, with both of his hands, and simultaneously squeezed it as he pulled her almost onto his lap. And as he did this, he felt her whole body shudder, almost violently, with excitement.

"Oh, Daisy," he said. He meant it to be a warning, but it came out instead sounding more like an invitation. Then she was scrambling onto his lap, facing him, straddling him, kissing him again, and pressing against him in a way she'd never done before.

"Let's go somewhere," she said, breathlessly, into their kiss. "Now."

"Where?" he asked, his arms circling her waist, pulling her harder against him.

"Let's go to the beach," she said, talking to him and kissing him at the same time. "Please, Will. Hurry."

"It's not a good idea," he said, pulling his lips away from hers. But he didn't say it with any real conviction, and she wasn't listening anyway. She grabbed the hem of his T-shirt and pulled it up over his head and then started kissing him again, her hands running over his bare chest. And he remembered the way she'd done this that first night, the night they'd gone to the beach, but her hands had been so hesitant then. So unsure of themselves. Now they felt hungry, greedy, as if they wanted to touch every single inch of him at the same time.

"Do you have any protection?" Daisy said, pulling her mouth away from his only long enough to get the words out.

"Protection?" he said blankly, as if he'd never heard the word before.

She nodded, her breath coming fast, her creamy cleavage just inches from his mouth.

"Yeah, I've got something," he said. And he did. He'd been carrying it around all summer, whenever he was with Daisy, without knowing if he'd ever actually need to use it.

"Then take me to the beach. But, Will? You're going to have to drive fast," she added, her hands touching his shoulders, his chest, his stomach. "Because I can't wait that much longer."

"Oh, God, Daisy." He groaned, because he couldn't wait that much longer either. He leaned over and nuzzled her cleavage with his lips, then traced its silky, sweet-smelling skin with his tongue. He needed to stop, now. He needed to drive to the beach. But then he remembered something.

"Daisy," he said, pulling his mouth away. "You said you didn't want our first time to be in the back seat of a pickup."

"That was before I knew how hard it was going to be to wait," she said, her breath soft against his ear. She started kissing him again, with even more urgency than before, and Will held her, held her so tightly that he could feel her cleavage against his bare chest, and, through her bra, the tender hardness of her nipples, too.

She wriggled in his lap, and Will sucked in a breath of surprise, surprise and almost painful arousal. "Oh, don't do that, Daisy." He groaned again, not really meaning it.

"Will, please, let's go to the beach," she said, against his ear, as her hands plucked impatiently at the button on his blue jeans.

The beach? Not a chance, he thought. They'd be lucky now if they made it as far as the back seat, and even that was going to be a stretch.

Then, from a few blocks away, came a sound,

just loud enough to register in his consciousness. It was an engine backfiring, and the time it took for Will to hear it, and to categorize it, was enough time to bring him back to reality, or to some form of reality, here in his pickup with Daisy. It wasn't supposed to be this way for them, he thought. He knew it; she knew it, too. She'd just forgotten it in the moment.

So with some supreme effort of will he didn't even know he had, he put his hands around her waist and lifted her off his lap, depositing her on the seat next to him.

"What's wrong?" she asked, staring at him, bewildered.

But he turned away from her and looked determinedly out the window. He figured if he looked back at her right now, with her messy hair, her unbuttoned blouse, her shimmery bra, and her silky white cleavage, he would completely lose it.

"Nothing's wrong," he muttered finally. "I just need to get a grip on myself." He reached for his T-shirt on the floor of the truck and pulled it back on, still without looking at her.

"What if I don't *want* you to get a grip on yourself?" she asked quietly.

"You do. Trust me."

She said nothing, and a few minutes later he glanced back at her again. She was buttoning her blouse, and when he felt the urge to tell her to stop, to leave it open, he knew he needed to look out the window again.

After a few more minutes had passed, she said softly, "I'm sorry."

"Sorry for what?" He turned back to her in surprise.

"Sorry to make you be the one to stop us. I feel like we're . . . switching places or something."

He smiled, then trusted himself enough to reach out and stroke her cheek with his fingers. "Maybe we are," he said. "But I'm willing to do that for you, Daisy. I don't want to just do the easy thing; I've been doing that my whole life. I want to do the right thing."

She thought about that for a moment. "Okay. But, Will, what if the right thing for us now is to be together? I mean, *really* be together?"

He kept stroking her cheek. "Is that what you want, Daisy?"

"Yes, Will. It is. I've wanted it all summer. But I don't think I was ready until now."

He felt another surge of desire for her, hearing her say those words, but he tried to keep his voice and expression neutral as he said, "Are you sure about that?"

"I'm sure," she said, taking the fingers he was using to stroke her cheek and kissing them. "But you're right about my not wanting it to happen in your truck. I mean, it didn't seem like a bad idea five minutes ago, but now, it kind of does. Still, there must be someplace else we can be together. Your apartment, maybe . . ."

Will shook his head. *Apartment* was overstating it. *Room* was more like it. And this room had a bed with creaky springs, cracks in the ceiling, and the not-so-faint aroma of motor oil permeating everything in it. He couldn't see Daisy there. But there might be someplace else he could take her.

"Daisy, you know how I work on Mr. Phipps's cars?"

She nodded, not understanding the connection.

"He told me I could borrow his cabin anytime I wanted it. I don't think he gets out there very often. It's out on Butternut Lake, *way* out on it. He said his nearest neighbor is over a mile away."

"And you . . . you don't think he'd mind?"

"No. I'll tell him I'm taking someone, too. I don't want you to feel like we're sneaking around or anything."

Daisy frowned, considering this, and then said, "But, Will, we will have to sneak around when it comes to my mom. She wouldn't stop me from going—she *couldn't* stop me from going—but she wouldn't be happy about it either. It's just simpler if I don't tell her, if I tell her, instead, I'm going to Jessica's house or something."

Will hesitated. He thought honesty was probably the best policy here, but then, when it came to parent-child relationships, he didn't have a lot of experience to fall back on.

"You do what you think you need to do," he said finally.

She nodded, suddenly preoccupied. "I can't go this weekend. I'm working Saturday and Sunday. But my mom said, in exchange, I could take next weekend off."

"Good, we'll go then. I have to work that Saturday, but I could leave early and we could get there before dark. What do you think?"

"I think . . . I think that sounds good," she said. Will noticed her face was pink, whether with excitement or nervousness he couldn't tell.

He looked at his watch. "I need to get you back to your apartment," he said. She nodded and started trying to fix her messy hair, the way she did every night before she went home. Watching her, he felt a wave of new affection for her. Then he felt something else, too . . . guilt.

"Daisy," he said, suddenly, "you don't feel like I'm pressuring you to do this, do you?"

"Pressuring *me?*" she said, pausing, her loose hair gathered in both hands as she got ready to put it in a ponytail. "Will, if anything, *I'm* pressuring *you.*"

He laughed and pulled her into his arms again. But he was thinking that the real pressure, for both of them, was that the summer would be over soon. Daisy would be going back to college. And Will? Will would be going somewhere too. Because for the first time in his life, he actually had a plan.

Chapter 15

"Do you want another Diet Coke?"

"No, I'm fine," Daisy said, smiling at Will.

"Do you want to leave?"

She shook her head. "Not yet. Finish your beer."

He nodded, but he made no move to drink it. Instead, he reached over and took her hand. "Are you . . . are you worrying? About this weekend?"

"Not *worrying*," Daisy qualified. "Just . . . *wondering*."

"Wondering, huh?" His gold-brown eyes rested on her. "There's a lot of that going on around here, isn't there?" he said, running his thumb over the back of her hand in a firm caress.

It was a Wednesday night, and Daisy and Will were sitting at their usual table at the Black Bear, listening to the jukebox. That Saturday, they were driving up to Mr. Phipps's cabin, and the knowledge of that seemed somehow to charge the very air between them, until Daisy thought she could almost hear it crackling with electricity.

Will smiled now and leaned closer. "What are you wondering about, exactly?" he asked, grazing her earlobe with his lips.

"Nothing," Daisy said, blushing and looking down at the table. What she was wondering about, actually, was something she'd been wondering about all summer: namely, was it possible to be *too* attracted to someone? And, if it was possible, what would happen to her this weekend? After all, if something as simple as Will holding her hand, or kissing her earlobe, left her light-headed with pleasure, how would his lovemaking leave her? Paralyzed, maybe? Or just completely catatonic?

"Do you know what I'll never get tired of, Daisy?" Will asked, next to her ear.

"What?"

"Watching you blush."

That was the last thing he said to her before someone passing their table did a double take, stopped, and came back. *"Will?"*

Then, with an almost physical effort, Will pulled his eyes away from Daisy and looked up at the woman standing beside their table. He tightened his grip on Daisy's hand. "Hi, Christy," he said, with what sounded to Daisy like a kind of resignation, a kind of inevitability. As if he'd been waiting, all summer, for her to stop by their table.

Daisy looked up at her too then, and, when she did, she had three thoughts in quick succession. The first thought, which was really more of a mental image than a thought, was *one small orange juice with ice, and one order of oatmeal with bananas and blueberries on the side,* which was Christy's usual breakfast order at Pearl's. Her second thought, as she sat there looking at her, was that Christy was a little overdone for a weeknight at the Black Bear. She was wearing a tight dress and high-heeled sandals. Her blond hair was perfectly blown out, and her permanently pouty lips coated with a shimmery pink lip gloss. Daisy's third thought was that even though she didn't know Christy very well—she and her husband, Mac, had only moved to town a few years ago—she knew her well enough to know she didn't really like her.

Daisy smiled at her now, though, with the reflexive politeness that twenty-one years of being her mother's daughter had instilled in her, and said, "Hi, Christy."

But Christy ignored her. "What are you doing here, Will?" she asked, and there was something about the way she asked it that made Daisy look back at Will, suddenly alert and interested to hear what he would say.

"We're having a drink," he said, indicating Daisy, and the beer and the Diet Coke on the table in front of them.

Christy looked at Daisy now, then looked back at Will, and then looked at their hands, still entwined together, resting on the little table between them. And Daisy, watching her, saw the exact moment it happened, the exact moment it all clicked into place for Christy. As it happened, it was also the exact moment it all clicked into place for Daisy, too.

"Unbelievable," Christy said softly, shaking her head. "You're dating Daisy? Daisy the waitress?"

Daisy knew she should have felt offended by Christy's choice of words, and tone of voice, but she didn't feel anything right now. She couldn't.

"Daisy's in college," Will said patiently. "She waitresses in the summer."

But Christy didn't seem interested in this distinction. "So *this* is the girl you're seeing?" she asked incredulously. "*This* is who you broke up with me to be with?"

Daisy watched Will. He was meeting Christy's shocked stare with a level gaze. "Yes, Christy, I'm seeing Daisy now," he said, matter-of-factly. Daisy had a feeling, though, that his outwardly calm appearance was requiring enormous effort to maintain on his part.

"Did you tell her about us?" Christy asked, looking at Daisy again, and Daisy was irritated at herself when she felt her cheeks grow warm under her critical gaze. "Did you tell her about all the nights we've spent together, Will?" But before Will could answer, she kept going, "I mean, seriously Will, Daisy? She's, like, practically in high school. Is she even old enough to be in here?"

"Daisy's twenty-one," he said. "She has as much right to be here as you do." He glanced around the bar then and found what he was looking for. "Why don't you go back to your table, Christy,"

342

he said. "It looks like your friends are waiting for you."

"Oh no," Christy said softly, so softly it made the hairs stand up on Daisy's arms. "I'm not done with you yet."

"Christy," Will said warningly, but it was too late. In a movement so sudden it made Daisy jump back a little in her chair, Christy picked up Will's half-full glass of beer and threw the contents of it in his face.

If there was more, Daisy didn't see it. She wrenched her hand away from Will's and ran for the bar's door, pushing it open blindly, hot tears already spilling down her cheeks. But when she found herself in the middle of the parking lot, she stopped and looked around in desperation. She would give anything, *anything,* right now to have a way to get home that wasn't in Will's pickup. But she didn't know anyone else at the Black Bear. Well, anyone else she could ask for a ride. She thought, for a moment, about walking back to Butternut, but decided against it. She was miles from town, it was pitch-black outside, and she didn't know these back roads that well.

So instead she walked over to Will's pickup and tried the passenger-side door. Locked. It figured. She had no choice but to stand there and wait, her humiliation palpable, until Will came out a few minutes later.

"Are you okay?" he asked, opening the door for her.

She didn't answer him; she didn't trust herself to. Instead, she climbed into the truck, slammed the door, and fastened her seat belt, concentrating the whole time on willing her tears to stop. Which they did, more or less. Because during the drive home, which seemed inordinately long tonight, only a few of them slid, hot and silent, down her cheeks. She was almost positive Will couldn't see them in the darkness of the truck, though he looked over at her frequently, and a couple of times he even started to say something before he stopped himself.

All this reminded Daisy of another night, the first night, the night that Will had driven her home from the beach. Tonight, though, was worse. Then, she'd barely known Will. Now . . . well now, she'd at least *thought* she'd known him. And she was struck by a realization that almost made her groan out loud with the knowledge of her own stupidity. What she'd found out tonight about Will and Christy was what her mother and Jessica had both tried to tell her about. They'd both known about it before she did. Hell, the whole town had probably known about it before she did. She sank down a few more inches in her seat, her humiliation complete.

Already, though, at least one coherent thought was forming in her brain: she wasn't going to tell her mother about this incident. Not that hearing about it would bring her mother any satisfaction; it wouldn't. She wasn't mean. Far from it. And she'd never wanted anything more than for Daisy to be happy. She would never, ever say *I told you so*. But she might think it.

By the time Will pulled into his customary parking space on Main Street, Daisy was ready, her hand already on the door handle. But when she started to open the door, Will finally spoke. "Daisy, please, don't go like this. Just . . . just hear me out, okay?"

She stopped and then closed the door. She still couldn't look at him, but she would listen to him, she decided. For a minute, anyway.

"First of all, you need to know something, all right?" he said. "I never saw the two of you at the same time. By the night we had our first date, it was already over between me and Christy. I wanted to give us a chance, Daisy, a *real* chance. I never saw her again after the night I came over to your apartment for the first time. I promise you that."

She'd meant to listen to him in stony silence, but now she felt anger pulsing at her temples. "Is that all you think this is about, Will?" she asked, turning to him. "Because it's not. I mean, it's part of it. But, Will, *she's married,* for God's sake. She has a husband. I *know* him." As she said this, though, it occurred to her that the only thing she really knew about Mac Hansen was that he was a lousy tipper. But, still, to have *this* happen to him? This seemed like a punishment that didn't fit the crime.

Will didn't say anything; he only nodded a little, and for some reason Daisy found this infuriating. Wasn't he even going to try to defend himself? Or did he think he didn't even need to?

"I don't know, Will," she said, "maybe you think I'm blowing this out of proportion. Maybe you think, 'So what if I had an affair with a married woman. It's no big deal.' And maybe you think it's old-fashioned, or quaint, even, for me to be upset about it—"

"I *don't* think that," Will interrupted.

But she wasn't listening. "Maybe you think, too, that because my own parents got divorced, marriage means less to me, Will, that I don't take it as seriously as I would if they'd stayed married. But that's not true. If anything, the fact that the two of them failed at marriage makes me take it *more* seriously." She stopped, a little out of breath.

They were silent then, for a moment, even though her mind was racing with questions. "Just, just tell me something, Will," she said suddenly. "Just help me understand this."

"All right," he said.

"How . . . how did it happen? How did you meet her?"

He hesitated. "I met her at a bar," he said.

Of course, Daisy thought. Where else?

"And how long . . . how long did you see each other for?" It was so strange, she thought. The *wanting* to know, and the *not wanting* to know, both at the same time.

He sighed and closed his eyes, just for a second, and Daisy knew she wasn't going to like his answer. "A year," he said.

"*A year?* Will," she said, shaking her head in disbelief. But she had more questions for him. It was like ripping off a Band-Aid. Once you started to do it, you couldn't very well stop in the middle. "And how often did you see her. Will?"

He sighed again. "It varied. Sometimes, I'd go a month without seeing her. Sometimes, if her husband was away, I'd see her two or three nights in a row."

Daisy rubbed her eyes, trying to block out the image of the two of them together.

"Daisy," Will said quietly. "Stop, okay? You don't need to know this."

"I *do* need to know this."

"Every detail?"

"Yes, Will. Every detail."

He sat in silence.

"Were there other people, Will? For you and for her?"

He shrugged. "There wasn't for me. I don't know about her."

347

"What about her husband, Mac? Did he ever find out about it?"

He shook his head. "No. Not as far as I know."

"And what, what was it . . ." She paused, struggling with the wording of this question. "What was it that you and Christy had in common?" she asked. "I mean, you seem so different to me. What did the two of you even talk about when you were together?"

For the first time since her interrogation started, she saw his exasperation begin to break through. "We didn't talk, Daisy. That's not why we were together," he said. And she knew, from his expression, that as soon as he said it, he regretted saying it. He started to say something else then, but she wasn't listening.

"Oh, God," she murmured, putting a hand to her temples.

"Daisy, what is it?" Will asked, alarmed.

"Nothing," she said. "It's just . . . thinking about the two of you . . . *not* talking. It's making me feel sick to my stomach."

"Then don't think about it," he said, reaching for her, but she moved out of his reach.

She heard him exhale then, slowly, "I'm sorry," he said. "About the sick to your stomach feeling. Thanks to you, I know what that feels like."

"Thanks to me?" she said, looking over at him.

He nodded. "I feel that way every time I think about you going back to college and . . ." He hesitated, and Daisy sat very still, because they never talked about this. Ever. About Daisy going back to college at the end of the summer.

"I think about you going back there," Will continued, "and . . . and meeting someone else. Or just being with someone else. Someone on your volleyball team, or in your apartment building, or in one of your classes. I don't know why I think about it, Daisy, because it's like torture. But I do. I imagine you with this person, this person who isn't even real, talking to him, or kissing him maybe, or just being with him, and it makes me feel sick to my stomach. Just like you said. That's jealousy, I guess. I'd never felt it before this summer."

She shook her head. They were getting off topic. Besides, there was another question she had for him. "Did you know she was married when you first met her, Will?" she asked. *Please say no.*

"Yes," he said. "I knew."

"You knew and you didn't care?" she asked, irritated that her tears were threatening to start again. *Don't you dare cry now, Daisy.*

"I don't know, Daisy. Sometimes, I think, I *did* care. I just didn't care *enough.*"

"What is that supposed to mean?"

"It's supposed to mean, Daisy, that before I met you this summer, I didn't spend a lot of time thinking about whether or not what I was doing was right or wrong. Sometimes, I wanted to; I

349

wanted to care. But most of the time, I was just glad I didn't care."

"I don't understand," she said, wiping away a tear.

"I didn't grow up like you did, Daisy," he said. "I've seen those pictures hanging on the wall in your apartment. The ones of you building a snowman, or eating an ice cream cone—"

"My childhood wasn't perfect—" she started to object.

"I'm not saying it was perfect. But someone . . . someone brought you up, Daisy. Someone taught you things. They took those pictures of you, and then they went to the trouble to buy frames for them and to hang them on the wall. Just like they went to the trouble to help you with your homework, and, later, to go to all those volleyball games you played in."

He blew out a long breath and glanced out the window of the truck, and then he looked back at her. "Look, I'm not feeling sorry for myself. And I'm not excusing what I did. What I'm trying to say is that I've been on my own, pretty much, for my whole life. My mom took off, and my dad . . . my dad's not a nice guy, Daisy. You'll just have to take my word for it . . ."

Daisy almost pressed him here for more information, but Will, she knew, didn't like to talk about his father.

"Anyway," he said, "except for the time I spent

with Jason's family, I was on my own. I just kind of . . . raised myself; you know, figured things out as I went along. Obviously, I wasn't very good at it. I made a lot of mistakes—and I'm still making them. But the difference now, the difference since you walked into the garage that morning, is that I *care* that I'm making them. You *make* me care, Daisy; you make me want to be a better person."

"Oh, Will," Daisy said softly, shaking her head. She felt an urge then to bury herself in his arms, and to forget about all this. But she wasn't ready to. Besides, her head ached, and the smell of the beer that Christy had thrown on Will was making her feel queasy.

"I've got to go," she said, reaching for the door handle. "I need to think."

Will nodded grimly, and this time, he didn't try to stop her.

Chapter 16

"Are you sure that roof is going to hold?" Walt asked doubtfully, looking up at the cabin's rafters.

"I hope so," Jack said, following his gaze up. "Depends on how long it rains for. But I think I did a pretty decent patch job," he added, in a slightly louder voice, so he'd be heard over the steady drumming of the rain on the roof. It was early morning, and Jack and Walt were sitting in Jack's living room at a table Jack had salvaged from a yard sale, drinking the instant coffee Jack had made on a hot plate. His entertaining skills, already somewhat limited, were now additionally hampered by the fact that he'd torn out the cabin's kitchen the week before. He'd already ordered new flooring, new cabinets, and new appliances, but until they came in some time next week, instant coffee and canned soup were his featured menu items.

"Jeez, it's really coming down," Walt said, looking out the window to where the rain was blowing in gusts across the lake. Jack agreed and started to lift his coffee cup to his lips, but he remembered then how awful the coffee inside it was and lowered it back down without taking a sip. He was thinking about trying to make a better cup of it when he realized Walt had asked him a question.

"I'm sorry, Walt. What did you say?"

"I said, did you sleep at all last night?" Walt repeated.

"Not really," Jack admitted. "I had that dream again. You know, the one I told you about."

"You told me about it," Walt said, nodding, his white handlebar mustache nodding with him. "And I told you then what I'm going to tell you now, Jack. I'm not qualified to analyze anyone's dreams. I'm not a psychiatrist. I'm just an old man who's willing to drag his sorry ass out of bed early in the morning, and drive out here, in the pouring rain, so that you can ignore me."

Jack laughed. The man had a point. He *had* been ignoring him. Still, Walt was wrong about the other thing, about needing to be a psychiatrist to analyze Jack's dream. It was the same dream he always had about Caroline, the one where she was waiting for him, in her nightgown, in her bed, and Jack was fairly certain that any fool could have figured out what it meant.

"Jack, I don't like it," Walt said now, shaking his head.

"You don't like the dream?"

"No, not the dream. The whole setup, Jack."

"What setup?"

"*Your* setup. Here, in Butternut."

"What's wrong with my setup? I have a goal, don't I? I'm fixing up this cabin."

"It's not *that* goal I'm concerned about; it's the other one. And don't act like you don't know what I'm talking about," he said when Jack feigned innocence. "I mean your goal of you and your ex-wife getting back together again."

"And what's wrong with that goal?" Jack asked, a little defensively.

Walt shrugged. "It's too . . . too open-ended, too far outside of your control. I mean, you're waiting for something to happen that might not happen. And if it doesn't happen . . ." His voice trailed off.

"If it doesn't happen, you're afraid I'll relapse."

"You're damned right I am," Walt said, scowling at him, and Jack was reminded of the fact that Walt had a reputation in Butternut for being ornery. Jack had never seen that side of him, though. He knew him as a tough, but patient sponsor, who would meet with anyone anytime of the day or night and listen to them for as long as they needed to talk. Caroline didn't like Walt much, he knew, but Jack figured he was lucky to have him in his life just the same.

Walt took another drink of coffee and said slowly, "You need to think about this, Jack. I know you want your ex-wife back. But what if she doesn't want you back?"

"She does want me back," Jack said. "She just doesn't know it yet."

"So you've said. But what if you're wrong, Jack? Have you ever stopped to consider that?"

"No," Jack said. *Yes.* But never for too long. It was too depressing.

"Well, maybe you should consider it then."

"I can't. Not yet. But whatever happens with Caroline, Walt, I won't start drinking again," Jack said, meeting his look head-on. "I can't go back there. I owe it to her, and to Daisy, to stay sober. And you know what, Walt? I owe it to myself, too. I mean, I'm not going to lie. I got sober for Caroline and Daisy, but I'm going to stay sober for myself."

"All right," Walt said, looking mildly placated. "But I want to see you at at least three meetings this week, Jack."

"Three minimum," Jack agreed, with a tired smile.

Walt nodded, satisfied, and took another swallow of his coffee. Then he grimaced. "My God," he said, "this stuff is awful. But you know who makes a good cup of coffee, Jack?"

"Who?"

"Your ex-wife. Best cup of coffee I've ever had."

Jack frowned. "But she says whenever you come in to Pearl's you complain about her coffee."

"Do I?" he said, amused. "Oh, I'm just giving her a hard time."

"Well, she doesn't like you," Jack said bluntly. "Neither do a lot of other people in town. They think you're mean, Walt."

"Do they?" Walt said. He looked pleased. "Well, that's fine by me."

"Why's that?"

Walt considered the question. "Well, because when people think you're mean, they have a tendency to leave you alone. And, for the most part, I like being left alone."

"But you're a sponsor."

"Well, I didn't say I wanted to be left alone *all* the time. Even I can't do without people entirely. But the thing is, I find most people annoying,

355

Jack. Recovering alcoholics, for some reason, I find *less* annoying."

Jack smiled. "Glad to hear it," he said. "But seriously, Walt, you're the best sponsor I've ever had."

"I don't know about that," Walt said gruffly. "But I do know that if you're waiting for me to give you a hug, it's not going to happen."

Jack laughed. "I won't hold my breath. But I am going to make another cup of really horrible coffee. What do you say?"

"I say you're quite the salesman." Walt chuckled, sliding his empty cup across the table to Jack.

"Damn it," Will said, slamming down the coffeepot. The coffee machine in the service station's office was broken, again, and Jason, as usual, was late for work, which meant there wasn't even anyone here for Will to complain to about it. He thought that was a shame, really, given what a foul mood he was in, and given how little sleep he'd gotten last night, and given how much he could really, *really* use a cup of coffee right about now.

"Damn it," he said again, fiddling with the settings on the unresponsive coffee machine. He yanked its plug out of the wall then, and he was just about to throw the whole thing into the garbage can when he heard a tapping on the office door. *That'll be Jason,* he thought, granting the coffee machine a temporary reprieve. Jason, who'd forgotten his keys again. But when he opened the door, he saw that it wasn't Jason. It was Daisy. Her mother's pickup was parked out front, the engine still running, and she was standing outside in the pouring rain, already soaking wet.

"Daisy," he said, pulling her inside and forgetting, for a moment, the ambiguous note she'd ended things on last night. "What are you doing here so early? And why are you standing out in the rain?"

"I needed to talk to you," she said simply.

"Okay, but let me get you a towel or something first," he said.

"No, don't," she said quickly. "I can't stay long. I left Jessica waitressing by herself."

"Well, in that case, we better hurry up and talk," Will said, trying to get a smile out of her. He didn't get one, but she let him take her by the hand and lead her farther into the office, so that was something, Will told himself.

"Have a seat," Will said, locking the door behind him and indicating one of the plastic chairs that were there for waiting customers.

But Daisy shook her head and leaned on the desk instead. He came over to her and tried to read the expression on her face. But it was unreadable. She looked tired, though, he saw with concern. Her wet strawberry-blond hair was bedraggled, and her blue eyes were shadowed with fatigue. He waited for her to say something, but she just wrapped her arms around herself and shivered a little shiver. This was going to be bad, he decided.

"I couldn't sleep last night," she said finally. "I mean, I couldn't sleep *at all*."

"Neither could I," Will said.

"But I did think, a lot, about you—about us. And do you know what I decided, Will?"

He shook his head.

"I decided that if you meant what you said about *wanting* to be a better person, then that's good enough for me. The *wanting* part. Because I think if that's the case, then the *being* part can't be far behind. Besides," she added, with a little sigh, "I'm not perfect either. I'm not even close to perfect."

"You're pretty close," he said, feeling the first tiny wave of relief start to break over him.

"No, I'm not," Daisy said. "If I were," she went on, her voice dropping, "I wouldn't . . . I wouldn't sort of hate Christy right now."

"Do you sort of hate me, too?"

"A little," she nodded, her eyes dropping to the floor.

He laughed. "Oh, Daisy," he said, pulling her into his arms. He held her tightly, and she held him back, and Will let himself feel, for the first time since Christy had stopped by their table last night, how afraid he'd been of losing her.

"I'm sorry," he said, tightening his grip on her. "I should have told you, right from the start. I should have told you that day I came into Pearl's and asked you out again."

"Actually, it's probably a good thing you didn't," Daisy said, pulling far enough away from him to look up at him. "That might have been a deal breaker for me," she added, with the ghost of a smile.

But Will was serious. "Daisy, look, I'm not defending Christy," he said, looking down at her and brushing a damp strand of hair off her cheek, "any more than I'm defending myself. But what happened between us wasn't her fault. It was *both* of our faults. I went into it with my eyes open. If I could go back, I'd do it differently. I wouldn't do it at all. And you know what else I'd do differently? I would have gone out with you in high school. Assuming, of course, that you would have gone out with me."

"Will, you barely knew me in high school," she said, shaking her head, and he thought about telling her about all the volleyball games he'd watched, but he kissed her instead, until something else occurred to him.

"Daisy," he said, stopping. "Do you want me to tell Mr. Phipps we don't need his cabin this weekend? Because we can wait. We can wait for as long as you need to wait."

"Oh no," she said, "we're going."

"You sure?"

"I'm sure," she said emphatically. "Because I can't live this way anymore."

"What way?"

She blushed and looked down. "Will, I think about us being together *all* the time—every waking minute, and some nonwaking minutes, too. It's exhausting. This thing . . . it needs to happen. The sooner the better. Maybe then I can think about something else occasionally." She looked back up at him, and for a second she looked so genuinely desperate that he almost laughed. But he stopped himself, because while he might think it was funny, she obviously didn't.

So he held her again, tightly, and she held him back, her wet clothes seeping into his dry clothes, and they stayed that way for a long time, until Will felt something in her give way. It was almost as if a tiny spring inside of her had been released. She let out a small, jagged sigh then and relaxed into him, and he knew something had changed between them. He knew she had let go of the last little piece of herself she had been keeping from him, protecting from him. She was in this now, with him, all the way, and it scared him, a little, to have that much responsibility for someone else. But because she was Daisy, he figured it would have scared him even more not to have it.

Chapter 17

"You're so quiet today," Will said, taking his eyes off the road long enough to look at Daisy. It was Saturday evening, and they were in his pickup, driving out to Mr. Phipps's cabin.

Daisy shrugged. "I'm just . . . enjoying the drive," she said, smiling at him, and he smiled back. But the truth was, she was nervous. No, she wasn't nervous, she was *beyond* nervous. She was more nervous now than she'd ever been in her entire life, and she'd been plenty nervous before in her twenty-one years on earth: nervous about standardized tests, nervous about championship volleyball games, nervous about college exams. But that kind of nervousness, she now understood, came under the heading of garden-variety nervousness. This nervousness was something different. This nervousness was in a league of its own. She stole a sideways glance at Will, wondering if he'd noticed it, but he was concentrating now on the notoriously twisty stretch of road that followed the contours of Butternut Lake.

"Not too much farther now," he said a few minutes later, and Daisy nodded. This was the problem with waiting so long to lose your virginity, she decided, watching the pine and birch trees slide by outside. The longer you waited, the bigger a deal it became, until now, at twenty-one, it was so big a deal that Daisy was a complete and total wreck. If she ever had a daughter, she decided, she would tell her not to wait; she would tell her to hurry up and get it over with, with the first remotely acceptable candidate. But then she smiled. Because what were the chances, really, of any mother urging her daughter to treat her virginity like some unwanted piece of baggage, to be gotten rid of at the earliest possible opportunity?

"You're smiling," Will said, sounding pleased as he looked at her again.

Daisy nodded.

"That's good," he said. "I like it when you smile." He took his hand off the wheel and reached over and took her hand, pulling it to him. Then, turning it palm up, he held it up to his mouth and kissed it gently. *Like a promise,* Daisy thought. And this simple gesture left her pinned weakly to her seat, almost overwhelmed by her need for him, because this desire was the flip side to her nervousness. This desire was beating through her veins and thrumming in her ears. There was nothing now, she knew, that would assuage it except what would happen between them tonight.

A moment later, Will needed two hands to drive,

so he put her hand back in her lap, and Daisy examined her palm, almost as if she'd expected his kiss to leave a mark on it. But there was nothing there, so she tucked her hand, which was feeling a little shaky, firmly beneath her thigh and looked out the window again.

Calm down, she told herself. *You're ready for this. You both are.* She'd been to see Dr. Novack, her family doctor, last week and had listened to his lecture about safe sex. It had been a little awkward, coming from the man who used to give her grape lollipops after she'd gotten her childhood vaccines, but Daisy had left his office with the desired prescription, and she'd taken it straight over to Butternut Drugs to be filled. And earlier in the week, Will had driven over to Ely, to a clinic there, to be tested for . . . well, for everything, she supposed. She didn't know all the details. But she did know that everything had been fine.

"Oh, by the way," Will said now. "I bought some groceries for dinner tonight." He indicated a cardboard box on the back seat of the pickup. "Nothing complicated, just stuff for spaghetti and a salad."

"That sounds great," she said, but she didn't think she'd be able to eat tonight. The only thing she'd been able to eat all day, in fact, was half a piece of toast for breakfast, and even that had been a challenge.

They lapsed into silence then. But a few

minutes later, Will said, "Here it is," and he slowed the truck and turned down a gravel driveway. He followed it a quarter of a mile through dense forest and then stopped in front of a large, A-frame cabin. Beyond the cabin was Butternut Lake, dusky blue in the evening light. As they got out of the truck, they were both struck, simultaneously, by the sense of isolation and quiet.

"Wow, he wasn't kidding when he said it was private," Will said, taking the groceries out of the back seat. "He said his cabin's the only one in this bay. The rest of the land is National Forest." Daisy nodded, swinging her backpack over her shoulder, and following Will up to the cabin's front door on unsteady legs. Will took out a key, fumbled with the lock, and pushed the door open.

"I'll turn some lights on," he said, moving through the shadowy front room, snapping on the floor lamps and the table lamps, and Daisy saw with relief that the cabin was rustic but also comfortable, its living room filled with thick rugs, deep couches, and a big fireplace.

"It's a little chilly," Will said apologetically. "Maybe we can start a fire before dinner."

"That'd be nice," Daisy said, looking around and wondering if she and Will would make love in front of the fireplace; then she blushed at the thought of being completely naked in front of him. No, they wouldn't make love in front of the fireplace, she decided. They'd make love in a real bed, with a full complement of sheets and blankets for her to hide underneath.

"We should probably get this stuff in the fridge," Will said, indicating the groceries he was holding, and he headed for the kitchen.

"Here, let me do that," Daisy said when Will put the box down on the counter. She wanted to have something other than her nervousness to concentrate on. But when she started taking things out of the box, Will came up behind her and put his arms around her waist. She dropped the head of lettuce she was holding onto the counter and shivered as he brushed her hair off her neck and grazed her skin with his lips.

"You know, Daisy," he said, his breath soft against her ear. "It's not too late to change your mind. We don't have to do this. We can just have dinner and hang out. I saw some board games on the shelves by the fireplace."

Daisy smiled, but his lips were nuzzling her neck now, making it hard for her to think clearly. "I don't know, Will. It's a long way to come for a game of Monopoly," she said. "I don't even get cell-phone coverage out here."

His arms tightened around her waist, and he started kissing her neck in earnest, and Daisy felt a warm, slow, liquid sensation slide through her whole body, temporarily overshadowing her nervousness. God, she loved the way he kissed her, loved the way he touched her. And suddenly, she was glad that he had so much more experience than she did, glad that at least one of them would know what they were doing tonight. *Oh, he'll know what he's doing all right,* a little voice inside her said, and an image of Christy, in her tight-fitting dress and high-heeled sandals, came into her mind. But she forced it right back out again. Will wasn't with Christy now. He could have been, presumably, if he'd wanted to be. But he didn't want to be. He wanted to be with Daisy. She flushed with pleasure, just thinking about it, and, twisting out of his arms, she turned to face him and kissed him on the lips.

But when Will started kissing her back, her shyness returned. Why couldn't she be brave now, the way she'd been brave that night in his truck? The night they'd practically undressed each other. But she already knew the answer to that question. She couldn't be brave like that now because then there'd been a built-in safety valve. She'd known they weren't going to make love in a pickup truck parked on a public street. But now, now they had the whole cabin to themselves; hell, it felt as if they had all of *northern Minnesota* to themselves. There was no one, and nothing, to stop them.

She felt Will's kiss changing now, getting deeper, harder, and she felt herself responding, sliding her arms around his neck, anchoring her body against his. In one fluid motion, without ever breaking his kiss, he put his hands around her waist and lifted her onto the kitchen counter. She wrapped her legs around his waist and pulled him closer to her.

"Oh, Daisy," he murmured through their kiss, and his hands moved to the front of her blouse, which he started to unbutton with great care and tenderness. Daisy felt herself tense up a little. Were they really going to do this now? She'd thought, somehow, there'd be something more leading up to it. Dinner, or talking, or cuddling on the couch . . . But then she realized that Will had been waiting for this all summer. And so had she, in her own way.

He finished unbuttoning her buttons, and then he stopped kissing her and looked down at the bra peeking out of her open blouse. Daisy squirmed a little, feeling newly self-conscious in the brightly lit kitchen.

But Will smiled and murmured appreciatively, "You wore it." She had on the same shimmery, lilac-colored bra she'd worn that night in his pickup.

"I did wear it," she said, and then she laughed. "I swear, Will," she said, "you look like a kid on Christmas morning."

"I *feel* like a kid on Christmas morning," he said, kissing her again. "I'm just wondering, though, is your bra, is it . . . you know, part of a set?"

Smart boy, she thought. But she didn't want to spoil the surprise for him, so instead she smiled and said, with a little surge of bravery, "Why don't you take me to the bed and find out?"

When Will woke up the next morning, Daisy was asleep in his arms, her head resting on his chest, her breath tickling his bare skin. He lay there for a moment, getting his bearings, and then he gently disentangled himself from her and slid out of bed. He winced as his bare feet touched the cabin's cold floor, and he almost got back into bed to take refuge against Daisy's warm body. But he didn't.

He didn't because he knew if he did, he'd wake her up. He knew, too, he needed to be alone right now; he needed to think. So he groped around on the floor for his blue jeans and pulled them on. Then he went into the kitchen, let himself out of the cabin's back door, and went down the steps that led to the lake. He paused there for a moment when he reached the dock, struck by the almost surreal beauty of the scene. The sun hadn't risen yet, but there was the faintest blush of pink in the eastern sky, while a cottony white mist hung over the gray, glasslike surface of the water.

He walked out to the end of the dock and sat down, dangling his feet over the side. He shivered a little as the chilly air bit into his bare chest. But it felt good, bracing. So he stayed where he was, enjoying the almost eerie quiet of the morning and thinking about what had happened the night before. They'd made love twice before going to sleep, and in spite of her nervousness that he would see her naked, and his that her first time wouldn't be perfect for her, it had still been everything he'd expected it to be. Then sometime during the night, Daisy woke him up.

"What is it?" he asked, reaching for her. He was surprised to discover how much the temperature had dropped. "Are you cold, Daisy?" he asked. "Do you want me to get another blanket?"

"No," she said, coming into his arms. "I'm not cold, Will. I want you. Again. *Now.*"

"Oh, Daisy," he groaned, indescribably aroused by her words, and by her naked, pliant body beside his. "I want you, too."

"Hurry," she said. And he'd entered her, immediately, amazed by how ready she was for him. They'd started to make love with a new sense of urgency, and with a deep, raw need for each other that finally stripped away his nervousness and her self-consciousness and laid them both completely bare. Daisy moved with him, hesitantly at first, but then with increasing confidence, until her movements were perfectly synchronized with his. And Will held on to her as if he were holding on for his life, anchoring himself against her, bracing himself as they moved together, faster

369

and then slower and then faster again, in some rhythm they had both instinctively agreed on, until finally, she arched her back, and tilted her head back, and cried out into the darkness, and almost simultaneously, he buried his face in the softness at the hollow of her neck and said her name, or something close to her name, anyway.

Afterward, they didn't say anything; they didn't need to. Will held Daisy, stroking her back and waiting for her ragged breathing, and her pounding heart, to slow down. When they did, when she sighed a deep, contented sigh and drifted off to sleep, her hair tumbling across his chest, Will lay there in the dark and felt more alive than he'd ever felt before. And in that moment he realized that what he and Daisy had done was make love. Now, for the first time, he knew the difference between having sex and making love. It had almost made him laugh, too, because when it came to making love, it turned out that he'd been as much of a virgin as Daisy had been.

Now, sitting on the dock, he wondered if it was possible that all those years ago, when he'd watched Daisy play volleyball, he'd known that no matter how different the two of them might seem to be separately, together they would fit together perfectly.

But an unsettling thought intruded now: he and Daisy were going to be separated from each other soon. He'd always known she'd be leaving to go back to college, but now he knew *he* would be leaving, too. He couldn't imagine, though, what it would be like for the two of them to be apart. *Far apart.* He needed to talk to her about it, but he just hadn't found the right moment. Still, he couldn't keep putting it off . . .

"Will?"

He turned around in time to see her coming down the dock, wrapped, towel style, in a bedsheet, a bemused expression on her face.

"What are you doing out here?" she asked, coming to stand beside him.

"I didn't want to wake you up," he said, reaching for her hand.

"I wouldn't have minded," she said, with a shy smile, gathering the sheet around her and sitting down beside him on the dock.

"I'll remember that next time," Will said, leaning over and kissing her gently on the lips. And then he pulled away from her and studied her thoughtfully.

"Are you blushing, Daisy?" he asked.

"Maybe a little," she said, blushing even more deeply.

"Why?"

"I was thinking about last night," she admitted. "I mean, the middle-of-the-night part of last night."

He smiled. "That was pretty amazing, wasn't it?" he said.

"I thought so," she said softly, looking down at the water as she dipped her pretty toes tentatively into it.

He studied her face again, then asked, "Do you always look so pretty in the morning?"

"Well, I've never thought so," she said, smiling. "But I've never had a night like last night before, so maybe I look different this morning."

He smiled back at her and ran a hand through her tousled strawberry-blond hair. Then he lowered her down onto the dock and lay down beside her.

She smiled and, turning on her side to face him, propped herself up on her elbow. "You know, Will," she said, "we don't have to leave for a couple more hours."

"I know," he said, playing with her hair again. "I was thinking we could play one of those board games now. Monopoly, maybe. Or Clue."

Daisy suppressed a smile. "Is that what you want to do, Will?"

"Absolutely," he said.

"Because I was thinking maybe we could do something else," she said, and with that, she peeled open the sheet and flung it onto the dock beside her. Will swallowed, hard, letting his eyes travel over her. "You are so beautiful," he breathed, unable to take his eyes away from her, and in that instant, he wanted her so badly he felt almost paralyzed by desire.

"You know, Will, you can touch me if you want to," she said, smiling mischievously.

He shook his head. "I can't," he said, still not taking his eyes off her.

She laughed. "Need a little help?"

He nodded.

She took his hand in hers and drew it to her body, then used his index finger to trace a line that ran down her buttermilk smooth skin, from the hollow at the bottom of her neck to her navel. But then she shivered violently and, dropping his hand, wriggled so that she was against him, her bare breasts pressing against his bare chest. Will moaned and wrapped his arms around her, pulling her into him and digging his body into her body. She wrapped the sheet around both of them then, closing them together inside of its cotton folds. And when Will bent to kiss her, and she opened her mouth to his, she tasted as sweet as the morning air.

"Daisy, are you feeling all right?" Will asked, looking over at her as they drove back to Butternut later that morning.

"I'm fine. Why?"

"You look . . . you look kind of flushed," he said, glancing over at her again.

"I'm a little warm," she lied, opening her window.

"Do you want me to turn on the air-conditioning?"

She shook her head. "No, the fresh air's nice." But Will still looked worried. So she smiled what she hoped was a reassuring smile and turned to look out the window, so he couldn't see her face anymore. She'd been trying, all morning, to ignore how much pain she was in, but she couldn't ignore it anymore. So now, she'd settled for trying to hide it from him instead.

It had started several hours ago. After she and Will had come up from the dock, they'd gone back to bed and made love again. Twice. Afterward, Will had fallen asleep, and Daisy, tired but too full of the blissful sensations of their love-making to sleep herself, had watched Will sleep instead. It had never occurred to her before that watching someone sleep could be interesting. But watching Will sleep was; in fact, watching Will sleep was fascinating. She could have done it all day. She loved the way his dark eyelashes looked against his suntanned skin, the way his bare chest rose and fell to the rhythm of his breathing, and the way his mouth, which had so recently been kissing her mouth, managed to look both sensual and masculine at the same time.

Thinking about that, she'd put out an explora-tory hand and skimmed it, lightly, down his bare chest. He'd stirred, but he hadn't woken up. So she'd let him sleep, partly because she figured he'd earned it, and partly because it was about that time that she began to feel a dull, aching sensation, right around her navel. She paid no attention to it at first. But as the minutes ticked by, the pain migrated down, and to the right, and sharpened, so that by the time Will woke up a few hours later, with the morning sun streaming in through the cabin's windows, the pain had progressed from mildly annoying to just plain worrying.

But she hadn't told Will about it. She hadn't wanted to spoil his good mood. And he was in *such* a good mood. The moment he woke up, he reached for her, nuzzling her and kissing her, and Daisy had known he'd wanted to make love again, but she was in too much pain by then, so she'd reminded him that they needed to be getting back. Still, his good mood persisted, and as they showered, had breakfast, and tidied up the cabin, he was affectionate and sweet, teasing and touching her at every opportunity. Were all men in this good of a mood after sex? Daisy had wondered. But then it occurred to her that she would have been in a good mood too if she hadn't otherwise been so miserable.

Now, sitting in the passenger seat of his truck, she stole a look at him. He was smiling, and humming along to the radio, something she'd never heard him do before.

"We'll be back soon," he said when he noticed her watching him, and he reached over and put a hand on her knee. "You sure you're feeling all right?" he asked again.

375

"I'm sure. I'm just . . . I'm just tired," she said. "Tired in a good way," she added quickly.

"Are you going to be able to get some rest today?" he asked, concerned

"I think so," she said, forcing another smile.

"Good," he said, giving her knee a final squeeze before he took his hand away, and Daisy found that even through her pain, she missed his touch, missed the warmth of his hand through the fabric of her blue jeans. She shifted around a little then, trying to find a more comfortable position, but she couldn't. Nothing felt right; *she* didn't feel right. She almost told Will then about how she felt, but he started humming along to a song on the radio again and she found that she couldn't.

So she gritted her teeth and tried, somehow, to tolerate the pain, the pain that was getting harder to manage with each passing minute.

What is wrong with me, she wondered, tamping down a rising sense of panic and trying to evaluate the situation calmly. *I probably just have the flu,* she told herself. *As soon as I get home, I'll crawl into bed and stay there for a couple of days. And I'll be fine.* But it didn't really feel like the flu. *So maybe I have food poisoning,* she reasoned. *I've had that before. It's no big deal. It's inconvenient, but not fatal.* There was a problem with the food poisoning theory though. She and Will had both had the same dinner last night, and Will was fine. Better than fine, she decided, stealing another sideways glance at him. He was positively exuding good health.

So Daisy considered the possibility that something else was wrong with her, something having to do with, well . . . with all the sex they'd had: twice before they'd gone to sleep last night, once during the night, and twice this morning. She hadn't even known it was *possible* to have that much sex in so little time. She'd assumed that men at least had some kind of inherent limitation built in to how often they could make love. But that wasn't true, obviously, because Will seemed to have an inexhaustible supply of sexual stamina. Or maybe, she thought, Will wasn't like most men; maybe he was superior in this way. And thinking about the way he'd touched her, the way his hands and his mouth had traveled over her body, it was almost possible to believe this was true.

But still, she kept coming back to this question. Was it possible to have too much sex? And, if so, was that what was causing the pain she felt now? But she decided, finally, that it wasn't, that it couldn't be. After all, Daisy hadn't just paid attention in sex education class, she'd taken notes. And what was it one of her college professors had said in a biology class? He'd said the human body was designed for sex. In her and Will's case, obviously, lots and lots and lots of sex. So whatever was wrong with her, then, was something else—

something that was getting scarier by the minute.

She felt a wave of nausea roll over her, *steam-roll* over her, really, so that for one appalling second she was afraid she was going to throw up right onto the floor of Will's truck. But the moment passed, and the nausea eased, though as it receded her scalp prickled with perspiration, and a dizziness descended over her. She put a hand out, reflexively, to brace herself against the truck's door.

"Daisy, seriously, what's wrong?" Will asked, but they were driving into town now, and she knew she could hold it together a little bit longer. Still, she had to tell him something, because if she looked as bad as she felt, she must look pretty awful.

"I think I'm coming down with something," she said, glancing over at him. "I'm going to go straight to bed. But I'll call you as soon as I wake up, okay?"

"All right," he said, pulling into his usual parking place a block away from Pearl's. "But let me walk you to your apartment."

She shook her head. "No, you better not. My mom still thinks I spent the night at Jessica's, remember? I'll call you later. I promise."

He nodded worriedly and started to reach for her, but Daisy pulled away. She knew she had a fever, and she didn't want him to feel how warm she was.

"I'll call you later," she said, grabbing her backpack, sliding out of the truck, and slamming the door behind her. Then she walked, at what she hoped was a normal speed, down the block. The pain was worse now, and she wanted to stop, or sit down, but she kept going. If Will was watching her, she didn't want him to be any more worried about her than he already was.

When she got to her building, she bypassed the door to her apartment and went straight to the door to the coffee shop. She'd ask Frankie to make her something to eat, she decided. She'd only pretended to eat something at breakfast with Will that morning. But now she would try to have a cup of tea, or some toast, or anything that might make her feel better.

But as she pushed open the door to Pearl's and walked inside, her stomach lurched, violently, and she changed her mind about eating. Instead, she tried to shut out the sounds of the coffee shop—the drone of voices, and the clink of dishes —both of which seemed somehow too loud this morning. She tried, instead, to focus on Frankie's massive form, rising up from beyond the counter. He was working the grill, and standing beside him, and talking to him, and looking worried was Jessica. *Jessica?* What was she doing here? She was supposed to have today off, and Daisy was supposed to be with her right now, having spent the night at her house.

"Daisy," Jessica said, catching sight of her. "You're back."

"I'm back," Daisy agreed, coming around slowly to the other side of the counter.

"Didn't you get any of my messages?" Jessica asked, looking agitated. "I left you seven voice mails."

Daisy shook her head. "No, I turned my phone off. I didn't get service out there."

"Well, your mom called my house last night," Jessica said, her lower lip trembling, something Daisy knew it did when she was upset. "I was out. But my mom told her you weren't spending the night at our house. I'm sorry, Daisy. I didn't want you to get into trouble."

"Jessica, it's fine, really," Daisy said, feeling dizzy again. "It's not your fault. It's mine; I should have told my mom the truth to begin with."

"I know. But, Daisy? She's really mad," Jessica said. "She called me this morning and asked if I could come in and help out, and when I got here, your dad was here, too. Your mom *asked* him to come, Daisy. He's upstairs with her right now."

Wow, her mom *was* mad, Daisy thought, mad enough to invite her dad over. But then Daisy reminded herself, for the hundredth time, that she was an adult now, and she didn't have to ask her mother's permission to do anything anymore. She was free to come and go as she pleased. But the pain in her side was taking up so much of her energy that she didn't have enough left over to work up any real sense of injustice over the situation.

"Daisy, what's the matter?" Jessica asked then, and even Frankie paused in his pancake flipping long enough to study her.

"You don't look so hot," he said, frowning.

"I'm fine," she said, a feverish chill racking her body.

"Well, why don't you sit down at the counter and I'll get a glass of ice water," he suggested, going to pour one.

But she shook her head. "No, I want to get this over with," she said, heading for the coffee shop's back door. She went through it, walked down the back hallway, and climbed up the stairs to the apartment, counting each one as she went as a way to counteract her dizziness. When she got to the top of them, she took out her keys, unlocked the front door, and walked, a little unsteadily, into the kitchen. Her parents were both there, sitting at the kitchen table, drinking coffee, just as she'd known they would be.

Her mother saw her first, and after relief flitted briefly across her face, her jaw set in a hard line of disapproval, disapproval and disappointment. Her father looked up too, but his expression was different. He gave Daisy a half smile, and an apologetic little shrug, as if to say *sorry about all the fuss.*

Daisy tried to smile back at him, tried to let him know how glad she was he was there, but the pain in her side tore at her again.

"Daisy?" her mother said, alarmed, standing up and moving toward her.

And Daisy's last feeling, before she fainted, was one of relief—because she knew the conversation she and her mother were going to have to have had just been postponed.

Chapter 18

After Will dropped Daisy off at Pearl's he drove around for a while, at loose ends. He was worried about her. On the drive home, and even before that, she'd been so quiet, so tense. And so . . . so flushed, each of her pale cheeks stained with a single feverish red splotch. Should he drive back to her apartment and check on her? But no, she'd said she was going to go straight to bed. If he went over now, he'd only wake her up. He'd call her later, he decided, after she'd had time to take a nap.

But he didn't drive back to his apartment yet, maybe because he couldn't stand the thought of being there now, in that depressing little space, after his euphoric night with Daisy.

So he drove back out to Butternut Lake, with no

real aim in mind but to pass the time. Once he'd gotten to the beach, though, where he and Daisy had gone that first night, and where picnickers and swimmers were now out in full force, he realized something. There was a place he needed to go, and a person he needed to see. It wouldn't be easy right now, especially so soon after being with Daisy, but it wasn't going to get any easier if he waited. It might even get harder. So with a feeling of resignation that bordered on fatalism, he turned his pickup around in the beach parking lot, and, taking one of the back roads that crisscrossed the area, he headed out to his dad's house.

When he got there, he parked his truck on the road—his dad had blocked his driveway by stringing a barbed-wire fence across it—and got out and started walking. He followed the fence into the woods, until he found a break in it. Then, being careful not to snag his clothes on the barbed wire, he slipped through it and worked his way back to the overgrown driveway. He walked down it for a quarter of a mile, passing several Private Property, Keep Out, and No Trespassing signs that his father had tacked to tree trunks.

When he rounded the final bend in the driveway, and the house came into view, Will felt the corners of his mouth twitch up in grim humor. His father's obsession with his privacy was totally unwarranted, he thought, looking at his unkempt front yard and decrepit house. Because the truth was, no one in his or her right mind would ever *willingly* come to this place, which begged the question, really, of what Will was doing here now.

He made his way up the barely visible path to the house's front door, stepping over the rusted-out car parts that were scattered around the yard. Will didn't know whom he'd gotten his affinity for car engines from, but it hadn't been his father. He'd always been a lousy mechanic.

Will climbed gingerly up onto the sagging front porch, testing it for stability. It held under his weight, but just barely. When he reached the screen door, he rapped loudly on its frame and called inside.

"Dad? Are you home? It's me, Will."

Silence. Will listened carefully. He heard the faint hum of talk radio, then footsteps from another room and an angry, incomprehensible mutter.

Will's body stiffened, and he almost, *almost,* left. But he didn't. *Suck it up, Will,* he told himself. *You knew you wouldn't get a warm reception. And you're not here for one either. You're here to say good-bye. So hurry up and get it over with.*

"Dad, I'll just be here for a minute, okay?" he called out. "I won't keep you long." He watched through the screen door as his father shuffled into view. He came over to the door and peered through it, but he didn't open it.

"What do you want?" he asked.

Will felt a flicker of anger, but he quickly smothered it. He needed to keep his cool. "I want to talk to you," he said.

"About what?" his father grumbled, still watching Will warily through the screen door.

"Dad, I haven't seen you in three years. Do I really need a reason to want to talk to you?"

Will heard his father sigh. "All right, come in," he said. He stepped aside and propped the screen door open, just wide enough for Will to angle himself inside the house.

He held his hand out then for his father to shake, but his father had already sidled away.

"I'm not really set up for guests here," he mumbled, gesturing around the small front room. *That's an understatement,* Will thought, looking around at the shabby, haphazard furnishings.

"That's all right," Will said, walking over to a rusty-looking lawn chair in the corner and sitting down on it carefully. His dad sat down—slumped down, really—on a nearby couch that had springs breaking through its threadbare slipcover.

"I'd offer you something to drink, but . . ." His father's voice trailed off. *But I don't want you to stay,* Will finished for him silently. He studied his father now. He'd been in his forties when Will was born, so he would be in his sixties now. He looked the same, more or less, as he had the last time Will had seen him. He was a little leaner, a little grayer, a little more grizzled, maybe, but basically unchanged. Now his father narrowed his blue eyes at Will—*mean eyes,* Jason had called them—and rasped uneasily, "What are you here for, Will? Spit it out."

But Will wasn't ready to tell him yet. Instead, he looked around the little front room, which, even on a summer day, had a chilliness and a mustiness about it that was hard to ignore. Will wondered what it was like in the dead of a northern Minnesota winter, and he barely repressed a shudder.

"Are you doing okay, Dad?" he asked. "Money-wise, I mean?"

"Why do you want to know?" his father asked, immediately suspicious.

"I just wondered if you had enough, you know, for groceries, your utility bill, stuff like that. I mean, you've got your heat on in the winter, don't you?"

"What's it to you?"

"I don't want you to freeze to death, Dad," Will said bluntly, his patience wearing thin.

"Nobody's freezing to death," his father said. "In fact, I'm doing just fine," he added, his chin jutting out with a pride that seemed a little misplaced, given his surroundings.

"That's . . . that's good, Dad. But if you needed money, you'd tell me, wouldn't you?"

"*You?* Why would I tell you if I needed money, Will?"

Will felt his jaw clench involuntarily. "So I could give it to you, Dad."

"Oh, I see. My son, the big-time mechanic, is making so much money now he has to give it away," his father said with a humorless laugh.

"That's not it," Will said, his patience slipping again. "But I've made enough money to put a little aside. And it's yours, if you need it."

"Well, I don't need it," his father snapped, his blue eyes suddenly blazing. "I don't need anything. But that doesn't seem to stop people from trying to give me something, does it? Last year, right around this time, someone came from some organization and wanted to know if I needed them to drop off lunch and dinner here every day. Like I was some old goat who couldn't even open a can of beans by himself," he said, disgustedly. "They said one of my neighbors— I'd like to know which one—told them I was a shut-in. I said, 'You're not a shut-in if you choose to be a shut-in.' And then I told them to get the hell off of my property and—"

"Yeah, okay, Dad," Will said, trying to cut him off. But his father wasn't done yet.

"Then, last fall, a nurse comes here. Said she's from the County Health Department. I had my doubts, though. She had some ID card, but it's not hard to make one of those yourself. Anyway, she says she's here to make 'a home visit.' Wants to do an exam and give me a flu shot. *A flu shot,* Will. I said, if you are still on this porch in ten seconds, I swear to God I will—"

"Okay, Dad, I get it. You don't need help," Will said, breaking in again. "I'm sorry I asked, all right? You're obviously managing fine on your own."

Will's father nodded, seemingly satisfied, and Will breathed a sigh of relief. He thought he'd succeeded in heading off his father before they'd gotten to his favorite topic, which was his hatred of everything and anything having to do with the government.

"Look, I came to say good-bye, Dad," Will said, cutting to the chase. "I'll be leaving soon."

"You left here the day you graduated from high school," his father pointed out.

"I don't mean 'here,'" Will said, gesturing around. "I mean this town. This state, actually." His father nodded but didn't say anything. Then, almost imperceptibly, his blue eyes narrowed.

"You in some kind of trouble, Will?" he asked.

"No," Will said, flinching. "That's not why I'm leaving."

"No trouble with the law?" his father asked challengingly.

"No, Dad," Will said, irritated. "That's not it."

"Hmmm," his father said, unconvinced. Then something else seemed to dawn on him. "You get a girl pregnant, Will?"

"No," Will said, exasperated. He almost told him about Daisy then, but he didn't. He didn't because he knew his father would never understand how he felt about her. He'd cheapen it somehow, make fun of it. And Will knew he wouldn't be able to stand it if he did. So instead he asked, "Why do you always have to assume the worst about me, Dad?"

"Why?" his father said, studying him coolly. "Well, maybe because that's what I've always gotten from you, Will. When you were in high school, I used to get a phone call from them every week at least. Once, I had to come in and meet with your counselor. Another time, it was with the principal. And it was always the same thing. You were cutting classes, smoking on school property, talking back to teachers. You were always in some kind of trouble."

Will only shrugged. "I didn't like high school, Dad," he said, trying to be patient. "You know that. But I've got another opportunity now."

"An opportunity?" his father repeated, immediately suspicious.

"Yes. I have a chance to . . . to do something better with my life. But I've got to leave here to do it, Dad."

Will waited for his dad to ask him more about

389

this, but he didn't. Instead, he asked, his eyes narrowing again, "You know who else left, Will?"

Will tensed. He knew.

"Your mother left," his father said. No, he didn't say it, really—he snarled it.

"I know that, Dad. That's not why I'm here. I don't want to talk about her. I came to say good-bye."

His father shrugged, looked away. "So say it."

Will felt anger flare up inside of him. "Forget it," he said, standing up. "I don't even know why I came here. It's not like I expected some kind of Hallmark moment from you, Dad. You know, like, 'Good luck, son.' Or 'I'm proud of you, son.' No, that's not your style, is it, Dad?"

"Sit down," his father barked, and Will, almost involuntarily, sat down.

"Now you listen to me, smart-ass," his father said, leaning forward on the couch. "You think you're so smart. You think you know so much. Well, you don't know *anything,* not one god-damned thing. You think it was easy? Raising a kid by myself? And your mother—*your* mother—leaving one night, in the middle of the night, and you, two, two-and-a-half years old, screaming your head off because she was gone." His blue eyes blazed.

Will felt his pulse quickening, and his adrenaline spiking. "You know what, Dad?" he said, louder than he'd intended. "I used to think about her leaving, too. I used to think 'what kind of mother would do that?' Leave a child alone with a man like you? But then I realized something." Will's anger was building, the blood thrumming at his temples. "I realized that she would have taken me with her if she could have. But she couldn't. She couldn't because she had to make a break for it. She had to get the hell out of here, and I would have just slowed her down. If she'd stayed here with me and you, Dad, she never would have made it. She would have just given up."

His dad started to say something, but Will kept talking, faster and louder, knowing he was losing control, and not really caring anymore. "You know what else I like to think, Dad? I like to think that wherever she is, or whatever she's doing, she's happy. And that she's had a good life, a good life with someone who cares about her."

His dad scowled at him. "Is that what you think, Will? Well, you know what? That's not what happened. You don't know anything. You're just like your mother," he muttered. "She was a loser, and so are you."

"I'm not a loser, Dad," Will said, an almost blind fury building in him. "But if I end up one, it'll be because you raised me. Maybe if you'd given me a little encouragement, Dad, or had a little faith in me, just a little, I would have gone to trade school, or college. Maybe I'd already be someone now, Dad. Maybe I wouldn't have to—"

"Get out," his father barked, standing up. "Get out right now."

"Don't worry, I'm going," Will said, getting to his feet and heading for the door. "I don't know why I came here anyway." He pushed open the screen door and walked across the front porch and down the front steps. He glanced back long enough to see that his father had come out onto the porch.

"Get off my property," he shouted after Will, his voice shaking with rage. "Get off it or I'll throw you off it."

Will kept walking, his breath coming faster now, as if he'd already been running, hard. He thought, for one wild moment, about picking something up—the rusted-out tire iron he'd just stepped over, maybe—and flinging it through one of the house's windows. But he didn't. He didn't because he knew that was exactly the kind of thing his father wanted him to do. So he just kept walking, just kept putting one foot in front of the other. "You're just like your mother," his father shouted again to Will's retreating back. "Do you hear me? Just like her. And don't you come back here again, either. I mean it. Don't you ever come back here!"

Will stumbled, once, as he rounded the bend in the driveway that took him out of sight of his father's house. He kept walking, almost blindly, aware that his father was still shouting after him, but unaware of what the words he was shouting were. And the next thing Will knew, he was back on the road again, back at his truck. He didn't remember getting there, but a deep scratch on his arm and a rip in his jeans told him he hadn't stopped to find the opening in the barbed-wire fence. He'd just gone right through it. He leaned over his truck, his elbows resting on its hood, his head down. He stayed that way for a long time, his heart pounding, his chest heaving, his stomach churning. He felt as if he was reeling from a punch—a hard punch—to the gut. He wondered now, not for the first time, if a punch to the gut would have been preferable to listening to his father's words. He knew everyone who'd ever met his father—Jason, Jason's parents, his high school counselor—had assumed that he beat Will. But he never had. Physical violence wasn't his father's style. Not once, when Will was growing up, had he so much as raised a hand against him. No, he'd preferred words. He hadn't been as bad when Will was a little kid, though he hadn't exactly been affectionate, either; he'd always been quick with a hard word and slow with a kind one. But he'd gotten worse over the years, and by the time Will was in high school, the man had gotten so bitter and mean that Will had learned to avoid him whenever possible.

Now, draped over the hood of his pickup, Will

tried, and failed, to draw in a lungful of air. He felt as if he was drowning, drowning on dry land, and for a second he almost panicked. But he thought about Daisy then, and he felt his panic recede a little. So he thought about her some more, starting with all the little things he liked about her, like the way her strawberry-blond hair always worked itself loose from her ponytail and then brushed softly against her creamy white cheeks; and the way she always looked a little surprised, just for a second, right before she laughed; and the way her head rested perfectly on his shoulder when they slow danced, as if her body had somehow been designed specifically to fit together with his.

He sucked in a little welcoming breath and felt his heart rate slow a little. He thought then about the bigger things about Daisy, about how she made him want more. Not more money or more things, just *more*—more of her, more of her love, more of the world she already lived in. It was a world so different from the one he'd grown up in. Hers was a world where people were, by and large, kind to each other. People made plans and had dreams in that world. And there, even when life wasn't perfect, people found ways to be happy.

He drew in a deeper breath now and realized his heart was beating almost normally. God, she believed in him, he thought, believed in him more than he believed in himself. And maybe that was enough for now, having Daisy believe in him.

Maybe the rest of it would come later, and he'd become the person who didn't just need Daisy, but deserved Daisy. He'd thought a lot about that lately, about how to change his life, change it in a way that would make a future with her possible. His trip to Duluth several weeks ago had been a first step in that direction. Unfortunately, it was a direction that would take him away from her, at least in the short run. But in the long run, he hoped, it would mean they could be together.

He pushed himself up from the hood of his truck and looked at his watch. It was later than he'd realized, he saw with surprise, and he wondered how long he'd been standing there trying to catch his breath. He needed to go; he needed to see Daisy. He slid his cell phone out of his pocket and checked to see if there were any texts from her. Nothing. He called her now, but she didn't pick up. He didn't leave a message, though. He didn't trust his voice to sound normal yet. He'd go back to his apartment, he decided, and do something about his arm, which by now was bleeding a lot. Then, if he didn't hear from her by this evening, he'd drive over to see her. He wouldn't tell her, yet, about his going away. That could wait, at least for one more day.

So he walked slowly, as if testing his legs, over to the driver's-side door and got into the truck. He started the engine and pulled out onto the road. And he never looked back.

Chapter 19

"Caroline, for God's sake, calm down. You're shaking all over," Jack said, sitting next to his ex-wife on a couch in the visitors' lounge at the hospital.

"*Calm down?* Are you serious, Jack? Daisy almost died, and I'm supposed to calm down?"

"She did not almost die," Jack corrected her gently. "The doctor said——"

"Oh, the doctor. *The doctor,*" she said, rolling her eyes. "What does he know?"

"Well, he just operated on our daughter, so I hope he knows *something,*" Jack said mildly.

But Caroline wasn't listening. "And that boy, Will. Wait until I get my hands on him. This is all his fault, I know it is."

"Because he gave her appendicitis?" he asked, raising an eyebrow.

"Because he must have known something was wrong with her. And after keeping her out all night, God knows where, he just dumped her on our doorstep, like a newspaper, and——"

"Caroline, that's not fair."

But she ignored him. "That's it," she said, getting up and pacing back and forth in the little room. "I have put up with that relationship all summer. I've looked the other way, while Daisy's walked around in a complete daze every day, going out to some dive bar every night. But when Daisy comes home from the hospital, I'm going to tell her *exactly* what I think about Will."

"She already knows what you think about him."

"Well, I'm going to tell her again. Less politely this time."

Jack sighed and ran his fingers through his hair. "Caroline, you can tell her whatever you want to, but if you think it's going to stop her from seeing him, you might be disappointed. She wants your approval, but she doesn't need it anymore. And I think that's as it should be, don't you?" he added, carefully. "I mean, she is an adult now."

Caroline stopped pacing and stood in front of him, hands on her hips. "There you go again, Jack," she said, glaring at him. "Taking her side. And *his* side, too."

"I'm not taking anybody's side." He shrugged. "But we don't know the whole story yet, do we? Maybe he didn't know there was anything wrong with her, Caroline. Or maybe he did, but assumed that whatever it was, it wasn't serious. The doctor said a lot of people with appendicitis mistake it for indigestion at first."

"Humph," she said, sitting back down on the edge of the couch. She was still wound as tight as a spring.

"And another thing," Jack said, bracing himself

for what he knew would be her response. "I think we need to tell him she's here, don't you?"

"What? No! Absolutely not. Why would you even suggest that?"

"Because . . . because I think he has a right to know. And I think Daisy would want him to know, too. She just doesn't want to bring it up in front of you."

"Well, *I'm* not telling him," Caroline said crossly. "I'll leave that to you."

She was silent for a minute and then added, "Honestly, Jack, I don't understand how you can be so casual about this whole thing. You act as if Daisy gets rushed to the hospital every day."

"Caroline, I'm not being casual about this," he said, tensing. "It scared the hell out of me. Following the ambulance here, waiting in the emergency room, waiting again while she was in surgery—those were some very long minutes, trust me. As long as they get. But unlike you, I'm somewhat reassured now. Maybe because the last time I saw Daisy, when the nurse finally evicted us from her room five minutes ago, she was eating a chocolate pudding and watching *Wheel of Fortune.*"

"Well, she's not out of the woods yet," Caroline reminded him. "There could still be complications."

"Her doctor said it was possible, but unlikely," Jack said.

Caroline leaned back against the couch cushions, and Jack watched as a little of her anger, and indignation, ebbed away and was replaced by tiredness.

"Did you get any sleep last night?" he asked.

"Very little," she said, rubbing her eyes. "Once Jessica's mother told me Daisy wasn't spending the night there, I imagined . . . well, I imagined the worst."

"Caroline, it's Daisy," he reminded her. "Even her worst couldn't be very bad."

But she didn't answer him, and Jack was left to wonder how she could be so unprepared for Daisy to grow up, so in denial about the fact that the daughter she'd raised was no longer a child, but instead a young woman. Then another thought occurred to him. Maybe if he'd stuck around and watched Daisy grow up too, the way Caroline had, he wouldn't be prepared for it either. Still, some facts had to be faced.

"Caroline," he said now, "you must have known, at some point, that Daisy would spend the night with a boy."

"Of course I knew that," she said, a little irritably. "And that's not what this is about, Jack."

"Then what is it about?"

"It's about . . . it's about something else, something Daisy said recently about Will."

"What did she say?"

"She said . . . she said he was her dream, Jack.

Or something like that, something that made me think she was going to do something crazy. So last night, when she wasn't at Jessica's, and she didn't come home, I thought . . ."

"You thought what?"

"I thought they'd run off together. You know, eloped or something."

"*Eloped?* Caroline, that's crazy. They're kids, for God's sake."

"Oh, so now Daisy's a kid? Because five minutes ago, you said she was an adult. Which is it, Jack? I'd really like to know."

"She's neither, Caroline. Or she's both. She's both at the same time, just like you and I were at her age. Nobody's completely grown-up at twenty-one. They're not supposed to be," he said. And then he chuckled a little. "Did you honestly think they'd eloped? I mean, do people even do that anymore? It's kind of outdated, isn't it? Kind of like a 'shotgun wedding.' "

"You mean like *our* wedding, Jack?" Caroline asked challengingly, turning to look at him.

"Well, yes," he said, surprised, even though he probably shouldn't have been. "But I didn't think of our wedding as a shotgun wedding."

"Maybe not. But that's what it was. I can still remember my mom trying to zip up my wedding dress before the ceremony," she said, with the ghost of a smile. "I think I gained five pounds the week before we were married."

"That dress fit you perfectly," Jack said. God, she'd looked beautiful that day. She'd absolutely glowed, the way a pregnant woman was supposed to. He almost told her that now, but he stopped himself. She didn't really look like she was in the mood for reminiscing. Still, there was one thing he was curious about.

"Does Daisy know . . . ?"

"That I was pregnant when we got married? No. I've never told her. And, amazingly enough, even with her natural mathematical ability, she's never figured it out. It helped, of course, that by the time she was old enough to put two and two together, we weren't celebrating our anniversary anymore."

Jack nodded, feeling suddenly depressed, depressed about all the anniversaries they hadn't celebrated.

"Are you sorry, Caroline?" he asked suddenly, turning to her. "Sorry that you got pregnant?"

"Of course not," she said automatically. "If I hadn't, there'd be no Daisy."

"Well, that *is* unthinkable," he agreed. "But what I really mean is, are you sorry about *us?* Sorry about us ever having gotten married?"

"Sorry?" she said thoughtfully. "No, I don't feel *sorry* about it. Not exactly . . . I feel guilty about it maybe, but not sorry."

"Guilty?"

She nodded. "Guilty about making you marry me."

"You didn't *make* me marry you," he objected. "I was in love with you, Caroline." *I still am.*

She shrugged. "Maybe. But that's not why you asked me to marry you. You asked me to marry you because you were trying to do the right thing, Jack. You didn't ask me to marry you because you wanted to be a husband or a father."

"I don't think I knew what I wanted, Caroline," he said honestly. "I think, to the extent that I wanted anything, I wanted you."

She smiled, a little sadly. "But *you* really were just a kid, Jack, weren't you? At twenty-one you weren't ready for any of it, were you?"

I'm ready now, he wanted to say. But he didn't.

"I've often thought since then that I should have said no when you proposed to me," Caroline continued, in the same musing tone. "You know, just to let you off the hook altogether."

"And what would you have done, Caroline?"

"Oh, gone it alone, I guess."

"Well, you basically did that anyway," he said, feeling about as low as it was possible for a person to feel. He looked away from her and examined an especially ugly painting hanging on the wall of the visitors' lounge.

"Hey, don't beat yourself up, Jack," Caroline said, noticing his expression. "You did your best."

"My best wasn't very good."

She shrugged. "You sent me money."

"It was never enough."

"Well, you weren't exactly rich yourself, were you?"

But Jack didn't answer. She could defend his actions. *He* wasn't going to. Instead, he thought about Daisy, whose hospital room was only about one hundred feet down the hallway from the visitors' lounge. He hadn't been kidding when he'd told Caroline that what had happened to Daisy that morning had scared him. It had scared the hell out of him. And it had been a huge relief to see her, just a little while ago, sitting up in her hospital bed, talking, smiling, and even teasing Jack about having gotten an unexpected day off from working on the cabin.

"Don't be too hard on Daisy about what happened," he said now, turning to Caroline. "Especially since you can still remember what it's like to be that age. I mean, it's the same age you were when you married me."

"That's what I'm afraid of, Jack," Caroline said, rubbing her eyes tiredly. And suddenly, sitting there beside her, Jack finally understood why Caroline disliked Will. All summer, he'd puzzled over it, especially since the one time he'd met Will in passing, he'd seemed like a perfectly nice guy. But now it all made sense. Caroline didn't see Will when she looked at Will, she saw Jack. And she wasn't afraid Daisy would make *any* mistake. She was afraid Daisy would make *her* mistake, getting involved with, and maybe even getting married to, someone like Jack. Someone who would be, as he had been, directionless, irresponsible, unfaithful . . . You could take your pick of adjectives. They all added up to the same thing. She didn't want Daisy wasting her time, her *life,* really, on someone who had as little to offer to her as Jack had had to offer Caroline.

"Jack, what's wrong?"

"Nothing," Jack said, sinking a few more inches into the couch.

"Have you eaten yet today?" Caroline said, frowning.

"Not really," he said. *Not at all.*

"Neither have I. We should get something in the cafeteria. It'll be terrible, of course, the usual selection of cardboard sandwiches. But if we go down there, it'll give Daisy time to take a nap. Besides, we can't stay here all day without some kind of sustenance."

"I'm not hungry."

"Well, you're not going to starve on my watch, Jack Keegan," she said briskly. "Let's go."

Ten minutes later, they were sitting at a table in the almost empty hospital cafeteria. Caroline was picking at a salad and Jack was trying, valiantly, to eat a particularly uninspired-looking turkey and cheese sandwich.

"Honestly, I don't see how they can charge money for this food," Caroline said, putting her fork down. "If I served this at Pearl's, I'd never have a repeat customer."

Jack nodded, but Caroline could tell he wasn't really paying attention to her. Finally, he gave up on his lunch too. "Caroline, I want you to promise me something," he said, pushing his tray aside.

"What?"

"I want you to promise me that when Daisy comes home from the hospital, you won't be too hard on her."

"Well, not *hard* on her, maybe, but—"

"But you might deliver a few well-placed lectures?"

"I might," she said, faintly irritated that once again Jack was casting her in the bad cop role.

"All right, look, lecture her if you want to," he said. "But remember, she's going to make mistakes. Fortunately for her, and for us, she's been blessed with good judgment. She won't make that many of them, and the ones she does make won't be irreversible. But you need to let her make them, Caroline. That's how people learn."

"Well, Daisy will have to find some other way to learn, Jack," she said stubbornly. "She can't afford to make mistakes."

"Of course she can," he said, exasperated. "They're a part of life, Caroline. Everyone makes mistakes. You can't hold her to a higher standard than everyone else."

But Caroline shook her head. "You don't get it, Jack. You just don't get it; you don't know how much is at stake here."

"You're right, I don't," he said bluntly. "Enlighten me."

She looked at him speculatively, trying to weigh what his response would be if she told him what she hadn't been able to bring herself to tell anyone but Frankie.

"All right, Jack," she said finally, "I'll enlighten you. But now you have to promise me something."

"Anything," he said automatically.

"You have to promise me you won't judge me."

Jack's eyes widened. *"Me,* judge *you?"* he said, amused. "Caroline, I think we both know I'm not in a position to judge *anyone.*"

"Well, that may be, but . . ." She paused and looked away, torn between her desire to finally unburden herself of this and her equally strong desire to protect her pride, or rather, what was left of her pride. But even if she didn't tell him, she reasoned, he would know soon enough. The whole town would know soon enough . . .

"Caroline, I'm not going to judge you," Jack said, leaning his elbows on the table between them. "But I'm also not leaving here until you tell me what this is about."

She sighed and picked at her lifeless salad again. "The reason there's so much at stake for

Daisy is because . . . because she's so close, Jack," she said. "Only two semesters away from graduating."

"I understand that," he said patiently.

"And if something were to go wrong now for her now, Jack, if something were to derail her plans for her future, she wouldn't have anything to fall back on, not even waitressing at Pearl's."

He looked at her questioningly.

"And I wouldn't be able to help her either. Financially, I mean."

"I . . . don't get it."

"Oh, Jack . . ." she said, and all at once she felt the fatigue, not just of the past day, but of the past several years, settle over her. "Jack, I'm about to lose it all." She raised her chin fractionally and met his eyes. "The building, the apartment, the coffee shop. Everything."

He stared at her wordlessly. But she nodded her head and went on. "It's true. I borrowed money from the bank, and now I can't pay it back."

"Wait, back up," he said. "When did you borrow money from the bank?"

"Seven years ago. I'd decided to take out a second mortgage with a balloon payment due at the end of the seven years. Business was good at the time, and I'd put some money aside for Daisy's college education. And I thought, 'Here's my chance.' You know that old adage, you have to spend money to make money? Well, my parents never had any money to spend on the business, so I figured I could borrow the money and do all the things they'd put off doing: replace the roof and the air-conditioning system, upgrade all the appliances, expand the seating area, buy new tables and chairs. You know, nothing crazy, just commonsense stuff. It was a solid plan, Jack. The bank loan officers thought so, too, and they gave me the loan."

"So what happened?"

"The recession happened, Jack. And it . . . it was bad."

"How bad?" he asked quietly.

"*Plenty* bad. It turns out that when people cut their budgets, they cut blueberry pancakes first," she added, with a little laugh. But that laugh sounded bitter, even to her. "I replaced the roof, but most of the other improvements I'd planned had to be put on hold," she continued. "Which turned out to be a good thing, because by the time I'd emptied out my savings account to pay for taxes and insurance and the payments for my first mortgage, that second mortgage was the only thing keeping the business afloat. During the bottom of the recession, things were so bad, I even thought about laying Frankie off. But I couldn't bring myself to do it. It's hard enough for an ex-con to find work in good times, and here . . . well, things weren't good. Bill Phipps was laying people off at the mill, and summer tourism was way down. Anyway, before I knew it, I'd used up the whole loan and . . ." She shrugged.

"How much was the loan for?" Jack asked, his brow furrowed.

"Fifty thousand dollars," Caroline said. Fifty thousand dollars; it might as well have been fifty million dollars.

"Have you missed any payments on it?"

"No, not yet. I've been able to keep up with those, so far. But there's a balloon payment of $44,500 due September twenty-first. And since there was no reset option on the mortgage, and they won't let me refinance the loan, I have to make that payment."

"September twenty-first. That's less than a month away."

She nodded.

"Do you have the money?"

She shook her head.

"Can you *get* the money?"

She shook her head again. Jack stared at her in disbelief. "Look," she said, defensively, "I've done the math. Backwards, forwards, and sideways. I've added up my worth a hundred times over, meager as it is. I've even thought of selling the few things of value I own, like Grandma Pearl's wedding china." *And my wedding ring,* she thought, but didn't say. She'd often wondered, over the years, why she'd kept it, in its little black velvet box, in her top dresser drawer. Now, of course, she didn't want to examine that question too closely.

"Are you sure they won't let you refinance your mortgages?" Jack asked.

"No, I tried, believe me. But John Quarterman can't help me. He would, if he could, but three years ago, the bank was bought by another, Chicago-based bank. And they said I'm not a good risk."

"And you don't have any other ideas?"

"Well, my employees, I mean my *employee,* Frankie, would like to help. He's willing to give me everything he's got. But everything he's got still isn't enough."

"Did you . . . did you ever tell Buster about any of this?" Jack asked hesitantly.

"No, thank God. Because if Buster had known, he would have loaned me the money. *Given* me the money, more likely. And then when I ended things with him, I mean, when we ended things with each other," she corrected herself, quickly, "it would have been . . ."

"Awkward?" Jack supplied.

"Awkward," Caroline agreed.

"But, Caroline, business has gotten better, hasn't it?"

She nodded. "It has. But it's all I can do now to keep up with the monthly payments on the two mortgages."

"So what happens when you miss the balloon payment?"

"I'll try to negotiate an extension with the bank that will give me time to sell the building and pay off the mortgages. After that, I should just about break even, I think."

Jack massaged his temples now. He looked like he was having trouble taking this all in. "So you're just going to give up?" he said finally. "You're just going to let Pearl's go without a fight?"

"Without a fight?" she echoed, feeling a pulse of anger at her temples. "Jack, I've been fighting for Pearl's my whole life—every single day. But this . . ." She paused. "This has got me beat."

"But . . . there's something I don't understand. I asked Daisy, last year, how the two of you were doing. Financially, I mean. And she said you were doing fine."

"That's because we *are* doing fine, as far as Daisy knows. I've never told her about any of this. And you're not going to either, Jack," she added warningly.

He shook his head slowly. "So many secrets in one little family," he said, a bleak smile tugging at the corners of his mouth. "But you can't keep this from her for much longer, Caroline."

"I know. She'll find out about it. But *after* the fact, after she's back at college." *Safely* back at college, she added to herself.

"Caroline—" Jack started to say, but she waved his objection away.

"No. She's not going back to Minneapolis with this hanging over her like some dark cloud. I'll tell her when I have to tell her. But by then, she'll be almost home free. The first member of my family to graduate from college. And the first member not to be saddled with debt from the get-go. Think about it, Jack. Three generations of us—me, my parents, my grandparents—have spent our whole lives trying to stay one step ahead of the bank. Daisy's life is going to be different. That's why she can't slip up now. She thinks she's in love with Will, I know. This all seems so wonderful to her, so magical. But it's not enough."

"No," he said quietly. "Not from your perspective, it isn't." He paused then and seemed to struggle with something. "But what will *you* do, Caroline, when Pearl's is . . . is gone?"

She flinched at those words. Because no matter how much that place had felt like an albatross hanging around her neck for the last several years, she still loved it, of course. How could she not? She'd spent so much of her life there, had so many memories there. Not all of them were good, of course, but many of them were. And it tore at her heart now, thinking about Pearl's belonging to someone else—or, worse yet, ceasing to exist altogether.

"Butternut without Pearl's," Jack said out loud, as if reading her mind. "I can't picture it. And I'm not sure anyone else in town can either."

She didn't say anything. What was there, really, to say? There wasn't a single person who'd grown up in that town who hadn't spun on the red leather stools at the counter, memorized the menu inside and out, and ordered the Butternut Burger five hundred times over.

But Jack, apparently, was less worried about her customers than he was about her. "What will you do, Caroline," he persisted, "if you have to . . . let it all go?"

"I'll be fine," she said, quickly. "I can always waitress. Or manage a restaurant."

"But could you work for someone else? You've never done that before."

"Well, there's a first time for everything," she said, with a nonchalance she didn't really feel.

"And where would you live?"

"Oh, some place," she said vaguely. "Frankie rents a apartment over the Laundromat, and I was thinking about doing the same thing. But they're tearing that building down; he'll have to find a new place to live now, too."

Jack sighed, and Caroline watched him as he picked up a little plastic creamer and, peeling the lid off it, poured it into his cup of coffee. The coffee would be lousy, Caroline knew, and ice cold to boot. Jack seemed lost in thought, though, as he stirred it distractedly, and Caroline was free to look at him, *really* look at him, and marvel once again at how much she liked looking at him, even in her current mood. God, he was something else. Even under the cafeteria's fluorescent lighting, and even with a day's growth of beard, and a line of worry between his eyes, he looked better than any man had a right to look. And as she watched him take a sip of his coffee, she wondered, if he'd been just a little *less* good-looking, would any of what had happened between them still have happened? Would they, for instance, have had the daughter who right now was lying upstairs in a hospital bed?

No, she decided, Jack's looks had only been part of the draw. His charm had been the rest, his charm and his all-the-time-in-the-world smile that she'd never been able to resist. That smile was nowhere in evidence today, she realized, as Jack put his cup of coffee down and started to systematically shred his paper napkin. No, he didn't look like he was even close to smiling. He looked . . . *he looked angry,* she realized with surprise. "Jack, that's not fair," she said, her own temper flaring.

"What's not fair?" he asked, looking up at her, and leaving a little pile of pulverized paper napkin on his tray.

"You're being angry at me. You promised you wouldn't judge me."

414

"I'm not judging you. And I'm not angry at you either. I'm angry at myself."

"Why?" she asked, taken aback.

"Because it all makes sense to me now, Caroline," he said, leaning closer. His voice was quiet, but urgent. "I've known since the first time I saw you at Pearl's, at the beginning of the summer, that there was something wrong. I saw it—the exhaustion, the stress, the worry—but at the same time, I didn't see it. Instead, I saw what I wanted to see, which was that you were still the same woman I'd fallen in love with. And you are. In so many ways, you are. But in one important way you're not. Because the woman I fell in love with wasn't carrying the weight of the world on her shoulders, and she didn't feel as alone as you feel now, as alone as you've felt for a long, long time. The woman I fell in love with actually thought, crazily enough, that she'd found someone in her life who would help her, and support her, and—"

"Jack, stop," Caroline said, stunned to discover that there were tears in her eyes. "Just stop, all right? I mean, what's the point of dredging all of that up now? What happened, happened. We both did our best."

"*You* did your best. I did . . . I did something less than my best."

"It doesn't matter," she said, blinking back the tears that still wanted to come pouring out. "None of that matters now. Can't you see that? What matters now is Daisy. And we need to be there for her, again, in a little while, and we can't bring all of this"—she waved her hand between the two of them—"with us."

"You're right," Jack agreed.

And Caroline took a deep breath, relieved that the urge to cry had passed, though in its place was an aching sadness that didn't feel much better.

"You go ahead upstairs without me, all right?" Jack said now. "There's something I need to do first."

Caroline nodded, uncertainly. He wasn't going to have a drink, was he?

But he caught the expression on her face and shook his head. "I'm not going to a bar, Caroline. There's someone I need to see."

She nodded, embarrassed that her thoughts had been so transparent. "That's fine, Jack," she said. "I'll hold the fort down here." She stood up, and, taking her tray with her, she started to leave the table. But Jack stopped her.

"Caroline?"

"Yes?"

"Could I . . . could I see the bank documents?"

"Which ones?" she frowned.

"All of them, anything having to do with the loan."

"Why?" she asked, genuinely perplexed.

"Because I might have an idea you haven't had yet, a fresh perspective on the situation."

She wavered.

"Look, it can't hurt, can it?" he said. "Just let me take a look at them, all right?"

"All right," she said finally. "But I've read the fine print, Jack."

"I know. But you'll still get all the papers together for me? By, say, early this week?"

"Why not?" she said, turning away again. After all, Jack was right; it couldn't hurt. It couldn't *help,* either. But it couldn't hurt.

Chapter 20

When Will walked into Daisy's hospital room that evening and saw her wearing a hospital gown and propped up on pillows on a hospital bed, he felt a jolt of fear. Even by Daisy's standards she was pale, and her blue eyes were shadowed with fatigue. As soon as she saw him, though, her whole face lit up and she looked better, much better. "Will, you came," she said, sitting up.

"Of course I came," he said, and as he walked over to her bedside he felt a rush of protectiveness for her. She looked so fragile somehow, so helpless in that gown, and in that bed.

"How did you even know I was here?" she

asked as he leaned over and kissed her, very carefully, on the cheek.

"Your dad came over to the garage," he said, pulling a chair over to sit down on.

"He did?" she said, her eyes widening with surprise. "He didn't tell me he was going to do that. I would have called you, Will, but I didn't have my cell phone. I was hoping that after my parents left I could use the phone at the nurses' station. But I'm so glad I didn't need to. I have to thank my dad later."

"So do I. But, Daisy, when I opened the door to my apartment, and I saw him standing there, I swear to God, I think my heart stopped beating. I knew he wouldn't be there unless something was wrong. And when he told me you were in the hospital . . ." He paused, unable to put the way he'd felt into words. "Just, just promise me you won't do something like this again, okay?" he said.

"I won't. I promise," Daisy said, looking faintly amused. "I mean, I only had that one appendix."

"You know what I mean," Will said seriously.

"I do, Will. And I swear, no more medical emergencies. Now, are you going to give me the flowers you brought or not?"

Will looked down at the flowers in his hands, which he'd completely forgotten. He gave them to Daisy.

"They're so pretty," she said admiringly.

"There wasn't much of a selection in the hospital gift shop," he said. "I'll do better next time."

"Next time, Will? Is bringing me flowers going to become a regular occurrence?" she asked, smiling and looking so much like herself again that Will felt his stomach begin to unclench.

"Daisy, if it'll make you happy," he said. "I'll bring you flowers every single day."

He took the flower arrangement from her then and put it down on her bedside table. There was another arrangement there, too, as well as a teddy bear. A "get well soon" Mylar balloon was floating in the corner of the room.

He reached for one of her hands and held it in both of his, then worried that it felt cold.

"Do you want me to ask the nurse for another blanket?"

She shook her head. "No, I'm fine. But, Will, did you see my mom when you got here?" she asked.

He nodded. "She's in the visitors' lounge." He didn't tell Daisy about the icy reception he'd gotten from her.

"She's really mad, Will." She sighed. "She said we needed to talk later, which is always a bad sign. I think . . . I think she's going to blame you for this somehow. Which is ridiculous, obviously. And do you know what else is ridiculous?" she added indignantly. "The fact that I'm old enough to drive, and vote and drink and gamble and own a firearm but, according to her, apparently, I'm still not old enough to spend the night with my boyfriend."

Will didn't say anything. He didn't want to take sides, especially since he thought her mom's anger at him was not entirely unjustified. He'd known there was something wrong with Daisy on the drive back. He should have pushed her harder to tell him what it was. In fact, he should have taken her straight to a hospital. Yes, she'd gotten to one eventually, but what if she hadn't gotten to one in time? No sooner did he have that thought, though, than he dismissed it. It was too terrible for him to even contemplate.

Still, he wondered, why hadn't Daisy told him she was in so much pain? He asked her that now.

But she didn't answer him right away. She just looked down at the hand he wasn't holding, the one lying on top of the bed covers. "I don't know," she said finally. "I guess because I didn't want to ruin everything. It was so perfect, up to that point, anyway."

He smiled at her and squeezed the hand he was holding. "You're right. It *was* perfect. But trust me, there was nothing you could have done to ruin it. But what happened to you, Daisy, after I left you at Pearl's?"

"Well, I went up to the apartment, and as soon

as I walked into the kitchen—where my mother was obviously planning some kind of intervention—I fainted. By the time I came to, they'd called an ambulance. It brought me here, and the ER physician examined me, and I got a blood test and a CT scan. And then they took me into surgery, and that was it. The surgeon did my appendectomy with something called a laparoscope, which means he only had to make a tiny incision. And I only have to spend a day in the hospital, too. I can probably leave tomorrow afternoon."

"That's good," he said, smiling. But there it was again, that unsettling feeling that things could have turned out differently.

"Hey, what happened to your arm?" Daisy asked then.

"Oh, that," he said, looking at the bandage he'd put on his cut after he'd gotten back from his father's. "It's just a scratch."

"It doesn't look like just a scratch," she said, reaching out to finger the bandage gently. Then she chuckled softly.

"What's so funny?"

"You and me," Daisy said. "We spend one night together, and I'm in the hospital and you . . . you don't look like you're doing much better, Will. I mean, there's your arm, and your jeans, too. What happened to them?"

He looked down. He hadn't changed out of his ripped jeans yet. They'd gotten caught on the barbed wire too. Looking back at her, he had to laugh. "You're right, Daisy," he said. "That was quite a night."

Daisy smiled at him then, a lovely smile, and, letting go of his hand, she moved over on the hospital bed and patted the now empty space beside her. "Come here," she said, a familiar, and reassuring, light returning to her blue eyes.

He looked at the open door to her room and hesitated.

"Please?" she asked, patting the bed again. "Just for a second. Nobody's going to come in. I promise."

He sighed, stood up warily, and sat down on the very edge of her bed, keeping his feet firmly on the floor.

"Oh, come on," she said, moving over a little farther. He wavered, then slid over next to her, and propped his feet up on the bed. But he kept an eye on the door.

"Now kiss me," she said.

"Daisy," he started to object, so she kissed him instead. Soon enough, he was kissing her back and marveling, for the hundredth time, at the softness of her lips. After a minute, though, he felt the tempo of the kiss begin to change, and he pulled away.

"We should stop now," he said.

Daisy nodded, a little groggily. "You're probably right," she said. "They gave me something for the pain, and I think it's making my head feel a little fuzzy."

"I'll let you rest then," he said, starting to get up, but she grabbed his hand.

"I'll rest after you leave," she said. "I promise. But can we stay like this? Just for a few more minutes?"

"Okay," he said, taking her hand in both of his and kneading it between his fingers. She settled back on the pillows and turned to look at him. And watching her lying there, he felt it again, that almost primal urge to protect her, that gut-level determination to guard her against any danger. He could do that, too, he thought. He was sure of it. A few hours ago, of course, he'd been sprawled out over the hood of his truck, barely able to draw in a single breath, but now he felt his whole body flooding with strength. He could keep Daisy safe, if he could just be with her, every second of every day . . . But therein lay the problem. He couldn't. And with that realization came a bottomless, terrifying fear, a fear that something could happen to her, something he couldn't anticipate or control.

And that wasn't all Will was worried about. A letter had been waiting for him when he'd gotten back to his apartment, the letter that would take him away from her more suddenly than he'd anticipated, but that would also give him a chance at a future with her. But he couldn't tell her about it now. She was too fragile. He'd have to wait until she was stronger.

"Daisy, promise me something, okay?" he said suddenly.

"Okay," she said.

"Promise me you'll be careful."

She smiled a little tiredly. "Will, I *am* careful. It's in my nature to be careful. You know that."

"I do know that. Just don't . . . don't take any risks."

She looked amused. "You mean, like jumping out of airplanes?"

"No, I mean, like when you're doing everyday things. When you're back at college and you're crossing the street, or riding your bike to class, or walking home from the library at night—just be careful, all right?"

Daisy was silent. They never talked about her going back to college, at least, not if they could possibly help it. Finally, she said, "You don't need to worry about me, Will, okay. My idea of risky behavior is studying too hard. Or drinking too many caffeinated beverages."

He smiled at her, slightly mollified, and then he lifted his hand to her cheek and stroked it gently. "I love you, Daisy," he said. And when he heard himself say it, he was as surprised as she was. He hadn't even known he was going to say those words until they were already out of his mouth.

Daisy looked at him wonderingly, her pale complexion transfused with a soft blush. "I love you, too, Will."

They sat in silence for a few minutes, and then Will said quietly, "I've never said that to anyone before."

"You mean, you've never said that to anyone you weren't related to," Daisy clarified.

But Will shook his head. "No. I mean I've never said that to anyone."

Chapter 21

"That's funny. I don't remember the service here being this slow."

"Jack?" Caroline said in surprise, looking up from the industrial coffee machine she was shoveling coffee grounds into. It was closing time, Pearl's was empty, and, left to her own devices, she'd been deep in thought. "How long have you been waiting there?" she asked, putting down the plastic scoop and wiping her hands on a dish towel.

"Not that long." Jack rested his elbows on the counter. "And don't worry. I'm not staying; I haven't forgotten our agreement."

"Our agreement?" she repeated, coming over to him.

"I'm not allowed in here, remember?" he said, his blue eyes amused.

"Oh, that," Caroline said, with a tiny shrug. "I hope we've gotten beyond that, Jack."

"Have we?" he asked, suddenly serious, and because Caroline didn't know how to answer that question, she busied herself with pouring him an iced tea.

"Have you been up to the apartment to see Daisy?" she asked, setting the glass down in front of him.

He nodded, sipping his drink. "She looks so much better, Caroline. She's finally starting to get some color back in her face."

"She is, isn't she?"

"She says she's ready to come back to work again."

Caroline frowned. "I don't know about that, Jack. It's only been five days since she came home from the hospital."

"Well, it looks like five days is all it's taken for a serious case of cabin fever to set in."

"Maybe," Caroline murmured, reaching reflexively for a dishcloth to wipe down the counter and noticing for the first time that Jack had put the folder she'd given him earlier in the week—the one with all the financial documents in it—on the counter beside him.

"Did you get a chance to go over those?" she asked, nodding at the folder.

"As a matter of fact, I did. That's the reason I'm here."

She stopped wiping. "So you agree with me that it's hopeless?"

He shook his head. "No, I don't. In fact, I want to set up a time for us to discuss it," he said, tapping on the file.

"What about right now?"

"I don't think so," he said. "Not at Pearl's."

"Why not?"

"Well, for one thing, there's no privacy here," he said, and, as if to underscore his point, Frankie chose that moment to come through the back door with a bucket and a mop. He nodded at Jack and Caroline, came around from behind the counter, and started stacking the chairs on the tabletops.

"And, for another thing," Jack continued, "I'd like us to discuss it over dinner."

"Dinner?"

"Dinner," he confirmed. "The meal that comes after lunch."

"I'm familiar with it."

"Good. Because I'd like you to come for dinner at the cabin."

She frowned and started wiping the counter again. She didn't know if that was a good idea.

"Oh, come on Caroline," he chided her gently. "Aren't you just a little curious to see what I've done with the place?"

She sighed. He had her there. Daisy had given

427

her occasional reports on it, but she was dying to see it for herself. But still, she and Jack alone together?

"This would be business, Caroline. Not pleasure," he said, reading her mind, and Caroline concentrated on wiping the counter again. Because she was still having trouble reconciling the old Jack with the new Jack. The old Jack, for instance, had had very little interest in business. Pleasure, of course, had been a different matter.

"I don't think so," she said, finally, more to herself than to him.

"Caroline, I promise, I'll be on my best behavior. This won't be a replay of the last time we had dinner together." Caroline felt her face grow warm at the memory. "So, don't say no on that account. Unless . . ." He trailed off, one corner of his mouth quirking up in a smile.

"Unless what?"

"Unless you don't trust yourself to be alone with me," he said, dropping his voice so Frankie, who was mopping nearby, wouldn't hear him.

"Oh, I think I can handle myself, Jack," she said coolly, nonetheless remembering another night when he'd taken her home from the Corner Bar and she'd practically pinned him up against the wall at Pearl's. "But I don't know how I feel about leaving Daisy alone yet," she added. "She says she's fine, but—"

But Jack shook his head. "Sorry, Caroline.

You're going to have to find another excuse. Daisy told me she's spending the night at Jessica's house tonight. She says if she doesn't get out of that apartment, at least for a night, she's going to go stir-crazy."

"Oh," Caroline said. She was running out of excuses.

"Look, what's the worst that can happen?" Jack pressed. "At the very least, you'll get a free dinner out of this."

"A free grilled cheese sandwich?" Caroline ventured.

"No, I have something a little more complicated in mind," he said. And Caroline didn't answer, because that was exactly what she was afraid of.

"All right," Jack said. "Forget dinner at the cabin then. How about a drink there instead?"

"A drink?" she asked, raising her eyebrows.

"A sparkling water," he clarified.

She hesitated again, but Jack took her hesitation for acquiescence. "Good," he said, smiling. "I'll see you tonight. Why don't we say six o'clock. Oh, and you can have this back." He pushed the folder across the counter to her. "I don't need it anymore."

She nodded, a little distractedly, already having misgivings about their plans.

"Well, I'd better get going," Jack said, and they said their good-byes. Even after he left, though,

Caroline kept standing there, dish cloth still in hand but not otherwise moving.

"Everything okay?" Frankie asked, startling her out of her reverie. He'd finished his work and was toting the mop and bucket into the back room.

"Everything's fine," she said, giving the counter a few more halfhearted swipes with the dish cloth. But what she was thinking was, *Did I really just agree to go to Jack's cabin for a drink?* She had to admit, with a grudging admiration for her ex-husband, that she had definitely not seen that coming.

"There," Jessica said proudly, as she examined her handiwork that evening. She and Daisy were sitting on the couch in Jessica's living room, and Jessica had just finished giving Daisy a manicure.

"What do you think?" she asked Daisy, blowing on her still-wet nails. Daisy's hands were resting on a pillow, which Jessica had covered with a dish towel and placed between them on the couch.

"I think . . . I think they look great," Daisy said, knowing, even with her limited experience with manicures, that this was not a good one. She had some insight now into why Jessica might have flunked out of cosmetology school before coming to work at Pearl's. But she smiled at

Jessica and said loyally, "It's very professional. Thank you so much."

"You're welcome." Jessica beamed. "It's the least I can do for my best friend, who happens to be recovering from an appendectomy. And do you want to see what else we're doing tonight?"

"Okay." Daisy smiled.

Jessica left the room and hurried back with her arms full. "Well, first of all, I bought all the trashiest magazines," she said, depositing a stack of glossy magazines onto the coffee table in front of Daisy. "I also rented all our favorite movies," she continued, putting a half-dozen DVDs, all romantic comedies that she and Daisy had already seen at least ten times, beside the pile of magazines. "And, last but not least, I bought Double Stuff Oreos." She produced a bag of them with a flourish. "Remember how mad your mom used to get, Daisy, when we used to buy these at the grocery store?" Jessica settled onto the couch beside Daisy. "There was Pearl's, right downstairs, with all those homemade cookies, and we wanted these instead." She laughed then, tore into the bag of Oreos, and gave one to Daisy. And Daisy smiled and ate it, dutifully, being careful not to touch it with her fingernails.

She listened then, or tried to listen anyway, as Jessica reminisced about their growing up together. But as had so often happened that summer, Daisy was having difficulty paying attention. It wasn't that she didn't want to be with Jessica; it was just that if she could have chosen someone to spend the night alone with right now, it wouldn't have been her . . .

Daisy had been with Will a couple of hours earlier. Since she'd gotten home from the hospital, he'd gotten into the habit of driving over to see her in the late afternoons, after Pearl's had closed for the day and her mom and Frankie had left. They were able to find a little privacy then, sitting in one of the back booths, where they talked and kissed, but mainly kissed. It felt wonderfully illicit in its way. But it felt a little torturous, too, to go from spending a whole blissful night alone together to stealing a few hours of kisses in a place where they knew they might be interrupted at any moment.

But it wasn't just the lack of privacy that Daisy was struggling with. It was Will, too. He was still sweet, of course, still incredibly solicitous of her. But he was something else, too. Quieter, maybe, or more intense. He seemed burdened by something. It was hard for her to put her finger on it. But she felt it, just the same. Once, he'd told her he wanted to talk to her about something, but no sooner had he brought it up than he dropped it. And when she'd pressed him about it later, he'd changed the subject. It worried her a lot, almost more than she was willing to admit to herself.

"Daisy, you're not listening to a word I'm

saying," Jessica observed ruefully, bringing her back to the conversation.

"You're right," Daisy admitted. "I'm sorry." She felt a rush of guilt then, because she knew she hadn't been a very good friend to Jessica this summer. In fact, she'd barely spoken to her recently, except when she'd asked her to cover for her when she'd gone to Mr. Phipps's cabin with Will.

Jessica didn't seem angry though. "You don't need to apologize," she said, fishing in the bag for another Oreo. "It's not your fault you can't pay attention. You're in love. And you only get to fall in love for the first time once," she added, with a smile, biting into her cookie.

"That's true," Daisy said, feeling a wave of gratitude for her friend. Jessica might never make a good waitress, she thought—she might never even make a *decent* waitress—but she had the sweetest disposition of anyone Daisy had ever known.

"Thank you for being so understanding, Jessica," she said, leaning over and giving her a hug.

"Oh, it's easy for me to be understanding about this," Jessica said, hugging Daisy back. "Because it just so happens that I'm in love right now too."

"You are?" Daisy asked, settling back into her spot on the couch and examining her friend. "When did this happen?"

"It's been happening all summer. I just didn't realize it until recently. For the first time, Daisy, I didn't fall in love fast. I fell in love slow, a little bit at a time, and then, suddenly, all at once," she added, flushing.

"That's wonderful," Daisy said, beaming at her. "But who is he?"

"Guess," Jessica said, her big brown eyes dancing with excitement.

"Um, okay. Is it someone who comes into Pearl's?"

"You could say that."

"Is it . . . Oh, I know. Is it that new guy who works at the hardware store? The one who likes his eggs practically raw?"

"Nope. Try again."

Daisy tried again, but it didn't take her long to exhaust the possibilities. There just weren't that many young, single men who came into the coffee shop.

"It's not one of your ex-boyfriends, is it, Jessica?" she asked, at last. "Because as far as I'm concerned, none of them ever treated you the way you deserve to be treated."

"No, it's not an ex-boyfriend," Jessica said. "And I agree, Daisy. They were all losers. Keep guessing."

But Daisy held her hands up in surrender. "I give up. Tell me."

"No, this game is too much fun," Jessica said

with childish pleasure. "But I'll give you a hint. You know him. Very well. You see him every day."

Daisy frowned. "I see him at Pearl's?"

Now Jessica was practically squirming with excitement. "Yep."

Daisy shook her head slowly.

"*And* you said he makes the best hash browns on the whole planet."

Daisy looked at Jessica in astonishment. *"Frankie?"*

Jessica nodded excitedly. "It's Frankie. We're in love, Daisy."

Daisy struggled to wrap her brain around this concept. "But Jessica," she said finally, and not unkindly, "he's so much older than you."

Jessica looked hurt. "He is not. I'm twenty-one. He's thirty-six. That's only fifteen years. Lots of people who fall in love have a bigger age difference between them."

Daisy nodded. That was true. But did Jessica know everything about Frankie? And if she didn't, was it Daisy's place to tell her?

She deliberated, briefly, then asked, "Jessica, what has Frankie told you about his past?"

"Everything," Jessica said promptly. "He told me he killed a man, in self-defense, and that he went to prison. He told me everything; he said he doesn't want there to be any secrets between us."

Daisy was relieved. She wasn't worried about Frankie's propensity for violence. Because while she didn't know all the details of the incident that had ended in Frankie being convicted of voluntary manslaughter, she believed, privately, that he must not have had any choice in the matter. Besides, he'd paid his debt to society, and he'd been a loyal and trusted friend and employee to her mother, though her mother, she knew, had always worried that Frankie was lonely. *Well, not anymore,* Daisy thought with a smile. Not if he cared as much about Jessica as she cared about him.

"Does . . . does he love you too, Jessica?" she asked her friend gently.

Jessica nodded, flushing again. "He calls me his little doll," she said shyly. "You know, because he's so much bigger than me. And because he can pick me right up, just like a little—"

"Yeah, I get it," Daisy said, reaching over and squeezing her hand. "That nickname requires no explanation. But you know what does? The fact that I've been so oblivious this summer. I mean, not even noticing the two of you falling in love with each other, right in front of me?" And it wasn't just Jessica and Frankie falling in love either. Something was happening between her parents, too. She was sure of it. Even now, they were having a drink at her dad's cabin. Her mother had insisted that they were meeting there to discuss business, but Daisy had her doubts.

Now she shook her head in bemusement. So . . . Will and her, Jessica and Frankie, and now, maybe, her mom and dad. "Jessica," she said suddenly, "is everybody around here falling in love this summer? I mean, do you think there's something in the water at Pearl's?"

"I don't know," Jessica said, considering this. And then her eyes widened with solemn wonder. "But you know, Daisy," she whispered. "Frankie and I *did* both drink the water there."

Chapter 22

The first thing Caroline saw when she turned into Jack's driveway that evening was a bright red mailbox with "J. Keegan" stenciled neatly on its side. *So Jack really is planning on staying here,* she thought, putting down roots and mailboxes at the same time. She remembered now what she'd said to him at the beginning of the summer about his living in Butternut. *I'll give you two weeks, Jack. A month, tops.* Well, she'd been wrong about that. What else, she wondered, had she been wrong about?

But she didn't have much time to consider this question as she drove down the gravel driveway, because the next thing she knew she was pulling up in front of the cabin, and Jack was coming out of it to meet her.

"Hey," he said, as she got out of her pickup. "You're right on time."

"Am I?" she murmured, staring at the cabin, and seeing it, but, at the same time, not really seeing it, because being here was giving her the strangest feeling, a feeling that was the opposite of déjà vu. She'd been here many times before, most recently a few years ago when she'd brought an ailing Wayland a casserole, but right here, right now, she felt as if she'd never been here before. It was totally different, and totally unfamiliar.

"Jack . . . what did you do to this place?"

"What *didn't* I do to this place?" Jack said, pleased by her reaction. "But come on inside. I'll show you around."

"All right," she said, following him up the cabin's front steps. There hadn't been any front steps the last time she'd been here; there hadn't been any front porch, either. But now there were steps and a porch, straight and smooth, and built out of a clean, pale yellow pine that hadn't had time to mellow and darken with age.

Jack opened the front door, but she paused for a moment on the porch to admire the window boxes, which were painted the same dark green as the trim on the cabin's windows, but which did not yet have any flowers in them.

"I built those last week," Jack said. "I had

some extra wood, and some extra paint, but the flowers . . ." He shrugged. "I'm not much of a gardener."

"They're nice," she said, thinking that they would look even nicer with some impatiens in them.

"Are you coming?" Jack asked quizzically, standing in the doorway, and she nodded and walked past him into the cabin's living room, where she stopped and looked around, momentarily speechless.

"What do you think?" he asked, but he didn't wait for her to answer. Instead, he led her through the rooms, explaining as he went all the work he'd done. And Caroline tried to pay attention to what he was telling her, but it wasn't easy. Her eyes didn't know where to rest. There was so much to see, so much to absorb: wide-planked pine floors, sparkling new windowpanes, freshly painted walls, a pretty tiled floor in the bathroom, and shiny new appliances in the kitchen. The rooms were still sparsely furnished, but they were so well lit, so comfortable, and so inviting that it was all Caroline could do not to curl up on the buttery leather couch in front of the living room fireplace and demand that Jack give her a book to read right then and there.

But Jack had other plans.

"I want to show you the back deck," he said.

"Jack, I can't believe what you've done with the

place," she said, as he led her out through a sliding glass door. "I mean, I knew you were working on it, but it's, it's . . ." She stopped when she saw that a string of tiny white lights had been strung through the arbor above the deck. They were glowing softly in the evening light. She turned to him in surprise, and he shrugged. "Believe it or not," he said, "I found a box of lights in the attic. So either Wayland decorated his Christmas tree with them, or he was a secret romantic."

Caroline laughed. "The first one, I think," she said, wandering over to the deck's railing and admiring the view of the sun setting over the lake in a swirl of pinks and golds and reds.

"Well, either way it seemed like a shame to let those lights go to waste," Jack said, coming up beside her. "And I thought they might be nice to look at while we had a drink out here." He gestured to a little iron table, with two iron chairs. On the table was a bottle of sparkling water, two glasses filled with crushed ice and lemon twists, and a plate with red grapes, cheese, and thinly sliced French bread on it.

"Jack, you didn't have to go to all this trouble," Caroline protested.

"It wasn't any trouble." He pulled out one of the table's chairs for her.

"Well, it's very nice," she said, hesitating. She'd never seen Jack play the role of gracious host before, and watching him do it now only added to her sense of disorientation. But she sat down on the proffered chair and watched as Jack sat down across from her, opened the bottle of sparkling water, and filled both of their glasses. Then he handed one to Caroline and picked one up himself.

"Are we celebrating your finishing the cabin?" she asked, holding her glass. "Because you've done an amazing job, Jack. You really have."

"Thank you, Caroline. That means a lot to me. But we're celebrating something else, too, the fact that we can now be in the same place, at the same time, without you wanting to kill me." He clinked his glass against hers. And he smiled that long, slow smile, the smile that had been her undoing more than once in her life. She took a long drink of her sparkling water, hoping to tamp down an odd feeling that had just begun. It was like the buzzing she'd felt in her head the night she'd drunk too much, only this buzzing wasn't in her head. It was in her body, her *whole* body. She wondered again if coming here tonight had been a good idea. She suspected it hadn't been. In fact, looking at the tail end of that smile, she *knew* it hadn't been.

"I'm sorry I don't have anything stronger than this," he said teasingly, indicating his glass of sparkling water. "But I don't keep any vodka in the house."

Caroline raised her eyebrows, amused in spite

of herself. "That's all right," she said. "I'm a nondrinker, remember? You said I should know my destiny. And my destiny, apparently, is to not drink."

"Well, not to drink the way you were drinking that night at the Corner Bar," Jack agreed. "But that was unusual for you. Most of the time, you understand moderation."

"And you don't, Jack," she said. It wasn't a question but a statement.

"No," Jack agreed. "For me, it's all or nothing," and he smiled that smile again. Caroline suppressed a little shiver, remembering what the "all" in the all or nothing had been like with Jack. *Stop it,* she told herself, and she took another large gulp of the sparkling water for good measure.

"Look," Jack said now, suddenly serious. "There's something else we need to celebrate tonight."

"Yes?"

"Pearl's," he said. "The best coffee shop east of the Mississippi. It's already served three generations of customers. Now, with any luck, it'll serve three more."

"It'll take more than luck," Caroline said sadly.

"I know," Jack replied quickly. "It'll take money, too. Which is why . . ." He paused here, seemed to consider something, then said, "Oh, never mind. This will say it better than I can anyway." And he reached into his front shirt

442

pocket, pulled out a folded envelope, and handed it to her.

She turned it over in her hands. It was unmarked.

"Open it," he said, his blue eyes suddenly serious.

Caroline opened it and slid out a check. It was written from Jack's bank account, made out to her. For forty-four thousand and five hundred dollars.

She felt a little sting of hurt surprise. "This isn't funny, Jack."

"It isn't supposed to be," he said, frowning.

"But . . . it's a joke, right?"

"No, it's not a joke," he said, looking faintly annoyed. "That's a real check."

She studied it. It *looked* real enough. But still . . .

"Jack Keegan," she said, tensing. "Where did you get this money?"

"I saved it."

"You saved it? The Jack I knew couldn't save a dime."

"Well, I'm not that man anymore. I thought we'd already been over that."

She put the check back into the envelope and put the envelope onto the table. He looked a little hurt, she realized. But she didn't care. She wasn't taking his ill-gotten gains.

"Oh, for God's sake, Caroline. If you're worried about my having robbed a bank or something like that, you can relax. I made this money the old-fashioned way. I earned it."

"How?"

"Working at an oil refinery. Once I stopped drinking, and playing poker, there wasn't much left to spend my money on. Not in Elk Point, South Dakota, anyway. Besides, I figured the more time I spent working, the less time I'd spend thinking about drinking. So I worked overtime, and I worked weekends and holidays, both of which, by the way, are high-risk times for recovering alcoholics."

She studied him carefully. She believed him, she decided. But she still couldn't take the check. Reaching over, Caroline pushed the envelope closer to him on the table.

He sighed and crossed his arms. "You're not going to make this easy, are you?"

She shook her head.

"Why not?"

"Because it's a lot of money, Jack. Too much for me to pay back."

"It's not a loan, Caroline."

"What is it then?"

"It's a . . . gift, I guess. But you've earned it, Caroline. All those years, raising Daisy by yourself, it's the least I can do."

"Jack . . ." She hesitated, struggling to come to terms with what she'd just learned. *Jack had the money. And he wanted to give it to her.* God knows, she needed it. But could she take it? Just like that? No, she thought. She couldn't. Because if there was one thing she'd learned about money, it was that it never came without strings attached.

"Look, just take it," he said.

"I can't, Jack."

"Why not?"

"Because even if I wouldn't owe you the money, I'd owe you something, wouldn't I?"

He look surprised—then angry. "Caroline, you think that's what this is about? You think I want you to feel beholden to me?"

"No, but—"

"Caroline, make no mistake about it. I want you back. Everything I told you that night at Pearl's still holds true. Nothing has changed. But if I can't have you back for the right reasons, I don't want you back at all. That said, I want you to take this money. In fact, I *insist* you take this money."

But she shook her head. "You worked for this money, Jack. You should save it or invest it."

"I'm *trying* to invest it, Caroline. In Pearl's."

"But it's not a good investment if there's not going to be any return on it," she pointed out.

"Trust me, Caroline. If it'll keep Pearl's open, it'll be the best investment I've ever made."

"Even if you can't get a cup of coffee there?" she asked, suddenly amused at the memory of their tense negotiations at the beginning of the summer.

"Even if I can't get a cup of coffee there," he agreed.

Caroline hesitated, then picked the envelope up off the table and slid the check out of it again. She held it by its edges and studied it carefully, thinking—*really* thinking—about everything Jack had said.

Finally, she looked back up at him. "All right, Jack," she said decisively. "I'll take it." Jack looked relieved, then pleased.

"I'll take it on *one* condition."

"Which is . . . ?"

"Which is that this check buys you a share in Pearl's. A partnership in it."

"Caroline," he said, shaking his head. "That's not necessary."

"Yes, it is—because I won't take it any other way. Certainly not as a loan, which we both know I can't pay back, or as a gift, which I'm too proud to accept because it feels too much like charity to me. But if I accept your check as an investment, that, obviously, would be different. Besides, I've often thought of having a business partner, someone to share the responsibility with, and maybe, who knows, the profits. It couldn't be just anyone, of course. It would have to be someone whose opinion I respect, and someone who, I hope, respects mine. But we'll make it legal, Jack. We'll have the business appraised and draw up an agreement."

"Caroline, I don't know what to say."

"Say yes," she said simply.

"But it's a family business," he objected.

"We have a daughter together. I'd say that makes us family, Jack."

Now it was Jack's turn to think.

"It's not a bad idea, is it?" Caroline asked finally.

"No. It's not a bad idea. But I don't want to do anything to jeopardize this new, um, friendship we have."

"Is that what it is, Jack? A friendship?"

"Well, for lack of a better word."

"Our friendship will be fine. Now, what do you say? Do you want to own a piece of a Butternut institution or not."

"All right. But I have a condition, too. I'd have to be a silent partner. Because I would never presume to tell you how to run that business, not when you already do it so well by yourself."

She nodded thoughtfully. "Okay, you can be a silent partner, Jack. But I'm going to take on another partner, too."

"Who?"

"Frankie. He's got some money to invest. Not as much as you, but enough to replace the air-conditioning system, I hope. And I think it's about time he had a stake in the business, don't you? Nobody, including me, has worked harder for Pearl's over the last several years."

"You're right," Jack said. "And he'll be an excellent partner."

"He will be, won't he?" Caroline was already

excited about having this conversation with Frankie. But then something else occurred to her. "Jack," she said, "if you're going to be a silent partner, what will you do . . . the rest of the time? You know, now that you've gotten the cabin fixed up?"

"It's funny you should ask that," he said musingly. "I've been thinking about it all afternoon, ever since Bill Phipps came by and offered me my old job back."

Caroline raised her eyebrows. "He did? What did you say?"

"I thanked him, obviously. But I said no. I told him there was something else I wanted to do."

"What's that, Jack?"

"I want to keep doing what I've done here," he said, gesturing at the cabin. "I want to keep fixing these places up."

"You mean, be a handyman?"

"No," Jack shook his head. "I mean I want to buy another cabin, fix it up, and sell it. And if I make a profit on it, I want to do it again. And, who knows, maybe again."

"So you'd renovate these places for a living?"

"Why not? I'll still have some money after you cash that check. And the timing is right. Interest rates are still low, and with the economy improving, more people from the Twin Cities are going to be buying weekend places up here again. I've taken a look at some of the cabins on the market, and they're pretty rustic, to say the least. Some people, of course, want a fixer-upper. But some people, especially busy people, want something they can move right into, some place easy, and low maintenance, where they don't lose that feeling of being in the North Woods, but they don't have to sacrifice comfort to do it either. I don't know yet, obviously, if I can make it pay in the long run"—he gave a little shrug—"but I've got to try."

She smiled. "You really liked working up here this summer, didn't you?"

"I did. I mean, don't get me wrong, it had its low points. I made a lot of mistakes, especially in the beginning. But I got the hang of it. And once I did, I liked working at my own pace. I liked being able to see my progress every day. And I liked that feeling of getting something right, even if was something little. You know, doing it the right way, and having it work, like planing a door so that it closes perfectly. Do you know what I mean?"

"Well, maybe not about planing the door," Caroline said, smiling. "But I think I know what you mean about taking pride in your work." And she felt that buzzing feeling again, only it was stronger this time and accompanied by a delicious warmth that was threatening to engulf her entire body. It was amazing how describing his work to her had transformed him, she thought, making him even more attractive than he already was.

Though, if she were honest with herself, he was already plenty attractive to her without having to say a single word.

The warmth spread a little more, but she took another sip of her sparkling water and tried to ignore it. For now, anyway. This conversation wasn't over yet.

"Jack, look, I think your idea about rebuilding cabins is great. I really do. If this place is any indication of the quality of your work, you won't have any trouble selling the next one. But there's something else I wanted to talk about."

"What's that?"

"Well," she paused, not knowing exactly how to broach this subject. "I, I know you've been sober for two years. But, Jack, a lot of recovering alcoholics eventually relapse."

"Caroline," he said, bemused. "Have you been watching one of those shows about addiction?"

"Yes, I have," she said. "I've been doing some Internet research, too. I know a lot more now about it than I did before. I'm not an expert on the subject, not by any means. But Jack, I must say, I'm really proud of you. What you've done . . . it hasn't been easy, has it?"

"No, it hasn't. But I've had two very powerful sources of motivation."

"But what if you relapse? Then what? What happens to our business partnership? And to our . . . our friendship?"

"I'm not going to lie to you, Caroline. It's a possibility; I like to think, though, in my case, it's not a big possibility. I've got a lot to lose, now that I've got you and Daisy back in my life. But all I can do is take it one day at a time—go to my meetings, meet with Walt, avoid triggers like going to bars or being around other people who are drinking." He shrugged. "That's about it. That's all I can do. I mean, the risk will always be there. But as someone who used to be a betting man, I have to say, I like my odds."

"So do I, Jack . . . Do you, do you feel like drinking right now?" she asked, looking at him steadily.

"No. Not even a little. I'd much rather be here with you, watching the sunset that we're not watching," he said, smiling.

Caroline smiled at him, but she ignored the sunset. She knew if she didn't keep going, she'd lose her courage. There was something she needed to ask him, something she knew he didn't want to be asked.

"Jack, there's something else. It's about your childhood."

"What about it?" he said, looking suddenly tense.

"I need to know about it, about what happened to you."

"Why?"

"Because you were right when you said we

451

had a lot of secrets in our family. We do. But I don't want to have them anymore. I need you to tell me what happened after your parents died, after you went to live with your aunt and uncle."

"There's not much to tell."

"I don't believe you," she said, not backing down.

"No, it's true. It's pretty simple, actually, what happened to me. My uncle beat the hell out of me," he said bluntly. "And my aunt . . . my aunt let him beat the hell out of me."

"Jack . . ." she said, her throat constricting.

He shrugged off her concern. "That's enough about that for now, okay? I promise I'll tell you more later. I'll tell you everything, if you want to hear it. But not tonight. Tonight, I feel like celebrating."

But as he said that, a leaf from a nearby tree fluttered down onto the deck and landed at Caroline's feet. Something about it caught her attention. She reached to pick it up and saw that it was already edged in yellow.

"Look, Jack," she said. "The leaves are already starting to turn."

"I know. Fall's coming; you can feel it in the air. This morning, I almost built my first fire in the fireplace."

And in that instant, watching him, sitting across from her, in the fading light, Caroline made another decision, a decision her brain had been working on subconsciously all summer.

"Can we have a fire tomorrow morning, Jack?" she asked suddenly.

"Tomorrow morning? Are you planning on coming back here?"

"No. I'm planning on staying here all night, assuming, of course, that I'm invited to stay."

The expression on his face then was deeply satisfying to Caroline. He had not seen this coming. It was hard to shock Jack Keegan, she thought. But she'd done it.

"You sure about this?" he murmured.

"Oh, I'm sure," she said, the sensation of warmth spreading deliciously through her whole body.

Only a moment later, it seemed, they were in Jack's room, and Jack was turning off the overhead light and leaving on a small bedside table lamp to glow softly and throw faint shadows against the wall. And then he was laying her down, carefully, lovingly, onto his bed. But he didn't immediately move to join her. Instead, he looked down at her, speculatively, almost worriedly.

"Jack, what is it?"

"Nothing. It's just been a long time, that's all."

"A long time since you've been with me?"

"A long time since I've been with anyone."

"How long?"

"Since I stopped drinking."

"That was two years ago, Jack," she said, her heart knocking against her rib cage.

"I know."

"Why, why so long?"

"You were the only woman I wanted to be with."

"Oh, Jack," she breathed, amazed and, to be honest, a little afraid. Afraid because there was a time when it would have been unimaginable for Jack to go two days without making love. But two years? She could only guess at the level of his need. And more than guess at hers. She felt it now, surging through her.

When Jack moved, it was with deliberate slowness and infinite patience, like the calm before the storm. He knelt on the bed, leaned down, and kissed her gently, then pulled away and smiled at her—that slow smile that was pure Jack, and that made desire unfurl within her, where it rippled and shimmied like a flag in the wind. She *loved* that smile, Caroline decided. It was a great smile.

Chapter 23

"Will, can you believe it? Frankie and Jessica, falling in love right in front of my eyes and I never even noticed it?"

"Yeah, I can believe it," Will said, reaching out to tuck a stray strand of Daisy's strawberry-blond hair behind one of her ears. "Because if you were like me this summer, Daisy, you've been a little distracted."

It was the next day, right after closing time at Pearl's, and they were sitting in one of the back booths talking. Or at least Daisy was talking. Will, who had come here to tell her something, something important, was finding it easier to listen than to talk.

"You're right. I *have* been a little distracted this summer. I can't imagine why," Daisy said, leaning over and kissing him on the lips. Will smiled at her, relieved that in the week since her surgery, she'd started to look like herself again. Still pale, yes, but a soft, creamy pale, not the worrying grayish pale of her hospital stay.

"You know, Daisy," he said now, running a finger down her cheek. "I didn't just come here to flirt with you. I came here because there's something I need to talk to you about."

"Will, you look so serious," she said, frowning slightly.

"Well, this *is* serious," Will said, his mouth suddenly dry. He didn't know what he was more nervous about, her reaction to what he was going to say or *his* reaction to *her* reaction to what he was going to say. Until this morning, it had all felt somehow unreal. Watching her face now, though, as the first shadow of anxiety flitted across it, it suddenly felt very real.

"What is it, Will?"

"I, I don't know how to start," he said, fiddling with the Coke Daisy had just brought him.

"Start at the beginning," she said, her jaw tightening. And Will realized his nervousness was contagious. He sighed. This wasn't going to get any easier for either of them. He needed to get it over with. Now. He took a deep breath.

"Okay, I'll start at the beginning. And actually, Daisy, it *was* the beginning. For us, anyway. It was the morning after our first date, our first real date, the one at your apartment, and I'd driven up to Duluth to pick up a car part. While I was there, I . . . I walked by this army recruiting office. I swear to God, I've walked by that place a hundred times, and I've never even thought about going in there before. But that morning, for some reason, I went inside. I have no idea why. But I started talking to the guy there, the recruiter. At that point, I wasn't thinking about joining the army. I was just . . . just curious, I guess."

He was watching Daisy for a reaction, but she didn't have one. Yet. She just looked alert, tense.

He took a quick, nervous sip of his Coke and kept going. "So the guy there, the recruiter, talked to me about all the job opportunities the army has to offer and how I might qualify for some of them with my background in mechanics. He suggested I take the army physical and vocational test. And I thought, 'What the hell,' right? I mean, what did I have to lose, really? So I passed the physical test and I did really well on the vocational test. I couldn't believe it. I've never done well on a test in my life. But the counselor at the processing center said, based on my score, I'd be good at aviation mechanics. The mechanics part didn't surprise me, I guess. But the aviation part did. I mean, I've read a lot about airplanes, but I've never worked on one. It didn't matter, though. The test measures your aptitude for something, not your knowledge of it. And he said the military would train me in aviation mechanics, and after my time was up, I could stay in the military or work in the private sector. I mean, it's so cool," he said, his enthusiasm breaking through his nervousness. "Here I've been working mostly on people's old, broken-down trucks and cars, and I could be working, one day, on airplanes or helicopters that cost millions of dollars to build."

Daisy didn't look like she thought it was cool, though. She looked like he'd said something to her in another language, something she was trying to translate into English for herself. "Are you saying, Will," she said, finally. "Are you saying that you . . ."

"That I enlisted? Yes." He nodded, looking into her eyes, her blue, blue eyes, and willing her, somehow, to be okay with all of this. "That's exactly what I'm saying, Daisy."

"Why . . . why would you do that?" she asked,

457

and there was something about her expression that told him she still didn't really believe him.

"Because it makes sense, Daisy. It makes a lot of sense. I know it may not seem like it now, but it does."

When she didn't say anything, Will tried again.

"Look, Daisy, I can't just keep doing what I'm doing at the garage. I mean, I spend most of my time babysitting Jason. And I'm just barely eking out a living doing it. I did think about other ways to get ahead. I thought about going to college or vocational school. But you know college is out, Daisy. My grades were lousy. All that time I spent in the bleachers, smoking cigarettes, I guess." He smiled at her, but she didn't smile back at him. "And I looked at some of the programs at the vocational college in Ely, too, but most of them have a two-year waiting list, at least. And I don't want to wait that long. I don't want to wait any longer than I have to."

"But when, when are you leaving?" she asked softly, and he saw that her complexion had gotten paler.

"Sooner . . . sooner than I thought," he said. "Originally, I signed up for the Delayed Entry Program, and they told me I had several months before I needed to report. That's why I didn't tell you right away. I thought I had more time. But then, the day you had your operation, I got a letter saying that my ship date had been moved up, and that I had to report to the Minneapolis processing center and then fly to Fort Benning, Georgia, for basic training in ten days. So I'm going sooner than I thought I'd be going." Will stopped talking. Something about the expression on Daisy's face made him stop.

"Will, that means you have to be there in a few days," she said.

"That's right," he said, nodding slowly. "I have to be in Minneapolis the day after tomorrow; I've already got my bus ticket."

"The day after tomorrow?" she echoed, and the last of the color drained from her face.

"Daisy, I know. I'm sorry. I didn't expect them to push up my ship date by almost six weeks."

"But, still, you waited until now to tell me?" she asked, her voice quiet. *Too quiet,* he decided.

"Yes," he said guiltily. "I waited until now. I know it was cowardly, and wrong, not to tell you sooner. But I knew as soon as I told you, it would hang over us. And you were so happy. And so was I. Then, we were going to Mr. Phipps's cabin, and I didn't want that to be about this, about us saying good-bye. I wanted it to be about us being together. I was going to tell you after we got back, but by the time I read the letter saying they'd moved up my ship date, you were in the hospital, and then, when you got out, it didn't seem fair to spring it on you right away."

"But now? Now it seems fair to spring it on me?" she asked, her voice almost a whisper.

"No, it doesn't seem fair."

Daisy looked away from him then, out the window of the coffee shop, and shook her head, slowly, and Will saw her eyes glaze over with tears. "So . . . so this is it?" she asked, looking back at him. "This is it, then, for the two of us?"

"*What? No.* God no, Daisy," he said, reaching for her. She let him take her in his arms, but her body didn't relax, didn't yield against his. "Is that what you think? That I'm breaking up with you? Because I'm not. Look, basic training is nine weeks. After that, I have something called Advanced Individual Training. That's where I learn my skill. But after six months, I'll get two weeks off, and I can be with you again. I can be with you for every single second of that two weeks."

"So we're going to be apart for six months?" she asked, pulling away from him. Her voice was trembling, and when she blinked, a single tear slid down her cheek.

He nodded, and he felt it too, the awful realization that he'd have to go for that long without seeing her. "Yeah, I know," he said. "It's a long time. But we'll write, and text, and talk, and do whatever we can do to stay in touch."

"But what happens after the training?"

"After that, I'll owe the army two years."

"Do you know where you'll be stationed?"

"No, I don't, and I won't have any control over that. But, Daisy, we can find a way to make this work. Other people do it. They do it all the time."

But she only shook her head. "I don't understand, Will," she said, her voice breaking. "I know we never talked about what would happen after this summer. But I thought . . . I thought . . ."

"You thought I'd stay here, and keep working at the garage, and see you on the weekends? Come down to Minneapolis, or have you come up here?"

"Something like that," she said, pulling a napkin out of the napkin dispenser on the table and wiping her eyes with it.

"But, Daisy, don't you see the problem with that? Only one of our lives would be going forward. Mine would be standing still. Or worse, it'd be going backward."

"Okay, but . . ." He saw her searching for another reason his plan wouldn't work. She found one. "But, Will, you said once you hated high school because there were too many rules. The army is *all* rules."

"I know that. But the reason I hated the rules in high school was because I didn't know what they were for. In the army, I'll know what they're for and why I'm there, Daisy. I'll know what I want."

"What do you want, Will?"

461

"I want you."

"You *have* me," she said, with a sob.

"No, I mean, I want you . . ." He paused here, struggling with how to say this. He'd never said anything like this to her before. "I want you for the long run, Daisy. That's why I have to have something to offer you, something more than I have now. Because I want you for good. I want you for the rest of my life." He kissed her gently.

She blushed immediately, as he'd known she would, but he kept going. He was desperate to make her understand. "Daisy, do you know what I've been thinking about since we got back from that night at the cabin? I've been thinking about what it would be like to live with you. To fall asleep with you every night and wake up with you every morning. I never thought I'd want that with anyone. But I want that with you. I mean, do you remember, at the cabin, when we were getting ready to go and I told you I needed to go check on something?"

She nodded, a little uncertainly.

"I lied. I went down to the dock, and I looked out over the lake, and I looked back up at the cabin, and I thought, what if we had a place like that one day? A place that belonged to us? Only we wouldn't have to lie then, or rearrange our schedules, or anything like that. It would be ours, and we'd live there together. That would be our life."

"Will, we can have a life together *now*," Daisy said, a little desperately. "Come back to Minneapolis with me, *please*. My roommates won't mind. You can share my bedroom with me and when I start classes you can—"

"I can sit on the couch in your living room and wait for you to come back between classes so I can make love to you?"

"Well, y*es*," Daisy said. "For starters, yes. That sounds like a good plan."

Will couldn't help but laugh. Because the truth was, right now, it *did* sound like a good plan, or at least the part about making love to Daisy did. But he realized then that he was getting sidetracked. They both were. If Daisy, for once in her life, was going to underthink this, then he was going to have to overthink it for her. Or maybe not *overthink* it. Maybe, instead, think about it just the right amount.

They sat in silence for a while then, Daisy crying quietly and Will trying to comfort her. Her blue eyes were red-rimmed, and her fair skin was blotchy and tearstained, but it struck him, nonetheless, that she'd never looked as beautiful as she did right now. And it left him feeling the same rush of emotions he'd felt at her hospital bedside that day, the day he'd told her he loved her.

"Look, I know this is a lot to take in," he said, pulling her into his arms again. "And maybe, right now, it feels like a mistake to you. But you

463

have to trust me here, okay? Because if there's one thing I've learned this summer, Daisy, it's that when it comes to you, I have to trust myself. I mean, that morning when I walked into the recruitment office, I already knew, somehow, how important you were going to be to me. And that afternoon, in high school, when I walked into the gym during one of your volleyball games, I—"

"Will, you didn't even know I played volleyball in high school. You thought I was a cheerleader."

"I knew you weren't a cheerleader," he said, kissing her wet cheeks. "And you know what? You would have made a lousy cheerleader, Daisy. And I mean that as a compliment."

"But—"

"I'll tell you all about it sometime," he said, as he stopped kissing her cheeks and nuzzled her neck instead. "About all the volleyball games I watched. But right now, I just want to know that you're okay."

She took a deep, shaky breath and wiped another tear away with a crumpled napkin. "I think so, Will. It's just . . . it's a lot to take in."

"Do you trust me, though, when I say we're going to make this work?"

She nodded, but her brow was creased with worry. "But, Will, what if there's another war? And you're sent somewhere halfway around the world?"

464

"I don't think that's going to happen," he said. "I mean, I could be wrong, but I think it's going to be a while before our country decides to fight in any more wars."

She nodded, but she didn't look especially reassured. So he pulled her back into his arms. "Six months will go faster than you think."

But she pulled away from him then. "That's another thing, Will," she said worriedly. "I don't know, honestly, if I can go for six months without . . . you know, us being together. I don't even know if I can go for six *minutes* without it."

Will laughed, but then he leaned down and kissed her. "That bad, huh?" he said, pleased, in a way, that she felt the same way he did.

She nodded seriously. "It's bad. I thought I would think about it less after we went to Mr. Phipps's cabin. But I've been thinking about it *more*. And it's worse, Will. It's so much worse."

He smiled and kissed her again, a long, lingering kiss this time.

She pulled away, her breathing uneven. "Is that supposed to make me feel better?"

"No," he admitted. "But I can't help it. You're not the only one who spends all their time thinking about it, Daisy."

"But what are we going to do about tomorrow night, Will? It's going to be our last night for six months. We *have* to spend it together." She hiccuped then and wiped at her eyes again.

He sighed. He'd thought about this, too. "I'd ask Bill Phipps if we could borrow his cabin again," he said. "But he's away on business now."

"What about . . . what about your place?" she asked.

"No, I'm not taking you back there," he said adamantly. "And I'm not taking you to a motel, either, even though, honestly, I've thought about it. But it would feel wrong somehow, sleazy. And you're anything but sleazy."

"Well, I may not be sleazy, but I *am* human, Will," she said softly, resting her head on his shoulder.

"Look, we'll figure something out, okay? But right now . . . I need to go. I'm sorry; I'll come back as soon as I can. But I need to tell Jason about this, too."

"Jason doesn't know yet?"

Will shook his head. He was dreading telling Jason only a little less than he'd dreaded telling Daisy.

"Does anyone else know?" she asked, sniffling.

"Ray knows."

"Ray?"

"Jason's dad. I figured I owed it to him to give him time to hire another mechanic."

"He won't find anyone as good as you," Daisy said loyally.

"He's not even going to try. He's selling the place and making Jason get a real job," he said, and he almost smiled then, because the thought of Jason actually having to work for a living was about the only thing he could find humor in right now.

"Okay, but don't go yet," Daisy said, holding on to him even tighter.

He kissed the top of her head. "I won't."

"How's she doing?" Caroline asked when Jack walked back into her kitchen later that afternoon.

"She's stopped crying, I think," Jack said, sitting down across from her at the kitchen table, where she was already on her third cup of coffee. He started to ask her then if it was always that hard, seeing Daisy cry. He'd seen her cry before, of course, when she was a very young child, and she'd bumped her knee or broken a toy. But this? This was different. This was worse. Something stopped him, though, from asking Caroline about it. Maybe it was the expression on her face. It was one of anxious regret.

"This is what I've been afraid of all summer," she said, topping off her already full cup of coffee. "Daisy getting hurt."

"Not *hurt,* exactly," Jack qualified. "Daisy told me that they're very much in love with each other. And that, army or no army, they want to stay together. They want to try to make this work, Caroline. Long term."

"Well, that was the *other* thing I was afraid of," Caroline said, but she smiled a little, and after a few moments of sitting in silence, she asked Jack, in a softer tone, "Did you . . . did you tell her about us, Jack?"

Jack shook his head. After spending the night at the cabin, Caroline had insisted that she get back home early, before Daisy got back from Jessica's. She'd told Jack that she wanted Daisy to find out about them the right way.

"So she doesn't know anything about our plans?" Caroline asked.

Jack shook his head again. He and Caroline had talked last night, in between lovemaking, and they'd decided that Jack would move back into the apartment, for now, but that after Daisy left for college later in the week, he would help Caroline pack up all her things and she would move out to his cabin, soon to be *their* cabin. The second, smaller bedroom there would be Daisy's whenever she came home to Butternut. And Caroline would offer Frankie, who was already looking for another place to live, the apartment above Pearl's. She was also going to offer him a partnership in the business, in exchange for his investment, and with the understanding, too, that if he was living upstairs, he'd be responsible for opening Pearl's every morning. Caroline was thrilled with the possibility of being able to sleep in occasionally—"sleep in" here meaning sleeping until six thirty A.M.—and she was thrilled with the prospect of letting someone else shoulder some of the responsibility for the business with her. There was another thing she was excited about too. She and Jack had agreed, sometime around sunrise, that after the summer season ended, they were going to do something together they'd never done before: take a vacation. Caroline wanted to go to Bermuda, and Jack had to admit, he was almost as curious about the pink beaches there as she was.

But now Jack felt blindsided by Daisy's tears. "Caroline, I'm sorry. I know I said I'd talk to her about us, but I couldn't, not when I saw how miserable she was. It just felt wrong, somehow."

Caroline nodded. "I know what you mean, Jack. It's strange to be so happy when she's so *un*happy."

"Are you happy, Caroline?" he asked quietly, reaching for her hand. It was incredibly soft, he realized with surprise, though how anyone who worked as hard as she did could have such soft hands, he didn't know.

"I'm very happy, Jack," she said, squeezing his hand and smiling a soft, wondering smile at him.

"So am I," he said, feeling it again, that pure, clear happiness he'd felt when he'd woken up after a very short nap in the middle of the night and discovered that he hadn't been dreaming. That Caroline was still there, still in his arms.

"Look," he said now, feeling suddenly energized. "It'll be all right. We just have to help Daisy get through this any way we can. That's what parents do, right?" he added, slightly out of his depth here.

"Right." Caroline nodded. "But where do we start? And where is Will, right now?"

"Daisy said he went back to . . ." He paused here. He knew Caroline didn't like the fact that Will lived at the service station. "He went back to his place to pack up his belongings," he said. "And then, I guess, he needs to tie up a few loose ends."

Caroline sighed. "His whole life is a loose end, Jack."

But Jack shook his head. "Caroline, you're going to have to stop doing that."

"Doing what?"

"Not liking Will without really knowing him," he said gently. "I mean, if it turns out they really are able to make this work, you're going to have to make your peace with him. From everything I can tell, he's not a bad person. He wants to do the right thing and give himself some kind of future. And I think he genuinely cares about Daisy. In fact, I *know* he does."

"How do you know?"

Jack shrugged. "I saw the expression on his face when he answered the door to his apartment the day I drove out there. He knew, right away, that something was wrong with Daisy, and Caroline, he looked so scared that my heart went out to him. You can't fake that kind of emotion. Not unless you're a very good actor. And I think his talents run more toward car engines."

Caroline looked conflicted. "But Jack, he has a past—"

"Caroline, *everyone* has a past. Even Daisy has a past now," he added gently.

She went silent then and sipped her coffee. "I think you're right, Jack," she said finally. "I think he does care about her. And do you know what else? I think until today, he's made her happy this summer. I've just been too stubborn to see it."

"Well, maybe," Jack said affectionately. "But your stubbornness was always one of your most attractive qualities. To me, anyway."

"Well, maybe to you. But it hasn't served Daisy very well lately, has it?"

He shrugged. "Oh, I don't know. You were just doing your job as a mother, a job, I might add, you do spectacularly well."

"I don't know," she said doubtfully. "Right now, I feel so helpless. I wish there was something we could do for her."

"Well, since you asked . . ."

She raised her eyebrows.

"Daisy told me that she and Will would like to spend tomorrow night together, but they don't have anywhere to spend it."

471

"And?" she prompted, with a little frown.

"And . . ." he said. "I told her they could stay here."

"With me?"

"No, not with you. You wouldn't be here."

"And where would I be?"

"At the cabin, with me," he said, caressing her hand. "Unless you can't think of anything for us to do there for another night."

"Oh, I'm sure we can think of something," she said, laughing, and she looked so young, and so pretty, that it was all he could do not to scoop her up and take her to her bedroom right then and there. But she suddenly became serious. "Jack? If I do spend the night, I can't stay awake all night again. I mean, I don't *feel* tired right now. I feel wonderful. But I'm not a teenager anymore. I've *got* to get some sleep."

He smiled. "Well, maybe a little," he said, leaning over and kissing her behind her right ear.

Chapter 24

"Is this okay? Being here?" Daisy asked Will the next evening. They were lying, entwined together, on the double bed in her room. They were still fully clothed, though probably not for long, because a few moments ago Daisy had decided she needed to feel Will's bare skin against hers, and she'd tugged his T-shirt up. He'd obliged her then by pulling it off over his head and dropping it on the floor.

"It's nice being here," he said, glancing around the room, an amused expression on his face. "It's just . . . it's just so pink." He nuzzled her neck with his lips. "I think all the pinkness might be lowering my testosterone levels."

Daisy smiled. "Somehow I don't think that will be a problem for you, Will," she murmured, her hand skimming down over his now bare chest, and stomach, and down over the waistband of his jeans, where it settled, *there,* on his satisfying hardness. She squeezed it, firmly, and Will groaned and started unbuttoning her blouse. But he was still in a teasing mood.

"Okay, but what about all those volleyball trophies," he asked, looking over at her nearby bookshelf. There were more than a dozen trophies there, each one with a miniature volley-ball player on it, poised and ready to spike a tiny volleyball.

"What about them?" she asked, leaving her hand right where it was, but wriggling around a little to make it easier for him to unbutton her blouse.

"Nothing." He shrugged. "It's just that they all look like they're watching us. It's a little unnerving."

Daisy laughed. "Don't worry about them," she said, leaning over to kiss him on the lips. "Because they are in for a real thrill tonight." He smiled, finished unbuttoning her blouse, and slipped it gently off her shoulders, kissing each one of them in turn once they were bare. Daisy sighed then, a little shakily, as he trailed kisses from her shoulders, across her collarbone, to the nape of her neck. He was edging down with his mouth to her milky white cleavage, his hand sliding inside her delicate, lacy bra, when he stopped suddenly and looked up at her, his face clouded with concern.

"Is this all right for us to do?" he asked. "You know, so soon after your surgery?"

"It's fine," Daisy assured him, trying not to squirm with impatience. "I asked Dr. Novack about it."

He looked surprised. "You asked him if you and your boyfriend could have sex?"

"No. I asked him if I could start exercising again."

"And?"

"And he said yes. He said to avoid strenuous exercise, but moderate exercise was fine."

"Moderate, huh?" he said, unfastening her bra, sliding it off her shoulders and dropping it on the floor.

"Is that all right?"

"That's fine," he said, with a caress of her bare

shoulders that made her want to squirm even harder. "Moderate should cover a multitude of sins." He smiled at her, his gold-brown eyes looking darker than they ordinarily did. "I love you, Daisy," he said, and then he pulled her into his arms and kissed her.

For the next several hours, it was quiet in the room, except for the soft, insistent sounds of their lovemaking. Occasionally, Daisy worried that they'd crossed some invisible line between moderate and strenuous. But in the end, she was fine. She was better than fine, really. Because by the time they fell asleep in each other's arms, the early morning sun shining through the window curtains and bathing them in a soft, pink light, Daisy felt absolutely perfect, not to mention completely and totally sated.

"Are you sure about this?" Jason asked Will that evening. They were at the highway junction outside Butternut that served as the town's bus stop.

"Yeah, I'm sure," Will said, shifting uncomfortably from one foot to the other and wishing Jason looked less miserable.

"Because it's not too late to back out," Jason said hopefully.

"Actually, it kind of is," Will said.

"Yeah, I guess you're right." Jason sighed. "I don't know who I'm going to play pool with now, though," he added forlornly. "Or darts. Or cards."

"You'll find someone," Will said. But he knew that wasn't really what they were talking about. He and Jason had been friends for as long as either of them could remember. And now, with Will leaving, Jason was lost.

"You know, Will, I've been thinking," Jason said, suddenly brightening. "I might enlist, too. I mean, I'm ready for a change, ready to see the world."

"Sure, why not?" Will said encouragingly. But they both knew it would never happen.

They didn't talk about it anymore, though, because at that moment, Daisy pulled up in her mother's pickup truck. She parked, climbed out, and started walking over to them. But when Will saw the expression on her face, his heart sank. She looked more miserable than Jason, if that was even possible.

"Jason," Will said quickly. "I need a favor."

"Yeah, of course."

"Will you stick around while I say good-bye to Daisy, and then drive her home? You'll have to bring someone back with you later to pick up her mom's truck and drop it off at her place again."

"I can do that," Jason said, and he looked relieved to have been given something to do.

Daisy came up to them then, holding back a little so as not to interrupt them. But Will grabbed her hand and tugged her over. Then he stuck his other hand out to Jason. They shook hands, and Jason started to let go, but at the last second he held on to Will's hand and pulled him into a hug.

"Take care," Jason said when he let go.

"You, too," Will said, a little gruffly, because this kind of emotion wasn't something their friendship had ever specialized in.

Jason walked over to his truck then and discreetly looked away, and Will took Daisy in his arms and held her tightly, relieved that even though there were a few people milling around, waiting for the bus, there was no sign of it yet.

"Are you going to be okay?" he asked Daisy now. Her arms were wrapped around him, and her face was buried in his chest.

"I don't know," she whispered into his T-shirt.

"Please tell me you're going to be okay," he said, holding her tighter. "Please. I need to hear that. Otherwise, I'm not going to be able to get on that bus."

She said nothing for a moment, then lifted her head, and said into his neck, "I'm going to be okay." But he could feel her tears against his skin.

"I love you, Daisy," he said, searching for her mouth with his and finding it. And he kissed her hungrily, not caring who saw them and marveling at the way the saltiness of her tears mixed with the sweetness of her mouth. He tried to memorize everything about her then, knowing he would need those memories over the long months ahead.

Then, on the periphery of their kiss, he became aware of two things at once. One was that the bus was pulling up, and the other was that it was starting to rain. Not a hard rain, just a dull, gray rain. *Perfect,* he thought. Even the weather was sad.

"Daisy," he said, pulling away from their kiss and looking down at her upturned face, "the bus is here."

"I know," she said, with a little hiccup. He smiled at her and bent to try to kiss the tears off her cheeks.

"Will, promise me something," she said as they heard the squeak of the bus door opening.

"I'll promise you anything."

"Promise me this isn't the end."

"It's not the end," he said, kissing away another tear. "It's only the beginning."

The driver had come down the steps of the bus now and had opened the baggage compartment and was helping the few passengers who were there stow their luggage.

"Now you promise me something," he said, giving up on kissing her tears away. There were just too many of them.

"Okay," she said.

"Promise me you'll go, now, before the bus leaves. Jason will drive you home and come back later for your truck."

"Go now?" Daisy asked, looking a little panicky.

"Yes, now. I'm sorry. I know it's cowardly of me, but I can't watch you, standing here, when the bus pulls away." *Because then I'll make them stop the bus, and I'll get off it. And then I'll have nothing to offer you, Daisy. Nothing except my love. And that won't be enough forever.*

"Please, Daisy," he said, aware that the passengers were boarding the bus now.

"All right," she said, a little sob escaping her.

He hugged her again, then let go of her. And Daisy, swiping at her tears with the back of her hand, tried hard to smile.

"Good-bye, Will," she said, and then she turned away and walked over to Jason, who, Will saw with surprise, gave her a hug. She hugged him back, and Will knew this was his cue to get on the bus. He stowed his duffel quickly in the baggage compartment and climbed up the steps, randomly choosing an empty seat next to a window. And he was relieved to see when he looked out that Jason and Daisy were already driving away in Jason's truck.

Good, he thought, knowing that Jason would get her home safely. But his relief was followed, almost immediately, by an ache that was both new to him and, in its way, already familiar to him. *So this is the downside of love,* he thought wryly, to distract himself. He already knew the upside. The upside was making love to Daisy in the big brass bed at Mr. Phipps's cabin as the sun rose outside.

And then, to stop thinking about a memory that was suddenly more painful than pleasurable, he looked around at the other passengers. A mother was sitting across the aisle from him, holding a fussy baby on her lap. And in front of him was a sulky-looking teenager, listening to his iPod.

Will looked back out the window, where the gray rain was falling harder, and felt so lonely that it made his throat burn and his eyes itch. The driver boarded the bus then and took his seat, pulling the lever that closed the doors. As the bus's engine came to life, Will felt a sudden desperation. He'd try to sleep, he decided. That would be the best thing, really. He yanked off his sweatshirt, rolled it up, and wedged it in between himself and the window. Then he rested his head on it, like a pillow, and closed his eyes. He felt the bus lurch forward and pull onto the highway. He kept his eyes closed.

When Daisy got home from seeing Will off, her mother was hovering in the front hall of their apartment, waiting for her. But if her worry for Daisy was apparent in her expression, at least she knew better than to ask Daisy how she was. If she had, of course, Daisy's crying would have started all over again, and it had already taken the entire drive home for her to get it under control.

"Daisy, honey," she said, gently, "I know you might not be hungry, and if you decide you're not in the mood to eat, we'll understand. But your dad's got some steaks on the grill downstairs, and we'd love it, both of us, if you'd have dinner with us."

Daisy hesitated. She didn't want to have dinner. She wanted to go straight to her room, lock the door behind her, crawl into bed, pull the covers over her head, and stay there until she had to leave for college later in the week.

"Daisy, look, I know the timing's not great," her mother said. "I'm sorry. But there are a few things the three of us need to discuss. If not tonight, then tomorrow, maybe, over breakfast."

"Does this have anything to do with Dad staying here now?" Daisy asked, gesturing at a suitcase parked in one corner of the front hall.

"Well, yes, your dad's going to be staying here with us, at least until you go back to college. And after that, well, that's what we want to talk to you about."

Daisy nodded distractedly and walked over to the entranceway to the little dining room that she and her mom rarely, if ever, used. Tonight, though, the table there was set with Grandma Pearl's wedding china, fresh flowers, and lit candles. A salad and roasted new potatoes had been set on it, too.

"It looks nice," Daisy murmured, and then she

turned away from the dining room and wandered over to the hall table, where something else had caught her attention. It was a framed photograph, and when Daisy picked it up and looked at it, she remembered the night it had been taken.

"Your dad brought that with him," her mother said, seeming suddenly shy. "He'd like to hang it with our other family pictures, but he wanted to make sure it was okay with you first."

"Of course it's okay," Daisy said, with something close to a smile, still looking at the picture. It was the photograph of her and her dad the night they'd gone to the fish fry. They'd talked about her mom that night, she realized, talked about her without ever actually talking about her.

Daisy smiled, thinking about that, and she was just putting the picture back down on the table when her dad came through the front door, carrying a platter of steaks.

"Daisy," he said, pleased to see her, but obviously worried about her too. Daisy sighed. There was no hiding her red-rimmed eyes and blotchy skin. He looked questioningly at her mother, and she raised her shoulders in a little shrug. "Daisy hasn't decided yet if she wants to have dinner or not," she told him.

"No, I've decided," Daisy said. "I'm starving. And those steaks look great." Both of those were lies. Food was the furthest thing from her mind right now. And the steaks, especially, looked unappealing, probably because her stomach felt as if it already had a lead weight sitting inside of it. Regardless of how she felt, though, she knew it was important that she have dinner with her parents tonight. A sea change had taken place in their relationship with each other, and her dad's suitcase and the framed photograph were only part of the story.

"That's great, Daisy." Her dad grinned. "I'll get these steaks on the table."

Daisy followed him and her mom into the dining room, and the three of them sat down, a little awkwardly, at the dinner table. It was all so new, she thought. So strange. And it occurred to her then to say something sarcastic about the situation, something like *Well, it only took eighteen years, but the three of us are finally having a family dinner together* or *Better late than never*. But she didn't say either of those things. It wasn't in her nature to be sarcastic, or to deny either of her parents their hard-won happiness. And it *was* happiness. She could see it, feel it. It was there, right beneath their concern for her, a deep, glowing happiness that gave off more light than the candles on the table. It made her mother look ten years younger, as if the tiny worry lines she'd had on her forehead and around her eyes had been magically erased. It made her father look different, too, Daisy thought, trying to figure out how. Then she realized what it was. It was the first time since she'd seen him again, over a year ago, that he hadn't looked lonely, that he hadn't looked as if he was somehow missing a piece of himself.

Now Jack looked at Caroline and Daisy and asked, a little self-consciously, "Do you two mind if I say something now, before we start dinner?"

"Of course not," her mom said, pleased, and Daisy tried to smile her encouragement at him.

"Okay," he said, taking both of their hands. "I'm not in the habit of saying grace, maybe because I've always had a kind of . . . *complicated* relationship with God. But as you may know, in AA we have to trust in what we call a higher power, and tonight has me wondering if that power, for me, at least, isn't God after all. I mean, how else to explain the fact that here we are, eighteen years later, sitting down to dinner together?"

He continued, "But whatever's behind it, it's more than I deserve. I know that. And I'm going to work very hard, every single day, to finish earning back the privilege of sharing my life with two beautiful, strong, intelligent women who are as kind as they are forgiving."

Jack paused, then, and looked at Daisy. "And, sweetheart? You need to know something. If you decide, one day, that you want Will to be a part of this family, we'll make room for him in it too."

Daisy thought he said this a little pointedly, for her mom's sake, but apparently that wasn't necessary, because as he was saying it, her mom smiled at her, squeezed her hand, and murmured softly, "It's true, honey." Daisy squeezed her hand back then, and, for the first time since the beginning of the summer, she felt their old closeness returning. She hadn't even realized until now how much she had missed it, how much she had missed *her*. She felt her eyes blur with tears.

"Well, that's all," her dad said, letting go of both of their hands.

"That was nice, Jack," her mom said, beaming at him, and Daisy, much to her annoyance, felt a tear slide down her cheek. She wiped quickly at it, and then, hoping to distract her parents from the realization that she was crying, again, she said, "Dad, can you pass the salad, please?"

Chapter 25

One minute Will was sitting on the bus, lulled by the sound of the engine and the gentle rocking of tires sliding over asphalt, and the next minute he was sitting on a lakeside dock, his bare feet dangling over the water. It was a perfect summer morning, he realized, glancing around, and the dock and the cabin on the bluff behind it looked a lot like Mr. Phipps's. Except they weren't, he suddenly understood. They weren't Mr. Phipps's, because they were his, his and Daisy's.

Daisy appeared then, walking out to the end of the dock. She was dressed in the short-sleeved cotton blouse that he loved—the one with the little blue flowers on it that matched her eyes—and blue jeans, and her strawberry-blond hair was down on her shoulders and slightly messy, just the way he liked it. She looked so beautiful, he almost turned away. But he didn't.

"Good morning," she said, sitting down next to him. She put her head on his shoulder. "What are you thinking about?" she asked.

He hadn't been aware that he'd been thinking about anything, but as soon as she asked him that question he realized he had been thinking about something.

"I was thinking that this was the best decision I ever made," he said.

"You mean, buying this cabin?" she asked.

"No, Daisy. Getting married. Getting married to you was the best decision I ever made." And he kissed her, kissed her soft lips and her sweet mouth as if he'd never stop kissing them again . . .

He jerked awake then, trying desperately to get his bearings. He was still on the bus, he saw, as his eyes adjusted to the darkness outside its windows. He was still sitting in his seat. There was the same woman and the same fussy baby sitting across the aisle from him, the same bored teenager, plugged into his iPod, sitting in front of him. Will sighed and leaned back in his seat, lifting his watch to his eyes. It was only nine o'clock. He had a few hours left to go yet. He closed his eyes and thought about his dream, about how real it had seemed, how real *she* had seemed. And in that moment, he missed Daisy so much that it was like a pain slicing through him.

He wouldn't think about it now, he decided. About them being apart. Will found his sweatshirt, rolled it up again, and wedged it against the window, putting his head down on it and closing his eyes. He'd try to remember the dream instead—every single detail of it. And, if he was really lucky, maybe he'd fall back asleep and dream it all over again.

About the Author

Mary McNear is a writer living in San Francisco with her husband, two teenage children, and a high-strung, minuscule white dog named Macaroon. She writes her novels in a local donut shop where she sips Diet Pepsi, observes the hubbub of neighborhood life, and tries to resist the constant temptation of freshly made donuts. She bases her novels on a lifetime of summers spent in a small town on a lake in the northern Midwest.

Reading Group
Discussion Questions

1. When Daisy arranges for a lunch between her estranged parents, without the consent of her mother, Caroline wonders if Daisy is trying to reunite her and Jack, even though they have been separated for eighteen years. Do most children of divorced parents harbor this wish? Is there an inevitable compulsion on the part of children of divorced parents to want to put the marriage back together, to mend what has been broken, even if it was an unhappy union?

2. Jack, now a sober man, returns to Butternut after eighteen years, with the hope of reclaiming his ex-wife and continuing the newfound relationship with his daughter, Daisy. Why does Walt, Jack's AA sponsor, think that Jack is putting himself in a vulnerable position that could cause him to relapse? During the course of the novel, does Jack have any moments where he acknowledges that alcohol is still a temptation that he must avoid?

3. Jack's "all or nothing" philosophy may be part of what drove him toward the extremes of drinking, gambling, and philandering. In what way does this very same philosophy help him to reestablish a life in Butternut, pursue an ex-wife who is angry with him, and maintain his sobriety?

4. Although Buster is a good man, he is too regimented and settled in his ways to give Caroline a fuller and deeper relationship. So why is Caroline ambivalent about ending things between them? And what is it that Caroline had with Buster that she was never able to have with Jack?

5. Being abandoned or beaten or verbally abused by a parental figure can cause long-term psychological, as well as physical scars. Both Jack and Will emerged from such a childhood. Jack, as a younger man, indulged in extreme behavior. Will made a "religion" of not caring. In what way were these behaviors coping, or defense, mechanisms? How and when do they both realize that these mechanisms are working against them?

6. Caroline wonders if she was right to keep from Daisy all the pain and anger she felt after Jack left them. Was she right to do this?

Parents who are divorced have been known to try to turn their children against the other parent. Except in extreme cases where the other parent has been abusive, is this ever a good policy? How does it harm the child?

7. Daisy is attracted to Will, a young man who is unlike her in many ways. It seems, at first, that it is simply "chemistry," that ineffable connection between two people, that draws her to him. But on closer inspection, Will has qualities that are deeply appealing to Daisy. What are they?

8. Daisy, despite the simplicity her name would imply, has a complex and judicious understanding of herself and those around her. She recognizes the shortcomings, or failings, of her father, her mother, Jessica, herself, and Will, but she is able to simultaneously acknowledge each person's strengths. In many ways, she is the book's central character; she is the one person with whom all the other characters freely communicate. How else is Daisy different from the other characters in the book?

9. Caroline declares that a leopard doesn't change its spots; that is, people do not change. But *Butternut Summer* is a book about

people who do change. Who changes and how? And what does it mean to change? Do we become different persons? Or do we get in touch with a part of ourselves that has been dormant or previously inaccessible?

10. Caroline has expectations for Daisy: she wants her to finish college, go to graduate school, and have a career that doesn't entail working in a coffee shop. She fears that Daisy will make the same mistakes Caroline did when she was young and thereby ruin her chances of having a different kind of life. Some parents want their children to follow in their footsteps and some parents explicitly do not want their children to follow their example. In what way are these two contrary wishes similar? And at what point do a parent's expectations become a burden to the child?

11. Daisy tells Caroline that she needs to stop focusing on Daisy and instead focus on her own life. This hurts Caroline, but she realizes it's true. Why is the poster of Bermuda important and how does it symbolize Caroline's shift toward articulating her own dreams?

12. Will is transformed through knowing Daisy. He doesn't want to disappoint her. And he is

driven to change his own life so he can be with her "in the long run." So why does he join the army, a plan that will take him away from Daisy for a couple years?

13. The book begins with Jack's arrival in Butternut and ends with Will's departure. Jack has been away from Butternut for many years, and Will has never really left the area. How are their journeys similar and how are they different?

Center Point Large Print
600 Brooks Road / PO Box 1
Thorndike, ME 04986-0001 USA

(207) 568-3717

US & Canada:
1 800 929-9108
www.centerpointlargeprint.com